The Devil's
Cold Dish

ALSO BY ELEANOR KUHNS

The Devil's Cold Dish

ELEANOR KUHNS

MINOTAUR BOOKS
NEW YORK

THE DEVIL'S COLD DISH. Copyright © 2016 by Eleanor Kuhns. All rights reserved. Printed in the United States of America. For information, address St. Martin's Press, 175 Fifth Avenue, New York, N.Y. 10010.

www.minotaurbooks.com

Designed by Steven Seighman

Library of Congress Cataloging-in-Publication Data

Names: Kuhns, Eleanor, author.
Title: The devil's cold dish / Eleanor Kuhns.
Description: First edition. | New York : Minotaur Books, 2016. | Series: Will Rees mysteries ; 5
Identifiers: LCCN 2016000054 | ISBN 978-1-250-09335-6 (hardcover) | ISBN 978-1-250-09336-3 (ebook)
Subjects: LCSH: Shakers—Fiction. | Murder—Investigation—Fiction | City and town life—Maine—History—18th century—Fiction. | BISAC: FICTION / Mystery & Detective / Historical. | GSAFD: Mystery fiction. | Historical fiction.
Classification: LCC PS3611.U396 D49 2016 | DDC 813/.6—dc23
LC record available at http://lccn.loc.gov/2016000054

Our books may be purchased in bulk for promotional, educational, or business use. Please contact your local bookseller or the Macmillan Corporate and Premium Sales Department at 1-800-221-7945, extension 5442, or by e-mail at MacmillanSpecial Markets@macmillan.com.

First Edition: June 2016

10 9 8 7 6 5 4 3 2 1

To Laura, again. My beta reader.

The Devil's
Cold Dish

Chapter One

When Will Rees finally arrived home, much later than he'd expected, he found his sister Caroline in the front parlor. Again. Since Rees and his wife Lydia had returned from Salem several weeks ago, Caroline visited often and always with the same demand: that Rees support her family. Almost eight years ago, in the spring of 1789 he had surrendered his farm to his sister in exchange for the care of his then eight-year-old son, David. Caroline and Sam had not only used the farm so carelessly it still wasn't as productive as it had been, they had beaten David. Treated him like a hired man instead of their nephew. Rees had sent his sister and her husband packing over two years ago, but Caroline still felt the farm should belong to her. And she was even more determined since last summer, when Rees's punch had left her husband, Sam, touched in the head.

This time she'd brought Sam with her, no doubt to impress upon Rees his culpability in Sam's disability.

"Look at him," she was saying to Lydia when Rees paused in the doorway. "My husband has no more sense than an infant." Although Rees did not like his sister putting pressure on his wife, his gaze went unwillingly to Sam. He was trying to catch dust motes floating through a patch of sunlight and humming quietly to himself. "I must mind him just as I would a child," Caroline continued. "Sam can't work or help at all." The truth of that statement sent a quiver of shame through Rees, although he knew he'd had no choice. Sam had attacked Rees and would have beaten him bloody if not stopped. "You see how he is—" Caroline gestured, her voice breaking. Rees eyed his sister. Dark rings like bruises circled her eyes, her hair was uncombed, and she looked as though she hadn't slept in weeks. Despite himself, Rees felt guilt sweep over him.

"I promised we would help you, Caro," he said, startling both women and drawing their attention to him. "I promised and we will." Lydia's forehead furrowed with worry when she saw his dirt-smudged clothing and the cut on his cheekbone. He acknowledged her concern with a slight nod; they would speak later.

"Finally," Caroline said. "You disappear for weeks and even when you do return to Dugard, you don't stay home."

"I've been home this fortnight and more," Rees said, keeping his tone mild with an effort. "I had an errand." He'd promised himself while still in Salem that he would try to treat his sister with more understanding and respect. But he was finding that promise almost impossible to keep. "Sometimes I suspect you come calling when you know I'm not at home." The words slipped out before he could stop them. Caroline's eyes narrowed.

"I've told you more than once your paltry help isn't enough." Her shrill accusation rode over his measured tone. She glanced at Lydia. "I'd hoped another woman would sympathize but I've been disappointed in that as well." Her furious countenance swung back to Rees. "Why don't you understand? I can't manage on my own. I want to bring my family here. To this farm. We can stay in the weaver's cottage. You aren't using it anymore, not since you and Lydia wed."

Rees sighed, tired of this well-worn argument. He didn't want Caroline and her family living so close. Rees knew his sister. Caroline would expect her sister-in-law to cook and clean for her family and would order her around like she was help instead of the mistress of this farm. As if that weren't enough, Caroline would find fault with everything. Her oldest, Charlie, would help David, but the two girls were too little to work much. "We've discussed this," he said. "You own your own farm."

"Charlie can have that farm. Oh, why won't you help me?" Caroline wailed. "You have plenty. This farm is rich. You have sheep and cattle as well as chickens and other poultry."

Rees could not bear to see his sister's anguished expression and looked at Lydia. She almost imperceptibly shook her head. Although a Shaker when he met her and well-used to offering charity, Lydia had no more desire to see them move in than he did. Lydia knew how difficult Caroline could be.

Caroline, catching Lydia's negative gesture, turned on her with a furious glare. "You think you've fallen into a soft bed, haven't you?" she shouted. "You greedy—"

"We'll help you bring in whatever you planted in your fields," Rees said, his deep voice cutting off his sister's charge. Caroline sent one final scowl toward Lydia before returning her attention to her brother.

"And what would that be?" she retorted. "Sam can't work. Charlie planted only a few fields and a vegetable garden."

"You must have hay," Rees said. He wanted to point out that she could have put in winter wheat last fall. The wheat, once it was harvested, would have given them a bit of cash. But he elected not to repeat something he'd said several times already. "If the fields went to grass . . ." Haying should have been finished weeks ago but perhaps something could be salvaged.

"Will you and David bring it in?" she asked. "Maybe I could sell it. I've sold the horses and most of the livestock . . . well, I had to," she said, catching Rees's expression.

"I'll help you in the garden," Lydia volunteered.

"Most of that's been eaten," Caroline said angrily. "It's not doing well anyway. I couldn't keep up with the weeds and now the squash has some kind of insect; the vines are withering. There isn't anything to put by for winter."

Rees sighed. "We'll offer you what we can," he said. "I promise you, you won't starve. I'll make sure your family always has food. But you can't live here. And that's final."

Caroline stared at him for several seconds. Rees had the clear sense she did not believe him. "But Will," she said, tears starting from her eyes, "what happens if it snows and you can't get to us? And my children are in rags, how will they be clothed? They won't be able to attend school."

Rees opened his mouth, but before he spoke his wife rose from the sofa and moved to his side. With the birth of their first child two months away she moved slowly and clumsily. "We will do everything we can do for you," she said. "Of course we don't want you and your children to live in privation."

"But you can't move in with us," Rees repeated.

Caroline's mouth turned down and her eyes narrowed. "You'll be sorry," she said. "You and this—this blaspheming wife of yours. Oh yes, I've heard what debaucheries those Shakers get up to in their services." Lydia flinched. "Come, Sam," Caroline said, sounding as though she was calling a dog. But Sam stood up and meekly followed her from the room.

"Blaspheming?" Lydia repeated. "Debaucheries?"

Rees frowned. "Don't pay any attention to my sister," he said. Caroline seemed to think Lydia should be ashamed of her Shaker past.

"Charlie," Caroline shouted to her son as she ran out the front door. "Charlie. We are leaving." Rees and Lydia followed Caroline out to the front porch and watched as she climbed into the cart. It, and the oxen Charlie used for plowing, were quite a comedown from the buggy and fine horses she'd once owned.

Charlie came out of the barn with David close behind him. Charlie was almost as tall as his cousin but his fair hair had begun darkening to brown and he had Sam's brown eyes. He wore the embarrassed and impatient expression of a boy with unreasonable parents. He and David slapped one another affectionately on the back and then he trotted rapidly toward the cart. He waved at Rees and Lydia before scrambling into the driver's seat. The battered vehicle hurtled down the drive in a cloud of dust.

"Don't feel guilty," Lydia said, turning to her husband with a fierce glare. "We will help them as much as we're able. And remember, Will, Sam attacked you. Besides, their farm would be more productive now if he hadn't spent most of his time gambling and drinking in the Bull." She did not say that Caroline could work harder but Rees knew she thought it. His sisters hadn't been raised to work the farm. Both Phoebe and Caroline had gone all the way through the dame school and, unlike many of their contemporaries, could read and write. Caroline fancied herself a poet and believed farmwork was beneath her. Unlike Lydia. Rees didn't know very much about her childhood and his wife avoided his questions, but he understood she had been raised in an affluent family from Boston. Still, her strong sense of duty and her years spent with the Shakers, where work was a tribute to God, had instilled in her a willingness to turn her hand to anything. Even pregnant, she'd thrown down her cooking utensils to help with the haying at the beginning of the month. And Dolly, Rees's first wife whom he had lost to illness along with the babe she carried, had loved the farm, just like David did now. David did the work gladly and although only sixteen he worked harder than most men. Thank the Lord, Rees thought now, most of the haying had been done by the time he had returned home. Of all the jobs on the farm, and Rees disliked the majority of them, he loathed haying the most.

"I'll take some of the cloth I purchased in Salem," he said, "and add some of the homespun so she can sew clothes for the children."

Lydia's lips twisted. "I suppose she'll want us to do that as well," she said. And then added quickly, "That was uncharitable of me. I'm sorry."

"Unfortunately," Rees said, "you're probably right. Caro hates sewing too. I swear, my sister could try the patience of a saint."

Lydia sent Rees a glance indicating she could say more if she wished. But she chose not to, instead closing the door to the parlor and preceding him down the hall to the large kitchen at the back.

Rees felt the familiar lift of his spirits as they entered. This was the room they lived in, a large room with east-facing windows and a door opening to the south. Rees's parents had added on a room to the side and a large southward-facing bedroom over it. Rees had always used that space for weaving, since the best light streamed through the windows. He and Lydia, once they'd married almost eight months ago, had chosen it as their bedchamber as well. Fifteen-month-old Joseph slept in the crib next to the bed and the other four adopted children occupied the rooms on the old side. But not David. He had moved himself into the weaver's cottage, claiming it was just for the summer. Rees suspected the boy would not return to the house even with winter. He said there was no room in the house. But while it was true the house was cramped now with five extra children, Rees thought David had moved less because of space and more because he resented these interlopers. Rees groaned involuntarily. David reacted to every perceived slight with hurt and anger, as though Rees had abandoned his son all over again. Rees sometimes wondered if David would ever forgive his father for leaving him with his aunt and uncle as a child.

Abigail, the Quaker girl who came in to help, glanced at them from her position by the fireplace but didn't speak. She'd returned to their employ with Lydia's arrival home and seemed even quieter than before. Jerusha, only nine but already a capable and stern young woman—well, she'd had to be with a drunken mother and the care of her younger siblings—looked up as Lydia and Rees approached.

"Where are the little ones?" Lydia asked. Jerusha nodded at the back door. Through it Judah, Joseph, and Nancy could be seen, running around and shouting.

"Nancy's watching them," she said. Turning her gaze to Rees, Jerusha said, "Your cheek is bleeding."

"Yes, it is," Rees agreed.

"Fetch me a bowl, Abby," Lydia said. "And put some warm water in it, please." She urged Rees into the side room and into a chair, despite his protests. "What happened?"

"Oh, Tom McIntyre had another customer. Mr. Drummond, a gentleman from Virginia by his accent. One of those land speculators. He was holding forth on George Washington and why he should have been impeached. I don't know why people can't leave the man alone." With last fall's election, John Adams had won the presidency and Thomas Jefferson the vice presidency. Washington had gone into retirement, a battered, aging lion.

"Was Mr. Drummond the one who did this?" She gestured to the cut upon his cheek.

"No," Rees said. Drummond had already left when the argument exploded.

"I suppose you had to speak up," Lydia said, her voice dropping with disappointment. "I love your sense of justice but I do wish you didn't feel the need to fight every battle." A former Shaker, she abhorred violence. Besides, she worried about the consequences, especially now after the serious injury to Sam.

Rees knew how she felt. He was trying to curb his temper, mostly because he wanted Lydia and his adopted children to be happy in Dugard. But so far he'd broken every promise to do better that he'd made to himself.

"We wouldn't have a country without the president's leadership during the War for Independence," Rees said, hearing the defensiveness in his voice. After fighting under General Washington during the War for Independence, Rees would hear no criticism of the man who'd become the first president. Those who hadn't fought, or who had only belonged to the Continental Army between planting and harvest, could not possibly understand what Washington had achieved.

Rees hesitated, fighting the urge to justify himself, but finally bursting into speech. "Mac and that Drummond fellow both favor

Jefferson and the French. Drummond said that President Washington's actions during the Jay affair smacked of treason. And when I said that the president had done his very best and that if anyone was guilty of treason it was John Jay, Mac said that the problem was that General Washington was a tired, senile old man." He stopped talking.

When McIntyre had called Washington senile, Rees's temper had risen and he had pushed the smaller man with all his strength. Since Mac probably weighed barely more than nine stone, he flew backward into the side of the mill. Flour from his clothing rose up at the impact, filling the air with a fine dust. That was when Zadoc Ward, Mac's cousin, jumped on Rees and began pummeling him. Rees had already had a previous fight with the belligerent black-haired fellow who was usually found in the center of every brawl. Rees had caught Ward bullying Sam in the tavern and would have knocked him down if Constable Caldwell hadn't broken up the fight and sent Rees on his way.

Rees permitted himself a small smile of satisfaction. At the mill, he'd put down Ward like the mad dog he was. But by then Mac's eldest son, Elijah, and some of the other mill employees had arrived. They'd grabbed Rees. In the ensuing altercation, Ward, who was looking for revenge, had hit Rees in the face and sent him crashing to the ground in his turn. But Rees had bloodied a few noses before that. He didn't want to admit to Lydia that he had participated in the brawl just like a schoolboy, but he suspected she already knew. She frowned anxiously.

"Well, you can hardly blame Mr. McIntyre for his unhappiness," she said, turning Rees's face up to the light. "The British have continued capturing American ships. Wasn't his brother impressed by the British into their navy? Anyway, it's not only the French who were, and still are, angry about Mr. Jay's treaty. You were the one who told me he was burned in effigy all up and down the coast. And that the cry was 'Damn John Jay. Damn everyone who won't damn John Jay and damn everyone who won't stay up all night damning John Jay.'"

"Yes," Rees admitted with some reluctance.

"And now, with the Bank of England withholding payments to American vendors, Mr. McIntyre might go broke and lose his mill."

"But none of this was President Washington's fault," Rees argued. "He has always striven for fairness. To be neutral in all things. Personally, I blame Mr. Hamilton."

"I'm certain Mr. Jefferson bears some of the responsibility," Lydia said in an acerbic tone. "He is so pro-French." Rees wished he didn't agree. Although he concurred with many of Jefferson's Republican ideals, the vice president *was* pro-French and a slave-holder besides. And Rees could not forgive Jefferson for turning on Washington and criticizing him. "Discussing politics is never wise," Lydia continued. "You know better. Passions run so high. And I see your argument resulted in fisticuffs."

"Mr. McIntyre struck me first," Rees said as Lydia dabbed at the cut above his eyebrow. The hot water stung and he grunted involuntarily. "You know how emotional he is." Mac had spent his life quivering in outrage over something or other, and for all his small size he had been embroiled in as many battles as Rees. But now, with the wisdom of hindsight, Rees was beginning to wonder why Mac had been so eager to quarrel with him. They'd always been friends. Yet Mac had been, well, almost hostile.

"He can't weigh much more than one hundred twenty or so pounds soaking wet," Lydia added in a reproachful tone.

"I know. This," he gestured to the cut, "came from his cousin, Zadoc Ward." In fact Ward would have continued the fight, but Elijah had held him back. "I knocked him down, though," Rees said in some satisfaction. Lydia did not speak for several seconds, although she gave his wound an extra hard wipe. "Ow," Rees said.

"I hope Mr. McIntyre will still grind our corn," Lydia said after a silence.

"Of course he will. Politics doesn't have anything to do with business," Rees said. "Tomorrow I'll ride over to pick up the three bushels I brought over this morning."

A scrape of a shoe at the door attracted Rees's attention and he looked over. "What did Aunt Caroline want?" David asked. As usual, seven-year-old Simon stood at David's elbow. After Rees and Lydia had adopted Jerusha and Simon and the other three last winter and brought them home, Simon had developed a severe case of hero worship for David. Now one was rarely seen without the other.

"Same thing as usual," Rees said. "To move in." Since Rees's return from Salem, David spoke to him only when necessary—or when he was shouting accusations. He hadn't forgiven his father for abandoning the farm during a very busy time when Rees traveled to Salem. Besides, Rees had left David to bear the censure of the neighbors. Rees knew many people in Dugard blamed him for Sam's condition, but it was David who'd suffered for it. In fact, during one of Rees's frequent arguments with the boy, he'd accused his father of running away and leaving his son to face the name-calling and worse. How much worse Rees didn't know. David refused to say but Rees could see how much it hurt him.

Nonetheless, David and Rees saw eye to eye about Caroline.

"I better count the chickens then," David said.

"Why?" Rees asked, catching Lydia's frown. "What's the secret?" For a moment no one spoke. David fixed his eyes upon Lydia.

She capitulated with a sigh. "Every time Caroline comes here, something goes missing, usually a chicken," Lydia said.

Rees stared from his wife to his son. "She's stealing from me?"

"Your sister's family is hungry," Lydia said. "I think they're eating them. And of course they need the eggs."

"Why didn't anyone tell me?" Rees asked. He had the clear sense that the entire story remained untold. And although he usually loved his wife's ability to see and sympathize with other people, in this case he wished she'd told him about his sister outright.

"This time Sam never left the parlor and Caroline went straight to the cart," Lydia said, turning to David. "I think the chickens are safe today."

"Charlie . . . ?" Rees suggested reluctantly.

David shook his head. "No. Charlie would never steal from us." He hesitated a moment and then blurted, "I hired him on to help us and promised we'd help with whatever little work he has. He's trying to support that family all on his own."

"I offered something similar to my sister," Rees said, directing a warm smile at his son, "but she turned me down."

"Charlie was glad of the offer," David said. He added with a wicked glint in his eye, "He hasn't finished his haying. You escaped most of that job here but I'm certain you won't refuse to help him bring in his hay." He knew his father hated this job above all others. Rees fought with himself, torn between the urge to refuse and the desire to placate his son. Finally, surrendering to his wish to please David, Rees nodded and stretched his lips over his teeth in what he hoped David would see as a smile. But he didn't fool his son. David laughed.

A fusillade of knocks sounded on the front door. Now what, Rees wondered, starting down the hall. Before he reached the door it crashed back against the wall. Sunlight streamed into the hall. Lit from behind, the figure was identifiable only by his odor: Constable Caldwell.

"Zadoc Ward has been found murdered," he said.

"What?" Rees said "When? How?"

Caldwell came into the hall and shut the door behind him. Although his shabby clothing was as dirty as Rees remembered, the constable had made some recent attempt to clean up. He'd washed his face and hands and tied his hair into a neat queue. "Where have you been these past few hours?" he demanded of Rees.

"You can't think I had anything to do with it," Rees said. He and the constable had worked together to solve Nate Bowditch's death last summer, and Rees counted the constable among his friends. In fact, one of his best.

Caldwell's muddy eyes flicked to Rees and focused on the scabbed cheekbone. "Earlier this morning witnesses saw you and Ward engaging in fisticuffs at the mill."

"Yes. So?" Rees said belligerently.

"If the positions were reversed, you would wonder about me," Caldwell said, keeping his gaze fixed on Rees's face. Unwillingly Rees admitted that was true. "So, where were you?"

"Here," Lydia said, the whisper of her skirts coming up behind him.

Caldwell nodded at Lydia respectfully but said, "Can anyone else confirm that?"

"My husband arrived home while his sister, Caroline Prentiss, and her husband were visiting," she said. Rees thought visiting was far too polite a term for his sister's scene but did not protest. "Also," Lydia continued, "Abigail Bristol is here. As you know," she added as a reminder of the many times Caldwell had visited and eaten at their table, "she comes every day but Sunday to help."

Caldwell heaved a sigh. "I had to check. You understand."

"How did Ward die?" Rees asked, brushing off the apology.

"He was shot." The constable grinned at Rees's stunned expression. "It wasn't a brawl. That would be no surprise since Ward bullied so many men in town. I'd have a lot of suspects then. But how many would take the time to plan a murder?"

Rees nodded. It was odd that Ward's murder occurred so soon after their fight this morning. Their previous brawl in the tavern had taken place only a few days earlier, but no doubt Ward had quarreled with many others between then and today.

"I won," Rees said. "I'd have no reason to go after Ward again."

"It would be more like Mr. Ward to try and murder my husband," Lydia pointed out. Rees, who knew she worried about his safety, put his arm around her and drew her close.

"I didn't really think you had anything to do with the death," Caldwell said, meeting Rees's eyes. "Are you coming to see the body then?"

"Of course," Rees began. At that moment David came into the hall with Simon at his heels.

"What's going on?" David asked.

"I have to go out," Rees said, purposely vague. "I'll tell you about it when I return."

David's mouth turned down. "Come on, Squeaker," he said to Simon. "Let's go outside and count the chickens." He threw an angry glance at his father before turning around and disappearing into the kitchen. Rees sighed with regret. But he had begun to find this placid life at the farm mind-numbing, although he'd tried to ignore his boredom for David's sake, and the lure of an unexplained death was too enticing to resist. He followed Caldwell out of the house.

Chapter Two

❧

Twenty minutes later Rees had Hannibal harnessed to the wagon and they were heading down the drive. With the excitement of a new investigation humming through his veins, Rees would have liked to pepper his good friend Caldwell with questions. But the constable was on horseback and almost out of earshot, so Rees had to curb his impatience.

To his surprise, they went almost due west, toward New Hampshire, not south toward the mill as he'd expected. Few farms lay in this direction; the rocky land rose into a series of jagged hills not amenable for cultivation. Rees had never been to the other side of this mountainous chain.

Caldwell turned off onto a wagon track that soon stopped altogether. *We're heading toward Bald Knob,* Rees thought. What was Ward doing out here? If the brawler had been killed in the street outside the Bull, Rees would not have been surprised. Whiskey and hot tempers led to many a riot and sometimes the participants were struck dead. Or perhaps by the mill; another worker might have tired of Ward's bullying. But here, far outside of town? It didn't make sense.

Caldwell stopped at the end of the track and tied his nag to a tree, next to the two horses already there. One was a farm horse, rough-coated and hard used. But the other? Rees stared. No one in Dugard had the funds to own an aristocrat like that.

Rees pulled up beside Caldwell. "The body is here?" he asked. Caldwell turned to Rees and inclined his head.

"That Virginia land speculator Drummond found him. Drummond and Zedediah Farley."

That explained the difference in the horses then, Rees thought, recalling his meeting with the beautifully clad Virginian this morning. "But what were these men doing here?" he asked, turning a puzzled glance at Caldwell. "Nothing much here but rocks and pine trees." Unless one of them had killed Ward?

"Drummond lost everything speculating on the western lands and thought Maine might be a good location to recoup his losses." Caldwell directed a sardonic smile upon his companion. "Besides, Magistrate Hanson introduced Mr. Drummond to an old friend of yours—Molly Bowditch. I understand they've formed an attachment."

Rees puffed out his breath in surprise. His investigation into the death of Molly's husband had laid bare her secrets, causing a scandal that rocked Dugard. She was now estranged from her children and from most of Dugard society, and only her friendship with Magistrate Hanson had saved her from worse. "Does he know her history?" he asked.

"Doubt it," Caldwell said with a grin. "And no one's likely to tell an outsider. Especially not someone from Virginia." He paused. "Anyway, I think there's something off about him, too. Not quite sure he is who he says he is."

As he talked, he led Rees into the forest. But Caldwell did not head left, toward Bald Knob. Instead he followed a faint trail up the gentler slope of Little Knob, Bald Knob's shorter companion. The evidence of a lightning strike several years ago remained visible in the burned trunks and blackened rock. But the scars were clothed in green and the fast-growing birches were already springing up and filling the emptiness with white trunks.

At first the shallow grade was easy, the granite protruding through the soil acting like stone steps. But soon the climb became much steeper. All conversation ceased as Rees and Caldwell hauled themselves upward from boulder to boulder. The birches thinned, giving way to maple and oak and then to evergreens. Mosquitoes whined about them and both men punctuated their climb with slaps. Rees's spirits began to lift. The sun fell warmly on his shoulders and the spicy scent of pine needles underfoot eased the frustration and boredom that had dogged Rees for weeks. Since his return from Salem, his life had been an endless succession of farm chores with only a visit to the mill once in a while for variety. He loved his family, and missed them terribly when he was on the road, but the relentless grind of farmwork oppressed him.

The sound of voices ahead carried through the trees to the two climbers. Rees turned and glanced over his shoulder at Caldwell. "Drummond and Farley," Caldwell wheezed. Rees put on a burst of speed. He was out of shape. Time was he could fly up these hills and barely break a sweat—and that was when he had walked all the way here from the farm. Now his thighs ached, he was breathing hard and perspiration clothed him in a clammy blanket.

"Nothing much up here but moose and bear," Farley was saying to the tall blond man next to him as Rees burst through the trees. Farley was five or so years Rees's senior, but they knew each other well enough to regard one another with mutual loathing. "Can't farm," Farley continued, spitting a stream of tobacco juice in Rees's direction for emphasis. "The soil is too rocky. My father thought he could take the lumber." He wore homespun and boots and carried a rifle in his right hand. His companion took a silk handkerchief from his pocket and mopped his face. In contrast to Farley, the tall blond was dressed in shoes, a pink silk embroidered jacket now marked with dirt, and a lacy neck cloth. Rees hid a grin. Climbing Little Knob must have been a struggle in that garb.

"Mr. Farley. Mr. Drummond," Caldwell said politely. Both men glanced at the constable and then fixed their eyes upon Rees. He wondered at the hostility in Farley's glare; it seemed unusually pointed. Surely the farmer did not suspect Rees of the murder? Anyway, although it was doubtful the Virginian knew Zadoc Ward, Farley definitely did. He'd suffered at the bully's hands so often Rees would have speculated about the scrawny farmer's guilt if Drummond hadn't been there as well. And if Farley suspected Rees of the murder, he would be thanking Rees rather than condemning him.

Rees acknowledged them with a nod and turned his attention to the body. The granite shelf on which Ward lay protruded from the hill almost as though it were a stage, bare of trees and vegetation. The sun shone upon the corpse, illuminating it. Rees could focus on nothing else. He hurried across the stony surface and knelt beside it.

Ward had been shot twice, once through the upper chest and once through the neck. Rees guessed that second wound was a head shot gone wrong. Not that it mattered; Ward was dead. His death had been fairly recent—his blood had formed a sticky darkening pool that had just begun to dry. "He must have come here straight from the mill this morning," Rees muttered. And the shooter owned a rifle and was an experienced marksman; no musket could hit a target with such accuracy. Rees glanced back at Farley, wondering if the rifle he carried had been fired. Rees reminded himself that many men in Dugard owned rifles and most were good shots. Ward himself had carried a musket, but it had dropped from his limp hand. The bags of shot and powder were still slung around his chest. He had not suspected anything and had made no effort to load his weapon.

Rising, Rees stared around him, searching for the shooter's location. There was nowhere on this outcropping for anyone to hide. Rees looked at Caldwell, who was now crossing the rock. Maybe another man had come up behind Ward? But he had not been shot in the back.

Rees returned his attention to the body. It was lying with the head toward Caldwell and with the feet facing the edge of the drop-off.

Rees walked to the edge and peered down. The steep rock face descended into a nest of trees and shrubbery about twenty feet below. No one had climbed up that way. He turned and looked across the ravine at Bald Knob. A rifle and an experienced marksman could easily make the shot from there.

"What's he doing here?" Farley's querulous voice sent a flock of black birds spiraling into the sky. The crows had already been at the body; Rees turned his gaze away from the bloody ruins of Ward's eyes and found Farley staring at him with angry hostility.

Farley was a short, bandy-legged man and his face was deeply creased. His wispy hair reached his shoulders in a frizzy gray fringe and he looked older than his forty-one years. Under Rees's glare, Farley grasped the leather bag hanging around his neck and stared at Rees nervously. Farley's world was filled with ghosts and bogeymen and omens; Rees thought him a superstitious fool. And his wife, the local wise woman and midwife, was no better, hanging apples shriveled into faces for good luck and putting ears of corn on women in labor. Rees suddenly decided he could not allow Mrs. Farley to deliver Lydia's baby. He wouldn't have that nonsense in his house. But where would they find another midwife?

"What do you mean?" Caldwell asked, interrupting Rees's thoughts. "Will is very experienced at solving these kinds of riddles, beginning when he was a soldier in the War of Independence."

"He was fighting with Ward just today," Farley interrupted.

"I know. Ward fought with everyone," Caldwell said. But he threw a nervous glance at his friend. Rees was also wondering about the coincidence of his battle with Ward mere hours before his death, but he couldn't let the implied accusation lie.

"You fought with him, too," he said. Both Ward and Farley had been in their cups and aggressive; the clumsy battle had been described to Rees as a regular Punch and Judy show.

"Not today," Farley said. He turned his pale eyes toward Rees. "And we all know what *you* is capable of. Your own brother-in-law . . ." Rees took an involuntary step forward. Farley jumped back.

"I'm sure there are others who hated this man," Caldwell said, his words clipped.

Farley did not reply, his gaze fixed balefully upon Rees and his hand clutched tightly about the little bag upon his chest.

"I'll go down," Rees said to the constable, "and wait for you below." He wanted to examine the hill nearby anyway. Caldwell nodded, his expression sympathetic.

"I'll speak with you later," he said.

———

Annoyance sent Rees running down the slope, jumping over rocks and careening around trees. He did not slow down until he slipped on a patch of damp granite and had to grab a tree trunk for support. Then he paused, breathing hard, and took stock. Farley was an idiot and many people in Dugard thought Rees a brawler, so why should Farley's opinion matter? Because Rees was already tired of the quick looks and veiled accusations he'd met every day in town since his return from Salem. And now Farley clutched at his amulet and looked at Rees as though he were a devil. Infuriating, but not worth breaking a leg because of it. Rees inhaled a deep breath and proceeded more slowly down the slope. He cut through the woods toward the other hill, crossing a small stream that was more mud than water and climbing through the litter of downed trees and leaves toward Bald Knob's summit.

Rees stood at the bottom of the hill for a moment, panting from exertion as he consciously pushed his anger aside. Philip, the Indian guide Rees had known during the war, had shown him how to look for signs of someone's passage through the woods. Rees looked up the slope before him, trying to identify broken branches and vegetation crushed by unwary feet. The marks were there and, once he looked for them, easy to see.

Rees began to follow the pale splintered twigs laboring upward until he reached the granite dome that formed the top. Breathless, his calves on fire, he paused to catch his breath. Saplings and underbrush clung to the small patches of soil on this rocky hill. Except for the whine of insects, it was silent and peaceful.

He followed the rocky path under the lacy veil of green until he could see Caldwell standing by the body on the promontory below. Rees could clearly hear the constable's argument with Farley, who wanted no part of carrying the body down to Rees's wagon. Clinging to the small bag at his throat with such force Rees wondered that the cord did not break, Farley cried, "No, no, I won't touch death. His ghost will come after me, it will."

With a derisive snort, Rees knelt on the granite and looked around. Trees and low shrubs grew thickly here; no one below could see a man hiding even if they should look. A cairn of small stones with a hollow in the center sat upon the rock slab. Rees thought the murderer had probably rested his rifle barrel on this support. To test his theory, he found a fairly straight branch and lay prone upon the ground, positioning the stick as though it were a gun. He stared down directly at the back of Caldwell's head, close enough to see his bald spot. Ward hadn't had a chance.

Although Rees scoured the area, he found nothing that identified Ward's murderer. Finally, he descended the slope, following the killer's trail all the way to the bottom. He examined the ground carefully but did not see any horse tracks or the grooves of wagon wheels. Had the murderer walked? Since this area was only ten miles out of town walking was possible. Or had Ward and his killer driven here together? Rees considered that possibility, realizing he'd seen no horse or wagon at the foot of the other hill. If Ward had ridden out here on his own, his horse or buggy would have still been there. Unless the murderer had taken it? Of course he had.

Rees turned his thoughts to a new question: who would go to such trouble to kill Ward? He was a bully and a blowhard, the kind of man who probably would have been killed in a brawl anyway. So why here? Ward had no business on Little Knob. Who would go to the trouble of luring him to this out-of-the-way place?

Head buzzing with questions, Rees started back up Little Knob to the body. When he reached the top he saw Farley and his companion were already gone. Caldwell had managed to drag Ward's body away from the cliff and was staring down at the corpse in dismay. "Thank God you've returned," he said to Rees. "The others left."

"I know," Rees said. He hastily sketched in his findings on Bald Knob.

"So, this murder was planned?" Caldwell said, aghast. "I thought, maybe an argument that got out of hand?"

"If it had happened in the Bull, maybe. You know that. But Ward was lured here." The blunt statement hung in the air. "Had to be. Otherwise he would have been killed at the tavern. No one would be surprised then." Rees paused, his thoughts veering off in another direction. "Was it to hide the murder? The body might never have been discovered but for Farley and his friend."

"That at least makes sense," Caldwell said, sounding somewhat relieved. "Farley told me someone suggested he show his father's property to Mr. Drummond. And why not? It's no good for anything except timber. So the killer probably hoped Ward would never be found, or at least not for a long time. Then these two men happened upon the body."

"They were here at this exact spot at the right time to find Ward?" Rees began shaking his head. "Coincidence? I don't believe it. No, they knew exactly where to look."

Caldwell caught Rees's gaze. "You don't think they had anything to do with the murder, do you? Why, Drummond never even met the man."

Rees shrugged. "Then Drummond and Farley were sent here, expressly for the purpose of finding the body."

"But why?" Caldwell looked around at the forest.

Rees did not reply although he thought he knew. If the murder itself was not the secret this mountain held, then it had to be the identity of the killer. He had wanted to be certain no one would know who he was. But he still wanted the body found. So probably not a casual brawler from the Bull. "Had to be a local boy," Rees muttered to himself. Who else would know the Knobs so intimately?

Caldwell nodded in agreement "And now I have to tell his wife. Although I bet she'll be relieved."

"He's married?" Rees just stopped himself from asking who would be desperate enough to marry Ward.

"Yes. And she'll want to bury him. We have to get it down from this mountain."

Ward was too heavy to carry. After some discussion, Rees suggested building a litter. He hadn't liked Ward, but he had been a living, breathing person just a few hours ago. And he would arrive at the bottom in one piece and with as much dignity as Rees could manage.

Branches of all sizes were strewn throughout the forest. By the time they'd found the right sizes and sorted out the decayed and broken sticks, the sun was high in the sky. Rees's stomach growled and he wished he'd brought something to eat and drink. If they were here much longer, he might be reduced to licking the water from the stone, like an animal. Now in a hurry, he ripped his linen shirt into strips (he tried not to imagine what Lydia would say) and lashed the branches together. Rolling Ward's body onto the litter took both Caldwell and Rees, and they quickly discovered Ward was too heavy to lift. They both needed to drag the stretcher. Then the first drop in elevation bounced the body off. Once it was back on the litter Caldwell removed his worn suspenders and tied the body in place.

Jerk, stop, jerk, stop. In a series of forward lunges, resting only when the litter needed to be heaved over rocks or untangled from the underbrush, they hauled the litter down. Rees didn't think he'd ever been so happy to see his wagon in his life.

After several minutes spent catching their breath, Rees and Caldwell considered the problem of wrestling the body into the wagon bed. Ward was too heavy for them to lift and beginning to stiffen besides. Finally Caldwell jumped up into the bed as Rees maneuvered the litter's front poles onto the edge. Then, with Rees pushing and Caldwell pulling, they managed to lever the stretcher up and in. For several minutes there was no sound but the two men panting and gasping.

"I could never have done that by myself," Caldwell said at last. Rees nodded in acknowledgment, still too breathless to talk, and climbed into the seat. It felt wonderful to sit, although he knew he would be sore tomorrow. Already his back and legs ached. He hoped Mrs. Ward would have help taking her husband's body from the wagon. Most of the branches that formed the litter had broken during the struggle to move Ward into the wagon. And Rees didn't think he had enough energy left to fight through another wrestling match with the corpse.

Chapter Three

Half an hour later they approached the mill. Ward and his family lived in one of the shacks across the road, close enough to hear the steady roar of the river.

These buildings were little more than crumbling hovels and the Ward home was more dilapidated than most. A wagon with a broken wheel occupied the front yard. Although the vehicle rested upon a tree stump as though the wheel was being repaired, the weathered wood and the tendrils of green creeping up the struts indicated a long stay in this position. Rees pulled up beside it. Then he jumped down and followed Caldwell to the splintered door. Bedraggled chickens fluttered away from him, clucking in distress.

The constable waited a long time before someone answered his knock. Finally a small child opened the door just wide enough to peer through. "I want to see your mother," Caldwell said. The door closed with a quiet snap. Rees and the constable exchanged a glance. Something was wrong—no child should be that silent. After another few minutes of waiting the wooden barrier swung open.

Rees could not tell the age of the woman who stood there, her face was so swollen. Bruising closed one eye and purple finger marks circled her throat. "Mrs. Ward?" Caldwell said in horror. She nodded. Her mouth was puffy too and Rees thought it must hurt to speak. He wished he'd hit Ward harder this morning. "I have . . ." Caldwell hesitated as though unsure what word to use. "News. News of your husband. He's dead."

"Dead?" Her eyes rested on Rees and his tattered shirt without curiosity. When he met her eyes her hand came up to shield her face from his gaze. Welts formed a bracelet around her wrist. Rees glanced quickly away and then, realizing that might seem even more insulting, looked back at her.

"We brought him home." Caldwell gestured to the wagon.

She limped out of the house, leaning upon a makeshift crutch and moving as though every step was agony. The glance she directed into the wagon was cursory. "Someone shot him?" Caldwell nodded. "Well, thank you?" She did not sound certain and Rees wondered if she wished her husband had simply disappeared.

When her eyes flicked again toward Rees, Caldwell said, "This is Will Rees. He helped me bring your husband down from—well, down. "

"Rees?" For the first time a flicker of interest glowed in her eyes. "The one married to the witch?"

"What?" Rees's voice rose. He knew Farley and some of his associates believed Lydia's past as a Shaker tarnished her with the shadow of witchcraft, their suspicions even stronger after Rees and Lydia's return from Salem, but he hadn't expected to hear the story here.

"Did you shoot him?" Mrs. Ward faced Rees and leaned forward, eager to know the answer.

"No," Rees said, steeling himself for the accusation that was sure to come.

"Well, thank you," she said. "If you did, I mean." Rees felt his mouth drop open in surprise. But then, as he looked at her wounds again, he understood. She might find her husband's death a relief.

"Do you know anyone who would want to kill him?" Rees asked. She offered another half-smile, the swelling on the right side giving her lips a lopsided twist.

"Everyone?"

"Mr. Farley and that Virginian found him," Caldwell said. He looked away from the woman, his gaze traveling over the battered cabin and the broken wagon. "I suppose Mr. McIntyre rented this place to you while your husband worked at the mill?" She nodded. "What will you do now?"

"Go home. While my husband was alive, my parents wouldn't take me back. He was my husband, they said. But now? Well, they'll have to, won't they? Me and my children." She nodded and raised a hand to her neck, a spasm of pain creasing her face.

As she spoke, Rees thought of Caroline. Mrs. Ward's bruises reminded him of his sister's—and the reason he'd taken her and his nieces and nephew in to begin with. Sam had hated him for it and badgered Rees, threatening him over and over until Rees struck him. And Rees, despite the censure and accusation he heard on a daily basis, still didn't know what he could have done differently. And what should he do now? He couldn't find a good answer.

"All right, Rees, let's get Ward out of the wagon." Caldwell's voice broke into Rees's thoughts. They looked at one another, understanding there would be no help with the body here, and moved to Rees's wagon.

The litter held together long enough to move Ward out of the wagon and into the cottage. Since it contained just two rooms and a loft, and only a few sticks of furniture, they placed the corpse upon the kitchen table. Several small children, very dirty and very silent, watched from the corner of the room. No one wept. Caldwell retrieved his suspenders and Mrs. Ward threw a ragged blanket over all.

"What's going on here?" Tom McIntyre stood just outside on the front step. "What happened?" His loud voice echoed through the cabin.

"Mr. Ward was shot to death," Caldwell said, moving forward to bar the other man from entering.

McIntyre's gaze went directly to Rees. "You shot him?"

"I had nothing to do with it," Rees said, his voice rising in irritation.

"We all know your temper," McIntyre said. "You were fighting with him outside the mill just this morning. It would be just like you to hide him up there in the mountains."

"I think you should be ashamed," Rees said, pushing the constable aside and stepping through the door. "Putting your cousin and his family in this shack." He gestured at the hovel behind him. "There's children here."

"You're a fine one to lecture me on family," McIntyre retorted. "We all know how badly you treat your sister."

Rees swore under his breath, wondering what Caroline was saying about him. Something terrible, no doubt, and even longtime friends like McIntyre believed.

"He was my cousin and I did right by him," Mac continued. "Without me, he wouldn't have had even this. Or a job. His wife and kids was his responsibility and it wasn't my fault he was a lazy drunkard. But I'm a Christian," Mac added with a nod. "They can stay a week or two before they leave. That gives them time to bury Ward and gather their possessions."

Rees's gaze went to the broken wagon in the front yard. "And how are they to do that?"

McIntyre shrugged.

"We'll get the blacksmith out here," Caldwell said. "He'll fix it." He stared at Rees hard, willing him to agree. Rees knew Augustus would do it, and probably for cost; Rees had saved his life the previous year. But Rees didn't like it. Anger filled him with heat and he wanted to lash out at someone. He didn't even know what—or who—he was angry at, but he felt as though he were bursting. "Go outside and walk around," Caldwell said in a low voice. Rees almost argued, but one look at the constable's expression encouraged him to stomp into the yard. McIntyre's sons had come over to see the excitement. They eyed Rees without speaking.

He circled to the wagon and squatted down to examine the broken wheel. Several spokes were missing and the iron rim was pitted with rust. Like everything else here, the wagon indicated lack of interest and care. But the rest of the axle seemed intact. Augustus could put on a new wheel and the wagon would survive another year or two.

McIntyre crossed the yard and joined the crowd. Rees could hear the low mutter of his voice as he explained what had happened. Rees knew they were talking about him when the group turned as one to stare at him. He rose slowly to his feet. Most of the men quickly looked away but some, Mac among them, held Rees's gaze for several seconds.

He can't really believe I had anything to do with Ward's death,

Rees thought. Aloud he said, "I'll be by tomorrow to pick up my corn." McIntyre did not react to his challenge but simply nodded. Then he and the other men standing with him walked across the field toward the mill.

"McIntyre agreed to pay for the burial, at least, being family and all," Caldwell said from behind Rees. He nodded, still watching the crowd cross the road. "Don't worry about—about the gossip. It'll die down."

"I've been telling myself that for weeks," Rees said, looking behind him to meet Caldwell's eyes. The constable nodded.

"I know you're angry, to be held responsible for Sam, especially when you were only trying to protect your sister. And now this thing with Ward. But don't lose your head. You already have the reputation as a brawler. The angrier you become, the more your neighbors believe you capable of anything."

Rees grunted and walked toward his wagon. He wasn't a brawler anymore, hadn't been for twenty years, but the people in Dugard wouldn't let his younger self go. He climbed into his wagon. If it were not for Lydia and the children he would abandon Dugard and take to the road. He could always find someone who needed yarn woven into cloth. But he knew if Lydia and the children were to be happy here he needed to make peace with his neighbors. He sighed. He would try to talk to McIntyre tomorrow.

Rees did not pull into his drive until after four. Although the sun had begun to drop toward the horizon, the air was even hotter now than it had been. David was already in the pasture behind the barn. He'd sorted out the milk cows and begun milking them. Rees could see the boy's straw hat rising above the shaggy brown bovine's back every now and then. He released Hannibal into the paddock and put the wagon in the barn.

Before going to help he looked around for Lydia. She was not in the house or in the dairy. He walked around the farm looking for her, finally spotting her working among the bee skeps. She was clad in her bee costume, a drape of white linen. Moving slowly and gently, she lifted the woven caps to inspect the honeycombs inside. Her movements looked, Rees thought, like a slow ritual dance around an altar. And although bees swarmed all about, lighting upon her head and arms, she never seemed to get stung.

Rees watched her from a distance for a few minutes. The bee skeps, woven from straw, were so pale they looked white. In some cases, the caps were glued to the bases with honeycomb and she couldn't look inside. Rees wondered what she would do with those. She was so tenderhearted she couldn't bear to kill the bees and used a mix of smoke and empty skeps to try to move the colonies from one home to another. She seemed to have some success but Rees knew she lost bees, sometimes most of a colony. She mourned the losses for days.

But the honey and the wax had to be collected for sale. With the eggs from the chickens and the cheese and butter Lydia made, the honey provided her a handsome income. Rees knew some of the local men wondered why he allowed his wife to keep that cash. But he thought since she'd earned it, it should be hers. Right now he envied his wife. She loved her bees and cared for them willingly while he disliked even the least of the farm chores that needed to be done.

Reluctantly he pulled himself away from the captivating sight and went to help David.

David was seated on his stool milking. Several pails brimming with milk were already lined up by the barn wall. Frowning with anger and frustration, he turned to stare at his father.

"Someone shot Zadoc Ward," Rees said, picking up a stool. There were only a few cows remaining. He chose the nearest and sat down, head resting on her flank. David would have known her name and spoken to her as he pulled her teats but to Rees all the cows looked the same. His hands were so sore from dragging the litter down the mountain he could barely close his fingers. The milk hissed into the pail very slowly. "He was found on top of Little Knob."

"We have another day's haying at Aunt Caroline's," David said in a flat tone. Rees turned to face David, willing the boy to look up. "Are you going to help? Or are you going to run off? Again."

"I'm sorry I left. But the constable came for me."

"If it were only today I wouldn't mind." David darted a glance at his father. "If you left once in a while I would understand. But you never stay home. It's like you hate being here, hate being with me."

"I don't hate being with you—" Rees began.

But David overrode him, speaking in a low, furious voice. "And when you do come home you bring a bunch of brats. You leave me behind but bring them home? I'm not good enough?"

"Of course you are," Rees said. "It's just that—"

But David jumped to his feet, knocking his stool over and spilling the pail of milk on the ground. As he ran around the barn Rees thought he heard David utter a guttural sob.

Rees also got to his feet, although more slowly, and followed his son. David sprinted north, toward the abandoned Winthrop property and its sheltering orchard. Rees knew he had no chance of catching him. After spending a few seconds staring in the direction David had fled, Rees sat down once again and finished milking the last of the waiting cows. He would have to talk to his son. And what would he say? By David's lights, his father had chosen the orphans over him.

Grinding his teeth in frustration—nothing he did seemed to placate David—Rees released the cows into the meadow with the rest of the herd and carried the milk into the house.

"What happened?" Lydia asked when Rees came through the back door. "And what happened to your shirt?"

"Caldwell and I had to make a litter to carry Ward—" He stopped and looked at the children sitting at the table eating their suppers of cornbread and leftover stew pie. They were regarding him with interest.

When Rees had first met them they had been cold, hungry, and ragged. But in the few months since their arrival from Dover Springs in New York, fed as much good food as they could eat, they had all filled out. None of the tattered clothing in which they'd arrived fit and they all wore mismatched pieces cobbled together until Lydia could sew new clothing. "Oh, David spilled a pail of milk," Rees said instead. Simon, who idolized David, looked up. Rees raised his eyebrows at Lydia, trying to indicate they would discuss this later.

"Put the rest of the milk in the pantry," she said with a nod of understanding. "It's cool there. I'll take it to the dairy after supper." Most of this milk was destined for butter and cheese. Like Dolly, Rees's first wife, Lydia was so skilled at dairying that her cheese and butter commanded high prices.

"Are you going to market this Saturday?" Rees asked, pouring some warm water from the kettle into the washbasin. He began to scrub his hands with the rough soap. Lydia hesitated. After a few seconds of silence, Rees turned to look at her.

"Maybe," she said. To Rees, her smile looked forced. "I really should begin pulling the honeycombs from the hives."

"What's the matter?" Rees asked. In the beginning of the summer she had loved going to market but lately she seemed reluctant. She held herself very still.

"Here's David," Simon cried in excitement.

Rees looked at his son, whose eyes were blotched red, and turned back to the basin. The water had gone cold and gray. Rees rinsed his hands and dried them on a linen rag.

"Don't worry about the milk," Simon said to David, trying to offer comfort.

Rees couldn't help himself; he turned around. Simon was smiling, his face alight with adoration.

"We'll milk again tomorrow, won't we, Squeaker?" David said in a husky voice. "You and me."

"Yes, you and me," agreed Simon with enthusiasm.

"Come on, Squeaker," David said. "I'll take you to the lake and we can go swimming." No one but David called Simon Squeaker. It was an insulting name but had become one of affection.

Rees glanced through the window. By the fingers of golden sunshine striping the yard and reflecting into the kitchen through the back door, he figured it was about seven. Less than two hours of daylight remained. "Be home before dark," he said. He felt unexpectedly bereft as he watched the two boys go into the sunshine, play fighting and chasing one another around the yard. Rees knew he had lost his chance for such a bond with David, who had been about Simon's age when Rees had left on his first of many weaving journeys.

Lydia inspected her husband thoughtfully and then turned to Jerusha.

"If you've finished your supper," Lydia said to the girl, "please take Nancy, Judah, and Joseph upstairs to bed."

"Do I have to?" Jerusha asked.

"Yes. But then you may go outside. I'll do the dishes tonight," Lydia said.

With a wide smile, Jerusha picked up Joseph, who was just beginning to walk, and urged the other two toward the front stairs. Nancy started to sob and protested she wasn't tired. Judah, seeing his older sister crying, burst into loud wails. Lydia closed the door to the front part of the house and the screaming faded to a murmur.

"What happened?" she asked Rees as she began collecting dishes.

"Sit down," Rees said, putting his hand upon Lydia's shoulder and pressing her into a chair. Fatigue etched dark shadows under her eyes. Even with the assistance of Jerusha and Abigail, who came mornings, the effort of caring for the five children and all the other work besides was wearing his pregnant wife down.

"But the dishes," she began, making as if to rise.

"I'll clear," Rees said, collecting the small plates left upon the table. He began scrubbing the places where the children had been eating. The amount of crumbs and other spills continually amazed him and if the mess was not wiped up immediately it hardened into rock.

"So, what did the constable want?" Lydia asked, breaking into Rees's thoughts.

"Zadoc Ward was found shot to death," he replied. Lydia paused for only a few seconds before rising to her feet and approaching Rees. She took his face into her hands and began examining him. "What are you doing?" he asked.

"Looking for wounds," she replied. "Investigating murders always seems to leave you with scars. I suppose I should be happy that this one only cost you a shirt."

Rees laughed and pulled Lydia into his lap. In the aftermath of his argument with David, Ward's murder had dwindled in importance. "Trouble is there are so many who might want that man dead," he said and kissed her firmly.

"Will, please. The children." But she made no attempt to climb from his lap.

"He beat his wife," Rees said. "She was bruised and limping and the children look half-starved."

"I'll take a basket over tomorrow," Lydia said instantly. "What is she going to do? Does she have anyone to take her in?"

"She says her parents . . ."

Several impatient knocks sounded on the front door. Rees kissed Lydia soundly and then, with a pained sigh, he helped her out of his lap and went to open the door. A frowning Caldwell was standing on the porch. "I have to talk to you," he said and brushed past Rees.

Chapter Four

c⁓

Rees hesitated for several seconds, not sure where to direct the constable. Despite Caldwell's recent efforts at washing he still smelled powerfully of tobacco and whiskey. Rees did not want to invite him into the front parlor. Although the coolest room in the house, the parlor housed their best furniture. The constable did not wait for an invitation. He began walking down the narrow hallway into the kitchen. "What happened?" Rees asked, hearing the resignation in his voice. He was already armoring himself against bad news.

Lydia had banked the fire in the kitchen but the room was still very warm. At the beginning of July Rees and David had moved the table closer to the back door, to catch every breeze, but Rees doubted it made any difference. Lydia was quickly clearing away the last of the supper things.

"Ale, Mr. Caldwell?" she asked. "Pie?"

"Yes, thanks. Both." His eyes rested on her belly for a moment and he quickly turned away in embarrassment. "I have bad news for you. Magistrate Hanson doesn't want you involved in the investigation of Ward's death."

"He doesn't?" Rees looked at the constable in disbelief. "Why not? Besides the fact that Piggy doesn't like me, I mean."

Caldwell grimaced. "That's the point, isn't it? He doesn't." Rees hesitated, considering. He'd known Piggy Hanson since they were boys together. Piggy had commonly told on the other boys to the adults and wouldn't let the truth get in the way of achieving his revenge on someone. Still, this seemed a little extreme even for him.

"All right, what happened? What aren't you telling me?" he asked. Caldwell's face worked; he didn't want to answer. "Come on," Rees said.

"Mr. Farley accused you of murdering Zadoc Ward."

The plate Lydia was holding clattered to the floor and smashed.

"He can't be serious," Rees said, not removing his attention from the constable. Lydia stepped over the smashed dish and went to her husband. As he put his arm around her, she peered intently into his eyes. After several seconds she nodded and stepped away to fetch the broom.

"You surely aren't surprised Farley accused you," Caldwell continued, sitting down at the table. He seemed more at ease now that the truth was out. "He said something on Little Knob. Remember?" He flicked a glance at the cut on Rees's cheek. "What's more, Farley isn't the only one who suspects you."

Rees remembered Farley's comment but had assumed no one would heed him. "Piggy Hanson is too smart to believe that."

"He is an especial friend of Molly Bowditch," Lydia pointed out, bringing the pie to the table. "And she blames you for ruining her life. Besides, I suspect the magistrate resents your interference in his land schemes. Remember, Will, you persuaded several of the local widows not to invest in Mr. Hanson's plan to develop the western lands. And rightly so," she added, turning a smile upon her husband. "They would have lost everything."

Rees nodded glumly. "That's true." He knew that, given the chance to remake the past he would do the same thing again.

"Maybe the magistrate wants to demonstrate his impartiality," Caldwell suggested. He paused and then, the truth forcing its way from him, added, "I might do the same, if it were me. It's a protection for you too. That way, when I find the murderer and it isn't you, no one will claim you corrupted the investigation."

Rees grunted and sat opposite the constable. "So, you're going to solve this one on your own?" He didn't realize how insulting that sounded until Caldwell shot him a glare.

"Yes. I don't need your help. And don't go around asking questions," Caldwell said. "I don't want to hear of that." Rees shrugged but did not promise. He couldn't push the words out.

"Do you have any ideas at all?" he asked instead.

Caldwell shook his head. "No one stands out. Ward fought with everyone, including Mr. McIntyre who gave him a job and a place to live. No matter how mean," Caldwell added, catching Rees's expression. "Certainly his wife had reason to want him dead. But as a member of the gentler sex—" Interrupted by Rees's derisive snort, Caldwell stopped. "What?"

"We both know the gentler sex can and will commit murder," Rees said in a dry tone. "And if Ward had been shot to death in the bedroom, I'd suspect her."

"I doubt his wife has the necessary skill with a rifle," Caldwell said.

"Certainly not for making the shot from Bald Knob to Little Knob," Rees agreed. "That was the work of an experienced marksman. Anyway, her long skirts, and the injuries inflicted by her loving husband, would have prevented her from climbing that mountain."

"That too," Caldwell agreed.

"I'll bring her a basket," Lydia said.

"I'm sure she'll appreciate it," Caldwell said. "But do it soon. She's burying her husband tomorrow and leaving immediately after. There's no reason for her to stay here."

"She's going alone? With just the children?" Rees asked.

"One of McIntyre's sons is going with her," Caldwell said. "As I understand it, her family doesn't live far away from Dugard. Just a day or so south in Massachusetts. Since Augustus couldn't get to the farm soon enough, McIntyre is lending Mrs. Ward a wagon. His son will bring it back." He paused and then added, "Most people seem relieved, not to say gladdened, by Ward's death."

"Well, I for one am happy to hear you won't be involved," Lydia said, turning an anxious gaze upon her husband. "This is one murder you do not need to solve."

Rees said nothing. Now he would spend his time wondering how the investigation was going, who said what to whom, and to what conclusions Caldwell was coming. And there would be nothing to look forward to, nothing but haying and milking and other farm chores. Rees could not help exhaling a heartfelt sigh.

"Maybe I should bring the basket over now," Lydia said, looking through the back door at the golden light outside.

"No need," Rees said. "I'm going to the mill tomorrow to fetch our flour. I'll bring you with me. Mrs. Ward lives in one of Mac's shacks across the road."

"Don't stop and visit," Caldwell said to Rees. Although he sounded teasing, his eyes were serious. "I don't want anyone claiming you were her especial friend and she hired you to kill her husband."

"But I met her for the first time today!" Rees exclaimed.

"Why would anyone say that?" Lydia said at the same moment.

"You know how people talk," Caldwell said, his eyes shifting away from Rees's.

"Someone's accusing me of that too?" Rees said, horrified.

Caldwell hesitated. "The rumor is making the rounds in the Bull," he said at last. "And there's already enough chatter about you there."

"Because of Sam Prentiss?" Rees asked.

Caldwell inclined his head. "That, and other matters."

"I can scarcely credit his popularity."

"He wasn't popular. But he was one of them. He spent a lot of time in the Bull. You—you're almost a stranger."

"Because I have better things to do with my time than spend all day in the tavern?" Rees said in a sour voice.

Caldwell smiled. "Some of them don't much like me either. I've had to put more than a few in jail. But you—well, some think you should have hanged for what happened to Sam."

For a moment everyone was silent. Then Lydia said with a hint of sharpness, "I believe envy has something to do with this as well."

Caldwell nodded. "That's true. But the envy is directed at more than this productive farm. You return from Boston and Philadelphia and New York with that town bronze. A lot of the men think you're arrogant."

Rees said nothing. He knew he was considered proud. Long ago he'd made a conscious effort to become someone different, and better, from the boy he'd been. And although the farm drew him back, he didn't think of Dugard as home, more like a half-forgotten memory from his past.

"I'll regret Sam and his injury for all of my days," he said at last. "But Dugard is not the world. And I've no patience for these petty squabbles."

Caldwell tipped his head to one side and opened his mouth, but chose not to speak. He bowed to Lydia and turned to go. Rees followed him to the front porch and watched the constable mount his nag and disappear down the drive.

Rees went back into the kitchen. For once the house was quiet. The younger children were in bed although not yet asleep—he could still hear muffled giggles. David and Simon had not returned from the pond. And Lydia had taken Jerusha out to the back steps. She now owned her first doll and was learning to sew by making dresses for it. Lydia had promised Jerusha a matching frock for herself. Since the girl's taste ran to flounces and bows, the task had become more involved than either she or Lydia had expected. Jerusha was currently struggling with the bodice of the doll's dress and had ripped out the seams so many times the cloth was beginning to fray.

"This is all part of learning," Lydia repeated over and over, particularly when especially tired of Jerusha's tears. But today Jerusha hummed softly to herself as she sewed, so Rees assumed all was going well.

Lydia looked over her shoulder at Rees and he gave her a reassuring smile. "I have weaving to do for the Widow Penney," he said.

He went up to his bedroom. Joseph, chubby thumb planted firmly in his mouth, was already asleep in the basket by the bed. Rees turned and looked at the loom. Since his return from Salem, he'd taken on a few weaving jobs. Not as many as he'd expected, though, and he would soon finish the twill upon which he was now working. He checked the tension and sat down. He began working the treadles, the soft rhythmic clacking filling the room. As the shuttle flew across the warp from right hand to left, all the worry of the day evaporated. He could feel it leave his body, as though it were a fluid leaking through the soles of his feet and disappearing. He relaxed and his thoughts turned involuntarily to Zadoc Ward.

Ward's murder did not surprise Rees. Ward was a bully and, likeliest, he had tormented the wrong man. But why then hadn't he been killed in town? Perhaps the shooter was so terrified of Ward he was afraid to be within punching distance? But why go so far away? And how had Ward been enticed to Little Knob? Only a powerful reason would draw him away from the comforts of the tavern. Rees unconsciously shook his head. He didn't understand the purpose behind such careful planning. Moreover, Rees admitted to himself that he found the proximity of the murder to his own brawl with Ward worrying. If someone else had fought with a man who was then found dead, Rees would be suspicious too. But in this case, the juxtaposition of the two events must be coincidence. Telling himself not to allow silly fancies to distract him, Rees turned his thoughts to Farley.

Maybe he was behind the murder? He owned a rifle and had the necessary skill. Then, perhaps, after murdering Ward, Farley had arranged for himself and Drummond to find the body? Rees mulled over that possibility for a moment and then regretfully shook his head. He couldn't imagine why Farley would kill Ward now and besides, Rees really doubted that little bantam rooster had the necessary intelligence to plan something like this.

And how, he wondered, could he find the answers when he had been expressly forbidden to participate in the investigation? He already knew he was going to disobey both Hanson and Caldwell. He had to. Not just because he needed the excitement of unraveling this puzzle, although that was part of it. Without this case to look forward to all he had was the drudgery of farmwork. But he felt even Ward deserved the justice of having his killer identified and punished. Maybe, while he wouldn't question anyone, he would engage in a few conversations. Surely some people would still speak to him.

He worked for some time, until the loom was in shadow and he could barely see the warp in front of him. "Hurry up, Squeaker," David called from outside. The front door slammed. Rees staggered to his feet, his knees stiff after sitting in one position for so long. He went downstairs and into the kitchen.

Both David and Simon were still damp from their swim. David's coppery mop, darkened and slicked down by water, looked almost as black as Simon's hair.

"We haven't had dessert yet," Simon was saying to Lydia, sounding shocked that she had forgotten.

Lydia laughed. "Of course. How silly of me." She brought out the raspberry pie and cut several large pieces. Simon poured cream over his and tucked in as though he hadn't eaten dinner just a few hours ago. He was wearing one of David's old suits and by the way the buttons strained across the chest the seams would soon have to be let out.

"Was it fun?" Rees asked.

"Yes," said Simon with enthusiasm. "Do you know the pond is full of frogs?"

David grinned at the younger boy. "Yes, and you jumped a mile when the first bullfrog started croaking."

"Did not."

"Did too."

"Jerusha finished the bodice of her doll's dress," Lydia said. "And a good job she made of it too." Jerusha smiled proudly and lowered her eyes to her plate.

Rees took a bite of pie and grinned around at his family. He had to admit there were compensations to less excitement. Like being home now. Maybe, for the good of his wife and children, he would step back from Ward's murder and allow Caldwell to look into this one on his own. With Rees making just a few suggestions here and there.

Chapter Five

B y four a.m. Rees was awake and in the pasture with David. Once the early chores were finished, Rees harnessed Hannibal to the wagon, and by six he and Lydia were on their way to the mill. Lydia had packed a large basket with freshly baked bread, eggs, cheese, and a jar of honey. She turned and smiled at Rees and he grinned back. Once away from the farm happiness swept over him. Land and livestock measured a man's wealth, but Rees frequently thought he would rather be a poor itinerant weaver than a farmer. And the worst task of all, haying, was still to come today. He shook off that thought so it would not lessen his pleasure in the day.

He let Lydia down near Widow Ward's hovel. The door stood open and a few battered chairs had been placed in the wagon bed. Once Lydia disappeared inside, Rees drove across the dirt road to the mill. It was just seven by his pocket watch. The sun had been up for some time and Rees could hear the turning of the huge millstone even from a distance away. His heart began pounding; he dreaded the inevitable remarks Tom McIntyre would make.

Rees pulled up beside the other wagons. The miller had promised to finish grinding Rees's corn by this morning. Hoping

McIntyre had done that, Rees went inside and up the small rise and around the wall into the mill proper.

To his surprise, Sam was there and McIntyre was just handing him a sack of something. Grinning and clutching the bag tightly in his hands, Sam brushed by Rees and disappeared outside.

Rees touched Mac on the shoulder to gain his attention. Here inside with the sounds of the fast-moving water in the river, the splash of the mill wheel turning and the rumble of the stone filling the space with an almighty roar, it was too noisy to hear the speech of a man standing only inches away. Rees put his hands over his ears, wondering how McIntyre tolerated it all day. Mac's father, Rees recalled, had gone deaf before he turned fifty.

Mac motioned Rees back outside and then gestured to his two eldest sons. Rees escaped with relief. Several minutes elapsed before the miller and his sons appeared. Elijah and one of his young brothers carried Rees's barrels on their shoulders; they dropped them into the wagon beds with a resonant clatter and went back inside the mill.

"Why was Sam here?" Rees asked. "Were you giving him charity?"

"He runs errands for us from time to time," McIntyre said. He glanced at Rees and then looked quickly away. Although five years older than Rees, the same age as Farley, the miller had been smaller at sixteen than Rees was as an eleven-year-old. He was still much shorter than Rees now. "Ward's funeral will take place in an hour. Mrs. Ward has Father Stephen coming. I hope you aren't planning to attend."

"You know I had nothing to do with his death, don't you?" Rees asked, fixing an intent gaze upon the other man. Hearing Mac say he knew Rees was innocent of murder mattered a great deal.

"You're not a murderer," McIntyre said. Rees released his breath in relief. Although he and Mac would never agree on politics, they'd known each other all their lives, and he couldn't bear having someone he knew so well believing him a killer. "Ward wasn't a good worker. Too busy drinking and fighting. With everyone." He fixed his gaze upon Rees. "I did wonder if you—by accident, I mean—you have that temper."

"Ward was shot," Rees reminded him. "From a distance by a coward." He knew he sounded hurt by Mac's implication.

"I know, I know." McIntyre took a step backward. Rees did not want to defend himself like a hysterical girl. He turned to the wagon and was surprised to see Lydia crossing the road, the full basket still over her arm.

"She wouldn't accept it." Lydia turned to face Rees. Her time outside in the sunshine helping in the fields and tending to the bees had browned her skin and streaked the hair around her cap with gold. "Oh, Will," she said, her voice breaking with dismay, "as desperate as she is, she wouldn't accept my basket."

Rees's belly tightened. "Because of me," he said. "Because she thinks I shot her husband."

"No. No," Lydia said, putting a gloved hand on his arm. "Not you. She said she heard rumors I was a witch." She tried to smile but Rees could see the tears just under the surface. "Mrs. Ward assured me she didn't believe in such gossip, oh no, but for the sake of her children . . ." Her voice trailed off and she swiped at her eyes. "They were so hungry, Will. I could see it. The way they stared at my basket. But Mrs. Ward was too frightened to accept the food."

Rees realized his hands were trembling with anger and his stomach was so queasy he thought he might throw up. "I see." He paused. They were both too upset to go straight home and anyway he had only haying to look forward to. "Let's stop at the Contented Rooster. Take of some refreshment and talk about this before we go home."

"Your sister is expecting you and I have to start pulling the honey from the hives."

"We won't be gone much longer," Rees said, lifting the basket from her arm and putting it with the flour in the wagon. "And it will be good to have a few moments where we can talk in peace."

"Very well." Lydia managed a slight smile. "That will be pleasant."

When Rees and Lydia entered the coffeehouse, Susannah Anderson, the hostess, stepped forward to greet them. She was a few years younger than Rees's thirty-six and they'd known one another since dame school. She was dressed in pale yellow sprigged cotton and, despite the matronly cap covering her blond curls, she looked like the girl Rees remembered from his teens.

As she approached, leaving the jolly group with which she had been conversing, a burst of laughter followed her. Rees glanced over at them. "Something amusing?"

"Oh, stories of old man Winthrop's ghost are circulating again." Susannah shook her head. "The poor man has been dead and buried the better part of ten years and still people talk about mysterious lights in his house and boys dare each other to steal apples from his orchard."

"I did that," Rees said with an answering smile. "Old man Winthrop was fearsome enough alive."

Susannah nodded but said, "Oh, the boys dare each other to go to his orchard at dusk, when spirits are most active. No one has had the courage yet."

"He was a notorious miser," Rees said. "If I believed in ghosts, his is the ghost I could see returning to protect his property."

"I agree. In my opinion, his parsimony killed him. It drove away his wife and children and when he fell ill there was no one to care for him. Why, his body wasn't discovered for over two weeks. But a ghost? You and I both know that is simply a tale."

"There are still people who believe in them," Rees said. "Even Father Stephen."

"Yes. And my own husband, Jack." Susannah shook her head, smiling with amusement. "Coffee?" Rees turned a look of inquiry upon his wife.

"Tea for me," she said.

"One coffee, one tea," he said. Susannah hurried away. As Rees pulled out the chair for Lydia he noticed that they were attracting furtive glances from the other customers. But when Rees tried to catch someone's eye, suddenly everyone was gazing elsewhere.

Susannah returned a few minutes later with a teapot, Rees's coffee, and a plate of scones. "You both look downcast. Is there anything I can do?"

Rees forced a smile. "Well, I've been told this morning that I am arrogant, and besides, that some people suspect me of murdering Zadoc Ward. And Lydia is also the subject of malicious gossip."

Susannah leaned forward to pat Lydia's arm as she said to Rees, "It is true I've heard you described as arrogant."

"And I'm certain less kind words were used," Rees said. Susannah laughed and Rees knew he was right.

"I suppose I would describe you as self-confident. You carry yourself with an air." She stopped and thought. "It's not that you think you know everything or even that you scorn the rest of us, but you wear your experiences from the wider world like a cloak. It's clear you've seen and experienced things most of us will never know. That bothers some of the men. It makes them feel . . ." She searched for the correct word. "Provincial. Lesser somehow. Don't worry. It's nothing important." The slam of the front door drew her attention to the two women who were entering. "I must attend my customers but I will return," she promised before hurrying away. Rees sat down across from Lydia and examined her countenance. When she noticed his regard she forced a smile.

"Don't worry," she said. "I'm fine." To prove it, she buttered the scone and took a bite. But Rees saw that she had some trouble swallowing. She clearly was not so calm as she claimed.

He turned and watched Susannah as she smiled at the two women and gestured to an empty table. But the elder of the women, her mouth pursed, turned to stare at Rees and Lydia. Rees could not hear what she said to her companion but they both turned and left. Susannah's smile faded but then, with a little shrug, she walked back to Rees and Lydia.

"I suppose they feared taking a dish of coffee with a suspected murderer in the room," Rees said. He gripped the coffee cup so tightly the handle broke off and the porcelain fell to the table and broke in half.

"Oh, Will," Susannah said. "Now look what you've done." She snatched up Lydia's napkin and pressed it to the spilled coffee. "Their leaving had nothing to do with you, nothing at all." She stopped short. But it was too late. Rees turned a surprised glance upon Susannah and then looked at his wife.

"Are you saying—Lydia?"

Susannah did not reply. Instead she pressed the napkin to the table long after the wood was dry.

"You mean they left because of me?" Lydia's voice broke.

Susannah stared at the wooden tabletop and the linen square crumpled in her hands without speaking. "There seems to be some . . . bad feeling against Lydia."

Rees said, staring at Susannah, "What have you heard?"

She hesitated, her eyes staring blindly through the window behind Rees as though the answer might be there. "I know there's been gossip."

"Mrs. Ward refused to accept help from me," Lydia said. Her voice trembled with hurt and when Rees looked at her he saw tears glistening on her lashes.

Susannah stared at Lydia's tears and sighed. "There's been a lot of talk. I mean, most people don't believe it but . . ." She stopped again, one finger tracing a faint line carved into the wood.

"What do they say?" Rees asked. And when she did not immediately reply, he persisted. "That Lydia practices witchcraft?"

Susannah nodded.

"There can't be many who believe that? Now? In this age?" Rees stopped and took a breath.

"More than a few. Many don't, but it's something to talk about. And Lydia *was* a member of that strange church."

"Not ten years ago," Lydia said in a peculiar voice, "Mother Ann Lee was suspected of witchcraft."

"And what happened to her?" Susannah asked in a hushed voice as though afraid of the answer.

"Nothing. She was eventually released," Lydia said.

Susannah nodded and began twirling a lock of her hair around one finger.

Rees remembered that nervous gesture from childhood. She knew something else she didn't want to confide. He reached across the table and put his hand on hers to still the motion.

"Tell me," he said.

"While the gossip about Lydia is serious," Susannah said, "I think it is more a nine-day wonder. It is Zadoc Ward's murder that is the more dangerous problem for you." Susannah raised her eyes and said anxiously, "Promise me you had nothing to do with his death."

Rees inhaled sharply, caught by surprise. "Of course I didn't," he said. "How can you even think that?" Although he thought she might mention his temper, she didn't. But she did not immediately assure him of her trust either. Rees stared at his old friend for several seconds. He was so hurt that one of his oldest and dearest friends thought he might be a murderer that he couldn't speak. He felt as though the ground underneath his feet had dropped away and he was teetering on the edge of a cliff. "There has been some discussion about your relationship with Mrs. Ward," she said at last, choosing each word with care.

"I met her for the first time when Constable Caldwell and I went to tell her of her husband's death," Rees said. He struggled to force the words through his trembling lips; it was as though he were communicating in a foreign language.

Susannah nodded. "I believe you. But you see how the story is growing."

"Who is spreading these rumors?" Rees asked. "Who?" And why? Gossip about Lydia, and Rees as the primary suspect in

Ward's murder. What was going on? He wondered again, this time with a sick feeling in his gut, if Ward's murder had been arranged specifically to implicate Rees. He didn't want to think so, but it was beginning to seem likely.

"I don't know who started the one about you killing Mr. Ward," Susannah said. "It was just everywhere, all at once."

"Did Ward brawl with anyone else lately?" Rees asked hopefully. Ward was a bully and picked on anyone he thought was weaker than he was. Rees had stepped in several times to defend Sam.

"Not more than usual," Susannah said. She touched his hand sympathetically. "I'm sorry."

"Was there anyone—have you heard of anyone with a particular grievance against him?"

"I'm sorry, no," Susannah said.

"A stranger maybe? That Mr. Drummond?" Rees knew he sounded desperate. Susannah shook her head.

Rees had hoped for another suspect. He dropped his head into his hand and tried to think. His thoughts were so full of concern for Lydia he could hardly focus on anything else.

"And the rumors about my husband's relationship with Mrs. Ward?" Lydia asked.

A faint pink tinted Susannah's cheeks. "I don't know."

"As though I would ever hurt Lydia in such a way," Rees said, turning to look at her and taking her hand in his. Lydia did not look at him but leaned forward a little.

"Do you know who's spreading those lies about us?" she asked insistently.

"No," Susannah said, her eyes shifting away from Lydia's gaze.

"And about Lydia?" Rees asked. "Who's spreading that gossip

about her?" Susannah shook her head, and her fingers began playing with the flounce at her waist.

"Who, Suze?" Rees demanded. "Tell me."

"It was Caroline," Susannah said. "She started the rumors that Lydia was a witch."

Chapter Six

I swear I'll kill my sister," Rees said to Lydia for the tenth time as he helped her into the wagon. He wished he had not eaten the scone. It felt like a lead ingot in his stomach. "How could she do this to me?"

"I know," Lydia said. She reached out and grasped his wrist when he climbed into the seat beside her. "I know. But you must master your anger. Rash action will not help resolve this."

He nodded, knowing she was recalling the blow that had hurled Sam to the mounting block. He took a deep breath but it did not calm him. Exhaling loudly, he picked up the reins and slapped them down upon Hannibal's back.

They rode home in silence. Rees did not trust himself to speak. He was furious with his sister and it took all his energy to keep himself from exploding all over again. But he was determined to speak to Caroline and demand an explanation this very day when he went over to help with the haying.

He deposited Lydia at his farm and unloaded the barrels of flour into the pantry. Then he climbed back into the wagon seat. His heartbeat began to speed up as he anticipated his conversation with Caroline.

It was already noon when he arrived and time for dinner. Of Caroline there was no sign but David, Simon, Sam, and Charlie were seated under a tree near the dilapidated house. Knowing Caroline's lack of domestic abilities, Lydia had packed a large basket for her menfolk this morning and David had just begun unpacking the freshly baked bread, a roasted chicken, hard-boiled eggs, and a wheel of cheese when his father pulled up. Charlie leaned with assumed nonchalance against the oak's trunk. But as Rees crossed the downtrodden weeds he noticed how his nephew eyed the food hungrily. David offered him a chicken leg and a hunk of cheese. Sam sat down without an invitation and grabbed a loaf of bread, tearing off a hunk with his dirty hands and stuffing it into his mouth. Rees shook his head. It was fortunate Lydia had packed enough for all of them.

"Where's my sister?" he asked.

"Inside," Charlie said.

Rising to his feet, Rees crossed the trash-strewn yard toward the house. He paused, foot on the lowest porch step, and listened. He could hear chickens clucking. He walked around the house to a fence made of stacked tree branches and peered over it. A small flock of chickens scratched in the dirt. Were these his missing poultry? All chickens looked alike to him. "David?" He called his son over, and when David approached Rees tipped his head at the flock on the other side of the fence.

"They're our chickens," David agreed. "See the hen with the torn comb? I saw that happen. Hawk tried to grab her. That's ours."

Rees swore and smacked his fist into the fence. Compared to the gossip that was distressing Lydia so, the theft of a few chickens was a small thing. But it was one more example of his sister's entitled behavior. Realizing that David had stepped back and was eyeing his father in concern, Rees forced a smile. "Caroline's behavior has become unsupportable. I will talk to her this very minute."

Turning, he stamped around the house. It was really little more than a shack. The front door hung askew from one hinge. The glass in one window had been broken and someone had tacked up a few boards across it. If it were not for the clucking of chickens in their enclosure, a passerby would think this place abandoned. Rees jumped over the rotting steps and banged on the door frame. He didn't dare touch the door itself, it might fall off completely. Then, although no one called out to him, he went in.

The smell, a combination of rotting garbage and unwashed bodies, hit him first. He tried to breathe in quick shallow breaths. When his nose had adjusted somewhat, he took a few steps farther in.

This was his first time inside and as he looked around he frowned with consternation. A wooden bench and a chair with a broken seat served as the sole furniture in the front part of the room. In the back, the kitchen half, Caroline sat at a wooden table with a carved oak cup before her. Even from the door Rees could see the faint sheen of greasy grime that covered the table. Dirty dishes littered almost every surface. Georgina, the youngest child, was eating an egg with her hands and yellow yolk smeared her face and the hair that hung unbrushed from her cap. Gwennie, the eight-year-old, bent over the spider, cooking another mess of eggs. "I'm sorry, Mama," she was saying. "All the yolks broke." Like her sister, Gwennie's clothing was ragged and dirty. The grayish tint to Caroline's apron and cap betrayed too long a span without laundering. Rees stared at his sister in shock. Caroline had always been the fastidious sister.

Gwennie bent precariously close to the flames as she poked at the eggs. But Caroline seemed not to notice. She stared blankly into her cup as though trying to read the future. "Caroline," Rees said. What was wrong with her? He crossed the floor in two strides and snatched up the little girl. "I think the eggs are done," he said to her as he moved her away from the fire. He wrapped a towel around the spider's handle and pushed it to the front of the hearth.

Caroline did not even turn her head to look at him.

He looked down at the little girl. "Have you eaten yet?" She gulped and shook her head.

"These are for my mother. She hasn't been eating."

Rees looked at his sister, really noticing her scrawny arms and angular, bony face for the first time. How had he not seen this before?

"Take Georgina out to the trough and wash her face and hands," he told Gwennie, lifting her younger sister to the floor. Both children could do with a bath. They smelled. "Then go out front and ask David to give you some food. He brought over a basket."

"Really?" asked Gwennie. He nodded and they ran out eagerly.

Rees sat down in the rickety chair across the table from Caroline. She slowly raised her eyes. "I want to talk to you about something," Rees said. She released her cup and looked at him, a faint light beginning to glow in their depths. She smiled slightly.

"It's a good time to move," she murmured. Rees ignored her comment, rushing forward with his question and eager to have this conversation finished.

"Besides the chickens you've stolen from me—"

"They're mine," she interrupted.

"No, they aren't. But forget that for now. I want to know why you've been spreading rumors about Lydia."

"Rumors?" Caroline said as though she didn't understand the word.

"Claiming she's a witch."

"I—well, it was only once or twice. And how does it feel to have your spouse badly treated?" For the first time since his arrival, Caroline spoke with some animation. "Are all the old tabbies ostracizing her? Well, good."

"Do you know what you've done?" Rees's voice rose in volume to a roar.

"Do you know what my life has been like?" Caroline shouted back. "Look at how I'm living, my children and me. I have to go ask Father Stephen for charity every Friday night. Every single week. Do you know how shaming that feels?"

"Sitting around in the kitchen doesn't help," Rees said in a judgmental tone.

"What do you expect me to do?" She began to sob.

Rees stared at his sister, his emotions a tangle of anger, frustration, and regret. He wanted to shake her, make her see her responsibility in this. At the same time, he wondered if he should be doing more to help her, and that guilt aggravated him all over again. "I've known other women who managed," he said. "Why, I knew a girl in Salem who ran her own shipping business."

"Did she have three children?" Caroline asked. "And a husband with no more sense than a babe? Because of her cruel brother?"

"Did you tell everyone I murdered Zadoc Ward to punish me?" Rees's voice rose with frustration.

"I don't know what you're talking about," she said with a sniff.

"But that's you, blaming me for everything. Mother and Father would be horrified."

Fearing his anger would drive him into saying something he would regret, Rees rose to his feet and stomped from the house. Then he paused in the yard. There were so many arguments he might have made. He half-turned, ready to go back inside, but reconsidered.

For two pins, he would go home and forget his promise to help with the haying. Of course, that would give his sister more ammunition to use in her pose as martyr. And he hadn't promised Caroline; he'd given his word to David. Rees looked over to the little group sitting under the tree. David, a chicken leg poised in front of his mouth, was staring at his father. Rees took in a deep breath. He had broken too many promises to his son through the last few years. He couldn't do that to David again.

Pasting a smile on his face, Rees joined the group and took something out of the basket to eat. His stomach was so twisted he could barely force a mouthful of cheese down.

"All right?" David asked.

"Of course," Rees said. Although his hearty tone sounded forced to him, no one except David seemed to notice.

When they all returned to the fields, David gave his father a scythe and directed him to a strip at the very beginning. Rees knew he would not catch up to the boys; they were too far ahead. He began swinging the scythe. He'd only gone a few feet when he began feeling the strain in his arm and back muscles. His soft weaver's hands began to hurt and he feared he would see blisters before day's end. And this field was not as easy as the haying at Rees's own farm. His grandfather had planted different types of grasses and now the fields contained red clover and alfalfa. This meadow had none of that but there was a healthy crop of weeds, mainly thistles, something David kept cut down in his grass. Some of the purple flowers here stood on stalks over Rees's head. His right arm quickly developed a score of little cuts from the long spines on the leaves. These stalks would have to be removed from the haycocks. The thorns would irritate the mouth of an unwary cow that happened to grab one. Rees hoped he could be excused from that horrible chore.

The weight of his sister's angry melancholy cast a shadow over him and he welcomed the heat of the sun on his shoulders and sunburned neck. He ran his fingers over the cut vegetation, the spines of thistles stinging like needles. Should he take in Caroline and her family? He shuddered. How could he even entertain such a notion with the proof of his sister's malice so obvious? But he still felt guilty.

Straightening up and staring unseeingly into the distance, he recalled the slight smile with which she had greeted him, and the comment he'd ignored. Oh no. She thought he'd finally surrendered and was planning to offer her the weaver's cottage on his farm. Rees closed his eyes in a spasm of shame. She had greeted him with hope and he had killed it and then made things worse with his clumsy accusation. Rees straightened and stared blindly over the field. Of course he couldn't know what she'd been thinking, could he? But not knowing did not ease his terrible regret.

"Looks like the hay at this end is dry enough," David said, coming up behind his father and making him jump.

"Yes, I see," Rees said, turning around.

"Are you all right? You look strange."

"Yes." Rees hadn't intended to say anything more but the words burst from him. "I talked to Caroline regarding the rumors she was spreading about Lydia."

"As nimbly as a cow in a cage, I daresay," David said. Rees nodded miserably. He knew he had to try harder.

"Maybe we should take them in to live with us," he said.

"No," David said. "No. And it's not just that I'm staying in the cottage. She'll come with Sam. Maybe if he was gone and it was just Aunt Caroline and Charlie and the girls, I might consider it. Even then you know Aunt Caroline would treat Lydia like help. But there is Sam."

Rees felt a new shaft of guilt pierce him. David had never confided all that had happened to him under his aunt and uncle's care, but he'd never forgiven them for it either. Not for the first time, Rees wondered how often and how cruelly Sam had beaten David. Remembering how Sam had treated his wife and children—why, Sam had broken Charlie's arm at least once—Rees shivered. "I'm sorry," he said now.

David shrugged, brushing it away. "The point is, just because Sam is touched, doesn't mean he's any nicer. And he'd be more trouble anyway. He has to be watched all the time because he wanders off. Then he can't find his way home. Charlie spends a lot of time searching for him. Sam is nowhere to be found now."

"He might be at the mill," Rees said, relieved that he had one answer at least. "I saw him there just this morning."

"I'll tell Charlie," David said. "He'll be glad." He looked down at the rows of cut vegetation. "I'll get you a rake. This stuff is ready for stacking."

For the first time ever, Rees bent his back willingly to the haying. Although at first all he could think about was Caroline, and how badly he'd bungled his talk with her, he was soon too physically tired to think much of anything. And that was best of all.

By the time David called a halt a few hours later—evening chores still had to be done at home—Rees was dazed with fatigue. Haying was hard physical labor and he was unused to it. Besides, he thought, watching Charlie and David joke and mock jostle one another, he wasn't sixteen anymore. He didn't have that kind of energy.

He drove home slowly, his arms and shoulders aching. By the time he pulled up the drive David had already been home for over an hour and had begun the milking. Rees released Hannibal into the paddock and went inside the house.

The kitchen smelled like honey and several small crocks were lined up on the table. Lydia had put the basket of honeycombs out on the porch. Flies, yellow jackets, and other insects buzzed about them, attracted by the sugary nectar still clinging to the cells. Eventually, she would clean the combs and melt them down and the white sweet-smelling wax would be made into her distinctive candles.

"You look tired," Lydia said, drawing a mug of ale from the barrel in the corner.

"I am." Rees sat down heavily in a kitchen chair. He ached all over and his hands were so sore he knew he would do no weaving today. He had to pick up the mug of ale with two hands.

Lydia sat down next to him. "What did Caroline say?" Rees looked at his wife. Her mouth was drawn down and she looked as though she had not smiled all day.

"She admitted to spreading the rumors," Rees said. He put down the mug, so clumsily he slopped ale across the table, and reached across to take her hand. "It's my fault. Caroline wanted to punish me through you. She thought the ladies in town would ostracize you."

"And I suppose they would, if I had any social connection with them," Lydia said. She turned her hand so that she could clasp Rees's freckled paw. "It's not your fault. I am shocked that Caroline would do something so cruel, but that must lie on her conscience, not on yours."

Rees nodded although he did not entirely agree. "She still wants to move in here," he said. Rising painfully to his feet, his back and legs protesting with every movement, he went to the sink and poured a jot of water from the jug into the basin. Although the water was warm from sitting in the sun, the liquid felt cool when he splashed it on his sunburnt cheeks. Every scratch on his hands stung and when he employed Lydia's strong yellow soap on his grubby fingers he had to keep himself from yelping in pain.

"I know," Lydia said from behind him, "that we are supposed to turn the other cheek and love even our enemies. But right now I just can't consider allowing Caroline to reside under my roof."

"David said something similar," Rees said.

"What did I say?" David said from behind Rees.

"That Caroline and her family should not live here," Rees said, turning. David carried two brimming pails of milk through the door. "But you should see how they are living. I just couldn't scold my sister for stealing the chickens."

"Your kind heart does you credit," Lydia said, rising to her feet. She began removing the crocks of honey to the pantry.

"What she means," David said, "is that you would be crazy to bring Aunt Caroline here. It would be like taking a viper into your bed. You would have to expect to be bitten."

"But I don't know what to do," Rees said.

"Write your sister Phoebe," Lydia said, reappearing in the pantry door. "Although Caroline left Phoebe's farm, we don't know whether Caroline chose to do so or whether Phoebe asked her, once Sam reappeared. But she knows your sister as well, if not better, than you do, so she may be able to propose a solution."

"That is a wonderful idea," Rees said, planting a kiss upon his wife's forehead.

"Go, do it now, while you are thinking of it," she said, giving him a little push toward the parlor. "I'll put dinner on the table."

Rees went into the parlor and took a sheet of paper and a pencil from his mother's lap desk. He carefully sharpened the pencil with his knife. He wrote, *Dear Phoebe*. He was still staring at the paper, blank except for the salutation, when Lydia brought in a bowl of hot stew and a chunk of bread. She looked over his shoulder.

"All this time for two words?" she said.

"I can't think how much I should say," Rees said. "Should I tell her about the rumors? Or mention that Caroline wants to move in with us? Or just say I need her help?"

Lydia squeezed his shoulder and quietly left the room. Rees licked the pencil tip.

He ate all the stew and the bread and still could not think what he wanted to say. Gradually the golden rays of sun that were pouring through the windows shifted position and soon Rees sat in shadow. He could barely see the paper. Finally he wrote: *Caroline is having trouble. I need help with her. Can you come?*

It did not even begin to address the situation but it was the best Rees could do. He folded it and, with a sigh of relief, left the parlor. When he entered the kitchen he handed it to Lydia. "Will you bring this to Borden's store tomorrow, when you go into town for market?" She nodded and put it inside the basket of honey crocks.

"Where is everyone?" Rees glanced around the empty kitchen.

"David and Simon are collecting eggs. Jerusha is putting the little ones to bed."

Rees sniffed. "What's burning?" He realized that he had been aware of the odor for a little while but had not paid attention. The acrid smell was much stronger in the kitchen, but he saw nothing amiss. The fire had been banked and only a few embers remained. He sniffed again and walked to the door. Although the sky was still streaked with light, the ground beneath lay in shadow. A reddish glow tinted the horizon. Lydia came up behind him.

"I smell smoke too," she said.

"Something's on fire." Rees said, descending the steps.

The stink of burning was much stronger outside and now he could see sparks flying in the air. He turned to tell Lydia to stay inside but found she was right behind him, a lighted lantern in her hand. "It's the bees," she said and lunged past him. Rees did not argue. He followed Lydia over the crest of the hill and down the slope.

Chapter Seven

❧

A yellow-and-orange blaze illuminated the hollow with a hellish light. Fire had consumed at least one hive and flames were leaping from a second. As Rees watched from the crest of the ridge he saw a spark jump to a third bee skep and the glow as fire took hold in the straw.

"It looks as though the fire is mostly at the southern end," Rees said, trying to reassure Lydia. "The other hives must be all right."

Lydia said nothing. She waddled down the slope toward the hives as fast as she could. Rees put on a burst of speed and quickly outpaced her. He joined David and Simon in the valley.

Simon was already by the hives, trying to douse the flames with buckets of water drawn from the pond. "David," Rees said, "get some more buckets from the barn." He took the one from Simon and began running back and forth to the pond, filling it with water and emptying it upon the skeps. David returned with two more buckets, and with the three of them dousing the hives with water, the fire was soon extinguished. The air smelled pungently of wet ash and charred straw.

Panting and sweaty, Rees dropped the bucket at his feet and surveyed the damage. Two of the hives were completely gone, burned to a few bits of black. Another was scorched upon one side; no telling if the bees inside had survived or escaped. Several others had been knocked to the ground. The buzz of frightened and angry bees filled the hollow with sound. Of the fifteen hives, only four remained standing and intact. Rees wondered if the smoke had affected them as well.

Heartbroken, Lydia burst into tears.

Rees covered the ground between them in two long strides. He gathered her in his arms. "I'm sorry, I'm sorry," he said, kissing the top of her head. He knew how much she loved those bees. Whoever had set the fire had struck her in the heart.

Simon stared at her in alarm. He still clutched an old bucket, the water leaking through the splints in a steady stream. "You did good," David told him. "You put most of the fire out by yourself." He looked at Lydia then back at Simon. "The damage would have been much worse without you, Squeaker."

"Some of the eggs got broken," Simon said. "I tried to be careful when I took them from the bucket. But one or two broke." His face creasing in anxiety, he looked up at Rees.

"That's not important," Rees told him. He wanted to pick up the child and hug him but knew that would offend Simon, who felt too grown up for such demonstrations. "David is right; the damage to the hives would have been much worse without you. Lydia may be able to salvage some of the skeps." He sounded dubious, even to himself.

"I don't think all of the bees are dead," Lydia said, her voice hoarse from the recent spate of tears. "Maybe some of the colonies escaped into the woods." Rees looked into the darkness, to the copse of trees behind the hives. Although he could hear the faint flutter of leaves, he could see nothing but a wall of blackness.

"We can't see anything now," Rees said. "It's too dark. Maybe tomorrow morning."

Nodding, Lydia stepped away from his embrace. "So many bees dead," she mourned. "All the honey and wax destroyed."

"Maybe this was an accident," David said hopefully.

"It's a clear night," Rees said. "Not a cloud in the sky. No, this fire was deliberately set."

"Who would do such a thing?" David asked, horrified. "Who in Dugard would be so cruel? And so destructive?"

Rees thought the question should be: who hated him and his family so much? He recalled Ward's murder and the reaction of his widow to Lydia's basket. "Caroline," he murmured. "She confessed to spreading rumors."

"Oh, I doubt she had anything to do with this," Lydia said wearily. Surprised by the relief that swept over him, Rees turned to look at Lydia.

"No?" he said.

"I've seen such defacement previously. At Zion." She looked up at Rees. "You know. The Shaker communities are frequently persecuted."

Rees knew. He'd seen the prejudice and persecution firsthand, not only in Zion but in Dover Springs as well. But here? In Dugard? Among people who'd known him all his life? And against his wife who, when she married him, left the Shakers for good?

"I can't really imagine Caroline crawling around in the dark, can you?" Lydia added.

"No," he agreed. He couldn't imagine her climbing Big Knob and shooting Zadoc Ward either, for that matter. And he remembered now that although she'd admitted to spreading the rumors about Lydia, Caroline had denied all knowledge of Zadoc Ward. "But if not her, who?" Had the same person who murdered Ward burned the beehives? He could not believe someone else in Dugard bore him the same malice. And he'd had firsthand experience with his sister, who was vindictive and petty. When they were children together, she'd hurled his prized collection of lead soldiers into the cow pond. He no longer recalled the quarrel that had precipitated the drowning of his entire army, but he very clearly remembered her mocking laughter. Although he'd managed to find most of the soldiers, he knew she'd intended to destroy them all. And she was barely punished. Since their parents believed Caroline delicate, they did not whip her. She was confined to her room for a week, but she swore thereafter that the punishment had been worth it. So, yes, he could see Caroline thinking of burning the beehives, even if she had to ask someone else to set the spark. He considered driving to her farm the next morning and questioning her. But, as he recalled their last discussion, he thought better of it. He didn't want to accuse her without some kind of proof, and he had another way of finding out where she'd been tonight. She'd told Rees that she applied to Father Stephen for charity every Friday night. Rees would ask the minister if Caroline had been there tonight.

Simon collected the unbroken eggs from the grass where he'd dropped them and he and David followed Rees and Lydia up the hill to the house. When they reached the top, they saw Jerusha, standing in the doorway and peering out. "What happened?" she called out. "Where did everybody go?"

"Someone set the beehives on fire," Lydia said, sounding so dispirited Rees put his arm around her shoulders and squeezed.

"But I put the fire out," Simon said, self-importantly.

"He did." Both Rees and David spoke in unison. Let the boy enjoy his good deed for a little while.

"I think everyone should bathe," Lydia said, struggling to speak in her normal tone. Rees looked at her when they stepped into the candlelight. She smelled of smoke. Black ashes flecked her apron and when she'd wiped away tears she'd left a long sooty streak down her cheeks.

"Ahh, we just went swimming," Simon said.

"Very well," Lydia said. "I don't have the energy to insist. Make sure you wash your face and hands . . ." She slumped wearily into a chair at the table and covered her face with her hands. The boys exchanged anxious glances with Rees and tiptoed away.

Confused and at a loss about the proper response to Lydia's grief, Rees sat down beside her. He couldn't tell if she was weeping, but she projected sorrow from every part of her body. Finally, he stood up and put the kettle on. He gathered towels and a bar of her fine Castile soap, used only for special occasions, and put them by her elbow. Hot water went into the basin and as she washed he made a pot of strong tea. Lydia seemed to recover. At least she smiled at him as she emptied her cup. But that night, after they'd gone to bed, he awoke to find her sobbing. She tried to muffle her cries in the pillow but they were clearly audible. The bed trembled with the force of her sorrow. As he rolled over to comfort her, he swore that when he found the person responsible, he would beat him—or her—senseless.

Rees slept poorly the remainder of the night, although Lydia finally fell into an exhausted slumber. After lying awake and staring at the ceiling for some time, he rose and made his way through the darkness to the kitchen. He stoked up the fire and put on coffee. Even David wasn't awake yet, although it wouldn't be long. He usually finished the morning milking around dawn.

Rees stood by the back door and looked outside. The stars burned brightly against the night sky; the morning star had risen and just below it was a thin line of gray. The air was pleasantly cool and scented by growing things. Rees inhaled and caught the acrid undertone of burning. With a sigh, he returned to the fireplace and helped himself to coffee. He ate the remainder of last night's cornbread and was just putting the plate in the sink when he heard the soft scuff of David's stocking feet on the stairs. A few seconds later, David came into the kitchen. He stopped short when he saw his father.

"Awake, already?" he asked.

Rees nodded and gestured to the coffeepot. "Coffee's ready."

"I don't know how you can drink that swill," David said.

"Lydia may choose to skip going to the market today," Rees said.

"I must go," David said. "I have livestock I've got to sell."

"Of course I'll go," Lydia said from the door. Rees turned. She was already dressed. The flesh around her eyes was flushed and swollen and Rees wished he knew how to comfort her. "I won't take the honey. We've lost the income from the hives." She stopped and gulped. Rees moved toward her, intending to pull her into his arms. But she held up a hand to stop him. For a few seconds she fought for control. "We will need the income from the eggs even more now," she said finally, her voice trembling.

"Would you like some coffee?" Rees asked. And, when she shook her head, he said, "I'll put the kettle on for tea."

"I'm going down to the hives," she replied. "I want to see how bad the damage is." Rees made as if to join her. "Alone," she said. "I want to look at them by myself. Please."

Rees nodded but he was not happy. He watched her disappear through the back door. "She'll be all right," David said. "Come on. You can help me milk."

Rees did not want to do farmwork but when he looked at his son, he saw David regarding him with concern. "It'll make you feel better," David said. Rees doubted that but he followed his son through the door and out to the barn.

By the time Rees and David brought the morning's milk to the kitchen, Lydia had returned. Her swollen face and red eyes betrayed a fresh bout of weeping. "How bad is it?" Rees asked in a hushed voice.

"Only one colony intact," she said. "I hope some of the queens escaped and are setting up new homes in the forest." She gulped and her eyes began filling again. Rees pulled her into his arms and hugged her tightly. After a pause, she stepped back and swiped impatiently at her eyes with her apron. "I think I might be able to rebuild. But it's the wrong time of year. In another few months they will go to sleep for the winter and it's likely I'll lose some." She stopped abruptly and turned away. Rees reached out for her but did not touch her. He felt so helpless and did not know how to comfort her.

"We'll look for them together," he promised. "Maybe you can lure them back." He didn't want them in the strip of woods behind the pasture anyway. Although black bears sometimes came out of the woods to raid the hives, the bears would be even more of a danger hidden within the screen of trees.

"Besides the eggs, I'll bring cheese and butter to market today," Lydia said.

"Are you sure you want to go?" Rees asked again. And when she nodded he said, "I'll accompany you."

"I don't think that's necessary." She forced a smile. "David always joins me. And I know you hate going to market."

"I do," Rees agreed. "But I'll go today. I plan to speak to Father Stephen. I don't want to think Caroline . . ." He stopped.

Lydia touched his wrist. "I know. But I'm confident she is innocent of setting fire to the beehives. I see a big difference between spreading rumors, which she might have done on a whim, and the planning necessary for driving ten miles and more to this farm, slipping onto the property without being seen, and then setting fire to the hives."

Rees smiled at his wife.

"You're right," he said. But he had to be certain, and Father Stephen would confirm—or contradict—Caroline's story.

The thud of feet hitting the floor above them drew Lydia's eyes up. "The children are awake and Abigail will soon be here." She filled a pot with water and put it over the fire. Rees nodded. He was glad of the Quaker girl and her help, especially now that Lydia was expecting a baby. He did worry sometimes about Abigail's relationship with David—they were both so young—but of course his son would be in town as well.

"I'll harness Hannibal to the wagon," Rees said. "We should begin packing what you want to bring to market. If you're really sure you want to go?" He looked at Lydia. She nodded.

"I do. I must." She managed a lopsided grin. "It is what I do every Saturday."

"Very well," Rees said, understanding it would be a comfort for her to return to the familiar. He went out to the barn for the wagon.

Chapter Eight

❧

Rees drove Lydia to market after breakfast. Although he tried to begin a conversation with his wife, she answered in monosyllables and after several attempts he gave up. They traveled the rest of the way in silence. David followed behind them with a wagon full of excess lambs and calves, mostly males. He was trying to increase the size of the flock and herd and for that he needed females. Rees wondered how much luck his son would have selling the livestock; most of the farmers currently had a surfeit of males.

Once Rees had set up Lydia's small table and she had arranged her cheese, eggs, and butter, he walked across the village square to the stone church. He'd been married twice in this Anglican church, and Father Stephen had buried both his parents. Rees had attended more funerals in this building than he cared to remember.

He hadn't been sure he would find Father Stephen. The pastor could have been at home but no, he was standing at the altar marking places in the Bible. He did not smile as Rees walked down the center aisle. "I wanted to ask you a question," Rees said. Father Stephen waited. "My sister, Mrs. Prentiss, said she and her family come every Friday night."

"They do. As you know, some of the local merchants donate food on a regular basis to be distributed to the poor and needy. That store is supposed to be used for those who are alone in the world, like some of our widows, not for someone like your sister who has a well-to-do brother living within a few miles of her."

Shocked by the minister's hostility, Rees did not speak for a moment. "We do help her," he said finally. Irritation made him add, "We regularly give them food and cloth, and I just spent the last day helping her son hay."

"You have sufficient for your needs," Father Stephen said in a stern voice. "Caroline has a justified claim upon you. Especially since you were the one who injured her husband." He paused and Rees pressed his lips together. He doubted he could fully express the nuances of his relationship with his sister. "Is it your wife who refuses your sister room in your house?" Father Stephen continued. "I know Lydia belonged to a strange faith before her marriage. A blasphemous heretical creed, I am told."

"The Shakers are good people," Rees said through his teeth.

"Are they even Christians? Who knows if they believe in good works?" Father Stephen continued.

"They do. But I refuse to discuss theology with you right now," Rees said.

"Hmm. Perhaps we should have that conversation as soon as possible. I haven't seen either you or your wife at services for some time."

Rees held his breath and counted to ten. "We were speaking of my sister," he said. "I think you do not fully understand the situation. I can imagine what she's told you."

"She does not need to speak at all," Father Stephen said tartly.

"We can see the results of your temper. You forget, I remember you as a little boy. You were always fighting with somebody."

"Will. Come and help." The frantic voice of Rees's friend George Potter penetrated the church. Rees turned to look. "Lydia is in trouble at the market."

Rees ran down the aisle and through the open door to the courtyard. Potter's face was white and sweaty with fear. Rees glanced at his friend and increased his speed. "What happened?" He threw out the question as he raced past.

"I don't know." Potter burst into a trot but could not keep up. Rees ran as fast as he could, his heart thudding with fear. Likeliest, Lydia was arguing with someone over the cost of a cheese. But he didn't believe it. Potter's expression had been too terrified for such a simple explanation.

At first, Rees couldn't see anything; the crowds were too thick. But even from the church he could hear the shouting and screaming. The crowd was gathered around something. Some of the people wore horrified expressions but most were flushed and shouting with excitement. Something was happening. He shoved his way through until he could see.

Lydia was hiding under her table. Shattered eggshells circled her in a ring of white, the yolks smearing the dirt like yellow blood. As Rees watched, a stone flew through the air and landed on her foot. If Lydia cried out, Rees could not hear it over the roar of voices. One young man reached under the table and began pulling Lydia from her shelter by her ankles. She tried to kick him away, losing one of her shoes in the struggle. But he held on and her white legs appeared as her skirt was rucked up.

Uttering a roar of rage, Rees forced his way through the throng and ran forward. He caught the fellow by his collar and began to shake him. "How dare you lay hands upon my wife? I'll kill you for this." The boy released Lydia's ankles and thrashed around like a fish on a hook, determined to break free.

"Murderer," someone shouted behind Rees. He felt the impact of a rock against his back. Grunting in pain, he turned and tried to see his attacker, involuntarily loosening his grip on his captive. With a mighty heave, the young man pulled away, tearing the grubby collar of his linen shirt. Rees was left with a handful of dirty cloth. But he knew who the lad was—one of Farley's boys.

He rushed to Lydia's side. Sobbing with fear and humiliation, she was attempting to smooth her skirt over her bare legs. Rees helped her to her feet and folded her into his arms, glaring at the people standing around them. One final egg came flying through the air. Rees felt it break against his shoulder. He craned his neck and saw another lad join Farley's son. Rees vowed he would find those boys. And beat them bloody until they cried for mercy.

"Let's get her to the church," Potter said, joining Rees in the square. Raising his voice, he shouted, "Nothing more to see. Go back to your business."

Rees looked around, defying those who remained to say or do anything further. Most dropped their eyes, unable to look at him, whether from embarrassment or fear Rees could not tell.

Potter took Lydia's other arm and together they supported her over the short walk to the church. Once inside, Rees pressed Lydia into a seat in the back pew and examined her. Blood streamed from a cut on her forehead. The handkerchief she pressed to the wound was already crimson and a thin line of red ran down her hand and into the sleeve of her gown.

"I'm all right," Lydia said, but her wobbly voice gave a lie to her words.

"It's just a scratch."

"More than a scratch," Rees said, trying to move her hand away. It was a long cut, although not deep, and blood was still seeping from it. He took out his handkerchief and pressed it to the wound. "What happened?"

"People started shouting," Lydia said. "Someone threw a rock." Rees stared at her as she put her face in her hands. He knew she wasn't telling him everything.

"Will," Potter said. And when Rees looked up Potter jerked his head toward the street outside. Rees hesitated, reluctant to leave his wife. Potter motioned emphatically toward the door and the bright sun beyond.

"I'll just be outside," Rees murmured. Lydia nodded but did not open her eyes. With a final pat on her arm, Rees followed Potter to the slate walk outside.

"It was an attack," he said baldly.

"I saw Farley's sons," Rees said.

"They came from the Bull, liquored up and ready for trouble. Caldwell is trying to hunt them down now." Potter hesitated, his eyes shifting from Rees's.

"What?" he asked. "What else?"

"They not only assaulted your Lydia," Potter said in a hushed voice. "They called her names."

A wave of nausea swept up from Rees's belly and into his throat. "What—what names?" He knew some, if not all, of the men in the Bull blamed him for Ward's death. That was clear. Were they attacking Lydia because of him?

"Witch. I heard one of them—he shouted, 'Thou shalt not suffer a witch to live,' as he threw a stone."

"What?" Rees stared at Potter. "They openly accused Lydia of being a witch?"

"It was probably just, well, you know." Potter shook his head in disbelief. "Probably just the worst accusation they could imagine."

"I'll wager everything I own that Farley was at the back of it," Rees said grimly. "He believes in witches and all manner of foolishness."

"Maybe. The constable can certainly tell you more. He saw it unfolding." Potter glanced over his shoulder, as though he could see the market from the church. Except for the stalls at the very end of Main Street, nothing else was visible and those few tables appeared to have been abandoned. "Take your wife home. Where is your wagon?" He looked around as though expecting it to spring up with Hannibal already harnessed to it.

"At Wheeler's Livery," Rees said, turning back to the church.

"I'll tell David where you've gone." Potter managed a lopsided smile. "He probably doesn't know what happened. He was at the far end, with the livestock . . ."

Rees nodded sharply and hurried inside. Although very pale, Lydia had sat up again and opened her eyes. Father Stephen was walking rapidly down the aisle with a beaker of water.

"I'm fine," she said when he glanced at her.

"I'll fetch your wagon for you," Potter said from the door. "Don't worry. Just take Lydia home. I'll tell David to follow you."

"Very well," Rees said. He joined his wife on the bench, eyeing her in alarm. Blood had run down the left side of her face and onto the white skin of her shoulder, revealed by her torn dress. Lydia forced a smile.

"I fear my gown is ruined. I'll soak it in cold water at home, but I expect the stains will have dried and set by the time we reach the farm."

"Don't worry about that now," Rees said. "What happened?" He leaned forward to examine the cut. It was so long it would probably leave a scar when it healed. And every time he looked at it, he would remember where that scar came from. "Who tore your dress?"

"I have such a headache," she said. "Oh, I didn't really see them. I heard shouting and suddenly there were eggs flying all about me. Then the stones . . ." She gulped. "The man in the stall next to me ran over and pulled me down, under the table, else I should have been more badly hurt. I don't know what happened next. I heard Caldwell's voice shouting and someone discharged a gun."

"What were they shouting?" Rees asked.

"Oh, just general epithets." She did not want to answer and her eyes shifted away from him.

"Lydia, Lydia Jane," Rees said, shaking her gently. "Don't lie to me."

"Witch," she said. "They called me a witch." Tears filled her eyes. "Someone shouted, 'Where's your broom? Have you killed any babies today?' The man who tore my dress—he said he was looking for a witch's mark. And then, when they started throwing rocks, I heard someone say, 'Thou shall not suffer a witch to live.'" She frowned and put her fingers on the handkerchief-covered wound. "He sounded older though. And more serious."

"Farley," Rees muttered.

"He accused you of murder," Lydia said, holding her torn dress closed as she sat up. "I heard him. He said you killed Zadoc Ward." Rees blew out a breath. So Ward's murder, and the implications against Rees, were connected to the accusations against Lydia. Who was doing this?

"Why would I kill Ward? My fights with him were trivial." Although his voice was shaking, he tried to sound nonchalant. He didn't want to frighten Lydia any further.

"Mr. Farley accused you of killing—or rather sacrificing—Ward for some foul rite."

"Farley is nothing but a superstitious lout," Rees said, trying to smile at his wife.

"Maybe so," Lydia said, looking at her husband anxiously. "But now his death and the accusations against me are connected."

"This is directed at me," Rees said. He paused, thinking. "Ward and Farley were not friends so . . ." He stopped. Farley was using Ward's murder to go after Rees and his wife. He needed to solve Ward's murder and find the architect of these attacks.

"I thought this was—I don't know—not serious. Just a pattern of the general distrust directed at the Shakers and Mother Ann Lee. But it is much more dangerous than I thought. I . . ." She swallowed convulsively, tears welling in her eyes.

"Mrs. Lee and her adherents were treated so with reason," Father Stephen said in a sharp voice. Rees jumped. He'd forgotten the pastor was there. "Doesn't that faith—your faith—believe in the end of the world? And that God is equally feminine and masculine?" He looked directly at Lydia. "All blasphemous teachings, but the most profane is that your Ann Lee is divine."

"She was touched by God," Lydia retorted passionately. "God granted her visions." Rees could feel his brows rising in astonishment. Lydia was the most practical of women, not one to believe in things she could not see or touch.

"So I've heard," Father Stephen said. "Her vision of an angel on the ship crossing from Great Britain to New York was the talk of sailors everywhere."

"She was right, wasn't she?" Lydia said. "The ship did not founder in the storm. They survived."

"That vision," Father Stephen said through his teeth, "could have as easily come from Satan as from God. Your sex is easily swayed by the Devil."

Rees gaped at the other man. "What are you saying? This is my wife. You married us here, in this very church."

Father Stephen, his lips so tightly pinched together a white line circled his mouth, turned his gaze to Rees. "You would not be the first man to be suborned by a fair face and form, unsuspecting of the rottenness within. Her red hair should have warned you."

Rees jerked Lydia to her feet. "We are leaving," he said. He had seen many strange events in his travels but none had had a supernatural cause. Although he tried never to argue these matters of faith, he did not believe either. People, in his opinion, caused their own Heaven or Hell. And these passions all too frequently justified cruelty to another.

"Beware," Father Stephen said to Rees's back. "Cast her off before you are tainted as well. Your birth and upbringing in this town will not save you."

Rees almost turned around. He was trembling with fury and, if he had not had Lydia clinging to his arm, the blood from the wound on her head still fresh and glistening, he would have punched the minister for his accusations, man of God or no.

Rees drew Lydia into the sunshine. Potter had drawn the wagon up to the gate. He waved from the wagon seat and hurriedly scrambled down. "Here you go. I saw Caldwell and he said he'll ride out after market is done and speak with you." Potter stopped talking and peered into Rees's face. "Are you all right?"

Rees reached out for the reins. "Fine." His voice was hoarse, unrecognizable. He turned to Lydia and extended his hand. She was trying to hold the ripped collar of her dress closed with one trembling hand and her hair had come unpinned and tumbled down her back. Her skirt was clotted with mud. Queasy with the intensity of his emotion, Rees closed his eyes and swallowed. When Lydia was settled he would return to town and find the young men who'd attacked her, a pregnant woman.

"You look—enraged," Potter said, taking an involuntary step backward. "Calm down."

"I'm fine," Rees said. It was so much easier to feel anger than admit to the fear that something terrible could have happened to Lydia and the baby she carried. He looked at her.

"I'm well," she said. "The baby too. Don't worry." Laying her hand upon Rees's sleeve, she smiled up at him. "We're both fine, I promise you."

Nonetheless, Rees lifted her into the seat, taking as much care as though she were exquisite china. He knew she was in pain when she gladly accepted his assistance; she usually climbed up by herself. He scrambled up beside her. Now that the danger was past he was shivering and sweating. He couldn't speak—when he tried his voice came out thready and weak—so he slapped down the reins. When Hannibal jolted into a walk Lydia swayed in the seat. "Do you need to lie down?" Rees asked anxiously.

"I can sit," she said, but she hung onto the side with such force her knuckles turned white and all the tendons in her hand stood out like cords. She was trembling like an aspen tree in a high wind. He took one hand off the reins for a moment to pat her shoulder.

"You know," Lydia said in a quavering voice, "I do not entirely believe in visions. But Mother Ann was a great woman."

"I understand," Rees said. "Don't worry about that now."

They did not speak again until they were clear of the town limits. Rees hadn't realized how tense he was and how tightly he was holding his shoulders until they left the town behind. "We're all right now," he said, feeling his solid muscles begin to soften. Relief left him so weak he wasn't sure he could hang on to the reins. Lydia nodded, her head moving jerkily. Her trembling had not ceased; quivers continued to ripple through her body. "I don't want you to go to Dugard again," Rees said.

"But—but market," she stammered.

"I mean it. Dugard isn't safe." He glanced at her and after a few seconds she assented with a nod. Rees turned his attention back to the road. Most of Lydia's eggs had been broken. Any that weren't had probably been stolen, along with the cheeses. The loss of both, on top of the destruction of the beehives, would seriously damage their finances. It had been a week of ill fortune and as he reviewed all that had happened, he wondered whose hand was at the back of it.

He considered his exchange with Father Stephen and recalled other sudden silences when he appeared, cold responses to his conversation and, in some cases, a sniggering attitude that had filled him with anger. He realized that since his return from Salem a few weeks ago he had been sensing something, an uncomfortable aura of dislike and suspicion, wherever he went. It may have begun with Sam's injury but now had expanded to a general aversion to Rees. It was almost as though his visit to Salem had given someone an opportunity to focus their anger and malice upon him and his family. He now knew that the notion someone was purposely targeting his family, something he'd considered nothing more than a wild fancy, was true. But who could it be? He tried to think, growing more anxious as he did so. He needed more information. With a shudder, he put aside the fear so that, although still a cold shadow upon him, it did not hobble him, and he turned a stern look upon Lydia.

"All right, Lydia," he said. "I want the truth." She met his gaze and shivered. "Tell me everything that happened before you joined me in Salem. Everything, including the cat that had kittens."

"Nothing happened," she began.

Rees cut her off, shaking his head. "Something's been going on. I know it. I'm just seeing the most recent attacks now."

She did not speak for a moment but Rees could see her thoughts represented in the small movements of her lips and eyes.

Finally she sighed. "Nothing happened when you were gone. But before you left . . ."

"You were keeping things from me?" His voice rose with hurt.

"David thought it best."

"David?"

"Don't be angry," Lydia said, putting her hand over his. "It didn't seem important at first." She hesitated and when Rees didn't speak she added in a rush, "I think we should wait for David."

Rees could not speak through the pain of the betrayal. He wanted to grab Lydia and shake her. Instead, he turned and dropped the reins gently on Hannibal's back, afraid if he didn't exercise the most powerful control he would lose his temper entirely. The horse jerked forward into a gentle trot.

Chapter Nine

When David arrived home a short time later, Rees met him in the drive.

"Charlie will bring the livestock home," David said to his father. And then, catching sight of Rees's expression, he asked, "What's wrong?"

"Come inside," Rees said. "I want to talk to you."

"I have to unhitch," David began, gesturing toward the horse and wagon.

But Rees cut him off. "Now. Lydia will not answer any questions without you." David swallowed, his Adam's apple moving convulsively. Rees turned and stamped into the house. After a momentary pause, David followed.

His eyes widened when he entered the kitchen and saw the wound upon Lydia's forehead. Although she had changed her torn dress the cut upon her brow and the dried blood streaking her cheek revealed the recent attack. "Mr. Potter said there had been a riot but I didn't realize . . ." David dropped into a kitchen chair and folded his hands so tightly together his knuckles turned white.

"What's been happening here?" Rees demanded. "Something led up to the burning of the beehives. And now this." His eyes moistened as he looked at Lydia. "And because I didn't know about it I couldn't protect my family."

David glanced at Lydia and she nodded at him. He shifted in his seat, eyes downcast. "I'm sorry. At first the little incidents seemed accidental and we ignored them." He looked up and met his father's eyes. "I guess we first realized something was wrong when Daisy disappeared. One of our best milkers."

"We thought at first your sister's family had taken Daisy," Lydia said, wringing a complaint from Abigail, who was trying to sponge the cut.

"But Caroline did not have an opportunity to take the cow," David said. "One day Daisy was just gone. None of the fences were damaged and the rest of the herd was still in the pasture." He met his father's eyes. "I searched and searched but it was Charlie who found her. Two laborers were driving her down the road. Charlie told me they claimed someone had sold her to them. Said we had more than enough and we wouldn't miss her. Mr. Caldwell told them that they could leave the area quietly or he would arrest them for cattle stealing. So we got her back."

"Then the door to the dairy was left open," Lydia said, wincing as Abigail dried the cut with a rough towel. Although the edges were beginning to close, the flesh around the wound looked red and angry. "Some animals got inside." Lydia sighed. "Not only was all of the milk ruined but the dairy had to be scrubbed, top to bottom. I thought maybe Abigail or Jerusha had forgotten to close the door but they swore they hadn't. And once the pigs escaped I was certain they'd told me the truth."

"The pigs escaped," Rees repeated. Lydia nodded and stretched out a hand to touch him. But she thought better of it and pulled her hand back.

Rees thought about his pigs. Most families kept a pig or two. On the frontier they were allowed to go feral and take care of themselves in the woods. But here in Maine, with the farmers scratching a living from the stony soil, many of the pigs were enclosed. At David's urging, Rees had purchased two sows and one had delivered a litter of piglets this past spring. Now they numbered thirteen in all. Or had numbered thirteen. "How many were lost?" he asked.

"One sow and two piglets. We recovered most of them," David said quickly. "The point is only Simon and I feed them. And the Squeaker doesn't even go inside the fence." He paused. Rees nodded, waiting. David had extended the enclosure into the trees so the pigs might scratch for acorns and such as well as eat scraps. "But someone unlatched the gate and let them out."

"At dusk," Lydia put in. "Oh my, we had a fine time chasing them."

"Could be they ran off. Or got picked up by hawks," David said. "But someone opened that gate. Had to be." Rees nodded slowly, the fear he and his family were being purposely targeted flooding into his mind. Not only was it obvious someone had opened the gate, but that someone had taken to visiting Rees's farm to hurt them.

"Whoever is unleashing their spite upon us," he said now, "is growing bolder and more malicious. He—or she—started with little things. But he has evolved to setting fire to the beehives. To accusing me of murder. And the attack upon Lydia cannot be a coincidence." Involuntarily his gaze turned to his wife and his throat closed up so he could not speak for a few seconds.

"Why didn't anyone tell me?"

"At first we thought it was just ill-fortune," David said, frowning in thought. "And then you left for Salem. In fact, that's the puzzling piece of all of this. Nothing happened when you were gone. The pigs were released the same day you left. I think no one knew you weren't here."

Rees considered this, growing more and more worried. He eyed the bandage about Lydia's head. Although *he* was the object of this spite, the malevolent person behind the attacks would not hesitate to assault the ones he loved.

Lydia brushed her hands over her cap, once again confining her hair, and rose to her feet. "Were you successful at market?" she asked David, putting an end to the discussion. He shook his head.

"Not very. Some of the farmers looked at the livestock as though it were tainted." David paused. No one said aloud that they were back to the previous topic, although Rees thought Lydia and David noticed it, just as he did. "I left them behind when Mr. Potter came for me," David continued. "Charlie said he would bring them home. He promised to keep an eye on them and anyway I suspect they would not be stolen. One of Farley's crowd told me he wouldn't eat one of my animals if he were starving."

"That seems excessive," Rees said. He wanted to protest that the fellow was simply exaggerating but after all that had happened, Rees suspected the man was simply stating the truth. No one interrupted the strained silence for several seconds. Simon's playful shout outside pierced the stillness like a knife. Rees turned and looked at Lydia. He wanted to scream and throw things. Who was behind these attacks?

"Aunt Caroline," David said as if he could hear his father's thoughts. "I think she has something to do with this."

"But Caro and her family were at church when the beehives were destroyed. I checked with Father Stephen," Rees said.

David did not look convinced. "So who could it be?" he asked.

Rees shook his head. "I don't know. But someone would have heard something."

"What about that Molly Bowditch?" Lydia said.

"Hello," Charlie said from the doorway. Rees experienced a pang at the thought Charlie might have overheard their comments about his mother. David waved him inside. Charlie was older than David, already seventeen. Although a tall boy, he was not as tall as David, and much stockier. "I brought the livestock," he said. "And Miss Lydia's chair and table."

"Oh, thank you," Lydia said. "I was so afraid I'd lost it."

He smiled shyly at her. "And the constable said he'd be by later."

"I'll help you put the animals in the pasture," David said, rising from the table.

"I was wondering," Charlie said as the two boys went out the back door. "Maybe I could buy a couple of lambs from you. And maybe a heifer or two. Not for cash money but for labor. I'll give you several hours of labor every day for them."

"You're already doing that," David said, his voice fading as they crossed the yard. "I'm sure I can spare some."

Rees thought Caroline might just steal them anyway—and then he mentally castigated himself for his uncharitable thoughts.

"I wonder if the constable caught the young men who were throwing rocks," Lydia said, taking plates and cups from the cupboard.

"I hope so," Rees said. He was eager to know their names. "I know Farley's boys were involved. Or at least one of them."

"You won't do anything, will you?" Lydia asked, looking up at him in concern. "You won't hurt anyone?"

Rees smiled at her. "Of course I won't hurt anyone," he said, meeting her anxious gaze with open-eyed innocence. He did not want to hurt them, just frighten them so much they never considered harming his wife or family again.

"The butter is churned," Abigail said, running up the back steps and coming into the kitchen. "David will put today's milk into the cold cellar and I'll start the cheese on Monday." The soft flush in her cheeks and secretive smile drew Rees's suspicious gaze.

"Where is David now?" he asked.

"Helping Charlie." Abigail cocked her head. "I hear wagon wheels. That must be my brother." She took off her apron and handed it to Lydia and put on her bonnet. Rees and Lydia exchanged a glance and then watched the girl disappear down the hall to the front door.

"He's never alone with her," Lydia said, turning a reassuring smile upon her husband. "Not even long enough for a true conversation."

Rees knew she meant to comfort him. He nodded and smiled but he was still worried. He knew the fire of desire and the shifts to which it would drive a man. He was not confident they had managed to keep Abigail and David from acting upon their feelings for one another.

Lydia went to the door and called in the children for supper.

———

Caldwell did not arrive until well after dusk, so late Rees had given up on him. As soon as Lydia finished cleaning the kitchen, they planned to go upstairs to bed. Even David had retired for the night; four a.m. came all too quickly. Rees was surprised to hear hoofbeats on the packed earth outside. Exchanging a worried glance with Lydia, he picked up a lighted lantern and went through the dark house to the front door. He opened it and went outside. Caldwell also carried a lantern. He handed it to Rees over the porch rail and dismounted.

"I'd given you up," Rees said.

"I've been busy," Caldwell said as he came up the stairs. "I started late and it took me much longer than I expected. But I promised I'd come and I'm here now." He blew out his light and followed Rees into the dark hallway to the kitchen.

Although the fire had been banked, the embers supplied a dim reddish glow. Lydia had lit some of her thick white beeswax candles and they bathed the table in a warm golden light. She'd already poured a beaker of ale. Caldwell sniffed at the faintly yeasty aroma and crossed the room at a rapid trot. Dropping into the chair with a grunt of exhaustion, he took off his hat. Rees eased the hat from Caldwell's hand just before he dropped it on the table and hung it up on a hook. Like most men, the constable wore a straw hat in summer and had exchanged his wool coat for one of linen. But it was still black, much patched, and wrinkled and faded now. But it could be washed and so he smelled marginally fresher than usual. He drained his mug in one long draft. "Haven't eaten or drunk anything since noon," he said by way of apology. Smiling, Lydia took the beaker and brought it to the jug to refill it.

"First off," Caldwell said to Rees, "I don't know all the names of the boys who attacked your wife." Rees grunted in disappointment.

"But I suspected Farley had something to do with it so I rode out to his farm and tasked him directly with it."

"Did he admit it?" Rees asked. He sat down across the table from Caldwell.

"I don't think I've ever met Mr. Farley," Lydia said, returning with a full cup of ale. Caldwell nodded his thanks as she put bread and cheese on a plate and lay it before him.

"He didn't deny it." Caldwell sliced the cheese onto the bread with his knife and took a big bite. "Thanks," he said through his full mouth. "Said he and some of the lads at the Bull were talking. And maybe some of his sons and their friends got excited." He rolled his eyes.

"So, he denied any responsibility," Rees said.

"Not exactly. He admitted he was at the market." Caldwell swallowed the mass of food in his mouth and took several enormous swallows of ale. "Of course we knew that. I think he got everyone fired up, but didn't expect them to go after Mrs. Rees." He bowed awkwardly from his seat to Lydia. "Have you ever been to his farm?" Rees shook his head. "Those witch balls hang everywhere and all the doors have a horseshoe above. Farley's scared. And he suspects Mrs. Rees of practicing the black arts, as he calls them. But he's uncertain enough that he did not lead the attack. If he'd been certain I think Lydia would have been hanged from the nearest tree." Rees gulped and turned to look at his wife. She was blindly wiping a pot over and over, although it had long since been dried. There was no color in her face and her skin looked as waxy as the candles around her.

"Even if I believed in such things," she said, looking at the constable, "I am no witch."

"Of course not," Caldwell said. "But Farley and his wife do believe in such things. And we can see there are others who are either credulous enough to listen to his fears or who pretend to. Someone set him off." Rees made an involuntary sound—he knew Caroline was the guilty one—and Caldwell turned his gaze to the other man. "For what purpose we don't know. And now, well, Farley told me you killed Zadoc Ward to use his body in some blasphemous rite. He may be a fool but he is a dangerous fool."

Rees exchanged a glance with Lydia. "I can hardly believe I'm hearing this. We are but a few years from the turn into a new century. We're not our superstitious grandparents." But he was not surprised.

"It's from envy," Lydia said, almost as though she were hoping this was so.

"Partly," Caldwell agreed. He paused and then added reluctantly, "There's a lot of sympathy for Sam."

"Of course," Rees said, bitterness welling up in his chest. "The man who gambled away his own farm and almost destroyed mine, as well as beating my sister and the children—poor Sam."

"No one should interfere between husband and wife," Caldwell said, his tone making it clear he was quoting someone. "Besides, your frequent absences from Dugard are hurting you. To some, you're almost a stranger. Sam is always here, a familiar sight. And your sister doesn't help your cause." A sudden jaw-stretching yawn interrupted him. His eyes closed and he forced them open again.

"You aren't going to make it home," Rees said. "You should spend the night here."

"All the beds are full," Lydia said, eyeing Caldwell's lank, greasy hair and dirty hands. Rees knew she was considering her clean sheets.

"I can sleep in the barn," Caldwell suggested. "I don't mind telling you I'm knackered."

"We'll make up a pallet here," Rees said, gesturing to the part of the kitchen used for a random assortment of activities. When his parents had built on another bedroom upstairs, this underneath space had been created as well. Rees did not know what his mother had planned for it, but since it held its own fireplace, he and Lydia used it primarily in the winter for their suddenly expanded family. "David rises early for chores and comes in here for breakfast, but he probably won't even notice you."

Caldwell nodded, yawning again. Lydia eyed him once more before disappearing upstairs to fetch a blanket and pillow. Rees noticed that she returned with the oldest she owned; the blanket's edge was ragged and there were several holes chewed through it by mice. But Caldwell didn't seem to notice. He took them with thanks and spread them out in front of the unlit fireplace.

Rees took a lantern outside to unsaddle Caldwell's poor overworked horse. Once the gelding was fed and watered, Rees released him into the pasture with the other horses. Then he went up the back steps and into the house. Lydia had extinguished all the candles save one. She'd taken off her cap and begun unpinning her hair. It glittered red and gold in the pool of light. The steady buzz of Caldwell's snoring, interspersed every now and again with a grunt or a gasp, sounded loud in the silent house. As Rees dropped his boots by the door, Lydia pushed herself up from the table. Smiling, she pointed into the other room at the man snoring in fits and starts on the floor. Rees grinned and nodded. "It must be tiring keeping the peace," he said, linking his arm with hers. They tiptoed upstairs to bed. Joseph, in the little bed beside theirs, turned over with a sigh. Lydia covered him with a light sheet, smiling down at his flushed face. When the baby arrived, Joseph would be moved to the other side to join his siblings and the newcomer would take his place in this crib.

Rees put his arms around Lydia and held her tightly. The depth of his feelings scared him. He would do anything to protect her and his family, anything including killing any man who threatened them. He prayed he would not be forced to cross that line.

Chapter Ten

Lydia spent a restless night, waking up with a cry more than once. Each time Rees held her until she fell back asleep. But he found rest difficult to attain; he was too angry—and too scared—to close his eyes. He promised himself he would find those boys and if Farley was behind the attack, well, Rees would think of some fitting punishment.

Finally, sometime in early morning, Rees gave up his battle for sleep and went downstairs. It was still dark outside. Caldwell was sprawled out across the quilt sleeping—no surprise there. Rees stirred up the fire and put on coffee. Then he went to the back door, expecting to find David outside and help him with chores. But David was already coming up the back steps. "Milking is done," he said.

"Oh. I planned to help."

"Who's that?" David jerked his head in the general direction of the other room.

"Constable Caldwell," Rees said. "He came by very late last night. And no, he doesn't know the names of the men who attacked Lydia." He paused, wondering if he should tell his son about the accusations of witchcraft. Deciding against it, he said instead, "Have you heard anything?"

David shook his head. "But then I don't frequent the Bull. And most of the men I know are too busy working on their farms to waste time on such foolishness."

Rees wondered if David was telling the entire truth. The boy did not meet his father's eyes and Rees detected a certain furtiveness in the quick reply. "Are you sure?" Rees asked. "Would you tell me if you knew?"

"Of course I'd tell you if I heard somebody talking about you," David said emphatically.

"What's going on?" Caldwell asked from behind Rees.

He turned. "Did we wake you?"

"I have to be getting back to town anyway. After a cup of coffee?"

Rees realized he'd smelled the coffee for some time, far longer than it should have been left to perk. He hurried to the fireplace and swung the pot away from the flames. "It's probably as strong as boot leather," he warned over his shoulder. Caldwell shrugged and followed Rees to the table. David took out what was left of last night's injun bread and put it on the table with a jug of fresh milk and a cone of sugar.

"Perhaps I'll ride in with you," Rees said, putting three mugs next to the coffeepot. "I want to talk to the Andersons. See if they know anything."

"Ask your friends only about Lydia," Caldwell warned. "Don't forget—you are not to involve yourself in Ward's murder, as per the magistrate."

"I remember," Rees said. He did not intend to comply, since he now knew that Ward's murder was tied to the attacks on Lydia.

"You remember it is Sunday," David said, helping himself to a huge piece of bread and coating it with butter. "The coffeehouse doesn't open until noon."

Of course it was Sunday. That was why Lydia had gone to market yesterday. In all the excitement, Rees had forgotten. He rubbed his nose thoughtfully. "I'll reach town before services begin," he said. A fury to resolve this situation had taken hold of him. He needed to find the person responsible and stop them. Now. Lydia might be seriously hurt next time. At the same time, he feared leaving Lydia at the farm without his protection. "I'll return as soon as I can."

David nodded and met his father's gaze. "Don't worry," he said. "I'll watch over her while you're in town." Rees inclined his head in gratitude. David understood both Rees's fear and his desire to protect his wife. The lad was more grown up than Rees cared to admit; somehow David's childhood had disappeared.

Caldwell ate the last bite of his bread and stood up. "I should see to my horse," he said, a guilty expression flickering across his face.

"I took care of him last night," Rees said. "He's in the pasture with our herd."

"I'll saddle him," David said, also rising to his feet. Turning to his father, he asked, "Do you want the wagon? I'll hitch Hannibal."

Rees nodded. "Thank you."

Caldwell followed the boy from the house. Rees pushed the coffeepot to one side of the hearth and put on a kettle of water. He could hear Lydia above him and the chatter of children's voices. They would all be down soon and Lydia would want her tea.

The sun had just peeked over the western horizon when Rees

and Caldwell started down the drive. There were a few people on the roads heading into town for Sunday services, but most of the farmers were still doing chores. The traffic would increase greatly within the next hour. When the constable turned west, toward the jail, Rees continued north, toward the coffeehouse.

The front windows were dark. Rees pulled around to the back. A faint mist from Dugard Pond hazed the air but the sun would soon burn it off; the first stray rays already felt warm on Rees's skin. He pounded on the back door. After a minute or so Rachel, the cook, opened the door. She smiled warmly. Rees thought back to the previous summer. Fearful for her son, who had been accused of murder and on the run, she had never smiled then. But now she was happy. "Why, Mr. Rees," she said. "What are you doing here? And so early too."

"I hoped to speak to Mr. Jack and Miss Susannah," Rees said.

"Well, he's already over at the church," Rachel said. "And Miss Susannah is dressing."

"Who is it, Rachel?" Susannah came up behind the cook and peered over her shoulder. Although gowned in her Sunday best, blue cotton with a ruffle at the hem, her curly blond hair lay down her back still confined in last night's plait.

"Will Rees. I should have guessed it would be you."

"I want to talk to you about something," he said.

"Of course you do," she said with a mocking smile. "Even though it is not even seven a.m. on a Sunday morning. Come inside."

The back door led into the kitchen but Susannah did not pause here. She led Rees through to the public rooms at the front. Rees noted that all the pots shone and the tables were scrubbed white; Rachel was doing well here. Susannah gestured Rees to a seat by the window and sat down across from him. "What is so important that it can't wait until this afternoon?" she asked him.

"Did you hear—someone threw rocks at Lydia yesterday."

"Yes." All light left her face and she frowned. "It was the talk of the town. Was she hurt?"

"One of the rocks hit her, left a bad cut." He gestured to his forehead. "Her dress was torn. And she was badly frightened. I fear someone is targeting my family and the next attack might seriously injure someone. Have you heard anything? More than you've told me, I mean."

Susannah hesitated. Finally she said, "There's something more than the usual envy but it is coming out of the Bull." She managed a mirthless smile. "And men claim women gossip. Caroline's malicious accusation against Lydia fell on fertile ground there. I haven't heard much here."

"We both know what my sister is capable of," Rees said. "But spreading rumors—and that's just Caroline's style of indirect malice—is different from attacking an unarmed and innocent woman." His voice rose, prompting Susannah to lean forward and pat his hand.

"Calm down, Will," she said. "Don't do anything rash."

"Me? Rash?" Rees tried for a light tone and failed. "Seriously, Suze, if you have heard anything, no matter how trivial, please tell me."

"Well, Magistrate Hanson is still angry with you for spoiling his land investment schemes."

The door to the kitchen opened suddenly, sending a breath of warm air through the common room. "Rees," said Caldwell. "I hoped you'd still be here. One of the McIntyre boys was waiting for me at the jail. There's been a murder at the mill." He stopped suddenly as though there was more to tell but he'd decided to hold his tongue. Horror contorted his face. Well, Rees was unsurprised by that. But fear shone from the constable's eyes and covered his face in a greasy sweat and it was that emotion that sent Rees into a wild run to his wagon outside.

Chapter Eleven

The village streets were deserted now since almost everyone was at church, and the two men quickly reached Dugard's outskirts. The constable did not head west, as Rees expected, but rode south. They passed near the road to Caroline's farm, and Rees wondered when Phoebe would receive his letter. Of course, she might not come. Caroline had not directed her malice just at Rees. Once, when they were children and Phoebe had a doll Caroline coveted but Phoebe wouldn't give up, Caroline had risen during the night and cut off all her sister's hair. Her explanation? Phoebe was selfish. And now, with Rees's farm, Caroline felt the same desire for something he owned and the same sense of entitlement. "I don't know if I would come," Rees said aloud.

"What's that?" Caldwell said, catching the sound of Rees's voice if not the words.

"Where are we going?" Rees shouted instead of repeating his involuntary comment. They had traveled through town and turned down the road by the carpenter's shop. This road paralleled the western branch of the Dugard River and connected the mill and, farther south, went past the tannery for the village.

"You'll see," Caldwell shouted in reply. He touched his mount's flanks and moved ahead.

Most of the land to the east of the road was farmland and despite the rocky soil the fields were thick with corn and wheat. It had been a good year so far. Fortunately. The previous winter had been unusually harsh. To the west, on Rees's right behind the screen of trees, was the river. He couldn't see it but could hear the water rushing over the rocks in the riverbed. The road made a bend, following the river's line, and some of the houses that comprised a small settlement around the mill came into view. A number of women and children were outside the houses, staring at the mill across the road.

Had one of the millers been killed? A fight over money maybe. Or had it been a brawl?

He followed Caldwell a few more yards, until the mill appeared. Painted red, it was set back just slightly from the road so that the mill wheel could drop down into the rushing stream. A cluster of men congregated outside, kept back by McIntyre's sons. Caldwell pulled up and eyed the crowd. "Damn," he said. "I'd hoped to keep this quiet."

Rees examined the faces of the men. Besides the mill workers, he spotted Sam standing among a number of tavern regulars. Everyone looked shocked and although there were a few muttered comments here and there, there was little conversation. Caldwell kneed his mount into a walk.

Rees took up the reins and followed the constable to the mill. Rees must have been here a thousand times during his lifetime. His parents had sent him here with rye and corn to be ground as a boy and now he did it for his own harvests. But today it felt strange to pull the wagon up to the side of the mill. Especially since he heard low mutters from the men standing along the road.

Caldwell dismounted and tied his cob to a post. Rees doubted the horse would run; the gelding moved slowly, head down, with exhaustion. Caldwell had been using him hard the last few days. As Rees tied up Hannibal beside the constable's nag, he realized something was different. Something was wrong. The enormous mill wheel was still. The grinding had stopped. Rees could hear the water in the river and the wind soughing through the trees, sounds usually completely submerged in the thrum of the turning millstone. During the summer, from July on, the stone turned almost every day until nightfall, grinding the bounty from the fields into meal and flour. The big wheel did not stop until after the first killing frost. Except for winter, when the frozen river held the waterwheel in place, the only time Rees could recall a pause in the mill's work was at the death of Mac's father.

Rees began to run toward the door.

"Wait. Rees, wait," Caldwell shouted as Rees went around him and through the door.

At first he saw nothing amiss. He ran up the ramp to the grain floor. A wall separated the millstone and the hopper above it from view; not a complete wall either. Rees could see some of the stone and the hopper above it through gaps between the boards. It didn't seem at first that anything was wrong. He turned left and went down the short narrow hall, out into the large interior of the mill. The dust that covered every surface puffed up from his feet and thickened the air around him with a faint white haze.

There were only two small windows high up in the back wall so the rear of the mill was in shadow. But a shaft of sunlight came in over the great wheel, shining upon the middle of the mill and illuminating Tom McIntyre.

His naked body had been tied upside down to one of the support posts. The flesh of his chest and legs was a startling white in comparison to his tanned face and forearms. Rees shuddered but forced himself to look at the body and notice everything. His ankles were tied securely at the top and the crown of his head rested upon the mill floor. Blood had pooled around his head, so much blood it was still not completely dry. The buzz of the swarming flies created a steady background hum.

A shovel, its blade darkened by blood and hair, had been tossed to one side. Rees gagged and had to stare over the mill wheel to the blue sky beyond for a few moments before turning back to the body.

McIntyre's arms had been stretched out and tied to the posts on either side of him. Someone, probably one of the miller's sons, had tied a strip of sacking around his waist to cover him. A pocketknife lay near his right hand, laying limply upon the floor. Although footprints marked the slurry of blood and flour on the wooden floor, the knife itself was clean of blood.

"Oh no, oh Mac," Rees said, his voice breaking.

"Good friend?" Caldwell asked, panting up behind Rees. Rees didn't know how to answer. No, he and Mac were not good friends, but Rees had known the miller all his life. Although they disagreed over politics, McIntyre did not deserve this end to his life. Nobody did. Rees stared at the body, almost too shocked to think. And to be posed in such a humiliating position; it was almost worse than the murder.

"Who found him?" Rees asked.

"Mac's sons. When they came in this morning. They said he stayed late to do some cleaning."

Rees went down on one knee to inspect Mac's head. He did not look peaceful. His wide-open eyes stared at nothing. "He was beaten," Rees said. "Did you see that?" He pointed to Mac's deformed head. The blood on the floor here was thick with brain matter. In this July heat the blood was already taking on the stink of rotting meat. Rees rose hurriedly to his feet and ran to the side, where he threw up the contents of his stomach.

The wheel occupied most of this wall. Breathing deeply to settle his rebellious stomach, Rees peered through the gaps between the spokes. He could see the trees on the other side of the river. A bird, a hawk by the width of the wings, took off from a branch and rose into the air, disappearing from Rees's sight into the glare of the sun. The peaceful bucolic scene was so at odds with the death inside the mill. Rees closed his eyes a moment, finally opening them and turning to face the constable. "Whoever killed him hit him over and over, long after he was dead."

"McIntyre wouldn't have stood still and let a stranger approach this closely," Caldwell murmured.

Rees nodded in agreement. "It was someone he knew, all right. And the killer was very angry."

"Must have been; he attacked Mac and then took his time staging this little scene. He came prepared to work after dark." Caldwell gestured to the row of white pillar candles lined up upon the grindstone. "Then the question becomes, why bother? Why not just shoot the poor fellow and be done?"

"I wish I knew," Rees said. "But I promise you, I'll find out." First Zadoc Ward and now Thomas McIntyre; what was going on?

For a moment Rees considered the possibility of two different murderers.

Ward had been shot from a distance, his murder almost anonymous, detached. But Mac's death was intimate, the bludgeoning and posing of the body personal and full of rage. The two victims were also very different. Zadoc Ward was a bully and not well liked, Mac was a pillar of the community and popular. His family had been here for generations. Why, Mac's great grandfather had built the mill.

"Why would anyone kill Mac?" Rees wondered aloud. "And do this to him?"

He gestured to the scene before him.

"I may have part of the answer. This is what I wanted to show you." Caldwell pointed to a patch of floor. "You have to be close to see it." So Rees crossed the wide planks back to the spread-eagled body tied to the posts. He stood behind them this time; he just couldn't look at Mac's face again. The blood had combined with flour dust to make a dark paste that had dried upon the floor. When Rees peered at the marks he saw a pattern: a crooked L and a deformed 7.

"What does that mean?" Rees wondered aloud. The marks were close to Mac's right hand. Caldwell squatted and turned over the limp fingers so that Rees could see the brown stain on the forefinger.

"This is why Elijah kept his brothers from cutting down the body. He thought his father might have left a clue to the killer."

"But it makes no sense," Rees said, his bellow echoing through the mill. "Seven? What does that mean? That there were seven killers?"

"You're standing on the wrong side," Caldwell said in exasperation.

"Anyway, Mac couldn't have written this," Rees said. "He was dying when he was tied up. He wouldn't have had the time to write a message. And his wrists were tied to the posts on either side. And the angle is wrong."

"Exactly what I thought," Caldwell said. "Come around and look at it from this side."

Reluctantly Rees circled the post. He did not look at the body but kept his gaze pinned to the floor. Caldwell put his hand down and bracketed the letters with his thumb and forefinger. "LY . . ." Rees began. Then his throat closed up and he couldn't continue. Caldwell straightened up.

"Someone wants everyone to believe that Lydia did this," he said.

Rees stared at the constable in horror. "Why accuse Lydia? She couldn't . . . And why would she . . . ?" Rees felt so light-headed he could barely talk. Farley would now feel he had clear proof of Lydia's guilt. "She never even met Mac."

"Of course she didn't do this," Caldwell said, waving away the suggestion. "Mac was a small man but no woman could lift him, tie him to the posts, and pose him. Especially not if she were in a delicate condition, as Lydia is. Besides," he added with a mirthless smile, "out of the entire town, I can be sure of only your and Lydia's innocence. Since I stayed at your house last night, I know exactly where you were."

Rees nodded. "That's true. But whoever did this did not know that." He looked at the candles on the flat round stone. There were six, all pure beeswax, and only partially burned. They looked exactly like the candles Lydia made and saved for special occasions. She would want to reuse these candles; any frugal housewife would, but the killer had left them here. "Lydia's candles were stolen and placed here to further implicate her," Rees said. While this staged scene might be an effort to deflect suspicion away from the real killer, Rees did not think that was so.

Beginning with Zadoc Ward's murder, no, before that, with the theft of the cow and the release of the pigs, and then Ward's murder and the attack upon Lydia's beehives, and now this, Rees and his family had been targeted. It was all part of the same malicious scheme. Rees shuddered. Despite the differences between the murders of Zadoc Ward and Tom McIntyre, both had been arranged to destroy Rees. Throwing suspicion on him for Ward's death had not done sufficient damage. But attacking Rees through Lydia—that had a powerful effect. Seeing Rees's reaction to the assault upon Lydia in the market had given the murderer a formidable weapon—and Mac had paid the price.

"Are you about finished?" McIntyre's eldest son, Elijah, paused at the end of the wall. "We want to . . ." A suppressed sob interrupted him.

"Was anyone here with your father last night?" Rees asked. Elijah glared at him and shook his head. "Of course not. No one. Just my father." A sob escaped him. "Who would do this?" He stared at Rees, and Rees felt the accusation almost like a physical blow.

"Do you have a bit of sacking?" Caldwell cut in before Elijah could continue his thought. Turning to Rees, he said, "Will you help me cut him down?"

Rees nodded. Although Susannah's information combined with Mac's death and the effort to incriminate Lydia had filled Rees with a desperate urge to see his wife, he didn't want Mac's sons to have to cut down their father. It was terrible enough to imagine this scene lingering in their memories for the rest of their lives. "Of course," he agreed.

Elijah, who could be no more than three or four years older than David, ran down the hall to the stairs. A few seconds later Rees heard footsteps thudding up to the top floor where the sacked grain was brought in and poured into the hopper. An empty sack with flecks of rye still clinging to it floated down from the upper floor. Rees took out his pocketknife and cut the sack's seams. The rough cloth opened into a sheet. He glanced at Caldwell. The constable nodded and knelt to begin sawing at the ropes around Mac's right wrist. Rees applied himself to the left wrist, keeping his face averted from the body. Usually he was not so squeamish, but he kept imagining Mac laughing and, during their final argument, calling Rees a silly fool for believing in President Washington. Dealing with the corpse of someone he knew was so much harder than with a stranger.

They got Mac down and stretched him out upon the floor. Caldwell knelt for one last look before covering the body with the hairy hessian cloth. Rees was breathing hard, not because Mac was so heavy but from the twin emotions of horror and fear. Poor Mac. And was Lydia all right? Had she been attacked during his absence? "I have to go home," he said, his teeth chattering so much he garbled the words.

Caldwell looked up at him. "I'm sure she's fine," he said. "But go on. I'll come by later and we'll talk."

Rees ran outside, barely noticing the glances directed his way or hearing the whispered comments. His entire being was focused on Lydia, on reaching her and assuring himself of her and his unborn child's safety.

Chapter Twelve

When Rees pulled up to the front porch, he didn't even un-hitch Hannibal before running inside. Lydia and David looked up in surprise as Rees crossed the kitchen floor in two bounds and gathered Lydia in his arms. He held her tightly, resting his cheek against the cap covering her red hair.

"What happened?" David asked, shocked.

Lydia struggled loose, remaining within the circle of his arms but far enough away to look into his face. "What did Susannah say?"

"Nothing much."

"Had to be something," she said, scrutinizing his expression. "You look terrible."

"Thomas McIntyre was murdered. His sons found him in the mill."

"Murdered!" David exclaimed. Throwing a quick look at Lydia, he asked his father, "How?"

"He was beaten." The image of the body tied upside down to the post flashed into Rees's mind, so sharp and immediate he could smell the blood. "It was terrible."

"Lydia is right; you don't look very good," David said, reaching out to grasp his father's shoulder. "I didn't realize you and Mr. McIntyre were such good friends."

"We weren't," Rees said, allowing David to draw him across the floor and press him into a seat at the table.

"Then what happened?" Lydia asked. "It's unlike you to be so distraught."

Rees did not reply, his attention captured by the candles in the middle of the table. They were identical to the candles in the mill. He began to tremble.

"What's wrong?" Lydia asked. "And don't tell me this is because of Mr. McIntyre's death. I've watched you investigate other murders and you scarcely turn a hair at the sight of a body. So what's different this time?" Rees hesitated, worrying over the best words for explaining without terrifying her. "What's wrong?" Lydia continued insistently. "Something happened; I know it."

Simon saved Rees. "Is dinner ready?" the boy asked from the back door.

Lydia directed an anxious glance at Rees and then turned away. "In just a few minutes. Jerusha can begin setting the table." Rees was relieved that the moment had passed. But as Lydia crossed the floor to the fireplace, she stepped behind her husband and said in a low voice, "We'll discuss this later." It sounded like a threat.

After dinner, Rees followed David out to the barn. "Why didn't you tell me people were talking against Lydia?"

Scarlet raced up David's neck and into his cheeks. "I didn't think it was important," he said. "It was just Aunt Caroline . . ."

"I wish that were true," Rees said.

"What exactly happened at the mill?" David asked. Rees shook his head. He didn't know how to describe the scene. "You know

I'll hear soon anyway," David said. "And it will be much embroidered."

Rees collapsed heavily upon a haycock. "That's true. Well, you know those young men who attacked her? They called her a witch. And Mac's body . . ." Rees stopped, fighting the wave of emotion that took hold of him. When he could speak again his voice trembled. "Mac was hung upside down, his arms outstretched. An upside-down crucifixion. A row of Lydia's candles sat upon the mill bed. And Mac's murderer tried to accuse Lydia by writing L-Y in Mac's blood on the floor."

As he spoke, David's face paled. "What? What?" He seemed incapable of saying anything else.

Rees pushed his hands over his face. "First I was made to look guilty of Ward's murder," he said. "And now the evidence left at Mac's murder implicates Lydia. Someone is trying to destroy me."

"This is wicked," David whispered. After a short hesitation, he added, "Could Aunt Caroline . . . ?" He was reluctant to absolve his aunt of anything.

"Not Mac," Rees said. "He was lifted onto the post. I could do it; Mac was a small man. But no woman would have the strength. But the rest? I don't know." For a moment he wondered if Farley could be at the bottom of this scheme. He was fit enough to climb Little Knob and owned a gun and he already believed Lydia was a witch. Maybe he hoped to manufacture proof of his beliefs? But Rees had a hard time believing Farley would kill a man in cold blood. And did he have the strength to lift Mac?

"What are you going to tell Lydia?' David asked, interrupting Rees's thoughts.

"I don't know. I don't want to tell her anything," Rees admitted in a burst of honesty.

"I think you should," David said. "She won't appreciate any attempt at secrecy. She would always rather know the truth, no matter how terrible."

Rees looked at his son. Of course David was correct. He met his father's gaze, equal to equal, and Rees felt a twist of regret. He had missed so much of David's childhood and now it was too late. Although David had not yet reached his majority in years, he was already a man. "When did you become so wise?" Rees asked. He wanted to sound teasing but failed.

"Just because I choose to spend my days on the farm," David said, his voice taking on an edge, "it does not mean I'm a stupid hick."

"I didn't mean that," Rees said. But the few moments of connection were lost.

"Are we going to the pasture, David?" Simon paused in the barn door.

"Right away, Squeaker." David glanced at his father and followed the younger boy out.

Rees sighed and looked around him. The barn was empty; all of the livestock had been put out to pasture. The doors to the upper floor were thrown open so the haycocks could be stored and sunlight illuminated the interior. Wondering if he and David would ever overcome the past, Rees walked back to the house.

He and Lydia did not have a chance to talk until that evening, as they were preparing for bed. Lydia was brushing her hair before plaiting it for the night by the light of a candle—a stub identical to those lined up in the mill. Rees could hardly take his eyes from it. "Now," she said, "tell me what you so obviously prefer to keep secret."

"It's just the details of Mac's murder," Rees said, attempting once again to shield her. She looked at him and waited. "Mac was hung upside down," Rees said at last. "Stripped naked. As though for some rite involving the black arts." He stopped again, hoping she would not ask any more questions.

Lydia put down the brush and folded her hands in her lap. "I suppose there was something there that implied I was the murderer," she said.

Rees stared at her, perspiration popping out upon his upper lip. "How did you know? There were candles and . . . well, never mind about that. How did you guess?"

"You are so distraught I knew it had to involve one of us—someone you love. And this comes hard on the heels of the incident at market." She shivered involuntarily and Rees hugged her to him. "People are afraid, Will." Lydia freed herself sufficiently to look into his face. "Not Susannah, I don't think a pack of wolves would scare her. But Mrs. Potter rushes past me without even a hello."

"I'm sorry," Rees said. "This is my fault. It all goes back to what I did to Sam."

"I thought so at first, but I'm not so sure anymore." Lydia shook her head, the skin around her eyes puckering with worry. "The Shakers have always experienced distrust and sometimes persecution. Because of Sam, Caroline spoke against me. But people believed her because of *my* past." She forced another smile. "It is I who should be sorry."

"I'll talk to Caroline again," Rees promised, his words muffled as he buried his face in her hair.

"I doubt she even knows what her malicious accusations have caused," Lydia said. When she leaned her forehead into his shoulder, her belly bumped into Rees and he put a hand upon it.

"You must not leave the farm," he said. "I don't want anything to happen to you or our child." She nodded into his shoulder.

"Don't worry, I won't. I have plenty of work here, besides bringing the bees and the ruined hives back to life." Her voice trailed off. Rees kissed the top of her head. He knew even the farm was not safe.

That night, after Lydia was asleep, he crept out of bed and went downstairs for his rifle. He took out his bag of black powder and the balls. Although he would need several seconds to load the rifle, he hoped the very sight of it would be sufficient to scare away any intruder.

Then he went outside into the dark. He waited by the back steps for a few seconds for his eyes to adjust. The farm where he'd been born and grown up seemed an alien landscape in the dark. The cries of loons drifted across the pond and a rooster crowed in warning. Rees looked at the sky. The crescent moon was up, shining as sharply horned and as bright as a scythe in the sky. Midnight was still several hours away. Rees set out for the front and the first part of his circuit.

He walked around the house and the outbuildings—barns, dairy, and chicken house. He did not want to leave the larger livestock to fend for themselves, but his farm was too large for one man to protect, and right now he had to be sure his family was safe.

After the first round, he had a route mapped out and his mind was free to wander. He began thinking of rifles, as opposed to muskets. Few men in town owned the more efficient—and more expensive—rifles, instead still possessing the old muskets passed down from their fathers. But Farley owned a rifle and, although older than Rees, had probably served in the Continental Army during the war. Farley would have killed his share of men. Tomorrow, after speaking with Caroline, Rees would drive to the other man's farm. It would be a trial; Caroline lived southwest of Dugard while Farley's farm lay to the northeast. But it had to be done.

Rees reminded himself not to ignore the women in Dugard. Although Lydia had most likely never fired a gun in her life, the same could not be said of Molly Bowditch. Rees knew she was at least a competent shooter. Had she taken Nate's rifle with her when she'd removed to the weaver's cottage? And would she even speak to Rees if he approached her with his questions?

The sudden eerie hooting of an owl made him jump. He realized he'd walked the last half of his circle without any awareness at all of his surroundings. He looked around him. The smell of pigs located him at the extreme eastern end of his circuit. Something rustled through the underbrush but all else was still. Reminding himself that he must keep aware of everything around him, he started walking again. Fatigue weighted his feet and filled his head with fog. He'd stood watch and patrolled many times as a soldier, but he didn't recall the heavy weariness that dragged at him now. Of course, he was no longer sixteen.

As he approached the farmhouse once again, David's voice came out of the darkness. "Father."

Rees gasped and almost dropped his rifle. "What are you doing here?" he hissed, his voice sounding unnaturally loud.

"I could ask the same of you." David sounded amused. "Expecting an attack?"

"Maybe." Put that way, Rees's fears seemed slightly absurd. "Why are you awake? Daylight isn't for several hours yet."

"More like two." David paused and Rees heard him shift his position. "I'd have to be up and doing chores in a little while anyway. Why don't you allow me to take over standing watch for the rest of the night?"

"Will you?" Rees asked. "Or do you think I'm a foolish old man?"

"I think you're right to do this. Somebody came on the farm, not just once, but several times. And then the latest attack on Lydia . . . Well, we don't know how much farther he—they are prepared to go."

A great sense of relief swept over Rees. "I'm afraid next time she, or one of the children, will be seriously hurt," he said.

"Yes," David agreed. Neither one voiced their underlying fear, that next time Lydia might be killed. "Get a few hours' sleep," David said. "I'll get an earlier start than usual, that's all." Rees hesitated. Somehow he felt as though he were shifting his responsibility to his son. Shouldn't he be protecting his boy? David added, "You won't be any good to us exhausted." So Rees handed his rifle and the powder and shot to David and went inside the house. David had lit a candle on the table. Rees picked it up and made his way upstairs, stumbling with weariness.

Chapter Thirteen

When he awoke the next morning he was alone and the room was full of light. He thought it was probably past seven, several hours after dawn. Yawning, he crawled out of bed. Although he'd taken off his shoes the previous night, he'd fallen into bed fully dressed. Today was wash day so he changed into his second set of breeches and shirt and went downstairs.

The large coppers were already boiling over the fire and Abigail, flushed and sweaty, was stirring the soapy water. Rees dropped his dirty clothing by the mound of children's clothing and looked for Lydia. "She's outside with Jerusha," Abigail said. Rees went to the top step and looked around. Lydia was helping six-year-old Nancy drape a linen square, a diaper, over a low bush. Jerusha, already experienced at nine, was hanging the clothing in her basket with speed. Rees exhaled heavily in exasperation; now he knew why the sleeves of some of his shirts were ridged with wrinkles. Lydia saw him and nodded. She spoke to the little girls, her voice so low Rees couldn't hear her, and crossed the yard to meet him.

"The pot of coffee is on the hearth," she said. "I hope it's still warm." She paused and glanced over her shoulder at the two girls. "And I hope these garments are dried by the time we are finished with the next lot. You would not believe how much laundry there is with all these children."

"Come inside and sit down," Rees said, eyeing her flushed face with some concern. "The girls can handle this chore for now." He extended his arm to help his wife ascend the stairs. Although their baby was not due until September, Lydia was already hugely pregnant and growing clumsy.

"Eat your breakfast," she said as she took the few steps across the floor. "We'll need this table cleared and scrubbed for folding the clothes." She sat down. Rees looked at the food on the table: the remains of a pie from the previous evening, a few stale doughnuts baked the previous week, and a handful of biscuits. No doubt the early risers had already eaten the more appealing of the leftovers. He poured himself coffee, which was barely warm, and began dunking the hardened doughnuts into it.

"Where's David?" Rees asked.

"In the north cow pasture with Simon. David wants to wean some of the calves."

"A little early for that, isn't it?" Rees asked.

"I believe David is planning to slaughter them in the fall."

Rees nodded in understanding. The heifers would become milk producers for Lydia's herd but most of the males would be turned into meat. Lydia brushed one hand wearily over her forehead. "He wants you to join him there."

Rees suppressed a groan as he rose from the table. He didn't dare refuse even though David had hired help; Rees knew his son would resent anything he perceived as his father shirking his responsibility to the farm.

By the time the cattle were sorted and Rees finally escaped, the morning was half gone. He changed from his clogs to his shoes and harnessed Hannibal to the wagon. Although he did not anticipate his conversations with Caroline or Mr. Farley with any pleasure, he was glad to leave the farmwork behind. He considered driving into town first and stopping at the coffeehouse for something to eat, but it was already late, so instead he drove directly to Caroline's.

As Rees pulled into the yard, he saw Charlie and the two girls laboring in the vegetable garden. Caroline was nowhere to be seen. Rees entered the grubby shack. His sister sat at the table in exactly the same position as before. It was as though she had not moved at all since Rees's previous visit. But when he stepped into the kitchen, a spark animated her expression. "Have you come to accuse me of something else?" she demanded.

"Just wanted to talk to you," Rees said, striving to keep his voice low and calm. "Tell you some news." She eyed him.

"And what's that?" she asked without curiosity.

"Thomas McIntyre was murdered." Rees watched her face closely but all he saw was surprise. "You didn't know?"

"Charlie hasn't gone to town in days. And Sam?" She gestured with weary resignation at the one window. Through it Rees could see Sam walking back and forth, his hands moving as he conversed with himself. "Even when he tells me something, I can't be sure it is the truth." She paused. "Do you remember when we were children, Will?"

"What?" Rees said.

Caroline removed her gaze from Sam. "I used to write poetry. More than anything I wanted to move to Boston, write poetry, and join a literary salon." Her expression softened. "It was my dream." Rees nodded in agreement although, until she mentioned it, he had not remembered anything of the sort. Now he recalled laughing until helpless over one of her pieces. It was all about the lark rising in the morn. Lark? A black-headed sparrow maybe. "Father wouldn't allow me to visit Boston, even in his company. He said I was only a girl and would get married."

"I've known other women who managed to free themselves from the expectations of their fathers," Rees said. He thought of Peggy Boothe, a girl he'd met in Salem, who'd managed to successfully run her own business. "I didn't realize you had aspirations to become a bluestocking."

"Maybe it's easier in a city. You probably don't remember—you were away with the Continental Army then—but Father introduced me to Mr. Borden, no doubt hoping I would marry that old man."

Since Borden, the owner of the local store, was only a little older than Rees, he thought it more likely his parents hoped to settle Caroline down. "They never approved of Sam," Rees said. "You chose to elope with him."

"I had to." Caroline's voice broke. "I was pregnant with Charlie. And now here I am, trapped on a hardscrabble farm. With a brother who won't help me," she added. "And one who only visits to accuse me of terrible things." Rees saw the suspicion that he had come for that purpose again flash into her eyes.

"That's not true," he said.

"Are you here now to suggest I killed Mr. McIntyre?" she asked, her voice rising. "Why, I would never hurt Mac. He gave me cornmeal and rye flour last winter. That injun loaf was all that kept us fed." Rees said nothing, assailed by guilt although he knew David had supplied Charlie with eggs and milk and even some pork. He waited for his sister to ask him for details about Mac's murder, but she did not. Instead, she stared listlessly out the window. Finally

Rees said, "You know some boys attacked Lydia, stoning her as a witch, because of your nasty gossip." He could not help the tone of accusation that sent his voice booming through the kitchen.

A faint pink stole into Caroline's cheeks. "I'm sorry. I was angry. I expected some of the ladies to take against her. Let your wife suffer so you can know what it feels like to have an unhappy spouse." She shrugged. "I didn't think anyone would take it seriously."

"Mr. Farley and his wife believe in witches," Rees said. Caroline rolled her eyes. Anger burned through Rees and he began shouting. "Do you know what you've done? Not only was Lydia attacked at market, but Mac was tortured and killed. It looked as though he was a sacrifice for some witch rite." Rees just stopped himself from blurting out the letters written in McIntyre's blood.

Caroline's mouth opened and she stared at him. "I had nothing at all to do with that," she cried. "Why do you blame me? How can you hate me so? I'm your baby sister. But you were always so hard on me." She began sobbing, her weeping interspersed with shrill piercing shrieks. Charlie and Sam ran into the kitchen.

"What are you doing to my mother?" Charlie demanded, his eyes wide and fierce in his flushed face.

Sam went to Caroline but did not know what to do. He paced anxiously behind her.

"I think you'd better leave," Charlie said. As Rees turned, the boy shouted after him, "And don't come back."

Frustrated, angry, and guilty, Rees went out to his wagon. He'd handled that badly, he should have spoken more gently and kept control of his temper. But he was afraid for his wife and family, and Caroline's gossip had given birth to a monster.

As he turned upon the road, he found Charlie waiting for him by the fence post. He had cut across a field and forced his way through a thicket of wild roses, making it to the road before Rees. Small cuts marked Charlie's face and hands with bloody scratches. "I wanted to apologize," Charlie said. "I know this isn't your fault. Since my father . . ." He lurched to a stop and looked away.

"I know," Rees said. He doubted Charlie would believe the truth, that Rees felt angry and upset enough for both of them.

"Anyway, my mother, well, she's different since then. She cries all the time. Anything sets her off." Rees ducked his head in acknowledgment, surprised at how relieved Charlie's apology made him.

"Thank you," he said. He paused. He knew it had taken courage for Charlie to approach him but didn't quite know how to express it. Charlie licked at a bloody scratch on his wrist. The sweet fragrance of the roses mingled with the scents of damp earth and fresh hay. Rees inhaled the summery perfume and as his nephew began walking down the road called out, "Where are you going now? I can take you." He wanted to do something for the boy.

A ghost of a grin touched Charlie's lips. "I'm going to your farm. I've been helping David and he's promised me a heifer."

"Well, climb up," Rees invited. "I'm heading in that direction anyway."

Rees was very glad when the journey ended. He did not want to discuss Charlie's parents with him, although Sam and Caroline were the link between uncle and nephew. Rees did not want to talk about Mac's body either. He knew Charlie would hear about it as soon as he went to town, but Rees did not want to be the one who gossiped about the gruesome details. So they discussed the heifer Charlie hoped to obtain. "I have a bit of pasture already picked out," Charlie said enthusiastically. "David promised me one of his bulls. He'll cover my heifer this fall. With any luck, she'll bear another female. I'll have milk for my sisters and at the same time I'll increase my herd."

"Sheep are better," Rees said, more from a desire to speak than from conviction. "They provide wool as well as milk and meat."

"Someday," Charlie said. "Someday."

Only when he dismounted from the wagon did Rees see anger contort the boy's features. Rees heaved a sigh, suspecting Charlie had remembered the scene they'd left behind them. Then David, with Simon running at his heels, came bounding across the barnyard. Charlie turned to greet his cousin, losing all interest in his uncle, and the two boys disappeared toward the pasture. Their laughter floated back to Rees's ears through the warm air.

"I hate Charlie," Simon said, scuffing his bare feet disconsolately through the dust. "He's mean." Then he burst into tears and fled into the house. Rees turned his wagon and drove back to the road. He pitied Simon but knew this was something he could not fix.

Rees had never visited the Farley farm. Zedediah Farley was older than Rees, old enough to have left school by the time Rees had begun attending at the age of six. And Farley with his old-fashioned views was not the sort of man Rees would seek out under typical circumstances. But he knew roughly where the farm lay, and although he usually would have resented the hour-long journey to the other side of Dugard, today he was pleased to have the time. His heart was still pounding from the confrontation with his sister and a layer of nervous sweat coated him from head to toe. His suspicions of her and the malice behind all that had happened to his family recently overwhelmed him with guilt, but he knew her too well to quickly dismiss her as innocent. So he needed a spell of time to settle himself, calm down, and prepare for the upcoming conversation with Farley.

Rees was tempted to stop at the Contented Rooster but steeled himself with his duty and rode on. Anyway, he saw the glances thrown his way by those he passed and the whispers that went from one to another behind concealing hands. Glad to leave that behind, he crossed the bridge over the eastern branch of the Dugard River and turned north. Not many lived in the hills on this side of town. The soil was even rockier here than it was farther south, and Rees could not imagine how the Farleys wrested any living from it.

He knew immediately when he reached the Farley property; two witch balls constructed of ash twigs hung from the fence posts bracketing a rutted drive. Haphazardly built stone walls paralleled the road on each side of the posts. Rees turned in. He could see gaps in the cornfield on his right made by outcroppings of rock; the Farleys had not succeeded in pulling all the boulders from the soil. On his left, potato hills crowned with green leaves circled the granite knuckles thrust through the dirt. Behind that field was one of buckwheat, flowering now with small white flowers.

The wagon bumped from side to side, jolting Rees until he thought even his teeth were shaken loose, as Hannibal picked his way toward the house. Now Rees began to see livestock: a handful of brown cattle in the pasture, a pair of oxen in a distant meadow, and a small flock of sheep. No horses. Rees was not surprised; horses were costly.

The land curved and the barn came into view, with the house

visible behind. Both were weathered, the barn larger than the house and swaybacked. Rees pulled into the yard in front of the house. Sometime recently, a second story had been added to the old house. Weathered a silvery gray, it sat on top of the original structure like a too-small hat on a big head. And a witch ball hung in every window. Some were of glass, probably imported from England at great expense, but most were made of twigs.

"What are you doing here?" Farley ran out of his house and aimed his rifle at Rees. He held his arms up.

"Looking for you," Rees said. Farley hesitated but he finally lowered his gun. Rees climbed down from the wagon seat. Farley paused a short distance away and stared at Rees in silence.

Mrs. Farley came to the door and paused. Rees could smell cooking; of course, it was almost noon. "What do you want?" she asked. Farley turned to glare at his wife.

"Go inside, Thankful," he ordered her. She regarded Rees through narrowed eyes. "Now." Farley's voice rose. She turned and retreated inside, her bare feet making no sound. Rees saw the fading marks of a bruise on her cheek. Farley spat into the dirt at his feet. "Witches, every one of them," he muttered.

He's afraid of his wife, Rees realized with a jolt.

Farley tipped his head back and looked into his visitor's face. "My sons ain't here," he said. "That's what you're looking fer, right?"

"They assaulted my wife," Rees said. But he already knew his concern would fall on stony ground. Farley had probably put his sons up to the attack. Farley shrugged. "I want to talk to them," Rees added firmly.

"They ain't here," Farley repeated.

Rees stared over the shorter man's head, through the door into the kitchen. Mrs. Farley was frying ployes, golden buckwheat pancakes, and a stack stood on the plate next to her. Far too many for just two. "You know," Rees said in a pleasant tone, "my father used to tell me that lying will send you to Hell just as fast as stealing will."

Farley erupted into speech. "You and that witch wife of yours better watch out, weaver man," he spat out. "I heard tell of Mac's death. Did you help her sacrifice a good man to Satan?"

Rees took an involuntary step back from Farley and the spit spraying from his mouth. But as he gazed into the blood-suffused face of the man, he leaned forward and said, "If you or your sons come after my wife, I will come after you. Understand? And I won't rest until I've put you either in jail or into the ground. I don't much care which."

"Git off my property," Farley shouted, raising the rifle again.

Although Rees doubted the weapon was loaded, he spun around and climbed into his wagon. From the elevation of his seat, he added, "You tell your boys what I said."

"You better watch it," Farley shouted after him. "And don't come here again."

Rees drove away, driving as fast as he dared over the deeply grooved ground. This was a new record for him—he'd been expelled from two farms in one morning. He felt as though he couldn't breathe until he reached the road outside. Then he stopped. He'd begun shaking and he sucked in great lungfuls over and over until he could hold the reins again. He was going to have more trouble with Farley, but was he the force behind the attacks targeting Rees's family? Rees still couldn't be sure.

Perhaps it had not been a good idea visiting. Every time he spoke to Farley, Rees felt disoriented, as though the world he knew had shifted to a reality filled with witches and magic.

Caroline's angry spite had found fertile soil in Mr. Farley's superstitious fears.

Caroline and Farley haunted Rees's thoughts all the way home. Could either have been the murderer? Both owned rifles. But Caroline could not have climbed Bald Knob in her skirts and both Caro and Farley were small and slight. Rees doubted either would have had the strength to lift Tom McIntyre. Nonetheless, it took great effort for Rees to push them from his mind when he finally turned into his own drive. He unhitched Hannibal and released him into the meadow. The gelding raced to the trough and plunged his nose into the water. Once Rees stowed the wagon in the manure-and-hay-scented barn he walked to the back of the house. He could feel his tension begin to dissipate in the soothing commonplace that surrounded him.

Every branch, every bush wore a piece of clothing. Jerusha and Abigail were walking around checking each piece for dampness. "Where's Lydia?" Rees asked. "Inside?"

Abigail nodded.

"Is dinner ready?"

"Soon."

Rees ran up the back steps, hoping he would not have to make do with stale doughnuts.

He found the kitchen hot and steamy. Even the buzzing flies sounded sleepy. The table had been pushed as close to the back door as possible while still allowing entry. Since the washing part of the laundry was done, the empty copper lay upended on an old piece of canvas, drying before it was stored. It would resurface next Monday. Lydia was bent over the spider, making pancakes. Although Simon was seated at the table, none of the younger children were present.

"I fed them first and sent them outside to play," Lydia replied to his question. She put a stack of the cakes before Simon and turned to her husband. "Are you ready to eat?" Flushed and perspiring, she looked both hot and irritable. The tendrils of hair hanging from her cap were glued to her forehead in damp curls. "After dinner, Abby and I'll begin ironing." Rees heard the rest of the sentence: so everyone should eat and leave the kitchen. But he was just so glad to see her he hugged her tightly.

"Really, Will," she said in annoyance. But she smiled at him.

"Pancakes are fine," Rees said, although pancakes did not excite him. In his opinion, they should be consumed only when there was nothing else but he did not express this view. Wash day was not a good time to cross a woman.

He took a chair next to Simon who had drowned his pancakes with maple syrup and was eating his way through with grunts of enjoyment. Lydia placed a plate before Rees. When Abigail and Jerusha brought in their baskets, they joined Rees and Simon, and a short while later David and Charlie came in for their meal. Like Simon, Charlie ate with a good appetite and great enthusiasm, appreciating a plentiful meal cooked and served by someone else. If he noticed Simon's ferocious glare directed his way, Charlie did not say so.

Lydia did not sit down with her own plate until the irons were lined up before the fire to heat, and then she collapsed the last few inches with a sigh. For several minutes, as everyone ate, the kitchen was silent.

David and Charlie took Simon with them, which made him smile, when they returned to their outside work. As the women cleared the table and began laying out the linens, Rees escaped upstairs. He was almost finished with his weaving commission and expected to cut it from the loom today. Besides, the bedroom, which was shaded by several large maples and had all the windows thrown open to catch any breeze, was much cooler than the kitchen below.

He wove the last of the yarn given him and rolled the finished cloth around the beam. This had been a simple job, just plain weaving, and had been quickly completed. Nothing else waited, and for the first time Rees wondered if his lack of custom was connected to Caroline's hateful gossip. Maybe the housewives of Dugard feared Lydia would curse the cloth and cause sickness or death to anyone who wore clothing made from it. No, that couldn't be true. This was Dugard, Maine, his birthplace and home.

But when his eyes fell again on the finished cloth he shivered.

Well, if he couldn't find more custom here in Dugard he would gladly take another weaving journey through the neighboring farms and villages. This time David would certainly understand.

Rees knotted the ends of the cloth to keep it from unraveling and carefully unrolled the yardage from the beam. He rerolled it into a bundle and tied it tightly with rope. He must make a trip to the Widow Penney soon to deliver her cloth.

As he stood up, Rees realized he could hear angry voices outside. Male voices, not the lighter tones of David and Charlie. Putting down the bundle, Rees ran out to the hall and started down the stairs. He met David coming up. The boy had lost his hat and his face was crimson with hurry. "What's going on?" Rees asked.

"There's trouble," David said. "Bad trouble. You'd better come now."

Chapter Fourteen

His heart pounding, Rees clattered after David. When they passed through the kitchen it was empty and Rees wondered if Lydia was already on the front porch. But when he stepped out, she wasn't there. David fell behind Rees but shadowed him so closely he almost stepped on Rees's heels.

For a moment Rees considered the group of men standing in the drive. It was not the entire town, but twenty or so men. Mr. Farley, frowning with such self-righteous rectitude Rees's gut clenched in fear, stood with his sons. The boys were grinning and one of them held a rope that he pulled through his hands with a sensuous delight.

Behind the Farleys stood the three McIntyre boys. Their faces were still flushed and mottled with grief. Elijah would not meet Rees's gaze. Some of the regulars from the Bull, including Sam Prentiss, filled out the mob. Rees began to feel queasy with the threat of imminent battle. "What do you want?" he asked.

"You know there've been two murders," Farley said. Although he spoke loudly, he licked his lips over and over. Rees realized Farley was not just nervous but terrified. Rees suspected Farley had already had this confrontation planned this morning, when Rees unexpectedly visited.

"I know," he said. And then, because he couldn't believe he was facing down a mob of people he'd known since childhood, he added loudly, "I've told you I didn't kill anybody. Not Ward. And certainly not Mac—Mr. McIntyre. We were friends. Our argument was over politics." He stopped suddenly, realizing he should have kept silent.

"We're not here for you," Farley said. He flicked a glance over his shoulder as though assuring himself of the men behind him. "We're here for your wife. We—she—will be arrested for murder. Murder by witchcraft."

Rees's mouth went dry as fear began to invade his anger. He felt the vibration in the air behind him as David moved. The door to the house shut quietly behind him. Rees did not turn around. His world had narrowed to the group of men standing in the dusty yard. "Witchcraft? Are you crazy? Lydia is no witch."

"The evidence," Farley said, trying to speak with the certainty of the law behind him, "is against her."

"Ward was shot," Rees began.

But Farley interrupted him. "So you say. If one of us had killed him, we wouldn't go to the top of a mountain. And what about Mac, huh? Not only murdered but hung upside down in a mockery of the Crucifixion, candles all around. Your wife's candles."

"Let us talk to your wife," said Elijah McIntyre. "Where is she?" He made as if to peer around Rees into the shadowy house behind.

"I don't know," Rees said truthfully, his thoughts moving at a furious speed. Farley turned around to confer with the others. Several of the men looked at Rees with suspicion. They were right to.

Rees wouldn't tell them if he did know. And he certainly would not turn Lydia over to them. He could feel the fear and anger coming off these men thick as smoke. Even if they did not mete out a rough justice of their own—hanging her from a convenient tree—Rees knew they would not be kind to her before delivering her to Wheeler's Livery. Since the jail had not yet been rebuilt, she would be confined to a stall and might not be released for months, well after the birth of her child. His child. He could not allow that to happen.

How quickly his passion for justice and his belief in law disappeared when it was Lydia at risk.

He looked over at McIntyre's sons. Not one of them could meet his gaze. "Do you believe this?" he asked. "Do you believe my wife killed your father with witchcraft? Why?"

For a moment none of the three young men spoke. Rees could see they were wild with grief, looking to blame someone, anyone, and yet the two eldest looked down at the ground in shame and discomfort. They didn't want to be here anymore.

"Someone killed him," Elijah finally muttered. "And he was strung up and the candles . . ." He broke into sobs.

Rees understood how emotion could move a man to do something that he would normally not even consider. And now Mac's boys were so angry and grief-stricken they were capable of anything. Rees couldn't look for help from that quarter. He wondered if he could dart inside the house and collect his rifle from the front parlor.

The door slammed shut behind him. He smelled the mixture of hay and sweat that marked David. "She's in the dairy," David said, his voice so low Rees could hardly hear his son. "I told her and Abby to stay there and lock themselves in."

Rees inclined his head in acknowledgment, moving so slightly he hoped none of the mob could see it.

"We want to check your house," Farley said.

"No," Rees said loudly. He clenched his fists, and adjusted his stance, ready to hit the first man who came up the porch steps.

"You can't hide her forever," shouted one of the men in the back.

"David, get the rifle," Rees said.

"Stall them. I'll get Charlie and ask him to ride into town and fetch the constable," David said. The house door snicked shut behind him.

"You can't beat all of us," Farley said loudly, showing his yellow teeth.

Rees looked at the men. Farley was shifting impatiently back and forth, back and forth, and the bruiser behind him, a big fellow Rees dimly recalled from the Bull, was slapping a cudgel into the palm of his hand. At the meaty sound of wood hitting flesh, an involuntary shudder swept over Rees. He dared not speak for fear his voice would tremble and betray his fear. When he thought he could trust himself, he said, "How do I know that once you are inside you won't hurt one of my children or destroy my property?"

Now it was Farley who looked surprised. "Why would we do that?" His voice squeaked. Rees wondered if Farley was really as naïve as all that. Surely he must know the type of man he stood with. His own sons were trembling with excitement, like attack dogs on a scent.

"We won't let them," Elijah McIntyre promised.

Rees hesitated. In the past, he would have dared them, knowing he could leave if it went badly, take an extended weaving trip, until all the trouble blew over. But he couldn't do that now, not when it would leave Lydia, his unborn child, and his adopted children in danger. The clatter of David's footsteps came up behind Rees but he did not turn around.

"Letting them look through the house will give the constable the necessary time to reach us," David whispered. Rees turned to look at his son. Underneath his summer bronze, David was pale. His freckles stood out in crisp definition.

"Are you going to let us in, nice like?" Farley asked. "Or are we going to come over you?"

"Very well," Rees said. "But I will accompany you. And if I see anyone stealing anything . . ." Farley raced forward. He had his foot on the bottom step before he paused and stared at Rees with a nervous expression. Rees folded his arms and stared down at the short, skinny man, daring him to ascend the stairs. In the sudden unexpected silence the birdsong in the maple sounded piercingly sweet. Rees could hear a cow lowing in the meadow. Then the other members of the mob caught up to Farley and with several men at his back, he was brave. They came up the stairs and pushed past Rees.

Farley and the McIntyre boys went up the hall stairs, David at their heels. Rees distinctly heard the thud of their feet above him. He followed Farley's sons through the hall to the kitchen. Grinning like a fool and whistling, Sam trailed after them. He seemed to view these proceedings as though they were a pantomime put on for his benefit.

Rees would have followed them up to the second floor and the bedroom he shared with Lydia, but Jerusha and her siblings had come inside and were standing by the back door. Jerusha was white with terror and she clutched at the door for support. "Are they going to warn us out?" she sobbed. "Do we have to leave?" She had lived with this fear in New York, before Rees and Lydia had adopted her and her brothers and sister. The three youngest began crying too.

"Of course not," Rees said. He had hoped he would never see that terrified expression on her face again. "It's going to be all right." But before he reached her she vomited with fright and began weeping harder. Rees picked up Joseph, the baby, and pulled Nancy and Judah to him. He couldn't abandon them; they were already scared, and he couldn't send them off to Lydia.

Rees watched as Farley led his group up the stairs. Rees tried not to listen to the thud of their footsteps overhead and the crash of something falling. Rees started for the back steps, the children at his heels. Mocking male laughter floated down the stairs.

At that moment Charlie jumped over the back steps and hurried into the kitchen. He was red-faced and sweating profusely. "I had to close all the gates," he muttered to Rees. "I'll go after the constable now. But first, I want to get my father out. David said he was here?"

Rees nodded and pointed at the stairs with his chin. "Up there."

Charlie took the stairs two at a time. "No, I don't want to go." Sam's protest was clearly audible. "I want to stay with Mr. Farley. I don't want to go home."

"We're all leaving now," Farley said, his voice floating down into the kitchen. Rees heard Farley's tread upon the stairs and a few seconds later all of them were coming down. "But wait." Farley looked past Rees and the children clutching at him. "Maybe Mrs. Rees went outside to hide."

"You've seen the house," Rees said, his voice sounding rough to his own ears. "She isn't here. It's time for all of you to leave." Judah began crying hysterically; he wasn't used to that angry tone.

"Not until we've found the witch," Farley said, his hand clutching at the amulet about his neck.

"I warned you," Rees said. "I'm telling you to get out now." He deposited Joseph in Jerusha's arms and stepped forward.

"My father said get out." David brushed past the other boys and joined his father. He looked at Elijah McIntyre. "You promised nothing would happen," he said.

Elijah exhaled and nodded. "We should leave," he agreed. "Mrs. Rees isn't here."

"We'll search the farm," Farley cried. "She's gotta be hiding somewhere. We'll find her."

"I said get out," Rees shouted. His stomach was twisted into knots and he was shaking so hard it felt like his bones were rattling inside his skin. But the beast, his temper, was rising and he was prepared to fight all of these men to defend his wife and family. "Get off my property. Now."

"Mr. Rees has asked you to leave." Caldwell's voice came from the front hall. Rees stared at him with a mixture of relief and astonishment; Charlie hadn't left to fetch him yet. Heads turned as the constable thrust his way through the mob. "I suggest you do so. Otherwise, I'll have to arrest all of you."

"You and who else?" sneered one of the men.

Caldwell looked over his shoulder. George Potter and Jack Anderson followed the constable into the kitchen. Rees realized he'd heard hoofbeats but in all the excitement he'd thought nothing of it. Potter carried two pistols. Although they were capable of only one shot each, the men scuttled backward when Potter waved them around. No one wanted to be one of those shot. Jack Anderson was even more fearsome. He carried a long and wickedly sharp kitchen knife.

"There are five of us," Caldwell said. He smiled. "And some of us are armed. That evens us up, doesn't it?'

Farley turned a look of hatred upon Rees. "She got away this time but we'll be back for her."

Rees took a step forward. "I told you to get out." He involuntarily lifted his clenched fist and for a moment he held Farley's gaze.

Then Farley, with a derisive snort, spat on the floor and stamped out of the kitchen. Gradually, the rest of the mob followed, Charlie pushing his father before him. Within a few minutes all were gone. Rees exhaled the breath he did not realize he'd been holding.

Caldwell turned to him. "Are you all right?" he asked. Rees tried to nod, his legs trembling so convulsively he thought he might fall. He tottered to a chair and collapsed into it.

"Surely they don't think you had anything to do with those murders," Jack said to Rees. He put the knife on the table. Rees looked at it and then raised his eyes to his old friend.

"I thought . . ." Rees stopped and moistened his lips. He thought he had never been so terrified in his life, not even during the war. "They came into my house, Jack, and threatened my wife," he said.

Chapter Fifteen

ⵣ

Rees had to assure himself of Lydia's safety. Leaving the constable and his other friends sitting at the table, Rees followed David out of the kitchen. The dairy was nestled in a copse of trees and so was not immediately visible from the house. Both Lydia and Rees had frequently complained about the distance but he was thankful for it now. Although his legs had been trembling when he stood up, by the time he reached the bottom of the back stairs, he was running in a clumsy stagger. Jerusha and the other children were close behind.

David called through the door, "Abby. Abigail."

Simultaneously Rees shouted, "Lydia."

The clatter of something heavy being moved from the door sounded within the dairy, and then the door opened. Lydia peered out. "What happened?" she asked. "David told us to . . ." Her words ended in a surprised gurgle as Rees snatched her into his arms and hugged her tightly. He was only dimly conscious of David clasping Abigail in his arms.

"Someone came to warn us out," Jerusha cried, clutching at Lydia's skirts. She began crying and all the other children except Simon joined in. Jerusha and Simon at least recalled their lives in

New York where the selectmen of their town threatened to expel
the family for being poor. Lydia freed herself from Rees's embrace.

"I'm sure that didn't happen," she said in a calm voice, her gaze
seeking out Rees's. "You must have misunderstood."

"It's all over now," Rees said. But he met Lydia's eyes and tried
to convey without speaking the seriousness of the situation.

"My Shaker family was frequently harassed; it means nothing,"
Lydia said, striving for a reassuring tone. "It will soon be time for
supper; you children should stay out here and play while I start it."

"Me too?" Jerusha said in surprise. Lydia usually insisted on
including Jerusha so that she might learn how to cook.

"You too." Lydia smiled. "You've had a fright. It will be good
for you to forget about it for a few minutes." She shot a glance at
her husband. "And Rees and I have to talk over a few things."

"Unless, of course," David said, "you all want to help me milk?"
Jerusha, shaking her head, hurried all the children but Simon away.
The boy trailed after David and Abigail toward the barn and the
pasture behind it.

Rees and Lydia began walking toward the house. Now that he
had an opportunity to tell his wife what had happened, Rees didn't
know what to say.

"David frightened us," Lydia said at last. "What happened,
Will?"

"A delegation came from town. Led by Zedediah Farley." Rees
spat out the name. "They wanted to arrest you, Lydia."

"Arrest me? For what?" Lydia asked. Rees could see the thoughts
moving behind her eyes. "Not for witchcraft?"

"Yes."

Lydia turned a horrified look upon her husband. "This is not

Salem one hundred years ago. I only hope cooler heads would have prevailed as they did with Mother Ann Lee ten years ago."

"Mother Ann Lee was not expecting a baby," Rees said. He sounded hoarse with fear and he paused to clear his throat. "We have no jail so you'd have been housed in the stables. And I am not so certain you would have been soon freed." He did not want to tell her about the rope.

Lydia did not speak as they climbed the stairs into the kitchen. Only Caldwell still sat at the table. He had found Lydia's ale and helped himself to a mugful. As Rees came inside, the constable said, "Mr. Potter and Mr. Anderson went back to town." He smiled. "They have businesses to run whereas I can sit here all day."

Rees was not taken in by Caldwell's flippant tone. "Thank you for coming to my aid, and so quickly. How did you know so soon? Charlie hadn't even left yet."

"I overheard one of the regulars in the Bull talking about it. I'm sorry; I was later than I expected to be. I didn't want to come alone. Mr. Potter was in his office but Jack Anderson took some tracking down."

"I am so grateful," Rees said.

"Indeed," Lydia agreed. "But surely we're safe now?"

Caldwell shook his head at her. "I don't think you are. Farley may be a superstitious fool but he is not the only man who . . ." He stopped to consider his words.

"Who views me with suspicion because I was a Shaker." Lydia finished the thought for him.

He nodded. "And with the recent murders—well, Zadoc Ward won't be missed but Thomas McIntyre was popular in this town—people's feelings are on edge." His lips curled up in a mirthless smile. "A deformed calf was born on one of the nearby farms yesterday. Mr. Farley, well, not only him, but several people in town have pointed to that as proof of witchcraft."

Lydia made a small sound of distress. Rees said nothing. He was struggling to understand how these people, people he knew and had grown up with, could be accusing his wife of something so ridiculous as well as threatening her with imprisonment and possibly hanging.

"But no one said anything to me last year when we married," Rees said finally, as though that would make a difference. "No one said anything at all."

"Someone lit the spark," Caldwell said.

"Caroline," Rees breathed. "She admits starting the rumor but she claims she had nothing to do with Ward or the attacks on Lydia."

"Maybe not." Caldwell's tone left no doubt he didn't believe that at all. "But someone fanned the flames. If not her, who?"

Rees did not speak for several seconds, his mind busy with the constable's question. Rees knew there were several people who disliked him, some from his childhood, like James Carleton and Piggy Hanson, and some from more recent interactions, like Molly Bowditch. And Rees mustn't forget Farley. But did dislike lead to this kind of planned assault on a person's life and liberty? Rees thought that kind of attack took both rage and hatred. Was Caroline that angry? Rees considered his own question. Maybe, he concluded reluctantly. And Sam certainly hated Rees enough to go after him, and besides possessed a wide streak of violence. It was Sam's steady harassment and attack upon Rees last year that had led to his injury, as Rees defended himself, in the first place. If Sam were not so clearly touched he would be Rees's first suspect.

Rees had been dimly conscious of buggy wheels on the drive

out front but had assumed they belonged to Abigail's brother, arriving to pick her up. The thunderous knocking on the front door made him jump. The force of the fusillade of blows upon the wood did not sound like Abigail's family, the quiet Quaker Bristols. As Rees stood, the door opened and heavy footsteps approached down the hall. Fearing that this new visitor was one of Mr. Farley's mob, Rees looked around for a weapon, any weapon. Caldwell rose to his feet as well.

But instead of Farley, the man who stepped into the kitchen was the magistrate, Cornelius Hanson. Rees sagged into his chair with relief. "Hello, Piggy," he said. "Would you care for a glass of ale?" Now that the initial wave of dread was receding, Rees was beginning to wonder why the judge had driven all the way out to the farm.

Hanson ignored Rees, turning to the constable instead. "What are you doing here?"

"I heard there was a disturbance," Caldwell began. His eyebrows had risen almost to the edge of his greasy hair.

"A peaceful inquiry, nothing more," Hanson said in a sharp voice. "But you brought a posse of armed men and threatened several of the town's leading citizens."

"Wait a minute," Rees said indignantly. "That mob was endangering my home and family. The constable saved us."

"You stay out of this," Hanson told Rees. "I believe Caldwell's friendship with you is clouding his judgment."

"Farley and the rest of his men were threatening my wife," Rees said, his voice rising.

Hanson flicked a glance at Lydia. "A day or so in jail wouldn't have hurt her. There have been two murders during this past week, in case you've forgotten. If she's innocent, she has nothing to worry about." Reduced to silence by this callous statement, Rees could only stare. He'd always viewed the pudgy, pink-and-white Piggy Hanson as foolish, indeed, somewhat ridiculous. But now he looked dangerous. "And you," Hanson continued, turning his gaze to Caldwell, "you should have discussed this ill-advised attack with me."

"You might have been on circuit . . ." Caldwell tried to interrupt.

". . . before haring off with a group of armed men." Hanson raised his voice. "I plan to bring this before the selectmen. We'll see if you keep your job." Leveling a final glare at Rees, a look of mingled anger and triumph, Hanson lumbered from the kitchen.

No one spoke until they heard the front door slam. "Maybe he is behind all of this," Rees said in a shaky voice. Stunned by Hanson's anger and open dislike, Rees was only partly joking.

"What have you done to him?" Lydia asked. She sat down at the table and put her trembling hands upon it.

"I teased him when we were boys." Rees stopped. That intensity of loathing arising from boyhood mischief seemed implausible. "Recently?" He paused to think. "I advised the Widow Penney and some of her friends not to invest in his land schemes."

"He doesn't like you, that's for sure," Caldwell agreed. "But I think this might stem from his friendship with Molly Bowditch."

Rees swore under his breath. When he'd investigated the death of his boyhood friend Nate, Molly's husband, Rees had uncovered many of the townspeople's secrets. Molly's had not been the only one but it had been one of the most shocking, and although she had her supporters, such as Piggy Hanson, many of her former friends now ostracized her. Her own son refused to speak to her. Molly blamed Rees for the change in her life and he supposed she would never forgive him.

"I'd better start supper," Lydia said, heaving herself up from the table. She stepped into the pantry to inspect the leftovers from the noon dinner.

"I should talk to Molly," Rees said. "And Piggy Hanson too." Caldwell nodded and fixed an intent gaze upon Rees.

"Yes. But you must know whoever is behind all of this won't stop. He'll keep going after you and the ones you love until he destroys you." Rees tried to swallow but couldn't get past the obstruction in his throat. Caldwell paused briefly and then added, "I think you'd better figure out, and quickly too, who hates you that much."

Chapter Sixteen

Rees went to bed but did not sleep. He spent the first few hours tossing and turning, finally arising with the moon. David had taken the first shift patrolling the farm, but Rees thought that since he couldn't sleep anyway, he would relieve his son. One of them might as well get some rest. David surrendered the rifle without protest and stumbled off to bed. Rees began his circuit. He was so angry and terrified he thought he might never be able to close his eyes again. The image of those men who had come to take Lydia was burned into his mind. And despite the assurances that had come from McIntyre's sons, Rees believed some of that mob would have hanged her with barely a moment's hesitation.

Before his marriage, Rees would have visited each of these men and fought out the problem. He would have risked his life to uncover the identity of his enemy. But when he'd fallen in love with Lydia, something inside of him had come to life and he couldn't do that now, not if his actions put Lydia and his unborn baby in jeopardy. He was, in fact, almost paralyzed with the fear something would harm them.

He needed to know his family was safe before investigating further. He just didn't know how to accomplish that.

Toward morning a light rain sprang up, hissing through the leaves like a swarm of bees and pattering on the ground. Rees was soon wet to the skin. But instead of seeking shelter under the trees, he lifted his face to the sky and let the rain cool his feverish cheeks. The eastern horizon blushed pink with sunrise. As Rees stood under the brief shower, his mind cleared and he knew what he had to do.

He heard the clatter of milking pails as David carried them out to pasture. Simon, David's little shadow, had followed his idol outside and the boy's high voice pierced the still morning air. "Right, David? Right?" Rees went inside, knowing nothing would happen now, not with his son out and about. Besides, everyone would be too busy milking his own cows to have time for making mischief.

Rees put his gun away. His powder horn had kept his powder mostly dry. Although barely sunrise, the air was already warm and humid and Rees knew today would be hot.

He went into the kitchen and started coffee. Every time he considered discussing his decision with Lydia his stomach clenched. But it had to be done. He stirred up the fire and pushed the pot over the flames. He needed the coffee today; fatigue rimmed his eyelids with sand and made him sluggish. But the sound of his wife's foot upon the stairs sent a quiver through him and he suddenly felt alert.

When she entered the kitchen and found him staring at her, she paused at the door. "What?" she asked.

"I think you should take the children and go somewhere safe until I find the person behind these attacks," Rees said. As soon as he spoke, he wished he had not expressed himself so baldly. Lydia stared at him, her eyes widening as she took in what he'd said.

"No," she said. "I won't. We will face this together."

"I won't be able to concentrate if I'm also trying to protect you," Rees said.

"Protect me?" Lydia's voice rose. "I'm no delicate flower. Besides, it's not a good time to travel, not with the baby coming."

"That's partly why I need you to go," Rees said, lowering his voice as he heard footsteps on the stairs. Jerusha's voice floated into the kitchen as she remonstrated with her younger siblings. "I don't want anything to happen to you or the baby. Or the children either." He stopped and looked over her head as Jerusha, dragging Joseph behind her, came into the kitchen.

"We'll talk about this later," Lydia said in a rapid undertone. She crossed the kitchen and disappeared into the pantry, reappearing with bread and cheese. Rees looked at the yellow brick. Oily and sweating in the heat, it did not look appealing.

Nancy and Judah ran into the kitchen. Jerusha released Joseph and he promptly made a beeline for the back steps. Lydia automatically moved a chair into the opening and he began to wail. On the surface this was a day like any other. The children seemed unaware of the tension between Lydia and Rees. And then Jerusha looked around and said, "Where's Abby?"

Both Rees and Lydia realized at the same moment that the girl had not made an appearance this morning. "Why, I suppose she's late," Lydia said easily. But she sighed and shot a glance at Rees. He nodded. It was likely that Abby's parents had elected to keep her home instead of sending her to a house where she would be in physical danger.

The chair blocking the back door scraped across the floor as David and Simon entered the kitchen. David's eyes were circled with shadows. He exchanged a sympathetic look with his father.

"What are you going to do today?" Lydia asked Rees. "Will you speak to your sister again?"

"Maybe," Rees said. He wondered if there was any point. She'd already admitted to starting the rumor against Lydia and claimed no knowledge of the murders or anything else. He wanted to believe her. "I suppose I could ask her about Sam," he said. He was beginning to wonder if Sam was quite as touched as he appeared—but Caroline would probably lie. "I'll see. I was planning to visit Piggy Hanson and also his good friend Molly Bowditch."

"Maybe you should refrain from calling the magistrate Piggy," Lydia said in a dry voice. "There is no point in offending him needlessly." Reed grunted. The fat little boy Rees remembered from his childhood had grown into a plump man who was very conscious of his importance in the community. Rees drank his coffee and helped himself to another cup. "He's arrogant," he said. "I don't want to encourage him."

Throwing him a glance, Lydia brought out the spider and put it on the hearth. She began slicing bacon and adding the pieces to the pan. "I know," she said. "But sometimes I think you take delight in offending the important men in town."

"What delight?" Rees replied. "I think Piggy knows something."

The pork began to sizzle, spattering grease across the stone. Rees knew she was cooking the meat for him. He crossed the floor and dropped a kiss upon her cap. "Don't worry," he whispered. Then he followed David outside to finish the milking and bring the pails to the cold cellar. Dug deep into the hillside, the cellar maintained cold temperatures all year round. During last winter, though, which began with an early frost in September and continued cold and snowy until April, the temperature in the cellar had dropped below freezing and remained there. A significant portion of the stored food, the wax shrouded cheeses, the barrels of brined meats and the collected produce froze. Rees hoped this coming winter's temperatures would not be so harsh.

After eggs and bacon and bread to wipe up the fat, Rees harnessed Hannibal to the wagon and set off for the Bowditch farm. Magistrate Hanson, Rees thought, probably followed town hours and would not be available until eight or after. But the Bowditch property was a farm and would have been in operation since before daybreak.

He hadn't been out this way since last summer, before his marriage to Lydia. And before his fight with Sam and the injury that resulted. The journey felt so familiar his last visit could have been yesterday. He noted that several of the fields left fallow by Nate were now under cultivation and wondered if he would see other changes.

He turned down the back lane. It was wider than he remembered and a crowd of boys and men thronged the barnyard ahead. With his heart beginning to pound in his chest, Rees pulled Hannibal into the shade and jumped out of the wagon. For a moment he paused on the grassy verge and examined the cluster of men on the other side of the lane. Although he saw several dark faces, he did not spot Marsh, and after a moment he walked up the path to the back door. The steps up to the porch were even untidier than before and the back door stood open. Rees knocked on the frame. Several minutes passed and Rees pounded impatiently on the wood again. Finally a scrawny child, his skin even darker than Marsh's, came to the door and eyed Rees cautiously.

"Is Mr. Marsh here?" Rees asked.

"I'll fetch him. Marse," said the child in a thick Southern

accent, ducking his head. He darted away. Rees followed the child into the hall. Despite the early hour, Rees was already uncomfortable and sweating. He wondered what the fall would bring: more heat or a sudden cold spell?

A few minutes later, Marsh came running up the stairs from the kitchen and crossed the hall, smiling broadly. He had been Nate's foreman and now served Nate's daughter, Grace, in that capacity. Once Grace had inherited the farm, Molly Bowditch had moved into what had once been the weaver's cottage. "Mr. Rees," he said, holding out his hand. But he quickly retracted it. Rees, who understood Marsh's hesitation—a black man who shook hands as though he were the equal of a white man would have to be crazy—quickly extended his own. Marsh's eyes lighted up with pleasure.

"How are you?" Rees asked. "And how is Grace?"

"She's doing well. But working hard, of course."

"I saw the new fields," Rees said with a nod. "It looks like she's taken on new hands?"

"Yes."

"I'm sure she values your guidance," Rees said. Marsh lowered his eyes, pleased but embarrassed too. He waited for Rees to explain the purpose of his visit.

"Is Molly Bowditch living here?" Rees asked. He thought so, but after the events of the previous summer Grace was estranged from her mother. Marsh's eyes widened in surprise.

"Yes. The weaver's house has been made over for her. But I doubt she'll speak to you." He stopped. Both men remained silent. Last summer Rees had been investigating Nate's murder. Along the way he'd uncovered several secrets. Molly's dark past had been particularly serious.

"I know," Rees said. "But I have to try. Someone is threatening Lydia, Marsh." His voice quivered in spite of himself. "She's been accused of witchcraft. And murder. The miller, Mr. McIntyre, was murdered surrounded by her candles. A mob came to my house." His voice shook and he stopped abruptly.

Marsh looked at Rees with sympathy. "I'm sorry to hear that. I know how that feels." He shook his head. "But I didn't hear anything." He joined Rees on the porch. Munch, Nate's big black dog, galloped over from the barnyard. He woofed at Rees in happy recognition and jumped up, putting his paws upon Rees's chest.

"Good boy," Rees said, patting the dog's head. Munch's doggy breath puffed into Rees's face. "Good boy. Get down now." Rees pushed the dog down.

Marsh began walking down the lane to the hollow that contained the weaver's cottage. "You'll see plenty of changes," he said. "I won't go down there. Not anymore. And Munch won't either. Molly doesn't like him and he returns the favor."

"Sounds like Munch has good judgment," Rees said, and was instantly sorry he'd spoken so tactlessly.

"Munch was always Nate's dog," Marsh said. "If you need anything," he turned to look at Rees, "just ask."

Rees smiled. "I will," he said, although he could not imagine what help Marsh could ever offer him.

He started down the steep slope to the small cottage situated in the hollow below. As soon as he crested the hill, he understood what Marsh had meant. Although the cottage looked the same, the grounds had been profoundly altered. The small fields where Nate had grown flax and various dye plants were filled with flowers and the two-wheeled track was now a drive. It went from the front of the cottage to what had been a path through the trees but was now a road to the street outside. Rees could have circled the farm and come to the cottage from that direction. A small barn had been built at the back of the cottage and Rees could hear the whinnying of at least a few horses.

As he descended the slope, Mary Martha, one of the kitchen maids—and Abigail's sister—came out of the cottage with a basket. "Mary Martha," Rees called.

The young girl froze. "Don't look so frightened." Rees broke into a trot, sliding down the hill in a dusty cloud. "It's me, Will Rees."

She nodded and came forward, moistening her lips with her tongue. "I know." As she stepped out of the shade into the sun, the red hair curling around the edges of her white cap took on the glitter of a new copper penny. "I don't really know why Abby didn't go to your house this morning. I know my parents don't believe in witchcraft, of course they don't, and anyway they know Miss Lydia so why would they believe it, but some people in town do and so my father doesn't want to put Abby in any danger . . ."

"I understand," Rees said, interrupting her. Mary Martha could talk for several minutes without taking a breath. "We guessed what had happened and I'll tell my wife that I spoke to you. Is Mrs. Bowditch inside?"

"I think so. I didn't see her this morning. She told me last night she wouldn't want to be disturbed so I just made coffee and tea and put fresh rolls and butter on the table."

"Thank you," Rees said, interrupting once again. He circled around the girl. But he paused before he stepped up to the door. Could he really enter this cottage? This was where Nate had been murdered. For Rees, just standing outside reminded him of the bloodstain left on the floor by the body.

"There's no one inside watching the door," Mary Martha said with an impatient edge to her voice. She might remember Nate's death but did not feel the complicated emotions that Rees associated with the murder. The girl brushed past Rees and jumped up to the massive granite slab to hammer on the door. "There you are. She's probably upstairs so you might have to wait." Then, with the happy assurance she had done her part to help, she started up the hill to the main house.

The door to the cottage was thrust open. "I told you, Mary Martha, I . . ." Molly's words trailed away as she realized just who stood outside. She was dressed only in a cotton petticoat and silk wrap and had clearly just arisen from bed. "How dare you come to this house," she said after a shocked silence. She went to swing the door shut but Rees, spurred into action, leaped up and blocked the door with his left arm.

"I just want to ask you some questions," he said.

"And why should I answer them?" she asked angrily. "You ruined my life."

"It's about the miller, Tom McIntyre. He's dead."

"Is he? I didn't know. A tragedy for his family, to be sure, but why should I care?"

"He was murdered," Rees said in an icy tone. He'd forgotten how self-centered she was. "And in a particularly nasty manner."

"Surely you don't think I had anything to do with it? Why, I barely knew the man." She stared at Rees with eyebrows raised in surprise. Her bewilderment seemed believable and Rees thought she might be telling the truth, but he knew very well that she was an accomplished liar. Footsteps clattering upon the stairs betrayed the presence of another person in the cottage. A tide of scarlet rose into Molly's neck and cheeks and she partially closed the door, but not before Rees saw black shoes with silver buckles and fine white silk stockings on the steps behind her.

"He was found in the mill, upside down, and surrounded by candles." Rees fixed his eyes upon her face, hoping to shock her.

"How terrible. But I haven't seen Mr. McIntyre since I was a girl," Molly said with a hint of hauteur. "Marsh deals with such things as the miller. I don't know anything. And I wouldn't help you if I did. Why are you even involved? You can't keep your long nose out of other people's affairs?"

"Lydia has been accused," Rees said.

Molly stared at him for a second and then burst into loud shrill laughter. "You've gotten what you deserve," she said, pushing the words between the gusts of hilarity.

"Is something wrong?" Mr. Drummond appeared behind Molly. Not for him a black coat. His was a beautiful yellow and patterned with a subtle sheen of silk threads. Lace edged the cloth tied around his neck. Rees nodded courteously, his initial surprise dissipating. A relationship between Molly and a suspicious Virginian seemed preordained.

"No," Molly said tersely. "Mr. Rees is just leaving."

"I had a few questions for Mrs. Bowditch," Rees said, sketching a bow. "I hoped that, from her place in Dugard society, she might know something." Missing Rees's sarcasm entirely, Drummond smiled. Molly's lips trembled and she shot Rees a look of hatred.

"If that's all, Mr. Rees?" she said in a frosty tone and slammed the door shut before he could reply.

Rees turned and walked toward the lane. Molly had clearly stated she did not know Mr. McIntyre very well and expressed a rather indifferent surprise at his death. Did Rees believe her? She certainly disliked him enough to want to do him an ill turn if she could. But Rees thought her surprise was genuine. Besides, Rees knew a woman could not have lifted the miller and tied him to the posts. Not without help anyway. Was Mr. Drummond so besotted he would do anything Molly asked, including murder? And of course Drummond had been one of the two men who had discovered Zadoc Ward's body. Coincidence, or something more? Rees couldn't answer that question now, but he would know the answer eventually, of that he was certain.

Chapter Seventeen

After an unproductive stop at Judge Hanson's empty office, Rees tracked the magistrate down to the Contented Rooster. The coffeehouse had begun to empty as the local merchants left for their businesses. But Hanson was still inside, seated before the window and enjoying a hearty breakfast of steak and eggs and a large glass of whiskey. He was stuffed like a sausage in a casing into a costly but wrinkled gray jacket. A large linen napkin was tucked into his neck cloth, protecting the lace beneath. He saw Rees enter and wiped his mouth on a corner of the napkin. "I will not offer Caldwell his job back," he said as Rees approached, "so do not even plan on asking."

"You took away his job?" Rees asked, shocked out of his own concerns. "Why did you do that? Because he broke up the mob attacking my family?" He pulled out the opposite chair and sat down.

Frowning, Hanson took a draft of tea and then patted away the perspiration dotting his forehead. "Please, sit down," he said sarcastically, gesturing to the seat Rees now occupied. "You have no sense of the order of things, Will. That's your problem. Never have had. You walk around with that damn-your-eyes arrogance.

No sense of the proper treatment of your betters." He gestured to Rees, sitting across the table. "You do not know how to behave."

"My betters?" Rees repeated "My betters? I have no betters. I'm as good as any man." He eyed the man sitting across from him, "And *my* respect must be earned."

A tide of red swept up into Hanson's cheeks. "I see. And I'm not worthy."

"I didn't say that," Rees said.

"But you did." Hanson shook his head. "It is you who think you're better than everyone. Half the men in town have suffered a beating at your hands."

"When I was a boy," Rees said, feeling his cheeks warm.

"You've made it clear to everyone in town that you don't want to live here; that this town isn't good enough for you. That we are just a stopover once in a while." Rees stared at the magistrate, for once bereft of speech. That accusation stung. "Every time you've come home, you've caused some kind of mischief. The rumor about Molly Bowditch was not the most current but certainly one of the most damaging."

"Preventing half the widows in town from losing their money in one of your schemes being the most recent," Rees said, expecting to get a rise from the magistrate.

Hanson wiped his lips. Although pink tinted his cheeks, he did not respond to Rees's gibe. Instead he said, "And Caldwell has permitted his friendship with you to affect his judgment. He should have known better." Rees leaned forward.

"They were threatening my wife, Piggy. Do you understand?"

"And how do I know she isn't guilty? I've heard those Shaker women never marry and believe they are the equal of men."

"You're not planning to tell me you believe in witches," Rees said. "I wouldn't credit it."

Hanson smiled, his thin lips stretching until they disappeared in the folds of his cheeks. "Do I think she used magic to bludgeon Mr. McIntyre and hang him upside down? No. But *she* might trust in her powers. And you might have helped her."

"Me? But you've known me all your life. You should know I would never commit murder. And Mac was my friend. Yes, we argued. But it was only politics."

"More than a few deaths have been caused by political arguments," Hanson said, somewhat dryly. "Besides, I don't know you." He smiled slightly as he inspected Rees's expression. "I knew the boy. I don't know the man."

Rees gaped at the magistrate. They had known each other all their lives, but now Hanson seemed like a stranger. Rees's anger was submerged by a coldness rising from the pit of his stomach. He began to shiver. "You really don't like me, do you?" He didn't much care for Hanson either—he was a bully cloaked in soft pink flesh—but Rees was startled by the depth of Piggy's loathing.

"You deserve a lesson in correct behavior," Hanson said, as though that explained everything. "And no, I do not like you or your family. You probably do not recall your father's articles about my father, accusing him of being a Loyalist."

"I don't remember them," Rees said. After a second's pause he added, "Was he a Loyalist?"

Hanson frowned. "Of course not."

But Rees heard the lie; Hanson Senior had been at least a sympathizer with the Crown. "He lost his property?"

"Yes. My inheritance. To the dirty rabble like your father." In the conflict of the times, loss of property was the usual result of such an accusation. And at that, Mr. Hanson had been fortunate to escape hanging.

Rees nodded. His father, as the town printer and editor of the local newspaper, could hardly be described as rabble, but arguing over something that happened twenty-five years ago did not seem important now. "That is a long time past," he said. "And both our fathers are dead."

"You don't remember how you bullied me?" Hanson's voice rose into a bleat. He cleared his throat and wiped his lips again, giving himself a moment to calm down. "You weren't content to tease me until I cried. No, you and Nate had to chase me home. You do remember punching me, don't you?"

"We were barely eight years old then," Rees said, his voice coming out hoarse. "I've grown up. I'm a different person."

"Are you? You bully people now, with those investigations of yours. Or meddle in things you do not fully understand."

"If you're talking about your land schemes—"

"Besides, the torture did not cease when we grew up." Hanson overrode Rees's voice. "Do you remember when we were thirteen and you and Nate abandoned me in the ice caves?"

"We didn't abandon you," Rees said. "We came back. And you'd found your way out by then."

"But I didn't know my way home, did I? I was cold and shaking, for all that it was summer. And I was terrified."

"We took you home." Rees stopped. What did it matter anyway? "I'm sorry," he said. "I'll apologize for the boy I was. Really, Piggy, it was a lifetime ago."

"And that's another thing. Do not call me Piggy." Hanson rose, tossing his napkin upon the table. "I am Magistrate Hanson to you. Never forget that."

Rees rose as well, towering over the shorter man. "And you don't forget that I will sup with the Devil himself to protect my wife and family." Hanson met Rees's eyes.

"From what I've heard, you and your wife regularly entertain him," Hanson said with a mocking sneer. He held Rees's gaze for a moment longer, making sure Rees knew Piggy was no longer afraid, and then he turned and stalked away. But he paused at the door and turned. "By the way, I've decided to appoint another one of your friends as the new constable. Mr. Zedediah Farley. How do you like that?" He laughed and went out the door, leaving Rees trembling. He knew that memories in Dugard were long and that slights could fester into resentments that lasted generations. But he'd never expected a boyhood grudge to develop into such hatred. Worse, Hanson's dislike was supporting those who would harm Lydia. And Rees didn't know what to do about it. This was not a case where he could fight someone, using his physical strength to overcome them. And Hanson, vindictive to the last, had not only blocked most of Rees's avenues for investigation but had now appointed someone who actively threatened Rees and his family.

"You look shaken," Susannah said, approaching the table and beginning to clear the used plates.

"I guess I didn't realize just how much the magistrate detested me," Rees said. He sounded shocked, even to himself. "I don't care, but . . ." His voice trailed away.

"If you didn't know that then you're the only one," Susannah said. She piled Hanson's used crockery upon the tray and nodded over her shoulder at Jack Junior. He scurried over. "And fetch Mr. Rees coffee and some eggs please," Susannah told her son.

"How are you?" Rees asked the boy.

"Fine," he mumbled and hurried away. Rees gazed after Jack Junior, surprised by the boy's rudeness.

Susannah wiped down the table and sat across from Rees. "Cornelius Hanson has never made any secret of his feelings toward you."

"But he hates me for my treatment of him when we were boys," Rees protested.

"Is that what he said?" Susannah considered that in silence. "Maybe. It is true that some people can't forget. Perhaps the magistrate relives these experiences over and over and they remain fresh in his mind. His dislike of you has been of long standing. Your father was a passionate Patriot; his was a Loyalist."

"He mentioned that," Rees said.

"But I know he resents other more recent experiences. Although the Widow Penney and other old women are grateful to you, the magistrate sees your effort on their behalf as interfering in his affairs. Besides, he lost a lot of money in those schemes, money he would have recouped from those poor old ladies."

"And all of those women would have been reduced to penury," Rees said as Rachel placed the plate before him. She offered him a warm smile. Rees wondered what had happened to Jack Junior, who should have delivered the food. Susannah must have wondered too; she turned to look into the kitchen. Rees began to eat, hungrier than he expected.

"You came home from the war something of a hero," Susannah continued, turning her attention back to her companion. "Mr. Hanson never went. Some people in town remember that. He expects everyone to treat him with groveling respect and you return home from your weaving trips with that urbane polish and the assurance that comes from knowing you are inferior to no one. He hates you for that."

"I can handle it," Rees said with a bravery he didn't feel. He pushed away his plate, suddenly losing his appetite. "It's Lydia and the children." He glanced away from Susannah, his gaze connecting with Jack's. Jack looked away. Then he looked back, offering Rees a jerky nod of acknowledgment. Rees turned his eyes back to Susannah. "You made Jack help Caldwell, didn't you?" Recalling Jack Junior's behavior, Rees added, "Is Magistrate Hanson pressuring you and your family?" She would not meet his eyes. "Susannah," he said sternly.

"Not the magistrate, no." She tried to smile. "But some others in town. Well, they're frightened. Some of them really do believe in witches. My own husband does. But he doesn't think Lydia is one," she hastened to add. "And Jack Junior has been teased."

"So Farley and all of that crowd are permitted to menace the ones I care about," said Rees through stiff lips. "Caldwell lost his job, just for protecting my family. You know, Suze, that now Farley, a man who believes Lydia is a witch, is constable. He won't let go until he's sent her to the gallows." Rees's voice broke. How could he protect Lydia and guarantee her safety? He couldn't, not in Dugard anyway. It was more important than ever that she flee to Zion before Farley brought another mob to Rees's farm.

Chapter Eighteen

He drove home like a fury, driving Hannibal so hard the gelding arrived panting and lathered up. With a promise to return, Rees looped the reins around the porch rail and ran inside. But Lydia was not in the kitchen. Only Jerusha was there, standing at the sink and swirling her hands through gray dishwater. Some of the breakfast dishes had been washed and dried but most were still stacked on the table, awaiting her attention. She looked up in surprise. "Where's Lydia?" Rees asked.

"In the dairy," she said. "What's the matter?"

Without replying, Rees spun around and retraced his steps to the front. He unharnessed Hannibal and walked him down the slope to the brick dairy. The horse needed cooling; foam flecked his smooth nose and spotted his mane and shoulders. David would be furious.

The door to the dairy was closed. Rees knocked upon it. He began walking the gelding around in a wide circle while he waited for Lydia to appear. Although it was probably only a few seconds, to Rees it felt like several minutes before she opened the door. "Will? What's the matter? I'm right in the middle of my cheese making. And what are you doing with that horse?"

Rees paused in front of her, pulling Hannibal to a stop. Because the dairy was nestled in a hollow and the brick floor dug a few steps down into the ground, the air inside was chiller than out. A breath of cool air touched Rees's face. He could see the panniers of milk spread out upon the shelves behind his wife.

"Caldwell is no longer the constable," Rees said without pre-amble. "Zedediah Farley has been given that post."

Lydia looked at him without comprehension. "That's too bad. But is it so important you had to interrupt me?"

"Farley is a superstitious fool. He believes you're a witch. He's the one who led the mob out here, to the farm. He would have taken you to town and imprisoned you. You and the children must leave here. Today."

Although Lydia's cheeks paled she shook her head. "I don't want to quarrel over this now, especially with the door to the dairy open and flies coming in." She blew a lock of hair out of her eyes. "We'll discuss this when I'm done." She shut the door firmly, leaving Rees and Hannibal standing on the other side.

"Foolish woman," Rees muttered. "Why can't she listen to me?" Hannibal whickered, almost as though he understood. Rees clucked and pulled on the bridle to urge the horse into motion. They walked up the slope but, before releasing the horse into the pasture, Rees found a rag and wiped him down. Rees could see David working in a distant cornfield, the straw hat bobbing up and down as he hoed. Rees knew he should help, but he wanted to speak to Lydia as soon as he could. So, instead of going out to the fields, he went back to the house.

But he was too restless to sit and wait. He pushed the kettle over the fire to heat more water for the dishes; Jerusha had washed only one additional plate since Rees had last been in the kitchen and the water in the dishpan looked slimy. Then he picked up the broom and applied it enthusiastically to the wooden floor. Sweeping had to be done constantly since dirt was tracked in from the yard every time someone came into the house. While the larger bits of mud and vegetation skidded away from the broom, the finer dust rose into the air, circling his head in a cloud.

He swept it out the back door. "My goodness, Will," Lydia said as she toiled up the slope to the house, "what are you doing?" Wisps of dark red hair, curly in the heat, fringed her white cap and her cheeks were flushed. Her long skirts and petticoats clung to her legs with perspiration.

"Waiting for you," Rees said, halting the broom. He leaned it against the wall. "Thought I'd do some work."

"Mmm," Lydia said, taking the broom and carrying it with her as she climbed the back stairs. "I usually dampen the floor a little to keep down the dust." Rees grunted without interest and followed his wife into the kitchen. Jerusha had taken all of the dishes from the pan and put them on the table. Lydia turned a stern look at the girl.

"I was going to empty the pan," Jerusha said defensively, "and put in fresh water." She glanced at the kettle and the steam pouring from the spout. "Let them soak in hot water." She stopped, eyeing Lydia in trepidation as she ran a finger over one of the dried plates.

"These need to be washed again," she said. "This is greasy."

"It's too hot to wash dishes," Jerusha whined.

"Unless you plan to cease eating, there will always be dishes," Lydia said as Rees picked up the pan and carried it down the back steps. "But go on outside. I have to talk to your father anyway." Rees hurled the dirty water into the weeds from the bottom of the stairs. As he returned to the kitchen he passed Jerusha, grinning and on her way to freedom. Lydia, who had poured the hot water from the kettle into the dishpan, put the empty pot on the hearth and turned to face Rees.

"Lydia," he began.

"I know you're worried," she said, interrupting him. "And I appreciate your concern. Do you believe I might spend more than an hour or two in Wheeler's stable?"

Rees shook his head, angry with himself. In his attempt to protect Lydia, he had not fully explained the danger and now it didn't seem as serious to her as it was. "You might possibly spend a week or more," he said. He did not want to mention the rope and the grin on the face of Farley's son as he slid it through his hands. "Caldwell would have done his best to protect you," Rees continued. "But not Farley. He'll want to keep you there until you go to trial."

"Trial?" She considered that a moment. "But then," she said in a reasonable tone, "when I appear before the magistrate, all charges will be dismissed. Just as they were for Mother Ann Lee."

"Perhaps," Rees said, the memory of Hanson's animosity fresh in his mind. "But I'm not willing to take that risk. Especially not when you're expecting." Involuntarily he gestured at her belly. "Besides." He paused, considering how much he should confide in his wife. "Magistrate Hanson, well, he doesn't like me very much. In fact, I think he will not stick at anything to serve me an ill turn. I need you and the children to go somewhere safe."

Lydia stared at him. "I know he doesn't like you. But this depth of animosity? What did you do to him?"

"Piggy has always been a bully." Rees took a turn around the kitchen table. "When my friend Nate and I were boys we punished him for teasing the girls." The memory of a small, slight six-year-old with flaxen plaits sobbing as Piggy pinched and slapped her appeared in Rees's mind, so fresh and sharp he might have seen it yesterday. "Abandoning him at the ice caves seemed fair and just at the time."

"I think that's what you told yourselves when you were cruel to another boy," Lydia said as she began sliding the dishes Jerusha had washed and dried into the steaming water.

"Perhaps," Rees said, although he did not agree. He and Nate had had their own code. "The point is that Hanson has never forgotten. And then I convinced the town widows not to invest in his schemes. Now he has an opportunity to punish me for it. So you won't be able to expect impartial treatment from him." He paused and watched his wife expertly scrub each dish. "Please, Lydia. I can't investigate this and resolve it if I'm trying to protect you and the children the entire time."

Lydia turned, her eyes filling with the easy tears of pregnancy. "I want to stay here, with you." She put her hand upon her belly. "Our child will soon be born."

"I know." Rees put his arms around her and blurted out the truth. "But I'm terrified something will happen to you both."

They stood for a moment in the embrace and then Lydia pulled back, wiping her eyes. "Even if I was willing to leave, where would I go?"

"Perhaps to your family?" Rees suggested. "I've never met them. And they don't know about . . ." He gestured to her swelling belly.

"No," she said in a flat tone that brooked no argument. "I would rather be hanged as a witch than throw myself on the mercy of my father."

Rees stared at her, wondering as he had many times in the past just what had happened between Lydia and her family.

"So you see," she said with a faint smile, "I have nowhere else to go. I have to stay here."

"You can go to Zion," said Rees. Zion was the Shaker community in which he'd met Lydia two years before. "You know some of the sisters from your time there. And you'll be safe." When Lydia did not respond, Rees hurried on. "We met the Elders and Eldresses when we brought Annie." After rescuing the young girl from an almost certain fate as a prostitute in Salem, they had brought her to Zion in June. "They'll take you and the children in, and I'm sure Annie will be happy to see you."

"We promised Jerusha and the others we wouldn't abandon them to the Shakers," Lydia said.

"I know. But this will only be temporary, until I discover the evil mind behind this. Besides, you will be there with them."

"Do you really want me to leave?" Lydia asked, staring into Rees's eyes.

"No. I don't. I'll miss you. But I couldn't live if anything happened to you." He touched her belly gently and felt an answering kick. The hair rose on the back of his neck and he said forcefully, "We have no idea how long you might be imprisoned. Do you truly want to give birth in a stable?"

Hysteria edged her involuntary laugh. "A stable was good enough for our Lord Jesus."

"I'm sure his mother would have chosen another place if she could," Rees said. "Think about what happened to your bees." A sudden shudder sent Lydia's body into a spasm and Rees put his arms around her. "I promise you, my darling, this is the only way to keep you and the children safe. I will come for you as soon as I can."

"Come from where?" David paused at the door into the pantry. "Are you leaving again? Now?"

Lydia and Rees parted and he looked at his son. "I'll be delivering Lydia and the children to Zion. They can stay there until I've resolved this . . ." He paused, searching for a good word. "Situation. This situation. Then I'll come home. I want to be sure they're safe."

David's gaze went to Lydia and he bobbed his head in agreement. "Good idea."

"You think I'm in danger too?" Lydia's voice rose in surprise.

David nodded again. "Mr. Farley really believes you're a witch. Put together with all the other things that have happened, well, I think it's dangerous to stay." Lydia glanced from Rees to David and back again and her hand went protectively to her belly. Rees saw the exact moment when she accepted the necessity of leaving. The eyebrows that had been moving up and down in thought settled and her mouth relaxed into sorrowful resignation.

"Very well, I'll pack some things for the children." As she hurried down the hall, Rees heard a muffled sob.

"I want you to go too," Rees said, turning to look at his son.

"No," David said. "You're going to need me to help run the farm, to do the chores, and guard it. Especially now that some of the boys I hired on as extra hands have stopped coming. They tell me their parents forbid them."

"All of them?" Rees asked in alarm.

David shook his head. "Not Charlie. Well, he's family. Not Freddie, but his family is so poor he doesn't have a choice. But several. And they don't want to talk to me. Good thing I still have some of the transients."

Rees sighed, staring at the floor. Everyone was trying to disassociate himself from trouble and this was such a bad time to lose the help. David needed it. Although the haying was done and most of the wheat was in, the corn would be starting soon. "I daresay we'll soon learn who our true friends are," Rees said.

"Yes," David said with a lopsided smile.

"I just don't want to see you hurt," Rees said, looking at his son. "I've failed you so many times."

"Not this time," David said. He hesitated and then added in a rush of words, "I wouldn't blame you if you did leave this time. Seeing a crowd outside our door—I'll have nightmares the rest of my life." He shuddered. "Besides, all of the trouble seems to be directed at you and Lydia. Not me. I think I'll be fine. And I have too many ties holding me here." When Rees did not speak, David added quietly, "I'm an adult now and this is my decision." He looked straight at his father, not impudent or defiant in any way but as one equal to another. Rees slowly nodded, his emotions a jumble of regret and pride.

"Very well," he said, his voice breaking. Where had his little boy gone?

"So, that's settled." David ducked his head. "I'll harness Hannibal to the wagon. You are taking the wagon, right? The buggy is too small for everyone." He hurried out the back door. Rees sighed and turned to the pantry to begin collecting whatever portable food he could find. They would have to spend at least one night on the road, maybe two, and eat as they traveled. Rees didn't want to spend more time away from the farm than he must; he was afraid to. What if something happened when only David was here? And David was badly hurt or even killed? Rees would never forgive himself.

Chapter Nineteen

⌁

The afternoon of the fifth day after departure, Rees finally pulled back into the drive to his farm. He was dirty, hungry, and tired, but at least he was finally home. The trip to Zion had been a grueling one, taking longer than Rees had expected, since Lydia tired easily and they'd had to stop frequently. The sun had beat down upon them mercilessly and the children had cried and fussed almost the entire journey. No one wanted to leave the farm and Simon, in particular, was inconsolable at being parted from David. More than once Rees was tempted to tell them why they were forced to go to Zion, but he didn't want to frighten the wits out of them. Lydia was scared enough for all of them, and angry too at being forced from her home. Rees knew it but they couldn't discuss it, not with five children listening to every word.

Now he pulled up the slope toward his house, eagerly anticipating a hot bath, fresh food that wasn't cheese, and a good night's sleep in his own bed. But as soon as he saw the wagon, with the ox between the traces, pulled up to the front porch he knew he would be denied all of those things. He pulled Hannibal to a stop. Sam and Charlie came out of the barn. Charlie hurried over and grasped the bridle. "I'll take care of the horse," he said, his expression somber. "You'd better go inside. My mother . . ." He paused when Rees groaned. Charlie smiled and offered Rees a hand to help him down from the wagon. He needed it. He had driven home as fast as he could, barely stopping, and his entire body seemed solidified into stone.

Sam caught up to his son. "I'll help," he said with a broad grin. Rees inspected the other man, a wave of guilt and pity sweeping over him. Sam's grimy cheeks were unshaven and his hair hung in rattails to the gray shoulders of his unwashed linen shirt. His breeches were so dirty Rees couldn't decide what the original color had been, and Sam had lost the buttons at the knees. He was bare-legged and barefoot and looked like one of the homeless men who wandered the roads. He smelled like something rotting, an odor so penetrating Rees stepped backward, gagging.

"Go back to the barn and finish raking out the stalls," Charlie said sternly. He rolled his eyes at Rees.

"I like your horse," Sam said to Rees as he reached out a hand to stroke the gelding.

"Uh, good," Rees said. "I have to go inside now."

"Father," Charlie said, sounding impatient. "We have work to do. In the barn. Go there, now." As Sam shuffled away, Charlie turned back to Rees. "I'm sorry. He wanders off. My mother told me to keep a close eye on him while she's here. And me and David with work to do." He shook his head. Rees directed a sympathetic smile at the boy before going up the porch stairs and into the house.

As soon as he opened the door he could hear his sister haranguing David. "You know your father won't come home. He's run away. Again."

"No, he hasn't. He's taken Lydia and the younger children away."

"Oh, but he left you here to face Mr. Farley, hasn't he? While everyone else is safe." This time David did not reply. "You can't stay here alone. You need us; we'll move in."

"No!" The word exploded out of David, very sudden and very loud.

"But you can't manage the farm and house without help . . ."

"He won't be alone," Rees said, walking through the parlor door. He eyed his sister, so angry that for a moment he didn't trust himself to speak.

She looked up at him, her eyes widening in surprise and dismay. "Well," she said, pursing her lips and frowning, "I didn't expect to see you."

"I told you he was coming home," David said. "I told you."

"I had to bring Lydia and the children to visit family," Rees said.

"I thought she had no family," Caroline said. Rees did not reply. His wife considered the Shakers her family. "I was just trying to help," Caroline added.

"No, you weren't," Rees said.

"Yes, I was. If Lydia is convicted of witchcraft and you weren't here, the farm could be forfeit. David could be evicted. But if I was here . . ."

"You might obtain the farm," Rees said. "Might." He glared at her. The fact that she was right about the possibilities did not ease his anger.

She stared up at him, her eyes filling with tears. As Rees looked at her, his annoyance began to lessen. His sister, younger by three years, looked so worn. Silver threaded her chestnut hair. He remembered her hair shining with red highlights, but there was more white now than red. Lines fanned out from the corners of her eyes and furrows grooved her forehead.

"I will be here with David," Rees said. "And Lydia will soon be home." He paused and then said, trying to be gentle, "You have your own farm, Caro."

"It's not a good farm, not productive like this one. It's not worth very much. We have no livestock—only chickens and the oxen we use for plowing."

"It could be, with work," Rees said, interrupting the litany of complaints.

"I'm not good at it, Will," Caroline said, sniffling. "You don't like it either. But at least you have a skill."

Her sudden unvarnished honesty reduced Rees to silence. Finally he nodded. "That's true. But I have my own family to care for. I'll offer you what help I can."

"Mother and Father charged you with looking after me," Caroline interrupted, her voice rising into a wail. "I don't understand why we can't move in here."

"Why didn't you stay with Phoebe?" Rees asked. "She was willing to look after you."

"I was neither wife nor widow. Sam, well, Charlie fetched Sam and brought him to Phoebe's and she told us to leave."

"What happened?" Rees asked. "Did Sam start beating you again?"

Caroline glared at her brother. "He never beat me. Ever." Rees stared at her. He knew Sam had and didn't understand why Caroline was telling him such a lie.

"You know that's not true, Caro," he said.

Caroline tossed her head and said, "You could arrange to sell the farm. That would be good for all of us." She smiled. "I could finally visit Boston."

"And what would you do about Sam?" Rees asked.

"He could stay here, with you. After all, it's your fault he's like this."

In an instant, Rees's sympathy fled. Caroline refused to take any responsibility for her poor choices. "No," he said. "Never." He was saved from blurting out a reply he would later regret by Charlie's arrival at the parlor door. "Are you ready to go home yet?" Charlie asked his mother. Sam stood next to his son, smiling. He was shorter than his son now but heavier, with a barrel chest and skinny legs. Even from the distance separating them, Rees could smell Sam's rotting-meat body odor.

"I like *your* farm," Sam said, staring directly at Rees. "I like your horses and your cattle." Enmity flashed into his eyes and then disappeared into his usual vacuous expression, so quickly Rees wondered if he'd imagined it.

"Yes, I'm ready. Since my own brother won't help me." Caroline jumped to her feet and flounced past Rees. She paused at the door. "I think you'd have been kinder if you weren't married. I wish you hadn't wed Lydia. She's changed you, made you hard. Maybe she's a witch after all and has cast a spell on you."

Before Rees could formulate a response, Caroline had joined Sam and started down the hall to the front door. Charlie paused, his face crimson. "Sorry. My mother . . ." Since no words could explain or make amends for his mother's behavior, he allowed his voice to trail away. After an uncomfortable few seconds, he looked at David. "I'll be back as soon as I've gotten them off." His footsteps clattered down the hall and the front door slammed behind him.

Rees collapsed into the horsehair chair behind him. His legs were trembling so much they couldn't support him. He looked at his son.

"This was her third visit," David said.

"Was she like that before?"

David nodded. "Yes. Not quite as tearful."

"I'm sorry," Rees said.

David shrugged. "You're back now so she probably won't return. Not immediately, anyway." He stood up. "I'll see you later. Charlie and I are working in one of the cornfields."

Rees nodded. "I'm going to eat something. Then I'll go down to the pond and take a swim."

David sighed. "I miss Squeaker. More than I thought I would." On that surprising statement, he followed his cousin outside. Rees smiled. At least this awful time had one silver lining; David was realizing how attached he'd become to Simon.

Rees sat in the chair for a minute or two after David's departure. He was still shaking. It was not so much the quarrel with Caroline. Although that had been unpleasant, it seemed to him when he looked back on his life that every conversation he'd ever had with his sister had become an argument. It was the rapid change in his emotions, from anger to pity to sympathy and back to fury, in the space of a few minutes that had exhausted him. Especially since the confrontation had occurred after some very difficult days.

Finally he pushed himself to his feet and lumbered into the kitchen. His legs felt both stiff and weak and he would have liked nothing better than to remain seated. But his stomach was growling and after he'd eaten his chores must be done.

It was the sound of buzzing that penetrated first. Then the smell hit him, a pungent rotting smell almost as though Sam was still here, waiting for Rees in the kitchen. Rees paused in the doorway and looked around. The dishpan with its mound of dirty dishes sat in the sink just as Lydia had left it five days before. More dishes were piled upon the table. Flies hung in a cloud over the food-encrusted crockery. He peered at the plates and bowls in the sink. It must be a trick of the light; it looked as though the food was moving. Then he jumped back, gagging. Maggots swarmed over the dishes.

He bent double, retching, his appetite disappearing. David had moved back into the main house and, busy outside, had done none of the inside work. Rees grabbed a bucket and stormed outside to the trough. He wished his son had at least kept up with his own dishes.

He discovered he could not just put the kettle to heat over the fire. The last embers were almost out. Although the fire had been banked and stirred up and banked again, the wood had burned into just a pile of ashes. No new logs had been added. Rees had to sweep out the residue of all the old fires, put in fresh wood, relight the kindling, and then, finally, put the kettle over the flames.

The spider with at least an inch of grease sat on one side of the brick hearth. It looked as though David had eaten only bacon these last few days. The leftover stew had grown a coat of white.

Choking, his fingers twitching away from the maggots, Rees carefully extracted the dishes from the dirty water and threw the slimy liquid out the back door. He thought Lydia would be furious if she saw the filthy dishpan. Rees rinsed it three times before finally adding the hot water.

Then he began washing the dishes with the strong yellow soap. As the water in the dishpan cooled and turned gray, he threw it out and added fresh, a chore that had to be done four or five times. It took Rees over two hours to finish washing the crockery. He scraped the bacon grease into the barrel in the pantry and finally filled the large kettle with water. That he put directly over the fire and set it to boil.

As he worked his thoughts returned to his confrontation with his sister. The only thing that would make her happy was Rees's surrender. For a moment he considered the possibility of taking her and her family in. Although Caroline was difficult, he conceded that he might still allow her and the children to live here. But not Sam. Besides the animosity that had existed between them for so many years, Rees kept remembering the flash of fully conscious hostility he'd just seen in Sam's eyes. For all that Sam was supposed to be touched, and Rees was beginning to doubt that, allowing him to live here would be like taking a wolf into one's bed. Rees would never allow Sam to live here again.

Rees paused in the kitchen and took stock. He was tempted to drive into town and eat a proper meal at the Contented Rooster. But that would mean harnessing Hannibal to the wagon once again and Rees just didn't have the energy. Besides, he was so hot and sweaty he could smell himself. When he licked his lips he tasted salt. He peered into the pantry to see if there was anything quick he could eat. But the bread was hard and moldy, and it looked as though David had eaten everything else, even the cheese.

Rees grabbed a linen towel, took the fragment of soap left from washing the dishes, and went down to the pond.

The water was warm but refreshing for all of that. Rees scrubbed himself from crown to toes and then submerged completely, rinsing away almost a week's worth of perspiration. He stayed in the water until the shadow from the sugar maple crept over the pond and the light took on the golden tone of late afternoon. Then he climbed out. Reluctantly he dressed in his dirty body linen and breeches and thrust his bare feet into his shoes. He tramped up the slope to the back door. The kitchen was empty and it looked as though the boys had not come inside. The kettle boiled enthusiastically; it was at least ten degrees hotter because of the fire burning on the hearth. Rees used the hook to move the pot away from the flames. Realizing how hungry he was, he made himself pancakes and ate standing up by the door. Then he went upstairs to change into fresh linen.

As soon as he entered the bedchamber, he realized his loom was lying on its side on the floor. He hurried to right it, only to discover one of the sidepieces had been wrenched off. Rees lifted the beam from the floor. The comblike reed had been bent and thrown to the other side of the room and the heddles were scattered around the floor in a shower of silvery pins. There were a few sparkling in Joseph's bed.

An unaccustomed burning formed at the back of Rees's eyes. He walked to the window and looked out, struggling to calm himself. He couldn't see either David or Charlie and wondered if they had gone to Caroline's farm to put in some work there. He exhaled a long breath. It would take only a few hours to reattach the wooden pieces and to straighten out the reed, collect the heddles, and reinstall them. Although none of the damage to the loom was irreparable, he felt personally violated. The motive behind this destruction hurt him more than a slap or a blow would have; it had been designed to destroy his livelihood. And it showed him that nothing, not even his bedchamber in his house, was exempt from the vandal's reach. Rees wiped his wet eyes on his sleeve. Although he could understand that some people might dislike him, the vengeful desire behind these personal attacks sent him into shudders of both fear and despair. Although he hated admitting it, Caroline possessed the necessary malice. But he did not think she possessed the strength. So who? Could it be Zedediah Farley? He had strength and malice and a rifle besides. But could he sneak onto Rees's farm without anyone noticing?

Charlie's statement about his father: "He wanders" began running through Rees's head over and over like a bad dream. Had Sam wandered up to this room and tried to demolish Rees's loom? Before Sam's injury, he would have been Rees's first suspect. Sam had not troubled to hide his hatred, envy, and conviction that he deserved all that Rees possessed. But once his head had struck that granite block, he had seemed to be a different person. As foolish and happy and sweet as a child. Unless it had all been an act to allay Rees's suspicion. Rees stared blindly into the gathering shadows. Had Sam just been playing the village idiot? Rees realized with an unhappy shock that this was exactly the conclusion to which his thoughts had been leading him.

Chapter Twenty

By the fading light, and the shadows creeping into the bedchamber he shared with Lydia—oh, how he missed her and the children, the whole house seemed empty—Rees thought it must be after six o'clock. He had never questioned Elijah McIntyre about Sam. When Rees had tried to talk about Mac's murder, Elijah had been too distraught. But Sam spent a lot of time at the mill. He'd been there when Mac's body was discovered; Rees had seen him in the crowd. And who would suspect someone who seemed as harmless as a child? Rees nodded to himself, guessing that no one at the mill really noticed Sam anymore.

Would Elijah talk to Rees? "I'll have to chance it," Rees said to himself. He needed to know if Sam had been at the mill the night of Mac's murder. If he hurried, he thought he could reach the mill, talk to Elijah, and still be home before dark. He raced downstairs and out to the barn.

When he arrived at the mill the yard outside was empty of wagons. But the mill wheel continued to turn and over the rumble Rees heard voices. He paused and listened. He thought he heard conversation. The McIntyre boys? He went into the mill, turning right instead of left and heading to the office once occupied by

Mac. Elijah sat at the desk, resting his head upon his hand, and flipping the pages of a ledger. A fine white powder coated every surface including his breeches and hair. Rees must have made some sound; Elijah looked up and saw him.

"What do you want?" he asked with a scowl.

"You've known me since you were born," Rees said. He held up his empty hands. "You surely don't believe I would ever harm your father."

Elijah said nothing for several seconds. "I've heard a lot of strange things about you and your wife," he said at last.

"Do you honestly believe a woman who is with child could murder a man, pick him up, and turn him upside down to tie him to the posts? Even with help." Another pause, a longer one this time.

"Well, someone murdered my father."

"Yes." Rees cautiously took a few steps inside the office. "I knew your father since we were boys together. We were always friends. He helped my family . . ." His throat closed up and for a moment he could not speak. Seeing Rees's expression, Elijah's eyes moistened and he gulped. "Please let me help you find out who killed Mac," Rees said. The pleading tone in his voice surprised him. Elijah wiped his eyes and nodded. Rees pulled out a chair and sat down. "I find it hard to believe anyone wanted to harm your father." He didn't want to confess his suspicion—that Mac had been caught up in a plot targeting Rees and his family. "Was there anyone left here with your father, you know, on that evening?"

Elijah shook his head. "I was the last to leave. Me and Sam Prentiss."

"Sam? Sam was here?" Rees almost felt like shouting. That was exactly what he'd suspected.

Elijah nodded. "But he didn't kill my father, if that's what you're thinking," he said.

"How do you know? Sam probably has the strength to lift your father."

"Maybe so. But we left together. I drove him home."

Rees felt all his excitement drain away. "Perhaps he returned to the mill," he suggested, knowing he was grasping at straws. Elijah now grinned openly.

"It would have taken Sam over an hour to go south on Duck Lane and then head west on the road to Bald Knob. Not only would it have been dark by the time he arrived, but my father would have already left for home."

Rees sat in a glum silence. Elijah was correct. Whoever hit Mac had done so soon after Elijah and the other boys had left, committing the murder in the last of the daylight. "Well, thank you," Rees said. He was not prepared to yield on Sam quite yet. Perhaps he'd had help? Even as he thought that, Elijah spoke.

"My father promised he would bring Sam home whenever possible. Otherwise, Sam gets lost. So I watched Sam go through his gate from the corner of Duck Lane and South Street."

Rees sighed. "Did you see anyone approaching the mill as you went home?" Elijah shook his head.

"It was about this time, already growing dark." He gestured to the wall as though Rees could see outside. He tried to think of another question but could not.

"My father liked you too," Elijah said suddenly. "He said you may have been misguided sometimes but you always tried to do the right thing."

Now Rees's eyes began to tear. Pulling his handkerchief from his pocket as he stood up, he tried to wipe away the water in his eyes. Elijah fought to control his sobs and Rees went behind the desk to put his hand on the boy's shoulder. For several seconds they remained in that position, mourning Mac together.

Finally Rees squeezed Elijah's shoulder and started for the door. "Catch him," Elijah said from behind him. "Please."

Rees turned and nodded. "I will," he said. "I promise." He went outside but for a moment he stood in the yard holding his handkerchief to his eyes. The sky was streaked with purple and blue as the sun dropped to the horizon. He blew out a breath, realizing he would have to hurry if he was to make it home by nightfall.

There would not be enough light left to collect the pieces of the loom. Just thinking about the destruction made him shake, not just from anger but also from anguish. He grieved for his broken loom and could hardly bear to think someone hated him so much they would destroy it. By the time he reached home and unhitched Hannibal in the last few rays of light, he was too upset to think. He burned off some of his emotion by continuing to clean the kitchen. He wrestled the pot and its cargo of filthy water to the door and dumped the still steaming water off the back steps. Most of the leftover food sloughed off in a gritty charred mass. Rees inspected the inside of the kettle. A good scrubbing with a handful of rags and it should be clean again. Hopefully it would be spotless enough for Lydia; she was particular about her cooking utensils. He collected some old linen cloths, most of them worn to threads by constant use, and began wiping out the inside of the kettle. His thoughts turned again to the damage to his loom and to Sam. Would it do any good to speak to Caroline again?

The clatter of hooves on the drive attracted Rees's attention. He put the pot aside and walked around the house. It was David. He dismounted from Amos and began stripping off the saddle and bridle. "Where were you?" Rees asked.

"Helping Charlie." David looked up. It was now almost too dark to see although a few streaks of pink and purple remained in the sky. "Is there anything for supper?"

"Pancakes," Rees said. "And bacon."

David grimaced. "I've had enough bacon, thank you."

Rees went inside to start the meal while David walked the gelding around the yard to cool him. The shadows had crept out from the corners of the kitchen and if it hadn't been for the fire casting its red light into the room Rees would have been blind. He fumbled his way to the candles and lit a few. Then he pulled out the cornmeal and started mixing.

David came through the back door about fifteen minutes later. "Pancakes on the table," Rees said as David took off his straw hat and hung it on the peg by the door. The boy sat down and took out his knife. He ate as though he were starving, devouring the food with single-minded concentration. When his plate was finally licked clean, he inhaled a deep breath and sat back in his chair.

"I've been so busy . . . and I've been up half the night guarding the farm."

And that was the only apology David was likely to offer for the dirty kitchen, Rees thought as he sat down across the table from his son. "You kept up with that?"

"Had to, didn't I?" David forced his eyes open with an effort.

"Any trouble?"

"Not a thing." He yawned. "Saw a couple of bears."

"My loom was broken," Rees said.

David's eyes popped open. "What do you mean?"

"Someone came into the house, went upstairs, and broke my loom into pieces, bent the reed." Rees couldn't continue.

"Is it completely destroyed?" David asked in a hushed voice.

"No," Rees admitted. "I think it can be fixed." He paused a moment and then added, "It may be unfair but I don't want Sam Prentiss in this house. Ever again."

David shot his father a quick look. "You think it was him?"

Rees hesitated. Although he believed Sam was the guilty party, there was no proof. Dislike and a history of conflict prompted Rees's conviction. "I do," Rees said at last. "It's exactly what that bastard would do. But am I sure? No. Could I be wrong? Most certainly."

David nodded. "Maybe you should just ask both your sister and her husband not to call upon us here." Rees nodded in agreement. After a moment of silence in which David yawned convulsively several times, he said, "I'm going to turn in. I'll take the second watch." As he went out of the door to the cottage, Rees began cleaning the kitchen once again.

Rees overslept the following morning, waking only when a burst of David's and Charlie's raucous laughter penetrated his bedroom from the kitchen below. He remained in bed for a few seconds, disoriented. After patrolling the farm until the early hours in the morning, he had finally gone to bed when David relieved him. But then, although dizzy with fatigue, Rees had found falling asleep almost impossible. The bed felt strange, cold and empty without Lydia, and he missed the sound of her voice. He even missed hearing the children's voices on the other side of the wall and Joseph's squeaks and mutters in his basket by Rees's bed.

Rees pulled his sluggish body out of the hot sweaty sheets and threw some water into his face from the ewer. Then he went down the steps.

Both Charlie and David had already gone outside. Rees peered into the spider. From the lacy brown remains left in the pan, Rees deduced the boys had eaten eggs. David had left the basket out for his father; there were a few eggs left. Rees decided to go into town and eat at the Contented Rooster. But first he would shave. His whiskers were beginning to form a ginger beard. He pushed the kettle over the fire and fetched his razor. While the water heated, he drank the rest of the coffee. It was almost too strong for him and, since it was the bottom of the pot, the coffee was gritty with grounds. It wasn't worth making another pot. Rees suddenly longed for Lydia with a physical ache. His eyes began to water. The house felt empty and unwelcoming and he now knew how much of his comfort depended upon her.

He arrived in Dugard midmorning. Buggies and farmers' wagons thronged Water Street but the coffeehouse was almost empty. To Rees's surprise, Caldwell was there, seated by the window, with the remains of a hearty breakfast in front of him. Rees crossed the floor, uncomfortably aware of the stares directed at him from the few other customers. Caldwell nodded at Rees without smiling.

"I didn't expect to see you here," Rees said as he helped himself to the chair across the table. Caldwell's usual roost was the tavern.

"I found I wasn't welcome at the Bull," Caldwell said in clipped tones. Rees, who didn't know what to say, made a gesture meant to convey sympathy and an invitation to continue. "I see now some of those men cozied up to me, thinking I would forgive their petty crimes. 'Cause I knew them, you know. Now that I'm not the constable anymore they don't have time for me."

"That can't be true for everyone," Rees said, knowing his comment was foolish. He didn't know what else to say.

Caldwell nodded. "You're right. The others are in Farley's camp." He paused. "You've heard, I suspect, that Mr. Farley," he spit out the name, "has been appointed constable?"

"Yes," Rees said. "I heard. And I'm sorry. If you hadn't come to my house . . ."

"You aren't to blame," Caldwell said. "Not this time anyway." He shot Rees a sharp glance. "You've made some powerful enemies."

"Some friends too, I hope," Rees said with a weak smile.

Caldwell stared over Rees's head and added, speaking softly as though to himself, "There's something sick here. Something wrong. I'm thinking I might move. Next town over maybe. Most of my brothers and sisters are gone from Dugard." But the corners of his mouth turned down.

"I'd miss you," Rees said. He felt both helpless and angry. Caldwell met Rees's gaze and nodded.

"I feel like I'm being forced out of town," Caldwell said, rising to his feet. "That's the only thing keeping me here—I don't want them to win." Rees inclined his head in understanding.

As Caldwell walked out of the coffeehouse, Rees moved to another table, sitting so he could watch the door. He noticed the furtive looks directed at the former constable as he left and a number of quick glances shot at Rees as well. Even Jack Anderson, a man Rees had known since they were schoolboys together, quickly looked away when he met Rees's gaze. Susannah said something to her husband, something sharp. Although Rees couldn't hear the words, the tone carried. Susannah pasted on a smile and approached.

"Breakfast, Will?"

"If Jack will permit it," Rees said.

Susannah grimaced. "I'm sorry. It's not you. He's frightened. All the stories we've heard about Lydia; he doesn't know what to believe."

"And you?" Rees's stomach began to churn and he was no longer sure he could eat breakfast.

"I've known you since we were babies." Susannah met his eyes with honesty and directness. "I know you too well to believe Lydia, or any woman, could bewitch you. And Lydia, if she's a witch I'm a spotted cow. But someone hates you, Will. Make no mistake about that. Hates you enough to go after you and yours. The rest of this," she waved her arms, "is fear. So I suppose the question is: who hates you so much?"

"Well, Piggy Hanson doesn't love me," Rees said, forcing a smile.

"Yes. And he'll take this opportunity to hurt you. But do you really see him creeping around your farm in the middle of the night?"

"I know. I was wondering about Sam."

"Sam?" Susannah's voice squeaked. "No. That's impossible. The strategy against you requires a devious mind. Sam had that but, even before his injury, he didn't possess the patience to see something like this through. And now?" She shook her head decidedly. "Not Sam. Although I don't want to cast aspersions on a member of your family, I'd sooner believe Caroline is behind it."

"He could be playacting," Rees said.

Susannah shook her head and Rees could see she didn't believe it. "He'd be the best actor in the world," she said. "I'll bring out your breakfast." She turned in a whirl of her yellow skirts, and walked quickly back to the kitchen.

Rees wished he had not agreed to breakfast. He did not feel comfortable here, in the coffeehouse or Dugard, anymore. He'd always felt like an outsider, even as a boy. Unlike his peers, who seemed mostly content to stay in Dugard, frequently on the very farms where they'd grown up or within five miles of them, Rees had always yearned for something different. Something more. From his earliest days he remembered his mother telling him that the grass was not always greener on the other side of the fence. Rees had never believed her. Every journey out of town had shown him that Dugard was not the world. It wasn't even a large part of the world. Starting with the war, Rees had traveled far away from this tiny corner in the District of Maine. Not just to Boston, but also to New York City and Trenton, New Jersey. At the conclusion of the war, he'd traveled to Philadelphia and out to Pittsburgh and everywhere in between.

With each journey out and the subsequent arrival home, Dugard seemed smaller, more closed off, and more smothering. Magistrate Hanson had been right, Rees conceded reluctantly. He didn't want to live here. He never had. And now someone was punishing him for that.

He ate as quickly as he could, barely tasting the food Susannah put before him, and unable to say afterward what had been on the plate. When he was done, he tossed a few coins on the table and left.

He would not be visiting Dugard very often in the future.

Chapter Twenty-one

He drove directly to his sister's farm, driving faster and faster with impotent anger. He didn't know what to do. And anger was so much easier for him to accept than the fear that threatened to overtake him. It was Caroline's fault, even if she had had nothing to do with the murders or the accusations leveled at Lydia by Farley. Caroline had started it with her initial rumor that Lydia was a witch.

Realizing suddenly that Hannibal was galloping, Rees slowed. Breathing hard, Hannibal dropped into a trot. He was covered with dust. And so was Rees, a fine brown coat from the dry roads.

They finished the journey at a more reasonable pace, arriving at Caroline's derelict farm close to noon. As Rees prepared to turn into the lane leading to the drive, a smart carriage with yellow wheels rattled toward him at a rapid clip. When the coachman turned toward Dugard, the carriage lurched and almost swung into Hannibal. He danced sideways and Rees had to struggle to bring the horse under control. He didn't want to see his wagon overturned. By the time he'd pulled Hannibal to a stop, the fine equipage was barreling down the road toward town. But Rees knew who was inside the carriage; one glance had been enough for him to identify Magistrate Cornelius Hanson, his balding head bent over something on his lap. Piggy hadn't even looked up and so had no idea his coach had almost driven Rees off the road. It was doubtful Piggy would have cared anyway.

Trembling, Rees urged Hannibal into the lane. This track led only to the drive into Caroline's barnyard and ended there. Piggy Hanson must have been visiting her. The question was why?

Rees pulled up to the rail and jumped down from the wagon. Since Amos was running around in the pasture behind the barn Rees knew David was already here helping Charlie. Rees leaped over the rotting front steps and went into the house without even a knock to announce himself. Caroline was in the kitchen washing dishes. She was humming.

"What did Piggy want?" Rees asked. She jumped, uttering a little scream.

"Why, Will, I didn't hear you come in."

"I asked you a question."

She smiled, her lips curling. "Just a friendly visit. I do have friends, you know, unlike you." Rees stared at his sister. She looked happy, as though she were a child promised a much-desired treat.

"I don't want you or Sam at my farm ever again," he said. "Especially not Sam."

"Why, Will, surely you don't believe he will hurt you."

Rees looked over her head at the back door. Sam was standing there, smiling and listening. "And not without a specific invitation," Rees said firmly.

Caro laughed. Rees wondered how many months it had been since he'd heard that sound. "You don't want me to visit? Very well. I won't. It doesn't matter. I don't want to live there anyway. I don't want to live on any farm," she admitted in a burst of candor. "I think it's time I move to Boston."

"What do you mean by that?" Rees asked in a sharp voice. She laughed again. Although she did not reply, Rees knew as clearly as if she had shouted at him that the magistrate had promised Caroline something. Rees was very afraid that something might be his farm. But she had just said she didn't want to *live* there. Did that mean she wanted to sell it and move to Boston?

"Where is Sam?' Caroline glanced around as though she thought he might be behind her. Rees looked through the door. There was no one there. In those few seconds, Sam had disappeared. "I suppose he wandered off. Again. I vow, he needs a keeper."

"Are you sure he has not improved?" Rees asked. "I wonder if his appearance and behavior are not all a sham."

Caroline burst into shrill laughter that was touched with hysteria. "Are you mad? Or are you just attempting to ease your own guilt? Of course Sam is not shamming. He can barely dress himself." Caroline turned her back on her brother.

"But everything will be better soon," she murmured, so softly Rees had trouble hearing her. "Go away, Will. I am not speaking to you anymore."

"Caro, turn around." But Rees knew his sister would not speak to him again; he recognized her behavior from his youth. Until Caroline decided to unbend, Rees would be invisible. As a boy he would sometimes allow his temper to get the best of him and he would punch her. A number of whippings at his father's hands for hitting a girl had cured him of that, but now, as frustration rose into a boil, Rees was tempted to spin her around to face him and demand answers. Of course, that wouldn't succeed either. She might look at him but with no more interest than if he were a wall. Muttering a curse, Rees turned and stamped out of the house.

He climbed up into the wagon. He was so furious he almost jumped back down and went inside. He needed answers. Why had Piggy Hanson visited his sister? Had he promised her Rees's farm? What had she really meant by her comment about moving to Boston? Was she, as Rees suspected, planning to sell his farm? He stared past the house to the fields beyond. This alliance between his sister and Piggy Hanson filled Rees with dread.

In the distance Sam was stumping through the cornfield with determined purpose. Was he playacting? Caroline had sounded genuinely shocked at the thought, but perhaps she was lying. She lied all the time to get what she wanted. Did she know what Sam had been up to? Was she Sam's accomplice? Or was *she* controlling Sam? Rees shuddered. He'd been so convinced that Caroline, despite her many flaws, could not be a murderer. But now he was no longer so certain.

He tried to put aside the anxious thoughts that went nowhere as he drove home. A host of chores waited for him, from checking the dairy and the cheese making Lydia had left behind to the wheat and cornfields. He also wanted to start on the repairs to his loom. Although he had no weaving jobs right now, he hoped to begin again this fall. He didn't want to be caught with a broken loom. Putting it back together might take only a few hours but he didn't know that for certain, and anyway he knew that many hours could be spent trying to resolve the unexpected problem. It was better to start early.

After tending to Hannibal he went into the kitchen to clean

up from breakfast. He'd only just begun when he heard the sound of horses' hooves on the drive; too many horses to be David and Charlie. He hurried out to the front porch. As he'd feared it was not his son but Farley. There were fewer men riding at his back today. The McIntyre boys were missing—so Rees's visit with Elijah had done some good—but Farley still had five men with him.

"What do you want?" Rees shouted.

Farley dismounted and came to the bottom step. As he put his foot upon the first one, his hand clutched the amulet at his throat. "We come for the witch," he said.

"There is no witch," Rees said, folding his arms across his chest. He heard Farley's companions getting down from their nags but didn't remove his attention from their leader.

"You know what I mean. We're here for your wife."

"My wife is gone, visiting family."

"So I heard." Farley's lips stretched, baring his yellow teeth. "But you could be lying. She's probably here, hiding. We're going to search."

"No, you're not," Rees said. "You searched once. That's enough."

"So, she is here," Farley said in triumph. He came up another step. Rees heard the thud of footsteps and two men moved behind Farley.

"She is not here," Rees said. "Get off my property."

"The magistrate gave me permission to search for the witch," Farley said. "I'm constable now, charged with keeping the peace. Two men have been murdered. I will search your house." He clutched the amulet around his neck so tightly his knuckles turned white.

"I told you, she's visiting family. And she had nothing to do with the murders."

"That will be decided in a court of law. Now, stand aside."

Rees shifted his stance and clenched his fists. "Don't come any closer. I told you to get off my land."

"Even if she ain't here, the magistrate said she could be tried in absent—absent something and convicted. And if she's convicted, all your property is forfeit. Everything: the land, the livestock, the clothes you're standing up in. So, it'd be better all around if she goes to jail nice and easy until she's brought up before the judge."

Rees shook his head. He didn't trust Hanson to treat Lydia fairly. Why, he might leave her in jail for months. Or confirm her guilt with the water test; if Lydia survived drowning she would be hanged as a witch anyway. "I told you she isn't here," he repeated, taking an involuntary step forward.

Too late he heard the whisper of a shoe behind him. One of the men had crept around the house and come in through the back door. Before Rees could turn, something smashed into his head and darkness descended.

He came to choking and gasping in a flood of cold water. David slowly came into focus above him. "What happened?" the boy asked.

Rees put his hand on the back of his head. He felt a swelling goose egg and his fingers came away red. "How long was I out?" he asked in a hoarse voice. The wound was already closing and drying blood had stiffened his hair into spikes.

"Don't know. I just got home. I saw you lying here." David put his arm under his father's shoulders and helped him into a sitting position. Rees groaned and the world spun around him. As the farm righted itself Rees carefully looked at the sky. The sun was dropping toward the western horizon; he'd been unconscious for hours. "How do you feel?" David looked down, his face pallid with worry. "You don't look very good."

"I have the worst headache." It felt like someone was striking at his head over and over with a hammer.

"Can you stand?"

Rees tried but every attempt resulted in the shakes and such dizziness he collapsed again. David tried to lift him but wasn't strong enough to take his father's weight. Finally Rees struggled to his hands and knees, and with many pauses to rest, he crawled into the kitchen. The wooden boards of the porch were stained a deep rusty brown with his blood.

David helped Rees into a chair. "Will you tell me what happened?"

"It was Farley," Rees said. "Him and his hired ruffians from the Bull. They came looking for Lydia. I refused to let them in."

"But Lydia isn't here," David said, sounding perplexed.

"I told them that. Repeatedly." Rees coughed, the vibration sending waves of pain through his skull. "We've got to check, make sure nothing was stolen."

David nodded and said, almost to himself, "I wondered why all the doors were open."

"Are the horses . . . ?" Rees sat up in sudden worry, clapping a hand to his throbbing head.

"I didn't count them," David said, "but there are horses in the pasture. I'll take a look now. And check on the rest of the livestock." He hared out the back door. Rees sat at the table for a few seconds more and then slowly, very slowly rose to his feet. The shakiness was beginning to fade and although the headache continued to pound in his head, he felt marginally better. He filled a basin with water and used one of Lydia's rags to wipe the back of his head. He gasped as his clumsy fingers touched the wound and pain surged through him. The rag came away red. He couldn't force himself to touch the swelling again. He tore one of the rags into strips and bound it loosely around his head. Then he made his way cautiously to the back door.

The brightness outside knifed into his eyes and he squeezed them shut a moment before gingerly making his way down the steps. He paused and waited for his body to steady before looking around. Everything looked as usual, untouched. He walked to the crest of the slope that led down to Lydia's hives. From this distance he couldn't be sure but he thought they appeared no different than before. He walked along the hill toward the eastern side of the farm. The weaver's cottage stood in a small hollow and Rees could see the door was open. He crossed the short distance and went inside. Nothing had been touched and after a few seconds out of the painfully bright sunshine he went back outside and closed the door. Then he angled north, toward the pigsty. He could hear them grunting even before he reached the enclosure. When he looked over the fence he saw them at the far end. None of them seemed to be missing.

With a sigh of relief, he started back to the house. But as he approached the dairy he noticed the door was open. He made his way to the small brick structure and peered inside. Lydia would have heated the milk in the panniers with rennet and put the resulting curds into molds. But Rees had hurried her away before she'd had the chance and now the stink of souring milk drove him back outside. And it looked as though a squirrel had already found its way through the open door. Rees closed it. Lydia would have to scrub the dairy again. If she was ever able to return. For the first time Rees considered the possibility that she would never be able to come home. Doing so would put her under the threat of imprisonment and death. He would not live without her and the rest of his family. So what would he do? For all that he had never wanted to stay connected to Dugard or this farm, they had been the constants in his wandering life. The prospect of leaving this familiar world forever sent a shaft of fear into Rees's heart.

He turned and vomited into the grass.

"What the Hell are you doing outside?" David demanded, trotting down the slope.

"Language, David," Rees said automatically as he wiped his mouth on his sleeve.

"You should be inside, resting. You look terrible," David said, taking his father by the arm. "Let's go back to the house."

"I wanted to check on the grounds," Rees said. But he gladly accepted David's help.

Chapter Twenty-two

David helped his father into the kitchen chair at the table and set about making coffee. "Nothing's missing," he said as he began grinding the beans. Neither spoke while the rattling sound filled the kitchen. As David measured the coffee into the pot, he continued, "It looks as though they went into the barn, the henhouse, the dairy, of course, as well as into the house and the basement."

Rees nodded and wished he hadn't. Pain rolled forward and throbbed behind his eyes. "But nothing was damaged?"

"No." David pushed the coffeepot over the fire. "They searched thoroughly but that was all." He attempted to smile, managing a lopsided effort that didn't fool Rees into believing David was unaffected by the invasion. "They were honest men."

"Would you look at my loom upstairs?" Although he suspected Sam of breaking it—he might not have participated in the murder of Thomas McIntyre, but he'd wandered about the farm enough to give him access to the loom—Rees knew it was possible one of these other men had done it. He could just see Farley lashing out with a foot. If so, that dirty dog might have taken this recent opportunity to finish the job, destroying the loom beyond any possibility of repair. David nodded and went upstairs. Rees could hear the clatter of footsteps above. David returned a few minutes later.

"Are the pieces pulled together into a pile?" Rees asked.

"Yes."

Rees exhaled in relief. "No further damage was done."

David pushed the perking coffee away from the fire. Wrapping a rag around his hand, he poured out a cup and put it on the table in front of his father. Rees put in a large lump of sugar and a dollop of cream. "I'll put the milk down the well to keep cool," David said and disappeared out the door. Rees took a sip of the hot liquid. Perspiration popped out upon his forehead and, although the coffee was not as strong as he liked, he began to feel better.

He fetched the cheese from the pantry and attempted a trip to Lydia's garden where he picked several ripe cucumbers. He didn't have the energy to do more than that. When David returned they ate their scanty supper. Rees intended to wash the dishes while his son finished up evening chores but fell asleep over the dirty plate before him. He did not wake until the following morning.

By then the sun had been up for hours. David had eaten eggs, his used plate was still on the table, and he'd disappeared outside. Rees dragged himself to his feet and had to clutch at the chair for support. His knees were so stiff they seemed ready to buckle under his weight. Rees shook them and took a few cautious steps. His legs began to come back to life. He realized his headache had diminished to a faint ache. He stirred up the fire and pushed the kettle full of water over it. Besides washing the dishes, he had to soak the dried blood out of his hair.

He put the dishes in the dishpan. As he poured hot water over them he heard a horse galloping up the drive. This time, before he opened the front door, he stopped at the parlor and took down his rifle. Although tempted to load it, he elected instead to carry the powder and shot with him. It was not Farley, as Rees feared, but Caldwell. He dismounted and came running up the steps. His eyes widened with alarm when he took in Rees. But, instead of asking what had happened, he said, "Promise me you didn't murder your brother-in-law."

"Murder? What are you talking about?"

"I was coming to see you anyway and I met one of my old acquaintances from the Bull and he told me he'd found Sam's body." Caldwell reached out to grab Rees's arm.

"Wait." Rees couldn't grasp what Caldwell was saying. "Sam's body? What happened?" He wrested his arm away from Caldwell. "I don't understand. Sam was murdered? No, that's not possible."

"Yes, Rees, it is. Will you listen? I just saw the body. Sam was found shot to death." He paused but this time Rees did not speak. "Come on. Don't you want to examine Sam's remains before Farley does? After that, well, it's unlikely you'll have a chance."

"Very well," Rees said, following Caldwell down the porch steps. "But when I saw Sam last he was alive." As though that made a difference.

"Can you get up behind me?" Caldwell put his foot in the stirrup and swung into the saddle. "We don't have any time to waste. Sam's body was found on your land and the farmer was heading into town to tell Farley."

"My land?" Rees stopped and put a hand to his head. It had begun to throb once again. "I didn't kill him."

"We don't have time for this," Caldwell said, leaning down and extending his hand. Rees grasped the grubby paw and hauled himself up onto the horse's back behind the saddle. The gelding jumped into a canter so suddenly Rees almost toppled off over the tail. He grabbed Caldwell's jacket and held on.

Caldwell urged the horse down the drive and onto the main road. He went right and they rode north a few miles. The fence here had fallen down in several places. Caldwell chose one of the openings and they trotted into a copse of trees.

"My father let this stretch go wild," Rees said. "To make a break between our farm and Winthrop's. He was a poor neighbor."

"The body is somewhere in here," Caldwell said as he jumped down. Rees dismounted more slowly and stood for a moment looking around him. "There," Caldwell said, pointing as he moved forward into the trees.

Sam lay sprawled on his back, half covered with the thick vegetation. Rees inspected the scene. It did not look natural. For a moment he couldn't put his finger on what disturbed him. Sam's body had fallen over sideways and Rees could clearly see the gaping hole in his temple. Black powder circled the wound in an ugly halo. He was dressed as Rees remembered and his legs were crooked, just as they would have been if he'd been kneeling. Weeds and last year's leaves covered him up to the chest in a green and brown quilt. But the long grass into which he'd fallen fluffed up around his head so that the body was obvious and Sam's face was recognizable. He'd been positioned so that although it appeared the murderer had tried to hide him, Sam could be instantly seen and recognized.

"Somebody wants it to look as though I killed him," Rees said in numb disbelief. Caldwell threw Rees a glance in which certainty and surprise that Rees could be so shocked were equally mixed.

"Of course," Caldwell said.

"I thought Sam might be behind the other murders and the

attacks on my farm," Rees continued. "But if he was, who killed him?"

Caldwell was no longer listening. His head was half turned toward the road. "They're coming," he said. Now Rees could hear the drumming of hooves on the hard-packed dirt road, still faint but growing louder with each second. "We can't go back to the road."

"C'mon," Rees said. "Get your nag and follow me."

While Caldwell ran to untie his horse, Rees stared at the body on the ground. He knew he might not have another chance to examine it and he wanted to remember as much as he could. Sam had never been a good man but he had not deserved to be murdered and discarded in the woods like garbage. Rees would do his best to find the man who murdered him.

"We're in full view of the road," Caldwell said. "Let's move."

With a nod, Rees spun around and set off into the woods where the trees would screen them. Caldwell pulled his horse behind him. They had to travel slowly; the ground was snarled with tree roots and scattered with granite boulders. If the horse tripped and broke an ankle they'd be in real trouble. Clouds of black flies rose up and settled around them.

Rolling his sleeves down to his wrists, Rees paused to orient himself. Many years had passed since he'd gone through this tree break and it looked different. Trees had come down and saplings grown up so everything was unfamiliar. After a second or two, Rees recognized the flat granite slab ahead and to the right and started walking again.

Although they approached the stone wall a few minutes later, they did not reach the gate for another twenty. The rotten boards were glued fast to the ground by years of leaves and vegetation, but one strong kick and the entire structure collapsed upon the ground in a shower of sticks. A flock of birds rose in a flutter of wings to the sky.

Rees and Caldwell came out at the bottom of the pasture behind the barn. Rees began walking up the hill but paused about halfway. He could hear loud, angry voices. Holding up a hand to stop his companion, Rees darted to the scattering of trees across from the house. He crept through the trunks, hiding behind every rock and bush.

David was standing on the porch facing Farley and the posse of men lined up on the ground. Even from the distance, Rees could see how frightened the boy looked. "We want your father," Farley said. Someone had given him a horse, probably Piggy Hanson, and the new constable now carried himself like a king. Rees realized that they had not stopped to view the body. Instead, while he and Caldwell had been hurrying through the woods, the new constable and his men had come straight here, to the farm.

"He's not here," David said.

"Where is he?"

David shrugged. Farley glanced at the men on either side of him and they shot off, one heading to the barns, the other going up the stairs into the house. Rees flattened himself to the ground. He didn't dare call out to Caldwell and prayed he had the sense to get under cover. "What do you want him for?" David asked.

"The murder of Sam Prentiss," Farley said.

David clutched at the porch rail. "I don't believe it," he said.

"No one's in the house," said Farley's man, appearing in the doorway behind David.

"Look around back," Farley said. The men scattered but no one even glanced behind them. Mosquitoes joined the black flies swarming around Rees. He buried his face in his hands. He could feel the stinging bites on his neck and ears but he didn't dare slap at the insects.

The men straggled back to the house. "I told you he wasn't here," David said as the last one reported his lack of success.

"We'll be back," Farley said in an ugly tone. He hoisted himself into the saddle. "If you see him, tell him to turn himself in. Magistrate Hanson said anyone can shoot him on sight."

The men galloped down the drive to the road. But Rees did not immediately rise from his hiding place. He feared one of the posse might take it into his head to try and surprise the fugitive. Besides, Rees's legs were trembling and he wasn't sure they'd support him.

"Rees," Caldwell called softly. Rees lifted himself to his knees. The other man was standing in front of the house, looking around him. Rees struggled to his feet with the aid of a young tree.

"Get out of sight," Rees hissed, brushing away the mess of leaves and dirt from the front of his vest. "They'll see you if they return."

David ran down the steps. "Get the horse into the barn, quick," he commanded, wresting the reins from Caldwell's hand and drawing the animal away.

"Let's go into the house," Rees said, climbing over the rocks to the road. He hoped no one came up the drive now; he didn't think he could run. He staggered across the drive and urged Caldwell into the house. Only when Rees had shut the door did he finally take a deep breath. He knew his feeling of safety was an illusion, but for the moment it would do.

"You're going to have to leave town," Caldwell said as Rees joined him at the kitchen table. "Why don't you go to your wife, wherever she is?"

Rees thought for a moment how pleasant that would be. "No," he said regretfully.

"You should listen to him," David said, coming through the back door. "Farley told me they can shoot you on sight. All men's hands will be turned against you."

Rees bowed his head in acknowledgment but said, "If I run now I'll never be able to return. I must stay here and find out who's behind all of this."

"I'd look at the magistrate if I were you," Caldwell said. "Or Farley. He is determined to see you and your wife hang."

"It's possible." Rees tried to grin. "Maybe they're in it together."

"The magistrate called in your friends Jack Anderson and George Potter and threatened them with jail if they helped you," Caldwell said. "I don't think you'll find any more aid from that quarter."

"I know he dislikes me," Rees said. "But to manufacture such a scheme? I don't think he even owns a gun, and if he does, well, he has no idea how to fire it." He met Caldwell's eyes. "Of all the men in the village, Hanson is one of the few who never fought in the war. I'd sooner believe Farley is at the bottom of all this. Him and his sons."

"In league with one another?" Caldwell suggested, sounding doubtful. He would have continued but David interrupted.

"None of this is important now. My father . . ." He stopped abruptly and turned to look at Rees. "You could be shot."

"You're right, lad," Caldwell said, his gaze swiveling toward Rees. "You need to get to safety."

"I'm not leaving here," Rees said. He was scared but he would never admit it to these two. "I meant what I said; I have to uncover the man behind this. And I can't do that if I'm at Zion. Or somewhere else far from Dugard." David and Caldwell exchanged glances and for a moment no one spoke.

"You can't stay on the farm," Caldwell said at last.

David nodded. "Farley'll come back and come back and come back," he said. "But there's nowhere else safe."

Rees said nothing for several seconds. Even if Potter or the Andersons were willing to take him in, Rees would be putting them and their families in danger. "I can't ask anyone to risk so much for me," he said at last.

Another silence. Rees glanced at the fireplace, wondering if he could put up another pot of coffee. But the fire had guttered out long ago by the look of the ashes.

"I might know of a place," Caldwell said finally. "My mother's." He raised his eyes to Rees and added, "She lives south of here, by the river, north of the tannery. It's a fair distance, but you'd have a roof over your head."

"I don't want to harm her either," Rees said.

"Likeliest no one will guess," Caldwell said. "Why would they? You've never met her." He paused and continued. "You'd have a long walk into Dugard, if you wanted to go to town, but it can be done."

Rees made his decision in an instant. "Well then, thank you very much. I won't stay long, maybe just a few days. Long enough to catch my breath and give some thought to—to . . ." His words ground to a stop. It was too hard to admit that someone hated him so much they would frame him for murder.

"We can't take the roads," Caldwell said. "Not the main ones anyway. There'll be two of us on my own nag so the traveling won't be fast."

"Maybe you should hide out until dark," David suggested.

Rees shook his head. "We can't risk it. Not here, anyway." He paused, thinking. "Why don't we go by way of the river?"

Caldwell rose to his feet. "Grab some food, clothes, whatever you think you'll need. I'll meet you in the barn." He disappeared out the back door.

Rees ran upstairs to collect another shirt and pair of breeches. When he came downstairs once again, David handed him a canvas sack. "Just a little food," he said, his face contorted with the effort of holding his emotions in check. Rees peered inside, seeing a hunk of cheese, a heel of a loaf of bread, and a handful of early apples. As he stuffed his clothing inside, David went to the front door and opened it. Stepping out onto the porch, he peered down the drive. "Come now," he said. He motioned his father forward.

Rees took one final glance around the familiar kitchen before hurrying down the hall and out to the front porch. "Godspeed," David said in a hoarse voice. Rees stared at his son. There were so many things he wanted to say, most of them beginning with "I'm sorry." He didn't know how to begin and he stared at David in silence. Finally David approached, arms lifted as though he wanted to embrace his father but wasn't sure how it would be received. Rees pulled his son into his arms for a hug. They were unaccustomed to displays of affection and the clasp was a clumsy one with too many sharp elbows and stiff arms. But David's hold tightened around his father and when they parted, both were teary eyed.

Chapter Twenty-three

❧

C aldwell and Rees did not cross the barnyard; it lay in full view of anyone coming up the drive. Instead they went down the slope into the hollow that contained the dairy and the pigsty. Rees, knowing he would not see these familiar landmarks again for some time, glanced from side to side. Every familiar object seemed to shine, glossy with his affection. He thought he had not appreciated his farm properly until then.

They went first into one of the cornfields. Rees hunched his shoulders and bent his head to make himself smaller, less visible. No one was working here, or in any of the neighboring plots. Still, Caldwell and Rees moved as swiftly and silently as they could. Sound carried easily over the open land and they did not wish to betray themselves to someone who might talk in the tavern. To further ensure they would not be noticed, they took a detour north, crossing onto the abandoned Winthrop farm. Although the miser's tumbledown cottage was not visible from this side of the property, Rees could see the orchard. One of the worst whippings he'd ever received from his father involved these apple trees. Like most of the boys, Rees had visited them regularly, climbing the trees to pick the apples. They were much prized, not so much for eating, but for missiles against one another. Besides, Winthrop was such a mean and unpleasant man that Rees and his friends trespassed just to annoy him. Now that Rees was himself a father and responsible for supporting a family, he had more sympathy for the man. It felt odd to Rees to realize that Winthrop, who'd seemed so old then, had actually been younger than Rees was now.

Overlaying the memories of his youth was the recollection of finding Winthrop's body a few years ago. No one had seen the man for some time, but since it was winter and few made it into town on a regular basis, no one thought about it. But with Christmas coming Mr. Borden, the shopkeeper, wondered aloud that he hadn't seen the old man. So one day Rees and David had crossed the fence and walked across the snowy ground toward the shack. Although deer and rabbit tracks streaked the snow, they hadn't managed to eat the remaining unpicked apples and the withered fruit as red as drops of blood still hung in the branches. Rees remembered thinking that that in itself was surprising. Winthrop supported himself primarily on the cider he pressed from those apples. He was very protective of them and would not willingly abandon even one piece of fruit, not if there was profit to be made from it.

When Rees and David entered the mean dwelling, they'd found Winthrop laying on the floor. He'd been dead for some time. Animals had been at him and his belly and side had been reduced to bones. The rib cage thrust its ivory points to the ceiling. But the cold had arrested the corruption and his body had frozen to the floor. Winthrop had died with no one by his side, leaving his little farm abandoned. Rees pitied the man but the miser had brought it on himself. He'd been a mean old cuss and once his wife had died the children scattered, leaving not just their father but the town. George Potter had been searching for the eldest son and heir this last year, without success. He hadn't, in fact, found any of the Winthrop children. Just the thought of dying in such solitude sent a shudder through Rees.

The sound of men's voices shocked him out of his reverie. He stopped moving and looked back at his companion. Caldwell put a finger across his lips. "Farley and his men returned to your farm," he said, barely moving his lips. With a nod, Rees hurried forward, as silently as possible, trying to keep his big body sheltered behind trees and underbrush.

A steep hill made up largely of granite comprised the descent from Winthrop's property to the river. Rees slid most of the way down to the riverbank, stopping every now and then in oases made up of spindly trees and shrubs. He heard Caldwell and his horse thrashing about behind him, and he hoped Farley and his men weren't close enough to hear it as well. When Rees reached more or less level ground he turned around. Caldwell's old horse was resisting his master at the same time he descended in tiny mincing steps. His eyes rolled wildly and he kept tossing his head. Rees sat on a boulder under a tree to wait.

Rocks, many as large as the one upon which Rees perched, made up the riverbank. Trees and other vegetation clung to the small patches of soil around the stones, forming a leafy green screen. Although traveling through the narrow thicket wouldn't be easy, Rees was counting on the band of forest to provide shelter on the journey south.

A few minutes later Caldwell and his gelding arrived on the bank. Both looked visibly shaken. Caldwell brought the horse to the water's edge so he could drink. "We could have been killed," he told Rees, turning with a glare.

"Ahh, it's not high enough," Rees said. "Anyway, we're safe

now." He cast a glance at the steep rock face. "With any luck, Farley won't guess we came this way." After a pause, he continued. "How long do you think it will take us to reach your mother's from here?"

Caldwell shrugged. "It usually takes me an hour or two, but that's on horseback and riding at a good pace. I guess, maybe this afternoon?" He turned to look at Rees. "Especially if we see anyone and have to duck under cover. That will slow us down."

Rees nodded and did not speak for a moment. "Thank you," he said finally. "I couldn't have gotten this far without you."

Caldwell shrugged. "I don't have a job here anymore. What can they do to me?"

Rees knew Hanson could hang Caldwell but did not say that aloud.

They kept to the trees as much as possible. Rees, on foot, scrambled easily over the deadfalls and around the rocks. It was Caldwell's horse that slowed them down; the ground was treacherous and the gelding was too large to squeeze through some of the openings Rees found. Caldwell began cursing in a steady monotone, his epithets punctuated by slaps as black flies and mosquitoes lit upon his neck and ears. Rees saw no one, not even river traffic, and would have enjoyed the walk if he hadn't been so jumpy. The canopy of leaves overhead kept them shaded and cool and every step sent the scent of pine into the air. He kept imagining he heard footsteps, although whenever he turned no one was there.

"They won't find you," Caldwell said. Rees grunted. He wished he could be certain of that. If he were the constable, he would search the riverbank, just in case.

They were traveling south beside the eastern branch of the Dugard River, a wide but fairly shallow course that ran from

Dugard Pond. Unlike the narrow and fast-moving western arm that connected to McIntyre's mill, the eastern waterway washed up against large slabs of granite, many of them fairly flat. During the early spring, the river regularly flooded and even now water filled the hollows in the stones. As a boy, Rees would come down here to swim and inspect the strange creatures in the pools. He remembered seeing the gundalows ply the river, trading coffee, tea, saltpeter, and sugar. The farm produce bartered in exchange went north to towns in Maine and south to Massachusetts. Now more of the goods came by way of the turnpikes, but keelboats still used the river to transport window glass, crockery, and pewter ware, poling their way north against the current.

Rees and Caldwell paused under the shadow of the trees and inspected the river. There were no boats now so they moved out onto the flat rocks. Able to ride for the first time in hours, they moved rapidly over the flat, hard surface. The sudden appearance of a boat, moving slowly north against the current, made a sudden dash into the forest imperative. And then, a short distance away, they had to circle through the trees to avoid a wagon pulled up to the riverbank. It seemed to be occupied by a large family—the parents were unfamiliar to Rees and probably on their way somewhere—but it seemed prudent to evade even their notice.

Caldwell's old horse quickly tired and the two men took turns walking alongside. Rees realized he'd gotten soft. He rode astride infrequently so his thighs began to hurt. He was not accustomed to walking such great distances either, and by midafternoon his pace was beginning to slow. His shoes had rubbed blisters on one heel and the sides of his feet. Instead of walking by the horse, Rees trailed behind, his gaze focused on the swaying black tail, and his thoughts entirely consumed with putting one foot in front of another.

"We're almost there," Caldwell said abruptly, his voice rusty with disuse. He cleared his throat. "Just around that bend." It was already late afternoon. Although the sky was still a bright blue, long shadows stretched from the line of trees across the bank and over the water. The last few hours had passed as though in a dream.

They rounded the last bend and Caldwell pointed ahead. "There," he said. A thicket of white linen that resembled an encampment of tents completely blocked the path ahead. Caldwell dismounted. "No one will see us," Caldwell said, turning to look at Rees. "But mind you don't touch the laundry. My mother will flay you with the rough side of her tongue if you put so much as a smudge on a sheet."

Through the haze of fatigue and hunger, Rees managed a nod. With refuge so close, he stumbled into an awkward run toward the drying linens.

He soon understood why the sheets appeared to be tents. Mrs. Caldwell had not draped the laundry on the available bushes as Lydia did; there was no vegetation here to use in that manner. Instead she'd tied heavy ropes from tree to tree, with a pole added here and there where a tree did not grow, and hung the laundry over the lines.

Once Rees stepped into the channel between the lines, he disappeared from view in almost every direction. He paused and took in a deep breath, safe in the forest of white. "Jericho," he heard a woman's voice say. "What are you doing here?" Rees directed his steps toward the voice, emerging very suddenly at the back of a shack. Inside the small space was a fireplace, the fire dying to coals, and several massive coppers ranged around the walls. Flatirons were positioned upon the stone hearth. "And who is this?" The question brought Rees's head around to the house about twenty feet back from the river and to the woman standing on the steps. Rees thought she was probably over fifty, although the arms bared almost to the shoulder were solid with muscle. Only a few strands of gray touched her dark hair but deep lines bracketed her mouth. Not smile lines either, Rees thought. The deep furrows were the marks of disapproval.

"Who are you?" she asked, the brown eyes so like Caldwell's sweeping over Rees.

"Will Rees. Weaver," he added as an afterthought.

Her expression lightened. "Are you the son of Martha Rees?" she asked. Rees nodded. "I laundered bedding for her from time to time, especially when your father became ill. I didn't realize you and my son were friends."

"Good friends," Rees said.

She acknowledged his comment with a nod and looked at Caldwell. "Why are you here?"

"I think we better go inside," he said. "And sit down while we discuss it." Caldwell sounded nervous and kept licking his lips.

He's scared of his mother, Rees thought. Not that he was surprised. She looked to be a tough old bird. Now Caldwell resembled a rabbit caught nibbling the greens in the garden, and expecting a spade across the head.

"Very well." Mrs. Caldwell turned and climbed the last step into the cabin. Caldwell gestured at Rees, inviting him to precede him. Rees didn't hesitate. He went up the slope and the steps as quickly as he could. He was tired and hungry and longing for a cup of coffee.

"Wipe your feet," Mrs. Caldwell ordered, gesturing to the woven mat by the door. As Rees obeyed, he looked around.

The cabin was long and narrow and the main room occupied the whole length. Opposite Rees and the door through which he'd come was the kitchen: a few shelves for dishes and a large sink. The front door was placed to the left with a flight of steps just past the opening and rising to the second floor. A large fireplace was located on the wall in front of the stairs so that the steps disappeared behind the chimney. Rees guessed that the second floor and the staircase to it had been added later.

But his first and strongest impression was of the strong odor of vinegar and the scrubbed white appearance of every wooden surface. The logs that made up the cabin walls had been washed, the bark peeled away by frequent and relentless scouring. A large washing copper, polished to a shine, rested against the wall by the fireplace. Even the fireplace was almost spotless. Black stained one side of the stones but Rees felt certain if he touched it he would not feel the greasiness of soot. Except for the still-smoldering wood from today's banked fire, all of the ashes had been cleaned away and the granite slab that made up the hearthstone glistened with recent washing.

Without being asked, Rees removed his shoes. He did not want to risk bringing even the slightest crumb of dirt into this home. Mrs. Caldwell smiled at him in approval.

Her son, however, clumped in without wiping his shoes and threw himself into one of the rocking chairs by the fireplace. Rees saw the exact moment when Caldwell recollected his purpose in visiting; he jumped to his feet and joined Rees on the mat.

"You must want something," Mrs. Caldwell said to her son in a sour tone. "Otherwise you would not comply with my wishes."

Turning to Rees, she said, "You look hot and tired. I can offer you cider or tea. Or water."

Rees stifled his sigh; he would really prefer coffee. But he accepted the cider and, at Mrs. Caldwell's gesture, sat down at the small table. Caldwell called for ale. Mrs. Caldwell disappeared into a room by the back entrance, a pantry positioned under the hollow left by the rise of the stairs. She returned a moment later with two full mugs and a loaf of bread. Visiting the pantry once again, she came out a second time with two plates, held together to form a closed carrier. Removing the top plate revealed a mound of sliced ham. Caldwell reached for a slice with his greasy fingers and she slapped his hand with a sharp crack. "Manners, Jericho," she said.

Porcelain plates and a silver fork came out of a cupboard. Rees thought that washing laundry must pay better than he would have suspected.

Mrs. Caldwell positioned the fork upon the plate of ham and began sawing slices from the loaf of bread. She offered both bread and ham to Rees first and he made a thick sandwich. Only then did she permit her son to take his share. For several minutes the cabin was silent as both men ate hungrily. Mrs. Caldwell waited until both plates were clean of everything but a few crumbs before she spoke. "Now that you have eaten and drunk, I want to know why you've come to me. What's the trouble? And don't even attempt a falsehood," she added, directing a stern glare at her son. "I can tell when you lie."

Chapter Twenty-four

Rees hesitated a few seconds. "Well," he said and then he looked at Caldwell. The other man flipped his hand as if to say, "This is your tale, you tell it." So Rees said, "This all started with the murder of Zadoc Ward."

"No," Caldwell interrupted. "Everything started with the rumor that your wife practiced witchcraft."

Rees hesitated for a moment. "Maybe so," he agreed. "Very well. My sister began spreading rumors about my wife." He paused. How much did Caldwell's mother really need to know anyway? "Thefts of livestock and petty destruction on my farm followed. I didn't know if that was connected or not. But then the attacks became more serious. And when the body of Ward was found shot to death, Zedediah Farley immediately suspected I had had a hand in it."

"Because you'd brawled with Ward," Caldwell put in.

"And because Farley thought Lydia might need the body for her rites." He stopped again, recalling with sorrow the desolation on Lydia's face when she saw the destruction of her hives. "Then the corpse of Thomas McIntyre was found, hanging upside down from a beam in his mill, with the marks of some kind of torture on him and candles all around." Rees's throat closed and he couldn't continue.

"I got wind of a plan to capture Lydia and bring her before the magistrate on charges of witchcraft," Caldwell said.

"I thought they might put her to the water test," Rees said, raising his eyes to Mrs. Caldwell. "Or press her . . ." His voice wobbled and he had to stop.

"Lydia is expecting," Caldwell explained to his mother.

"Our first," Rees said.

"Oh my," Mrs. Caldwell said in a hushed voice. "When is she due?"

"September." Rees stopped again, pulling out his handkerchief to wipe his eyes.

"Fortunately," Caldwell continued, "I was able to gather some of Rees's friends and we arrived in time to prevent any violence."

"Was she arrested?" Mrs. Caldwell asked. Rees shook his head. Just remembering those few hours made him shake. He turned to Caldwell.

"She was in hiding," the former constable said. "And Rees was able to spirit her away. But I lost my position over it."

"And Farley, the man who believes with all his heart and soul that Lydia is a witch, was put into Caldwell's place by Magistrate Hanson."

Mrs. Caldwell pursed her lips. "It sounds as though you have some powerful enemies."

Rees nodded. "And then my sister's husband, Sam Prentiss, was found shot to death. Of course Farley suspected me. He and his men came out to the farm to arrest me. And if it weren't for your son, Caldwell here, I would have been caught and probably strung up without even a chance to defend myself." Rees could still hardly believe it.

"So, you're on the run," she said.

"No," Rees said firmly. "I'm not. I want to stay in the area and find out who is doing this to me. I will find out who is doing this." He said the last with such intensity it sounded like a vow and both the Caldwells stared at him.

After a moment of silence, Mrs. Caldwell said, "If I were you, I'd look to my family. No one else can get so close and do so much harm."

Rees nodded. "At first I thought it might be my sister, but although she admits to spreading rumors, she swears she did nothing else. And I wonder how she, a woman, would lift the body of a man. And then I considered my brother-in-law but he was the most recent murder victim."

"And he was touched besides," Caldwell said. "Foolish."

"I wonder." Mrs. Caldwell turned to the sink and began putting the dirty dishes into the dishpan as she stared unseeingly through the window. "Is there a man other than her husband that your sister is close to?"

"No," Rees said quickly, although his thoughts went unerringly to Piggy Hanson.

Mrs. Caldwell fixed her eyes upon Rees. "Now you're lying to me."

"I'm not," Rees protested, sounding even to his ears like a guilty schoolboy. "But I did see the magistrate visiting her."

"There. I knew it. Most likely he and your sister cooked up this scheme between them."

"He's married." Rees's voice trailed away. He recalled meeting

Mrs. Hanson, a faded, gray woman who, although ten years Piggy's junior, looked decades older.

"I say, look to the connection between the magistrate and your sister." She paused and added in a cynical tone, "My experience tells me that someone is unfaithful to his wedding vows." She paused a moment and Rees was certain she spoke of her own past. "By enacting this elaborate story, she manages to free herself of her husband and blame the brother. If you pretend for a moment your sister is no relation to you, I think you'll see the truth to what I am saying." Mrs. Caldwell waved the dishrag for emphasis.

"I'm not sure that's correct," Caldwell said. "The magistrate doesn't like you, that is true. But enough to serve you such an ill turn?"

Rees shrugged with uncertainty. "But why accuse Lydia?" he asked. He did not like agreeing with Mrs. Caldwell, but her suggestion made sense. Caldwell frowned at Rees as though he were particularly slow-witted.

"Because a guilty verdict of witchcraft results in the confiscation of all goods and properties. And your sister has desired your farm for years."

Rees recalled Caroline's happiness the last time he'd visited her. She had told him that. "Piggy Hanson has promised my property to her," he said, appalled by the cunning behind this scheme. Then he remembered Caroline's other offhand comments; she'd asked about selling and mentioned moving to Boston. Was that her plan?

"And the magistrate is helping her, for whatever reason," Caldwell said, throwing a quick look at his mother.

Mrs. Caldwell attacked the plates aggressively and soon they were stacked on the table, ready to be returned to the pantry. "Mr. Rees can stay with me a few days," she said. "No more. I have customers coming and going—I don't want to take the chance someone will see him and bring the storm down upon my head. And before sleeping in the bed upstairs, I want both of you to bathe." Rees nodded in agreement. Even a few days would allow him a chance to investigate from a place of relative safety. He didn't think he would wish to stop with Mrs. Caldwell for much longer than that anyway. He would spend all his time trying to clean up any infinitesimal speck of dirt she might see.

"Why should I bathe?" Caldwell protested. "I'm fine." Rees left the table and walked to the back door.

"You stink of horse and sweat and whiskey," his mother said. "You will bathe or I won't permit you in the house."

"My entire childhood was spent washing," Caldwell said, his voice rising. "I'm a man now. I don't see why I should have to obey these queer whims of yours."

Rees picked up his shoes and his pack and went down the back steps, the sound of the quarrel fading behind him. He was still hot and sweaty from his trek through the woods, and his face stung with a crust of salt. He was certain he stank as well, even though Mrs. Caldwell had been too polite to say so, and a bath seemed a small price to pay for his safety. Anyway, he wanted to consider Mrs. Caldwell's suggestions. Unfortunately, they made sense, too much sense, and he knew if Caroline had not been his sister, he would probably have thought exactly the same. He couldn't see a romantic attachment between Caro and Piggy but maybe the angry spite they shared was enough of a connection. And while Rees didn't want to believe his sister capable of such guile, Piggy had that ability in abundance.

Positioning himself behind the washhouse, so that he could not be seen at all from the house, Rees shucked his clothing and cautiously stepped off the flat granite boulders into the water. It was as warm as it got, now at the end of the day, but it was still chilly enough to take his breath away. He ducked completely under and scrubbed his hands over his body. Then he climbed out and sat on the rocks to dry.

"My mother sent down a towel," Caldwell said, appearing with a large linen square. Ragged with long use, the cloth was soft and absorbent and Rees gratefully wrapped it around himself. "I will be sleeping in the washhouse," Caldwell said.

"Over a bath?" Rees asked.

Caldwell turned his head to look at his companion. "I've spent my life washing or being washed until my skin was red and sore. When I was younger I sometimes went to school in damp clothes. Not a pleasant experience during the winter, I can assure you. My mother just had to scrub my breeches the night before. And if I hadn't been sleeping in my shirt, she'd probably have laundered that too. Well, now I am a grown man and I won't allow her to dictate to me."

Rees kept silent although he thought both mother and son too extreme in their views.

"Anyway," Caldwell said, "I daresay you'll be sleeping upstairs in the bed, now that you've bathed."

Rees heard the sourness in Caldwell's voice and hesitated only an instant before replying, "No, I'll join you in the washhouse." How could he fail to demonstrate his loyalty to a man who had not only lost his job but was now risking his freedom to protect Rees's? Caldwell grinned. Rees dressed in the clean clothing he'd put in his pack and in the last golden rays of the setting sun, they climbed the slope to the house for supper.

Mrs. Caldwell offered them the last of the ham and greens from the garden; Rees saw that she was not much into cooking. She handed out threadbare quilts and Rees and Caldwell left the house once again. While Caldwell went outside to relieve himself, Rees spread his blanket on the dirt floor of the washhouse and lay down. It was dark inside the shack but pink still streaked the sky. Rees closed his eyes. Worn out by the emotional and physical toll of this very long day, he fell instantly asleep.

He was jerked out of slumber by a gunshot and sat bolt upright. A quick glance to his left told him Caldwell was gone. Although the sky outside was dark the moon hadn't risen yet. Orange light cast strange patterns from the front of Mrs. Caldwell's house to the side and a rumble of diffuse shouting echoed over the river. Rees tiptoed barefoot out of the washhouse and climbed the slope. From the safety of the shadows, he peered around the house. Zedediah Farley and a group of men, some of them holding torches, stood on the beaten dirt at the front. Mrs. Caldwell defied them from the front step. She had wrapped a shawl around her chemise and petticoats and her gray hair straggled over one shoulder in an untidy braid.

"I told you," she said in a loud voice, "no one is here but my son."

"We know he's here," Farley shouted back. "You ain't doing yourself any favors by protecting him. He's a murderer."

And how, Rees wondered, did Farley know he was here?

"He's not here," Caldwell said, coming through the house to stand by his mother.

"We know he is." Farley spat to one side. "You helped him escape. And what's wrong with you? You're a former constable."

Any thoughts Rees had of rushing forward to the defense of the Caldwells died. Doing so would not only make liars out of them but also put them in more danger than they were in now.

And how had Farley found out? Only David knew the plan and Rees would swear on the Bible that his son would never betray him. A momentary suspicion that David had done exactly that overwhelmed Rees with paralyzing grief. But then he shook his head. No, David would never do that, of course he wouldn't. Rees returned his attention to the drama playing out before him and realized he'd missed a few seconds. In that time Farley's men had grasped Caldwell in their hands and were shaking him like a terrier with a rat.

"I came to visit my mother," Caldwell protested.

"Search the house," Farley told two of his fellows.

In the ensuing struggle, Mrs. Caldwell was knocked from the step to the ground and Caldwell was beaten into quiescence. Then he was tied up and dragged away with his nose streaming blood.

Rees hesitated, quivering with the desire to run out and protect those who'd protected him. Then, sick with guilt, he withdrew, moving as quickly and silently as he could back to the washhouse. He grabbed his pack and went around to the back of the small shack. There he lowered himself into the bone-chilling water and began walking north through the water, against the current, staying as close to the granite boulders of the shore as he could. The water was chest high and the bottom rocky and hard to navigate with bare feet. He was no more than twenty feet away when the mob found the washhouse. Rees heard a great shout go up, but of course he was not there. Men carrying torches came out on the rocks and held the flames high, trying to see into the black water beyond. Rees kept moving, as silently as he could, as the men, disappointed to lose their quarry, set fire to the washhouse. The flames leaped up, casting a ruddy glow upon the river.

Rees realized that he might soon be visible. He had to make a choice: crouch down and hope no one saw him or strike out for the opposite shore. The river was shallow here so if he was going to swim across this was his best opportunity. He lay down in the water and with as little splashing as possible, began moving away from the bank. Fortunately for him, the shouts of the men and the loud crying of Mrs. Caldwell meant that any sound Rees did make could not be heard. He paused in the middle of the river and looked back over his shoulder. Someday he would have to make the destruction of the washhouse right with Mrs. Caldwell.

Then he turned and swam into blackness, his destination—the bank on the other side—invisible in the dark.

Chapter Twenty-five

Rees could swim but he was not proficient at it and he soon began to tire. The movements of his arms and legs became jerky, and water foamed up around him. Because he couldn't see the opposite shore, he had no way of orienting himself, or even any sense of the distance he still had left to travel. He inhaled a gulp of water and went under. Oh Lord, he was going to drown! But his toes touched bottom and although the inky water still reached his chin he knew he was approaching land. He fought his way through the last of the water with a mixture of swimming and walking and finally was able to put his hand on one of the rocks lining the shore. He hung there for a moment, gasping and coughing. His legs were trembling. Then he began pulling himself along the rocks, looking for a place to climb up.

He flopped upon the rock, half out and half submerged for a long slow minute, too weary to drag himself from the water. Finally, with one great effort, he hauled his legs out of the river and onto the stone slab. He lay on his belly, panting and waiting for his heartbeat to slow. He had traveled much farther than he'd expected and he did not think he could be seen. The fire had largely consumed the washhouse and was dying down. A rush of guilt swept over Rees that an act of kindness should have such a terrible result. But he couldn't dwell upon that now. The men were beginning to search the riverbank, both north and south of the Caldwell home, their torches bouncing through the air like fireflies, and he needed to get moving. Rees scrambled to his feet and, crouching, began to hurry toward the forest. He immediately slowed to a careful walk. The sharp stones dug into his feet, bruising the tender skin. He had not gone barefoot for many years, not since childhood, and his skin was soft. He paused to put on his shoes and that's when he realized he had left them in the washhouse. Well, they were gone now. He stifled an oath and then looked over his shoulder, afraid someone might have heard him. But the shouting of the searchers covered any small sound he might make. They had not heard him and Rees made as much haste as he could into the darkness.

He felt the exact moment when the sharp rocks underfoot changed to smaller pebbles, then to softer dirt mixed with pine needles and twigs. He couldn't see where he was going so he had to move cautiously, foot by foot, until the orange glow of the fire faded to barely visible behind him. One unwary step and he stubbed his big toe hard on a rock protruding from the ground. He scraped his blisters open on the woody shrubs he blundered through. After he crashed into a tree trunk he began walking with his hands outstretched in front of him. He could feel a bloody scrape on his cheek where he'd connected with the bark. Despite the danger of pursuit, he had to stop. He couldn't see where he was going and had no idea even where he was. As he thought that, he crashed into something knee high and lost his balance, toppling to the ground. Stretched out full length upon soft mossy ground, he decided he might as well remain here for the night.

He pulled himself to a sitting position and took stock. Although shoeless, he still had his pack. Like his clothing, the canvas was damp from his swim in the river. When he opened it he found everything inside was wet. He would have to hang out the clothing to dry as soon as he found a place of safety. The sodden bread fell apart in his hands but the apples were unharmed and the cheese, although wet, still seemed edible. He took a few bites but was far too tired to eat. Although he was soaked and shivering, his eyes kept closing and it took every ounce of determination to open them again. Well, he would need something for breakfast tomorrow morning. And, for the moment, he was free and as safe as he could be. With a sigh, he lay down and abandoned himself to sleep.

He dropped instantly into a dream. He was back in the river, fighting to stay afloat. But this time Lydia and the children were with him. Joseph floated by—not the older Joseph who could walk—no, this was the baby as Rees had first seen him, with the tail of a very dirty diaper snaking out behind him in the dark water. "Da-da," he called to Rees before disappearing downstream. Jerusha and Simon went by, clinging to a piece of driftwood. And then there was Lydia, flailing helplessly in the black water. "Will," she cried, "help me. Help me." Rees tried to reach her but the harder his arms stroked the water, the farther from her he went.

"Lydia," he shouted as she went under for the last time. "Lydia!"

He sat up with a jerk, Lydia's name still on his lips. The gray predawn light sifted like mist through the trees surrounding him and with a start he remembered what had happened. His clothing was still damp and he was shivering with both cold and fear. It's just a dream, he told himself. But it was also a warning: he could lose everything he held most dear.

He looked around. Last night he had come to rest in an old graveyard and slept the night among the tombstones. In fact, he had tripped over a small marker: a child's, he thought. He knew exactly where he was; in the abandoned Beloin burying plot. The last of the family had moved away forty or fifty years ago. The cemetery was reputed to be haunted and Rees, a skeptic even as a child, had once stayed overnight on a dare from his friends. He thought now that Piggy had probably hoped even then that something would carry Rees away.

He struggled upright with the aid of a stone, although he felt somewhat guilty of disrespect, and began stamping his cold, numb feet and slapping his arms around his chest until the blood began to flow. He would not allow anything to happen to his family. As the terror left by the dream subsided, his anger began to build. Someone would be called to account for this, he would make sure of it. He began walking once again, heading north toward town and the eastern bridge. He needed to cross the river to Dugard. Besides speaking to George Potter about the farm, Rees needed to find another place to hide so he could carry on his investigation. Now he had at least a four-hour journey, maybe five—barefoot.

The sky went pink with sunrise and the faint mist wreathing through the trees burned away. Rees gloried in the warmth, spreading his arms wide so as to catch every golden drop of sunshine he could. His damp clothing began to dry. But as the sensation returned to his feet, he began to feel every scrape and cut left by yesterday's mad journey through the woods. His soles were rubbed raw and he sought out the paths carpeted with pine needles. The layers of brown leaves cushioned his tender feet.

He reached town about eight-thirty, as close as he could guess by the sun. By then he was limping. Although the bridge over the river was not yet crowded, some early farmers and day laborers were crossing. Rees did not stick out. Some of the laborers were barefoot as well, although, if one looked closely, it was easy to see Rees's feet were pale and soft, not brown and as hard as shoe leather. He was also pickier about where he stepped, dodging the piles of horse apples as well as the stones. Once across and into town, he avoided the main streets, instead sneaking his way through the narrow alleys separating the buildings. He was not planning to travel far, only to George Potter's. He crept through the tiny alley separating the blacksmith's from the gun shop, sprinted across the street, and climbed over the fence into the small backyard. The horses in the stables stamped restively and one whinnied. Rees froze but no one made an appearance. He hurried across the rocky courtyard as quickly as his painful, bleeding feet would allow. But once behind the house he couldn't decide whether to throw pebbles at the second-floor window of Potter's office or knock on the door.

Deciding to try throwing stones first, he grabbed a handful and hurled them at the glass. No one appeared. As Rees started climbing the stairs, Potter flung the door open and, grasping Rees's arm, jerked him inside. "What are you doing here?" the lawyer asked. "Get upstairs, quickly, before anyone sees you."

"Who is it?" Mrs. Potter called from the kitchen.

"No one," Potter shouted back as he glared at Rees. "One of those annoying crows." Rees climbed the stairs very slowly and quietly. The office door was open and he entered, collapsing into the nearest chair with a gasp of relief. Potter had not followed and when he came up the stairs a few minutes later, heralded by a loud clatter of crockery, Rees knew why. "I told my wife I would take breakfast in my office," he said, closing the office door behind him with a foot. "I guessed you wouldn't have eaten anything either." He inspected Rees with a gaze that went from disapproving to concerned. "I expect you were sleeping rough. But what happened to your feet?"

"I forgot my shoes at—I forgot my shoes." Rees didn't want to chance involving the Caldwells any more than they were already.

"Farley locked Caldwell in Wheeler's Livery," Potter said, pushing over a plate of fried bacon and several hunks of bread slathered with butter.

Rees fell to. "Caldwell had nothing to do with anything," Rees said, his mouth full.

"You know," the lawyer said, "Magistrate Hanson has a shoot-on-sight charge on you." He had brought up a teapot and although Rees didn't care for that beverage he was looking forward to it. But when Potter poured the liquid into the cup, it smelled enticingly like coffee. Rees's hand trembled as he reached for the cup.

"I know."

"Then why are you here?" Potter's voice was sharp. "You're endangering my family."

Rees had hoped for a friendlier welcome. The food in his mouth suddenly seemed too much to swallow and he struggled for a few seconds. When he could speak he said, "Piggy is avenging himself on me."

"For the Widow Penney and others?"

"Probably. He's hated me since childhood. I suspect Molly Bowditch has a lot to do with this." Unwillingly he thought of his sister but he said nothing about her.

"Possibly. Although gossip has it that Molly will be marrying that Virginian, Drummond, and moving away." Rees said nothing. "If it makes you feel any better, I believe Drummond is a liar and a thief."

"It doesn't," Rees said. A future for Molly, no matter how uncertain, was still better than Nate's fate. She certainly had reason to hate Rees and if she had come after him with a loaded pistol Rees would have been unsurprised. But she didn't seem cunning enough for the scheme that had been laid against Rees, and besides, she did not have the strength to pick up a man and tie him to a beam. "She and Piggy Hanson have been friends for many years," he said at last.

Recalled by the mention of the magistrate's name to their current problem, Potter threw a glance out the window. "I can't provide a refuge for you here. That will put my entire family into danger. Between Farley threatening to arrest every woman he suspects of witchcraft and Hanson blaming you for the murders . . ." His words trailed away. He couldn't meet Rees's gaze. "I hope you understand."

"You've known me all my life," Rees said. "Do you really believe Lydia is a witch? And I'm a murderer?"

"Of course not," Potter said, too quickly. "But you do have a terrible temper and the relationship between you and Sam was never good."

"I see," Rees said. And he did see. Potter had not been convinced of Rees's innocence for all he'd freed him from the charges.

"Farley's threatening to hang Caldwell," Potter said. Rees could not repress his horrified gasp. "Farley's sure our former constable had something to do with your disappearance. Caldwell did, didn't he?" Potter slapped his desk. "I must say this for Caldwell. He's loyal. He continues to swear he had nothing to do with you and was only visiting his mother." He paused and added, "Susannah Anderson is making sure he's fed."

Rees wanted to stop by and thank her but didn't dare. He would be putting her family at risk too and he didn't want to repay a kindness with an injury. Not again. "I stopped here for a definite purpose," he said. "Farley told me the magistrate could try Lydia of witchcraft and enact a sentence, even if she weren't here. Is this true?"

Potter sighed. "It is. But it hasn't been done very often and you would think in this enlightened age we could behave with more reason." He hesitated and when he spoke again he sounded glum. "Piggy doesn't like your wife very much. He's told me more than once she does not behave as a proper woman should. You know, beaten down and docile like his wife. So, if you are convicted of murder and she is tried and hanged as a witch, your farm will be forfeit."

"But David should inherit it," Rees said, although this was nothing more than what he expected.

"He would under normal circumstances, but the farm is forfeit before inheritance laws come into effect."

"Then he must buy it," Rees said. "Will you do that for me? Write up a contract in which I sell my land to him." Rees turned out his pockets and the coins bounced upon the desk. "Date it a month ago or so."

"I'll have to secure his signature," Potter said. He rose to his feet and walked around the office. "But I suppose I can do that." He paused and looked at Rees. "You do understand this is skirting the edges of the law."

"And taking everything I would leave to him isn't?" Rees asked in a bitter tone. "Especially on trumped-up charges?"

Potter eyed him for a moment and then nodded. "Very well. I'll do it. But don't come here anymore."

Rees stared at his old friend. If pressed, Rees would have admitted to disappointment, but actually he was too hurt to speak. How could someone who knew him so well treat him so coldly? "I won't," Rees said at last, holding on to the front of the desk while he stood. The hour's rest had not done his feet any good. They stung now worse than ever.

Potter looked at Rees's stance and then down at the bloody feet. "Dear Lord." He looked at Rees with more sympathy. "You won't get a town block on those. Let me find something." He disappeared from the office and Rees sat down again. He finished all the crumbs on his plate and drank the last drop of coffee in the pot. No telling when he'd drink coffee again.

He had just put his cup back into the saucer when Potter returned. "Try these," he said, handing over a pair of moccasins. Rees gratefully slipped his feet inside. They were a trifle small, but the fur inside offered some protection to his scrapes and blisters. He walked around the office a few times. He was still limping but it was better.

"Thank you," he said.

"Go through the stables," Potter said. "That way none of my neighbors will see you." With a nod, Rees turned. Potter grasped his elbow. "Good luck, Will. I will be praying for you."

Rees crept down the stairs and padded to the back door. He could hear the Potter family, still at breakfast. He went out, closing the back door silently behind him and scuttled across the yard and into the stables.

Chapter Twenty-six

Rees had never been inside the stables before and was surprised by the number and quality of Potter's horseflesh. Rees hadn't realized how fond of horses Potter was. If he were willing to sell one or two, Mrs. Potter could have the house outside of town that she wanted. A large opening, wide and high enough for a carriage, opened onto Maple Street. Rees walked behind the stalls and peered cautiously through the open door.

In the short time he had spent inside Potter's office the streets had become much busier. Rees's heart sank; there was no way now for him to cross Wheeler's Lane without being seen by somebody. Unless . . . Rees took the battered straw hat worn by Potter's groom and clapped it on his head. Then he bridled the horse nearest the door, a small mare fit for a lady, and with one hand clamped firmly on the bridle and the other in his pocket he pulled the horse outside. He kept his head lowered and his eyes fixed upon the ground; just a servant bringing his master's horse somewhere.

"Wait. Where you goin' with that horse?" The groom's shout from the stable behind Rees startled him into a run. "Stop. Thief." Other men took up the cry and now everyone was looking directly at Rees.

Normally he would have paused. He had no intention of stealing the horse but this time he couldn't afford to be recognized.

He dropped the bridle and slapped the mare on her flank. She jumped and took off, running south on the lane. As Rees had hoped, Potter's groom and most of the others ran after her. But there were a few who turned toward Rees. He ran toward the blacksmith. If he could just reach the fence and climb over it, he would be in the alley that ran parallel to Water Street. But his sore feet slowed him down and he knew he wouldn't make it.

"Hey, you. Here." Augustus opened the door into the smithy and gestured. Rees raced toward him. As he passed through the door, the blacksmith jerked Rees inside and shut it behind him. "Quick. Up to the loft." Rees went up the ladder as fast as he was able and crouched behind a stack of old tools. Augustus knocked down the ladder and went to the forge. Barely a minute later the door burst open and two men panted inside.

"Where is he? Where's the thief?"

"No one's come in here," Augustus said.

"We saw him."

"You calling me a liar?" A pause. Rees peeked around the stack of iron implements in front of him. The two white men crowded Augustus. Although free, he was taking a big risk. Rees felt afraid for the boy. Augustus swung his hammer and smiled, his teeth very white in his brown face. "But I did see someone go through the gate down there, into the yard. He ran for the back fence. Big man, right? I thought it was Mr. Potter's groom."

The two men ran through the big opening into the yard and headed for the back fence. Augustus stoked up the fire as though preparing for the day's work but Rees could see the tension in his well-muscled arms. After a few minutes that seemed to Rees like hours, the two men walked back through the yard. "He got away," said the heavier of the two.

"You wouldn't mind us looking around a bit, would you?"

"Go ahead and then get out. I told you what I saw." Augustus began pounding on a horseshoe with deafening clangs.

The men briefly poked around the smithy and then returned to the yard. They disappeared to the back. Rees guessed they were planning on searching the stables at the back; that was what he would have done. Augustus kept up his relentless hammering until Rees's head began to pound in rhythm. Finally, as the shoe went into the water with a hiss, there was blessed silence.

"They're gone," Augustus said softly. "But I suggest you stay there a bit longer, just in case they come back."

Forgetting Augustus couldn't see him, Rees nodded. His thudding heart was gradually returning to normal and he was desperate to urinate. Finally he heard the ladder going up. "We've got to get you inside," Augustus said. "You aren't safe here."

Rees came out from his hiding place and cautiously descended the ladder. Now that his body was calming down, he felt his feet and wanted to scream with the pain. When he looked down at the moccasins, he saw blood seeping through the leather. Augustus saw it too. "Come on," he said. He looked through the door and, seeing nobody, he hustled Rees along the outside of the wall to the house behind it. With his inheritance from Nate Bowditch, he had purchased the smithy from the former owner. "My apprentice just went to the Contented Rooster to fetch my dinner. He'll be returning soon. And the fewer who know of your presence, the better." He pushed Rees up the steps into the kitchen.

No fire burned on the hearth and the sink was empty. Rees guessed Augustus took all of his meals at the coffeehouse. Since his mother worked as the cook there, the arrangement made sense.

Augustus pulled up two chairs and sat down in one. He gestured Rees into the one opposite. "Give me your foot," he said.

Rees obeyed and as Augustus gently slipped off the moccasin, Rees asked, "Why are you doing this? I'm a fugitive, to be shot on sight. And now, I suppose, a horse thief as well."

"How can you ask?" Augustus said. "I know something about being a fugitive." He raised his eyes to Rees who, the previous summer, had hidden Augustus at the farm.

"You aren't afraid you might be protecting a murderer?" Rees asked. "Or that the magistrate will punish you if he discovers you've helped me?" The hurt and bitterness at what he felt was Potter's disloyalty colored his voice.

Augustus shook his head. "You proved I didn't murder my father. And you took me in so the slave takers did not capture me and bring me south. All that I have," and he gestured around him, "is due to you."

Some of the ache in Rees's heart eased. "I won't forget this," he said and was embarrassed by the break in his voice.

"Your feet are badly injured," Augustus said after a moment's silence. "I'll put some of my mother's salve on them and wrap them, but the best thing for you to do would be to stay off them for a day or two."

"I can't stay here," Rees said. "Every second I remain puts you in danger."

"I have a place where you'll be safe for a few days. They'll be looking for you. It won't take the magistrate and new constable long to figure out you were in town and tried to steal a horse."

While he worked, his long-fingered hands spread salve over Rees's wounded feet and wrapped linen strips around them. Despite the calluses from his profession, his hands were surprisingly gentle.

"You are very skilled at this," Rees said.

"I've had a lot of practice, especially with feet battered by long walks."

Rees looked at him. Augustus met Rees's gaze with a level stare of his own.

"People traveling north, I would guess," Rees said. He thought of the little boy he'd seen at the Bowditch farm and wondered.

Augustus did not respond to the implied question, saying instead, "If you insist on leaving, I have a horse I can lend you. She's old, been worked cruel, but I think she'll get you around if you don't push her too hard. And best of all, I acquired her in trade from a man just passing through so no one will recognize her. As long as you keep your face hidden under a hat and make sure no one sees that fiery hair of yours, you should be safe leaving town."

Rees nodded hesitantly. What would he do with a horse? And what was safe? Right now he had no place to stay. He certainly couldn't return to his farm; Farley and his men would be watching it constantly. Rees had no money, no food, nothing, so how could he even care for a horse?

"You can't walk far on those feet of yours," Augustus said, seeing Rees's uncertainty. "You can either stay here or take the horse." He paused. Rees still didn't speak. "Look, I'm close to the bridge. You can slip over. Return the mare when you no longer need her." Rising to his feet, he continued, "I have some cornmeal and a bit of oatmeal I can give you. Nothing more, I'm afraid." He grinned. "I don't cook much. Most of my meals come from the Contented Rooster."

"Augie. Augie." A boy's shrill treble sounded from the yard outside.

"Oh, that's my apprentice." Augustus hurried through the back door and Rees heard the mutter of conversation. It faded as though the two young men were walking away from the house. Now, with a few minutes of safety and quiet, Rees pondered his options. Although he would prefer to shelter in a building with a roof, that was not as important as isolation. He needed a place where people did not go and, offhand, he couldn't think of anything that was still close to town. With the pain in his feet soothed and his belly full, Rees found his eyes drooping. The uncomfortable night before with its broken slumber began to tell and although he tried to stay awake, his eyes finally closed for good.

He awoke late that afternoon to the sound of Augustus tiptoeing into the kitchen. Rees rolled his head, trying to loosen his stiff neck, and said, "Why didn't you wake me up? I need to leave." He looked at the napkin-covered plate sitting on the table in front of him.

"When my apprentice came over with my dinner, he told me Farley's men were guarding the bridge. I didn't see the point in waking you up after that. Better you slip out of town after dark. Maybe head south."

Rees removed the napkin from the plate. The beef gravy had congealed into a shiny brown puddle and the meat was cold but he eyed the food hungrily.

"Go ahead," Augustus said. "I left it for you. I got another plate from my mother. I told her I was especially hungry."

Rees began to eat rapidly. Augustus's mother was a wonderful cook and even cold, the food was delicious. As the cobwebs of sleep began to clear from his brain, Rees said, "There won't be much traffic after dark and I'll stand out. It would be better to travel when there are other people." He paused. "I'd guess Farley has men stationed on the south road too. That would normally be the route I'd take home. In fact, if he's smart, he'll have men at every road."

Augustus sat heavily in the chair across from Rees. "So you can't leave then. You'll have to remain with me until they give up the search."

"No." Rees shook his head. "Every extra hour I stay here I put you into danger. Besides, if I'm to discover the twisted mind behind this, I need to have more freedom. There's got to be a way for me to slip out." If his feet were better, he knew he could creep out after dark and walk the ten or so miles home. But they weren't and he doubted he'd get ten yards. Anyway, Farley almost certainly had men watching the farm in case Rees tried to seek refuge there. And he wouldn't risk putting David in danger.

"Well, you can't wear Henry's hat," Augustus said. "He's been whining to anyone who will listen that the horse thief took his favorite straw hat." Rees took it off and examined it in surprise. Frayed with much wear, the brim bore a greasy smudge from frequent handling. "But, the good news is, he described the thief as a black man."

"What?" Rees looked up in dawning hope. But further thought dashed his tentative excitement. "But Farley and several of those men know me."

"Yes," Augustus agreed. "And you are memorable." He hesitated and said again, "I think you would be safest if you stayed here. You have nowhere else to go."

Rees nodded his head in acknowledgement, although he'd thought of a possible sanctuary. He didn't want to confide in

Augustus; the less he knew the safer he would be. Instead he said, "Maybe I have to make myself so visible no one really sees me."

"Huh?" Augustus looked at him. "What do you mean?"

"My old Indian friend, Philip, told me once that sometimes, before attacking a white settlement, one of the braves would pour whiskey down his chest and reel into town. While he lay in a doorway, counting all the guns, the people who passed saw only what they expected: a drunken Indian. I need to do something similar."

"It's too risky," Augustus said, shaking his head. "Especially if one of those men is someone who knows you well."

Rees acknowledged the truth of that. "I'll need another hat. And some soot."

While Rees dragged one hand over the sooty bricks of the fireplace and used the black to darken his hair and eyebrows, Augustus ran upstairs for another hat. When he returned to the kitchen, he stopped stock still in amazement. "What do you think?" Rees asked, turning around so that Augustus could see him completely.

"You look very different," Augustus admitted as Rees used some ashes to streak his face and clothing.

"Do you have any whiskey?"

Augustus nodded at the jug on the mantel. Rees swirled the whisky in his mouth before swallowing it. He poured a liberal amount over his chest. "God, you stink," Augustus remarked tactlessly.

"Good." Rees put on the moccasins and clapped the new hat on his head.

Since it was too big, the brim sagged over his eyebrows. It was newer than the one Rees had borrowed from Henry and a slightly darker color. Rees hoped this would be enough.

"If you're set on this dangerous course," Augustus said, sounding as though he still hoped Rees would reconsider, "I'll saddle the mare."

"I'll accompany you to the stables," Rees said although every instinct urged him to stay in hiding. But he would have to test his disguise sometime and there were only one or two men in the yard by the smithy. He picked up the whiskey jug and followed Augustus down the stairs, trying to change his limping into a convincing stagger.

No one paid them any mind and they made it to the stables without comment. As Augustus went for a saddle, Rees inspected the old horse. She was a nondescript brown and had been used hard but she seemed biddable enough. "I want the saddle back," Augustus said. "Remember that."

Rees turned and clasped the young man's hand, clapping him on one shoulder at the same time. "I won't forget this, Augie," he said.

"Just stay alive," Augustus said, his face creased with worry. "I wish you wouldn't do this."

"I must," Rees said. With a heavy sigh, Augustus tied a bag of cornmeal and a bag of oatmeal at the back of the saddle.

Rees mounted. His heart was pounding like a runaway horse. Taking a deep breath, he rode out into the sunshine.

Chapter Twenty-seven

Ｗhen he approached the gate, the men standing by it moved out of his way. Their eyes passed over him and they looked quickly away. They saw exactly what Rees wanted, a drunken laborer on an old horse.

Rees began to sing tunelessly, an old army song that he barely remembered the words to. The few ladies nearby looked away, disgusted, as did most of the men. Those that did notice him laughed and went on their way. In fact, everyone he passed tried to avoid looking at him.

But the real test, passing the three bruisers watching the road from the shade of an old maple, was still to come. Sweat began running down the back of Rees's shirt and he was so breathless the lyrics came out in puffs. ". . . my girl . . . back in derry-o . . ."

"Where you goin', old man?" One of the men, his bored expression lighting up with malicious glee, sauntered over toward Rees. He caught the horse's bridle. A shiver of fear went down Rees's spine.

"Hey," he said, his word coming out in a croak.

"You goin' ta give us a drink?" one of his partners asked, joining his companion. "Maybe we should toss you into the stables to sober up." He laughed again. Rees's legs felt boneless and he feared for a moment that he would slide right off the mare's back and land in a heap on the road.

"Leave the sot alone. He ain't the one we're looking for," said the third, barely looking at Rees.

The first speaker wrested Rees's jug from him and drank the last of the whiskey. "Ah, it's all gone." He threw the jug to the side of the road where it smashed. Rees put all of his fear into a scream that would have done a woman proud. The boys began laughing.

"Get outta here." The second speaker slapped the rump of Rees's old horse and she jumped forward so suddenly he almost fell off. "Can you ride, old man? Can you ride?" The two boys doubled over with their amusement. But Rees didn't care. He let the old mare gallop as long as she could. He was out of Dugard and riding south.

Rees planned to turn into the abandoned Winthrop property and hide in the empty shack. With its reputation as haunted and its proximity to both his farm and to town, Rees thought it was the best he could hope for as a hiding place. But when he approached the lane leading into the overgrown plot, he was still riding among a crowd of farmers. He didn't want anyone to even wonder about the abandoned farm so Rees continued on his way, maintaining his persona with snatches of drunken-sounding songs.

He was glad he hadn't intended to go home to his farm. Several men were congregated at the end, passing a whiskey jug from hand to hand and watching the travelers pass them without interest. Rees rode by without glancing over.

When he went round the next bend, and was out of sight of the men, he slowed his old mare into an even more leisurely walk. The wagons and horses rapidly increased the distance between them, leaving him behind. As soon as he saw no one behind him, and the pack in front of him was a significant distance ahead, Rees urged his horse off the highway and into the thicket. Dismounting, he pulled the mare deep into the vegetation. Although the last golden rays of sun still illuminated the road, it was already dark within the trees.

Rees guided the mare forward. They were on his farm—well, he had to start thinking of it as David's now—and circling around at the bottom of the hill. The trees thinned and Rees paused. He didn't see anyone but that didn't mean one of Farley's men wasn't at the top of the hill watching for him. It would be dark soon and Rees could wait for that extra hour. He stroked the mare's nose but she did not seem disposed to whinny. She began nibbling at the bushes, seemingly content to wait in silence. Rees sat down, awkwardly since his legs were stiff from riding, and leaned his back against the tree. He found these enforced pauses almost as difficult as the running. At least then he had the sense he had control over his life instead of waiting for something terrible to happen.

Through the leaves screening him from the meadow, he could just see the tops of the bee skeps. And how were the few remaining colonies faring, without Lydia there? He yawned and straightened out his legs. The shadows extended across the wildflower-spotted meadow and began creeping up the slope to the house. Rees wondered what David was doing right now. Were these ruffians tormenting him? Rees couldn't see the house and except for the lowing of the cattle and the relentless crowing of the roosters, all was silent. But wait, Rees saw movement. He snapped instantly to alertness and went on his knees to peer through the branches. Someone was walking at the top of the hill and Rees did not think it was either David or Charlie. The man walked into a patch of sun and there was a quick sharp flash as the light reflected from a metal barrel. Rees exhaled his breath in a faint hiss; he had been right to be cautious.

It took almost another hour for the light to disappear from the sky and Rees thought it was one of the longest hours he could remember. The mosquitoes came out in clouds, whining about his head and drawing blood with little stings. Rees rose to his feet and untied the horse's reins from the branch. He began picking his way cautiously through the narrow band of trees, mostly oak and maple. He promised himself that if he survived this, he would plant a row of evergreens. They would provide much more cover.

By the time he circled around the southern end of the property and began climbing the rise that led to the dairy and the pigsty, the sky was completely dark. The stars were out and the moon was beginning to rise. Rees could hardly see where he was going and was moving forward on memory and smell. He paused at the end of the pigpen and looked toward the house. He could see the faint glow of a candle. As he climbed the shallow rise, the boy sitting within the golden glow came into view. David's hair glittered like copper and for a moment Rees considered walking across the yard to the house and slipping inside. He longed to reach out and embrace his son, one last time. But he didn't dare. He knew at least a few of Farley's men were still about and Rees would only endanger someone he loved so very much. With a sigh, he moved on. He would find the one behind this scheme, that he swore. And when he did, well, he didn't know what he would do but it would be terrible.

Once Rees was in the cornfield he moved more quickly. Some

of the corn had already been harvested, the stalks cut to stubble, so the walking was somewhat easier. The mare's hooves made a faint sound on the soft dirt. Rees sped up, knowing the wall separating the two properties lay just ahead.

Suddenly someone by the barn pushed back the shutter on a lantern and light spilled across the field. "Who's there?" a voice quavered. It sounded like a young boy. Rees froze.

"See somethin'?" That was a man. The lantern was suddenly held high. "Nothin'. You're just spooked. I told Mr. Farley Rees wasn't likely to come back here. He'd be a fool to. And he ain't a fool."

The shutter shot over the opening with a bang and the fields were plunged again into darkness. Rees slowly, carefully eased his way right, toward the wheat field, and away from the barn, drawing the mare behind him. He paused after the first few steps and listened but he heard only the pounding of his heart. He pulled the mare forward and they went on, faster this time.

He urged her over the stone wall at the end and paused to orient himself. He had arrived deep within the orchard; Winthrop's shack was a good distance to the west. But the waxing moon rode high in the sky, and it illuminated the aisles between the rows of fruit trees in a faint silvery light. Rees groaned. More walking. His calf and thigh muscles ached and every step was agony. He knew some of the cuts and scrapes on his feet had reopened. He could feel the crawl of blood across his skin. But it was almost over. And the longer he stood here, the longer it would take him to reach the end of his journey. He forced himself to walk forward; one foot in front of the other; that was how he would finally arrive at Winthrop's shabby little cabin.

One foot in front of the other, he repeated it to himself over and over as he plodded wearily through the trees. One foot in front of the other. It was a shock to see the dark bulk of the cabin looming up before him and know he had finally reached his destination.

Since Winthrop's paddock was as tumbledown as the cabin—Rees vaguely recalled Winthrop owning an old cob with knobby knees and a swayback—Rees unsaddled his mare and pegged her out. He did not believe she would try to run; she was wheezing with weariness. First thing tomorrow he would have to find Winthrop's well and give the poor old horse water. But for now Rees was too tired to think of anything at all except rest. The final few steps seemed impossible. Rees shoved open the door, staggered into the cabin, and dropped both saddle and saddlebags on the floor. Then he lay down, rested his head on one of the bags, and dropped into sleep.

By the time he awoke the sun had been up for hours and he could hear birds chirruping all around him. Although he was painfully stiff and every movement hurt somewhere, for the first time in many days he felt safe. He had shelter, some food that he could supplement with Winthrop's ripening apples, and, once he found the well, water. Rees pushed himself into a sitting position, his back protesting with every movement, and looked around.

The cabin was just as Winthrop had left it although in much better shape than Rees expected, at least from what he could see of the main room. A table, accompanied by a bench and chairs, sat between the sink and the fireplace. There were no obvious signs of animal activity. There was still wood stacked on one side of the hearth and only a small heap of ashes in the grate. Winthrop had been a neater man than Rees would have expected.

Rees's gaze returned to the fireplace. Did he dare light a fire and cook his food or would the smoke betray him? A fire would offer him the possibility of cooked food, oatmeal and cornmeal and possibly even meat if Rees could recapture his boyhood skills with a slingshot. He levered himself to his feet. He wasn't sure. Winthrop had been something of a hermit so his cabin was set far back into the woods; maybe no one would notice, especially with the smoke from Rees's farmhouse close by. But he didn't want to be forced to run again.

His thoughts conflicted, Rees pushed open the door and went outside. He paused on the battered porch and stared into the trees. No one knew where he was and for the first time since he'd fled from the Caldwell home he felt relatively safe. He was struggling to wrap his mind around Sam's death. Rees had begun to feel quite certain Sam was the villain behind both the murders. He owned a rifle and knew how to use it. He was well able to climb Bald Knob, frequented the mill on a regular basis so no one would even notice him, and had enough access to Rees's house to steal Lydia's candles.

But now he himself had been murdered. So who was left? Caroline? Mrs. Caldwell's suggestion about Caroline and Piggy Hanson popped into Rees's head. Was it possible? Rees tried to imagine the foppish magistrate climbing a mountain and failed. But Farley could do it. That would mean Caroline and Farley were working together. For several seconds Rees considered the possibility. On the surface, this seemed not only conceivable but likely. Caroline and Farley shared sufficient malice. If Rees did not know them, he would look more closely at that solution. But he did know them and he couldn't imagine such an alliance. Farley disliked women for one thing, and Caroline, who fancied herself as a cut above the regular run of humanity, thought Farley was beneath her.

Still, Rees found he could not completely dismiss this as an option.

"Damn," he said aloud in frustration and set off to find the well.

Chapter Twenty-eight

After spending several fruitless minutes searching, Rees concluded that old man Winthrop had been too stingy to dig one. Rees looked around him. He knew the river lay to the east but he suspected a brook lay much closer to the cabin. Very faintly he could hear rushing water. When he followed the sound, drawing Augustus's old horse behind him, he discovered the indistinct remnants of a path down to the rocky banks of a fast-moving stream. Rees brought the mare to the edge so she could drink her fill. Winthrop had clearly expected his family to haul all the water they used. Shaking his head at such miserliness, Rees looped the reins around a shrub and knelt on a smooth granite boulder. Cupping his hands, he scooped up the chilly water to his mouth. It tasted of leaves and stone. As Rees drank his fill he pondered the problem of water and decided he would have to return with the old kettle now hanging from the fireplace hook. He would not want to walk here every time he wanted a drink of water and battle the swarms of black flies and mosquitoes.

He quickly washed in the cold water. As he turned and reached for his shirt, he spotted something tucked under the shrubbery lining the banks. An old broken bucket. He turned it over and over in his hands. No doubt one of the Winthrop children had stashed it here. Rees thought it could be repaired.

He walked back to the cabin swinging the bucket. Now that he had found a safe shelter, food, and water, he wondered again whether he might light a fire. Once he'd eaten, he could extinguish the blaze and set to his investigation. If it were winter he would have to but now? Rees sighed. He didn't dare light the fire. If someone saw the smoke, he would be on the run once again.

Sam's body had been dumped scarcely an hour's walk from the cabin. Seeing the corpse with Caldwell seemed more like a year than two days ago. Rees wondered how Caldwell was doing. Was he still imprisoned in Wheeler's Livery? Was he being fed? Rees pulled his wandering thoughts to a stop. How he missed his loom right now. Somehow it always helped him think. And Rees needed to focus. The sooner he discovered the intelligence behind this web, the sooner Caldwell would be set free. And since Sam was the most recent victim, and had been murdered close by, Rees would begin there, by reexamining the location where Sam had been placed.

But first Rees spent some time sweeping the ashes from the hearth and scrubbing out the old black kettle. He fetched water from the stream and made oatmeal. While it was soaking, he inspected the wooden dishes stacked upon the few shelves that passed as a kitchen. To his surprise, they appeared clean and intact. He climbed the ladder to the loft. Everything seemed just as it had been when Winthrop died. Although the loft was empty, the room at the back of the cabin included a bed and a cedar chest full of linen sheets and blankets. The straw mattress and the bedding covering it had been thoroughly chewed but all the bed coverings in the chest were whole although a little musty. Unlike the kitchen, which was relatively free of dust, in here all the surfaces were filmed with gray.

His spirits rising, Rees returned to his breakfast. He found a spoon and ate standing up over the hearth. The cereal was glutinous, the uncooked grains chewy, and it was bland without salt or flavorings but it was filling. Rees ate until he could eat no more, scraping the bottom of the kettle with the spoon. He refilled the kettle—he would have to repair the water bucket as soon as possible, the walk to the stream was already becoming burdensome—and set off for the edge of Winthrop's property and the Dugard road.

Even if the location of Sam's body had not been permanently fixed in Rees's head, he would have found the place easily. Dried blood coated the ground where Sam's head had lain. The dark reddish brown of old blood coated both the rocks protruding from the soil and the vegetation around them and the number of flies hovering over that patch filled the air with a steady hum.

Rees closed his eyes and called the scene to mind. Sam had been sprawled on his side, head toward the road. Rees opened his eyes and glanced around him. Why here? It was not so far into the forest that Sam and his killer could not be seen from the road, if a slow-moving passerby cared to look. Rees glanced at the road. Although he couldn't see it, and was in fact hidden by the trees and thick vegetation beneath them, the road was too close if the killer wanted to hide the body. "He wanted Sam's body found," Rees muttered, certain now. "He wasn't trying to hide it. Not for long anyway."

And the pistol shot would be audible for some distance. For the first time, Rees wondered how the farmer had come upon Sam's body so soon after his death. Had he been within earshot, traveling? Or had he been warned? Rees stared blindly at the vegetation at his feet, the imprint of the body still visible in the crushed stems. And why a pistol? These smaller guns carried only one bullet and did not have the accuracy of a rifle. So why hadn't the killer used his rifle, as he had on Ward, who had never even seen his killer and had been left where he fell? McIntyre—well, Rees did not want to think about his death. But like the miller's death, Sam's murder had been intimate. Rees shut his eyes once again. Sam had been kneeling when he was shot. Close range too; the wound on his temple had been black with gunpowder. Rees's eyes popped open in horror. The killer might have felt some hesitation at the murder of Zadoc Ward but he had quickly lost his reluctance. The murders of both Mac and Sam had been up close and personal and these men would have known exactly who the killer was. Sam, in fact, had knelt and waited for the shot to come.

"Dear Lord," Rees muttered, trying to understand why Sam would so tamely go to his death. Had he been drunk? Or dosed with laudanum? Had he not understood what was happening? Rees shook his head. He couldn't believe that Sam, as touched as he'd been, would willingly kneel down and wait to be shot, like a lamb to slaughter. And yet that appeared to be exactly what had happened.

Unless . . . Rees stared unseeingly at the green around him. He'd begun to suspect two people were involved in Mac's death. Perhaps there were two here as well? Of course, Rees had wondered if Sam were one of those two, but that no longer seemed possible. He was back to Caroline. And Farley?

The clatter of wagon wheels approaching on the road broke into Rees's reverie. He stepped back, deeper into the woods, and held himself still until the wagon was past. When all was quiet once again, Rees returned to the bloody ground that bore witness to the recent murder. Now that he knew in what position Sam had been in, Rees could clearly see the prints left by his knees. He moved around, trying to step lightly so as not to corrupt any of the marks. He quickly distinguished the place where the killer had stood, but there were no identifying traces that Rees could see. Rees stood just behind the crushed grass that marked the killer's position and pretended to raise a pistol. The killer had been shorter than he was. For Rees the angle would have been awkward. But he couldn't tell by how much. He did not think the murderer had been as short as Caroline. Perhaps a bit taller. Unwillingly Rees's thought returned to first Piggy Hanson and then to Zedediah Farley. Rees lowered his arm. Although he couldn't blame her for wanting Sam out of the way, he still didn't want to believe her guilty of murder. Could he believe Piggy was guilty? Or Farley? Reluctantly, yes.

Frustrated with more questions than answers, Rees retreated into the woods and headed back to the cabin. He walked as quickly as his painful feet allowed, barely noting the strip of forest around him as he considered Sam's murder. He did not want to suspect his sister but his thoughts returned to her over and over. Rees could think of no one else who could easily persuade Sam to kneel and wait while a pistol was put to his head. But he would almost certainly obey Caroline.

The cabin and the overgrown clearing looked exactly as it had earlier that morning. Rees peeked through the door. There was no sign that anyone had been here. Rees walked to the stream where he'd tied up the nag that morning. She was still there. Rees felt a lift of his spirits at this further proof of his safety.

He untied the horse and led her back to the cabin from the stream. He'd hidden the saddle and bridle under a haystack inside the deteriorating barn. Once he'd unearthed the tack, he saddled the old cob. Then he picked a few of the hard green apples and ate them. They were so sour his mouth puckered, but he was too hungry to care. He ate a handful of oatmeal with a cup of cold water. He did not want to speak to Caroline again. Besides the difficulty of questioning his sister, leaving his refuge would be dangerous. But it had to be done. And he had to speak to Molly Bowditch as well. He saddled the old mare, mounted, and set off.

He did not reach the road by way of the drive, choosing instead to ride over Winthrop's overgrown fields. The land sloped upward. Once Rees crested the hill, he looked down upon the east-west road and decided he would visit Molly Bowditch first instead of Caroline. Molly had driven him away during his first attempt, but Rees felt he must at least make a second effort. Believing that he had destroyed her life, and taking no responsibility for her own part in it, she had every reason to hate Rees enough to kill him. And he would much rather believe Molly was guilty of the three recent murders than Caroline.

Rees pushed his queue up under his straw hat so that his bright red hair was no longer visible. He would have to hope that everyone still believed he was on foot and that from a distance he looked like every other farmer.

There was not much traffic, most of the farmers were in their fields at this time of the day, and Rees avoided all that he saw. His journey was a series of gallops interspersed with leisurely walks to maintain a good distance from all who might recognize him. At last he reached the lay-by at the entrance to Molly's cottage. Most of the trees had been cut down to make a lane wide enough for a carriage, but Rees stayed in the shadow of the remaining foliage until he reached the field that stretched up to the door. He paused under an oak and inspected the cottage. He saw no movement at all and wondered if her carriage was in the stable at the back or if she had gone out. After several moments of hesitation, he stepped out from under cover and started across the yard. He walked slowly, cautiously, prepared to fling himself to the ground at the slightest hint of trouble. Somewhere nearby a dog began barking. And when Rees circled the cottage and looked at the stable at the back, he saw that the door was open and the carriage was gone. With a sigh of both relief and disappointment, Rees walked around the cottage. Marsh, with Munch beside him, was standing on the front walk waiting for him.

"I saw you." Marsh gestured over his shoulder at the large farmhouse at the top of the hill. "What are you doing here?"

"I came to talk to Molly."

"Last time you got chased off like a dog," Marsh said. "That wasn't enough for you?"

"Did you hear about Sam Prentiss?" Rees asked, looking straight at the other man.

Marsh nodded. "I heard you shot him." Although as a black man and a servant Marsh was not accustomed to meeting a white man's eyes, he raised his head and looked straight at Rees. "Did you?"

"No." He hesitated for a second or two but decided he could trust Marsh. "No doubt Piggy Hanson will hang me if you turn me in. And give you some reward besides. But I swear to you I did not kill Sam Prentiss. Or Zadoc Ward or Thomas McIntyre either. I had to send Lydia away to protect her and the babe she's carrying. And all the children as well, save David. I need to discover who is behind this plot against me." He paused and waited. Marsh nodded, not as though he agreed, but to show he was prepared to listen. "I thought Molly Bowditch might be at the bottom of it. She hates me, maybe with good reason, and we both know she shoots and rides as well as a man."

"She does, but she's been fair taken up with that Virginian. And although she might have shot Mr. Ward or Mr. McIntyre, I know she did not kill your brother-in-law. You see, she rode off in her carriage the day before Mr. Prentiss was shot. And, from what I've heard, Sam was still warm and pouring his blood into the ground when the constable found him."

"Rode off? To where?" Rees's voice rose.

Marsh smiled slightly. "Why, to Virginia. She told us she was marrying Drummond. And she took all her bits and pieces with her. Including her jewelry."

"I daresay no one told Mr. Drummond about Molly's past," Rees said.

"Maybe. Maybe not. All I know is I wouldn't trust that Drummond as far as I could spit. And Mrs. Bowditch may not own land, but some of those earbobs and other trinkets are worth a fair amount."

"You think Mr. Drummond promised marriage but is planning to rob her?" Rees heard the surprise in his voice.

Marsh shrugged. "I don't know." Rees nodded. "Miss Grace doesn't like him," Marsh added. He did not need to say anything more.

Rees thought about Molly for a moment and then put her aside. "She could not have killed Sam," he said, returning to his primary concern. Marsh shook his head. Now Rees had no excuse at all to prevent him from questioning his sister. "I'd appreciate it," he said, looking at Marsh, "if you didn't mention my visit here."

"Of course not," Marsh said. "And I don't want to know where you're hiding neither." He examined Rees. "You look rough. Do you need anything? Food? Water?"

"Food," Rees responded immediately.

"Go down, wait by your horse," Marsh said with a nod. "I'll be by directly."

Rees hesitated, thinking about the reward. He didn't think Marsh would betray him, but then he'd expected more from Potter. Marsh glared at him. "Get along, now." So Rees turned and went down the drive to the entrance. But he took cover under the trees just in case someone else came to meet him besides Marsh.

In less than twenty minutes, Marsh—and Munch—trotted down the hill with a canvas sack. As Rees left the copse of trees, Marsh said, "I gathered what food I could. Cheese. A bit of ham. A jug of ale. I didn't want you coming up to the house. Mary Martha is in the kitchen and, as you know, she can't help but talk."

"Thank you," Rees said, accepting the bag. He held out his hand. Marsh took it.

"Be careful now," he said. Then he turned and hastened up the hill.

As Rees mounted the horse, he reflected upon the difference between the two black men and Potter. The former could lose their lives, but they'd helped Rees nonetheless. Potter was too afraid of Piggy Hanson to assist someone he claimed as one of his best friends. There was a lesson in there somewhere, Rees thought.

Now he must face his sister.

Chapter Twenty-nine

Rees did not dare approach his sister's farm from the front. He elected to sneak up from the rear, a feat that was not so easy since the neighboring farmers kept their fields cleared and planted and there was little cover approaching the back of Caroline's farm. So he rode along a stream and cut through a field of barley to reach the property line. It was instantly recognizable. Left untended for several years, the trees had grown up and the stone wall marking the division had vanished under a coat of greenery. Once inside, Rees found his cover. But carving a path through the thicket of trees, downed trunks, and other vegetation, especially without knocking his head on a low-slung branch, was a challenge. This bit of forest had been untouched for a long time. Many of the evergreens were sickly and coated with the greenish growths that took root when the tree was beginning to die.

He could hear at least two horses in the paddock before he could see them. Since the horses owned by Caroline and Sam had been sold long ago to pay bills, leaving only a pair of oxen, Rees knew his sister had a visitor. He crept a little closer, finally coming up against the weathered wood at the back of the barn. He peered through the cracked boards. By twisting his head, he could see the corner of a buggy. A plain, ordinary buggy, not Hanson's sleek, stylish carriage with its yellow wheels and gilt trim. After a moment of indecision, Rees decided to chance meeting Caro's visitors. He crossed the yard at a run, jumping over the rotting steps, and darting through the open door into the shadowy shelter beyond.

He heard only Caroline speaking. By the tone of her voice, he suspected she was giving instruction to her daughters. He moved through the front room until he could see into the kitchen. Caroline stood over Georgina and Gwendolyn as they washed and dried dishes.

Rees's gaze traveled around the room. It looked like a different house. The old ashes were gone and the hearth stones scoured clean. The floor had been swept, the table scrubbed, and the air smelled of vinegar and soap.

Caroline turned suddenly and started to see her brother standing in the door. Rees had a moment to take in his sister's changed appearance—her neatly combed hair was caught under a sparkling white cap and she wore a fresh apron over a newly laundered dress—before she burst into angry speech. "Are you here to murder me too?"

Rees stared at her. "Murder you? I'm not the murderer. I was wondering about *you*."

She cast a quick look at the two children, both staring at the adults with wide eyes, and said, "Go outside and play, girls. I need to speak to your uncle for a minute."

Neither adult spoke as the children disappeared through the back door. Caroline crossed the kitchen to shut the back door. Then she turned to face her brother. "How dare you accuse me! You shot Sam, everyone knows it."

"I didn't shoot him," Rees said. "Did you? He would obey you . . ."

"What are you talking about? Why would I kill Sam? Now I have no husband at all."

"Perhaps living as a widow is preferable," Rees said.

"To living with a husband who can't even dress himself?" Caroline regarded her brother, her face set in lines of anger. "And whose fault is that? Yours. You hurt him. Why won't you take responsibility for that?"

"It was an accident," Rees shouted. "I didn't intend to injure Sam. He came at me . . ."

The back door opened and slammed into the wall with a crash. Rees jumped and stared. His sister Phoebe glared at him and Caroline both. "I could hear you yelling all the way to the well," she said, depositing the bucket on the floor.

"You came to Caro's farm?" Rees asked. He'd expected her to reply to his letter or come to his farm.

"My husband and I drove down from Rumford to collect Caroline and the children. We thought they could come home with us." She looked at Rees and he understood what she did not say. Now that Sam was dead she was willing to take in Caroline and her children once again. Phoebe had never liked Sam and had made it clear he was not welcome in her home.

"It's good to see you," Rees said, moving forward to hug her. "Even under these circumstances." Phoebe was taller than Caroline, lanky almost, and she had not escaped the curse of the red hair and freckles. But her hair had darkened with age as her freckles had faded, so she was no longer the homely little girl Rees remembered.

"But she won't come," Phoebe said in annoyance.

"I told you," Caroline said, irritated in her turn. "I don't want to lose the farm."

Phoebe turned a fleeting glance upon Rees and he understood that Caroline didn't mean this farm. She meant *his* farm.

"I already know you spread malicious rumors about my wife," Rees said in distress. "Did you do it so that my farm would come to you when I was hanged as a murderer?" He regretted the accusations as soon as they left his lips.

"Will!" Phoebe gasped.

"I didn't murder my husband," Caroline cried, tears flooding her eyes. "I didn't. You did. You know you did."

Rees could feel the beast rising. Using every ounce of his control, he said through gritted teeth, "I didn't kill him. How can you believe I would? When I hit him, he struck his head by accident." Without realizing it, he approached Caroline until he stood only a scant few inches away. He towered over her, intimidating her with his size and strength.

"Oh, are you going to strike me now?" Caroline cried at him. "Well, go ahead." She placed her hands over her face and sobbed into them, peeking through her fingers. Now he really did want to hit her.

"Weeping will not help you," he said. "Mother and Father are not here." How he hated it when she wept her false tears.

"Stop it, stop it now," Phoebe said, thrusting an arm between them. "I don't know why I always have to be in the middle of you two."

Her interference gave Rees pause and he stepped back. He paced around the kitchen twice, trying to calm himself.

"He's so cruel to me." Caroline wept, turning to her sister for comfort.

"You two have been like dogs over a bone since he was in dresses," Phoebe said with little sympathy. "You've always wanted what he had, Caro. When he went to school, you had to follow him. When he apprenticed to the weaver, you pleaded with Father to allow you to apprentice out as well. Do you remember what Father said?"

"That I was a girl and would marry," Caroline said in a sullen tone. Phoebe nodded.

"Yes. Will is the oldest, and a boy. Of course he had to learn a trade. And of course he inherited the farm."

"Dolly and I bought it," Rees said.

"But it isn't fair," Caroline cried at the same instant.

"Perhaps not. But it is the way of the world. And you'd best make your peace with it," Phoebe said.

"Will injured Sam and left him touched," Caroline said. "Then he refused to care for me and my children. Now my husband is dead, probably at the hands of my brother. Why shouldn't I have the farm?"

Phoebe turned a look of disgust upon her sister and shook her head.

"My wife and I were willing to help you," Rees said angrily. "Willing to offer food and clothing. David has been here several days a week helping Charlie with this farm and has paid his cousin to help with ours. But none of that satisfies you. You want to behave like a lady, ordering Lydia and me around as though we are servants. You are selfish and spoiled and I suspect Mother and Father are turning over in their graves."

Caroline slapped him as hard as she could, the crack of her hand hitting his cheek ringing through the kitchen. "I'm sure Corny Hanson would be interested to know you're still in Dugard," she hissed. Rees lifted his hand to hit her back but Phoebe grasped his arm and pulled with all her weight. Rees shook off Phoebe and stepped back.

"Go ahead and hit me," Caroline screamed. "You brute."

"Stop it," Phoebe shouted, grabbing Caroline's shoulders and shaking her with all her strength. "Stop it. This is just what you used to do as a girl." Caroline pulled away.

"Why are you taking his side?" She screamed and slapped Phoebe in her turn and then began sobbing wildly into her hands.

"I think you should go," Phoebe said to Rees, holding her wrist to her cheek. A scarlet handprint flamed against the white skin. She stepped to the water barrel and dipped a corner of her apron into it so she could apply the cool damp to her face.

Rees acquiesced to his sister and retreated. When he went through the front room he heard Caroline follow him. He turned to see her grab Sam's old musket. Rees laughed mockingly. But as he crossed the yard she ran after him. "I hate you," she screamed from the porch. "I hate you." She fired the musket. The ball went wide, smacking into one of the trees ten feet to the side with a thud. Rees could not believe she'd shot at him and turned to stare. He knew Hanson had set a "shoot on sight" order but hadn't expected the shooter to be his sister. And she would do it again. She'd begun the laborious process of reloading, pushing the ball down the barrel and tipping in black powder after it. Phoebe ran onto the porch and grabbed Caroline's arm. Rees didn't wait to see who proved the victor. Although muskets were notoriously unreliable and his sister was no marksman, Caro might be lucky and hit him next time. He fled into the woods, out of sight. From behind he could hear the screams of his sisters as they fought over the gun.

Reaction set him trembling. He leaned against the tree trunk for support and waited for his heartbeat to slow. After a moment or two, he reeled forward, toward the mare waiting so patiently a ways farther in. But once he reached the horse, Rees could not mount. His shaking legs wouldn't hold him.

What was wrong with Caroline? She could have killed him. Even a poor marksman with a musket could succeed sometimes. Taking hold of the bridle and drawing the mare behind him, Rees staggered into a trembling walk, eager to leave his sister behind.

When he reached the end of the forest and was facing fields, he used the crumbling stone wall as a mounting block and managed to clamber onto the horse's back. He turned her head toward Winthrop's cabin.

The journey took a long time and it was well into afternoon before they approached the property. Rees never pushed the horse into a gait faster than a walk. He couldn't. The shivering that afflicted Rees did not ease for some time and he felt as though he could barely hold the reins. He spent the first half of the trip wondering aloud how Caroline could be so cruel. He knew she could be a murderer; hadn't he just seen proof? But as the anger and the fear gradually dissipated, he began to consider his own part in the argument. He'd allowed himself to be drawn into his sister's clutches yet again. He should know better, should have learned by now how to pull back.

He had not handled the argument well and Phoebe, not for the first time, had received a blow meant for him. If he had kept his temper, perhaps he could have elicited more information. After all, he *was* willing to help his sister. He knew he was responsible for Sam's injury, although Sam bore some of the blame too. But with

Caro, nothing was ever enough. As a boy, his refusal to share his lead soldiers with her had earned him a blow to the head. He still bore a scar where she had hit him under his hairline. Although the blood streaming from his forehead meant that he did not receive a whipping from his father that time, his parents insisted he allow Caroline to play. He'd walked away. And once she saw his display of disinterest, Caroline had hurled the soldiers into the pond. Sometime later he'd gone into the water and recovered all he could find.

He shook off the memory. Now what should he do? The farm was not a lead soldier. Besides, he no longer owned it. It belonged to David, assuming George Potter had done what Rees asked of him. That did not mean Caroline would not still want it, of course.

And had she allowed envy and her rivalry with her brother to consume her to such an extent that she'd murdered Zadoc Ward, Thomas McIntyre, and finally her own husband, Sam Prentiss, all to incriminate Rees? It seemed so.

By the time Rees reached the lane into the cabin, the setting sun had dropped toward the western horizon and light bathed the line of trees with gold. Rees rode into the forest. For the first several yards, sunlight lay in stripes across the vegetation but as he rode into the woods and the trees thickened, the shadows deepened until the ground underneath the forest canopy was almost dark. A shaft of sunlight illuminated the overgrown clearing in which the cabin sat. Rees stopped short. An unfamiliar horse was tied up outside. Farley had found him.

Chapter Thirty

Rees had taken a few steps back into the underbrush when the fact that there was only one horse penetrated. Farley was too much of a coward to confront Rees without help, so almost certainly the visitor was not Farley. Who then could it be? After a moment's indecision, Rees tied his horse to a branch and hurried as quickly as he could through the clearing to the shack. The front door was firmly closed so he could not see in. He stepped over the deteriorating stairs onto the porch, treading as lightly as he could. But the rough board creaked in protest and he froze. No shouts came from within and after a moment he threw the door open.

David and Abigail Bristol sprang apart.

For a few seconds that seemed to stretch on for eternity the three people stared at one another. Then Rees said, "What the . . . ? What are you doing here?" Then he felt a fool for asking such an obvious question.

"I thought you were hiding," David said in his turn. And then he rushed forward and embraced his father. "Dear Lord, I have been so worried."

Rees hugged him back. "It has been an adventure," he said, his glance taking in the old quilt upon the floor and the open basket with the remains of a picnic hastily stuffed inside. "How long have you been meeting here?" he asked, too shocked to sound anything but calm.

David and Abby exchanged a glance. "For a while," David said at last.

"Since you and Lydia were in Salem," Abigail said. Although her cheeks were pink with embarrassment, her gray eyes met Rees's straight on. "My parents refused to allow me to work at the farm without Miss Lydia present."

"I see," Rees said. And he did. Since the young people couldn't see one another openly, they'd found a way to meet on the sly. He recalled all the times where David, supposedly in a faraway field or in the pasture with the cattle, could not be found. "And you two have been meeting here even after Lydia and I returned."

David and Abigail nodded.

"It was private," David said. "We figured no one would come here, not with everyone afraid of Winthrop's ghost." He forced a lopsided grin. "Of course, you aren't afraid."

"No." Rees didn't know whether to be angry that they had been meeting behind his back or relieved that Farley had not found him.

"You look . . ." Abby stopped and tried again. "Are you hungry?" She gestured to the basket. "We have bread and cheese and a jug of cider."

Rees crossed the floor and lowered himself to the quilt. With the food from Marsh still in the saddlebags and now this bounty, he would be set for a few days. "Starving," he admitted. "I don't dare light the fire."

"We've lit a fire on occasion," David said, sitting down as well. "No one noticed."

"I must go," Abigail said, putting on her bonnet. "I've been away longer than I intended already and my parents will be looking for me. Keep the basket," she added, turning her gaze upon Rees. "I'll fetch it later."

David jumped to his feet and walked her outside. Rees heard the low murmur of their voices and guessed they were making plans for the next meeting. He sighed. To him, David at sixteen was still a child. And so was Abby, younger than David by two years, for that matter. But they were clearly ready for marriage. And it had better be soon, lest Rees's first grandchild was born a scant few months after the wedding. The sound of hoofbeats faded into the distance. David returned, his face pink. "Who knows about this?" Rees said. "Anyone?" David shook his head. "Not even Charlie?"

"No. We were afraid Charlie would tell his mother and she would tell the Bristols," David said simply. Rees took a big swallow of cider. He didn't know what to say. Warning David about the possible consequences of these secret and private meetings with Abigail seemed like closing the stable door after the horse had bolted. "I would have asked her parents for permission to marry," David said stiffly, clearly reading condemnation in his father's silence, "but I have nothing to offer her yet."

"What do you mean?" Rees asked.

David shrugged. "No farm."

Rees smiled briefly. "You do have a farm. Since I didn't want to risk losing the farm to Piggy Hanson or my sister, I signed the farm over to you. George Potter has the papers."

"So, that's why I received the letter . . ." David turned his gaze upon his father. "I never answered it."

"I suggest you ride into town first thing tomorrow," Rees said. "As early as possible."

"And what are you doing here?" David asked. "I thought you were well on your way to Zion and Lydia."

"No." Rees shook his head. "I told you—I want to find out who is behind this crusade against me. Although I believe I know now," he said, his voice breaking.

"Who?" David asked.

Rees hesitated. "I want to find some proof first," he said finally. "I want to be sure. I don't want to accuse anyone based on just opinion." He added in a grim tone, "That's been done to me and I know how it feels."

David nodded and for a moment they sat in silence. "Well," he said at last, "I'd best be getting back." He jumped to his feet. "There's still most of the milking to do. And Charlie is likely wondering where I am."

Rees pushed himself upright more slowly. "I hope—I'm sorry if I left you with all the farmwork. And someone trespassing onto the farm and damaging the property, besides."

"That at least hasn't happened," David said. "There's been nothing since you left."

Rees stared at his son in silence. Then he nodded. Of course the vandalism had ceased; the anger had been directed at him. Caroline might not like David very much, but she did not bear him the same hatred she directed at her brother.

"I have to get back," David said again. He paused, his expression awkward. "Look," he said, "don't worry that I'll just take the farm. When everything is sorted, we can switch the ownership back to you."

"We can talk about it, afterward," Rees said. He was beginning to believe he didn't want to live in Dugard anymore, not after all that had happened. He clapped his son on the back. "After all, you're the farmer."

David shook his head, too uncomfortable to meet his father's eyes. "Be safe," David said. "I'll come when I can and bring food." With one final glance at his father, he hastened through the door. Rees followed him to the porch and watched his son lope through the clearing and disappear into the shadows under the trees.

As the sun began to set, Rees lit the kindling in the fireplace and fried slices of the ham given to him by Marsh. More of the bread and butter from the Bristols' basket and the last of the cider made an excellent dinner. By the light of a candle stub, Rees used a little water from the pail to wash the spider, which he then hung on the hook by the fireplace. Tomorrow he must fetch fresh water from the stream; he would do it when he brought the mare back to the cabin in the morning. He pushed the basket into the corner by the chimney and looked around him, trying to see the cottage as a stranger might see it. The old quilt was still on the floor, but Rees would bring that into the other room to sleep on. He did not want to lie down upon the bed with its fusty layer of old bedding. He imagined he could see the imprint of Mr. Winthrop still there.

He picked up the candle and his satchel and carried them into the other room. He used a little more of the water to wash his face and hands. What would Lydia think of him now, he wondered. He was unshaven, and his clothing was torn and dirty. If it were not for the gift of the moccasins, he would be barefoot. He no longer resembled a weaver and farmer; he looked more like one of the homeless men who wandered the roads looking for work.

With a gasp, Rees removed his footwear. The wounds on his

feet were beginning to scab over and heal. He dropped his dirty breeches upon the moccasins and lay down on the quilt. At least he was still free, with a full belly and a roof over his head. And, with any luck, he would soon put an end to this adventure. He just had to find proof that Caroline had been behind this all along. And he would hate to do it, he thought, his eyes moistening. His baby sister: a murderer. Even though he knew she was guilty, he still hoped he was wrong.

He awoke suddenly, disoriented, and sat up. It was late and the sliver of the moon was just visible above the trees. Rees couldn't at first understand what had awakened him. Then he heard a clacking coming from outside. He sat up, breathing hard. The clatter of two sticks being knocked together was growing louder as it approached and now he could hear the faint sound of footsteps in the grass. He jumped up, thrust his feet into the moccasins, and dragged on his breeches. He tossed the quilt onto the bed and turned to the door. Then he heard a footfall on the porch. He would not be able to escape the cottage that way. He turned to the window.

Winthrop had put glass in only two of the house's windows, the two at the front. His wife, when she was alive, had used greased paper, but that was now shredded by the elements. Rees put his feet through the opening and pushed the rest of his body after, dropping onto the ground with his sore feet. He uttered a grunt of pain.

"What's that?" Farley said in a quavery voice. The faint gleam of lantern light sprang into life. Rees went to his knees and ducked his head. For a moment he considered playing ghost and trying to frighten the men away. But if that didn't succeed, the men would know with certainty that he was here. It would be better not to give away his presence.

"I don't hear anything," said a second voice, after a moment of silence. "You're imagining things." But his voice trembled.

"Besides, if Rees was here," said a third in a sour voice, "that rattling of the sticks would've warned him away."

"For all we know," Farley said in an aggrieved tone, "that witchy wife of his flew in on her broom. Everyone knows knocking two sticks together warns away the witches."

"Warns away everything," muttered the third man.

"Doesn't look like anyone's been here since Winthrop died." The second voice spoke again.

"I tell you, Rees is long gone." The third voice belonged to a skeptic.

"But he saw smoke." Farley paused and then added in a lower tone, "If it were up to me, I'd burn the place down."

"Someone's been here. Look, a basket with food still inside."

Rees, crouching underneath the window, longed to rise up and peer through the window. Maybe he would be able to see across the room, through the door, and into the main room beyond. But he didn't dare.

"A basket of food?"

"One of you check the loft," Farley said. "You look around outside."

Rees began to ease carefully away from the window, his moccasin-clad feet making no sound. He planned to move back into the long grass and hide out of sight of the lantern light but a shout from the front of the shack arrested him.

"Constable Farley. I found fresh horse dung. From today, I

think." As Rees moved back toward the wall, footsteps clattered through the house to the front porch.

"He's been here then," Farley said.

"Hey, what are you folks doing here?" David's voice came from a distance. When Rees peered cautiously around the house, he saw a lantern bobbing up the slope from the farm.

"Why are you out so late, boy?" Farley asked. Rees, who saw the glint of yellow light on the metal rifle barrel, knew what David had been doing out so late: patrolling the farm.

"I saw lights up here," David said.

"You know your father is hiding out here?" Farley moved forward. Although more than a head shorter than David, the man managed to appear menacing. "You been feeding him? Protecting him, a murderer."

"We found fresh horse dung," put in Farley's companion.

"No, I . . ." David stopped and started again. "My father didn't take a horse with him. Everyone knows that."

"Maybe you gave him one," Farley said.

David shrugged. "Come down and check. I didn't."

"Maybe we'll just take you in, since you're helping him escape justice." Farley raised a hand as though to strike David, and Rees, without thinking, stood up and ran around the corner of Winthrop's shack. He had to protect his son, even if it meant risking his freedom. Anyway, there were only three men here and one of them was still inside. Maybe David and Rees together could defeat them, even though the other side had the advantage of numbers.

Since both Farley and his deputy had their backs turned, they didn't see Rees. But David did and he held up his hands. "No," he said emphatically. "No." Rees stopped, paused, and then moved back, out of sight around the cabin wall. But he remained poised to run out again if David needed him.

"Don't want to go to jail, eh, boy?"

"Tell us the truth. Is your father here?"

"I have been meeting someone," David admitted, reluctance in every line of his body. "But it's not my father."

"Who then?" demanded Farley.

"It's a girl," guessed the man standing beside him. "Isn't that right? Nice and private up here."

"But it's haunted," Farley said. "Only the most desperate of men would risk angering a ghost."

"Oh, this boy here wouldn't let a ghost get in the way of a little bundling," the deputy said with a coarse chuckle. "Would you, boy?"

The third man appeared in the doorway. Laughing, he said, "There's a quilt on the bed. And look at the initials on this basket. S. B.: Solomon Bristol. Right, David? Didn't one of Mr. Bristol's daughters work for your mother?"

"Stepmother," David said automatically.

"I suppose we'll be hearing the banns called any day." Even Farley laughed.

Rees could see the tension in David's body and guilt swept over him. Although he was not happy that David had been meeting Abby here, the secret was his and he should not have to confess it to protect his father.

"Yes," David admitted. "I've been meeting Abigail Bristol. She rode her horse up here today, just this afternoon. She brought the basket. I don't want her father to know. Please don't tell him. Please." The plea sounded thoroughly genuine to Rees's ears.

"I should tell him," Farley growled. "A man has a right and a duty to safeguard his daughters."

"He'll find out soon enough," said one of the men, nudging David with rough suggestion.

"If you hear from your father," Farley said to David, "I want to know about it. You hear me?"

"Yes," David said.

"Yes, sir."

"Yes, sir." David sounded as though the honorific was choking him.

After a few moments spent collecting their lanterns, and a few more jokes at David's expense, the men began walking away, toward the road. Farley picked up his sticks and the sound of them banging together gradually faded.

Rees came out of the sheltering shadows. "I am so sorry," he said.

"What were you thinking?" David demanded. "They could have seen you and then all of this would have been for nothing."

"I wasn't going to allow anyone to hit you," Rees said.

"I can take care of myself," David said angrily. "Or I could if I didn't have people trying to help me and spoiling everything when they did it."

Rees clamped his tongue between his teeth. He understood that David's anger stemmed not so much from his father putting himself in danger, but from the sudden and very public reveal of his most closely guarded secret.

"I hope Abby will still speak to me after this," David added.

"I'm sorry," Rees repeated.

"Huh." David turned and stomped away, toward home. The clearing settled back to darkness and silence. Rees stood outside until the faint glow of David's lantern disappeared. Then he made his way back into the shack by touch. He might as well try to get a little more sleep before morning, although he doubted he would be able to close his eyes at all.

Chapter Thirty-one

Rees spent a fitful night starting awake at every sound. The sudden thud of footsteps outside sent him rolling under the bed. But when no one entered the cabin and he heard nothing else, he rolled back out. When he stood up and looked out into the gray light of early morning, he saw a herd of deer, cropping grass and standing on their hind legs to reach the low-hanging fruit. No wonder Winthrop's family never seemed to run short of venison. When Rees appeared at the window, the deer took flight, their hooves hitting the ground with the same sound that had awakened him.

Rees lay down but knew he would not sleep again. The world outside was waking up. A catbird mewed in the trees and the mournful cry of a mourning dove sounded close by. Besides, the light was growing stronger. Finally he rose and went into the main room. He used the last of the fresh water for washing and inspected the remaining food in the basket. The bread had hardened and he wasn't sure about the ham. He sniffed it cautiously and wondered if he dared light a fire. But no, he did not; that was why Farley had come to this shack in the first place, despite his fear of Winthrop's ghost. Someone had seen smoke from the chimney. With a sigh, Rees picked up the kettle and headed for the stream. It looked like stale bread and cheese and water for breakfast today.

As he followed the path to the water, the sun peeked over the horizon, sending shafts of golden light through the trees. Despite his fatigue Rees felt his spirits rise. He would unravel this knot, he was certain of it. And everything would return to normal.

The placid old nag seemed content where she was, tied up within reach of the stream and with plenty of forage around her, so Rees left her there. From the shelter of the trees, the cabin still looked abandoned. But Rees paused and examined the dilapidated structure carefully. It was possible Farley or one of his deputies would return, despite David's sacrifice the night before. Rees approached cautiously, slipping in around the back door that hung tilted upon only one hinge. He smelled coffee. His heart began to pound. Then he thought that Farley would certainly not bring coffee. David's lanky form stepped into view.

"I thought you might be missing coffee," he said with a shy smile, pointing to the pot burning a circle into the table.

"You are a saint," Rees said fervently, and covered the final distance to the wooden slab in two bounds. He squeezed David's shoulders, moved that his son should make this effort to please him.

David had also brought two mugs and a pail of fresh, foamy milk, still warm from the cow. He poured out the coffee. It was as black as ink and Rees could smell it, potent and slightly burned, but he was not going to complain. David took a chunk of sugar from his pocket.

"I hope it tastes all right," he said, eyeing the dark beverage uncertainly. "I don't often prepare it. In fact, this is only my second time."

Rees poured out a cup and added milk from the pail, slopping a white puddle on to the table. He used the handle of his pocketknife to hammer off a chunk of sugar and drop it into the coffee. He took a careful sip, but the coffee had already begun to cool. Even under the sweetness of the sugar, he could taste a faint scorched flavor. David poured himself a cup and added milk and a hefty chunk of sugar but he pulled a face when he sipped it. "How can you drink this stuff?" he asked. Rees grinned and took another healthy swallow. After several days without coffee, drinking it again felt like greeting an old friend.

"When you get to my advanced age, this beverage will taste like nectar of the gods."

David snorted and for a moment they drank their coffee in a companionable silence. "Did you mean what you said yesterday? About the farm?" David asked. Rees looked at his son. He couldn't meet his father's eyes but stared at the table, his lean, tanned fingers tapping nervously at the cup.

"I did. Why?" An unwelcome suspicion crossed Rees's mind. "Abby isn't with child, is she?"

David's face flamed with color and he shook his head vehemently. "No. But I know people will believe so." He shot his father an angry look. "And some will quiz her with nasty jests."

"They will anyway, even if you and she are planning to marry," Rees said with regret. People always wanted to believe the worst.

"Perhaps. But once we're wed, that will end. I hope so, at least. I don't want her to feel ashamed." He paused and then added in a rush, "I don't care about the farm for myself. But I want to have something to offer."

"I meant it. Mr. Potter should have the papers waiting and you need to sign them." Rees paused and then continued. "Even if I didn't, I'd support a marriage between you and Abby. And you could still live at the farm."

"Don't you worry," David said, raising his gray eyes to his father's blue. "You and Lydia and all the kids will always have a home here."

The sight of his first wife's eyes in David's face sent a pang through Rees. What would Dolly think of everything that was happening? He wondered what her brothers and sisters, most of whom still lived in Dugard, believed. They had kept themselves away from him. But at least they weren't among those calling for his hanging.

Rees sighed. What would he and Lydia do? Move to the weaver's cottage? With all those kids? Abby would want her own kitchen and home, and she should have it. But so should Lydia.

"Do you know who is doing this?" David asked, breaking into Rees's thoughts.

"Not exactly."

"I think you should look at Aunt Caroline." David flushed when his father looked at him but did not lower his eyes.

"I have," Rees said carefully. He didn't want to say too much to David and worsen an already terrible relationship with his aunt, just in case Rees was wrong about her guilt. "I just can't imagine her climbing to the top of Bald Knob to shoot Zadoc Ward. And anyway, she's no marksman. You know that." He thought of Caroline firing at him and shivered. She might not be a marksman, but she'd tried to shoot Rees anyway.

"But Uncle Sam was," David said, interrupting Rees's thoughts. "What if she told him to do it and he did and then she killed him later?"

Rees stared at his son and then nodded slowly. If Caroline and Sam had been working together, well, that would explain how they'd managed to tie McIntyre to the beams in his mill. Or if Caroline and Farley had been working together. But would Farley kill the miller just on Caroline's command? "Mac was hit in the head by something, probably a shovel," Rees said aloud. "And I already know from Elijah that Sam couldn't have done it. Elijah drove Sam home." He paused, recalling with a shudder the sound of the bullet hitting the tree next to him. "I don't want to think of Caroline smacking someone in the head with a shovel, but I know she has the passion to kill."

"Mr. McIntyre wouldn't have been expecting a woman to hurt him," David said in a rush. "And Uncle Sam, well, he would need someone to tell him what to do, wouldn't he?"

Rees shook his head, not contradicting David but expressing his unwillingness to accuse his sister. Rees would rather believe Sam or Farley—anyone else—was the captain of this plot and Caroline the cat's-paw. "Maybe the murderer is someone I haven't thought of at all," Rees said in a final gasp of hope.

"Maybe," David said, avoiding his father's eyes. "I have to go. I haven't finished the milking yet." He pushed his half-empty cup of coffee across the scarred table. "Today I'm helping Charlie at his farm." He added, only half-jokingly, "I hope Aunt Caroline doesn't try to kill me."

"Of course she won't," Rees said. But the protest sounded weak to his ears. Caroline had shot at him. Would she hesitate to shoot David? Probably not, if she were angry. "Be careful." The words were wrung from him. David nodded solemnly and went out through the front door.

Rees drank the remainder of David's coffee, although it was rapidly cooling, and moved the coffeepot to the hearth. Then he tried to decide what to do. In other circumstances, he might return to some of the people of interest in the investigation and ask further questions. But this time he was afraid to do so. He didn't dare drive to Dugard and chance revealing himself. That was likely to bring Farley after him—if someone else didn't shoot Rees first. He risked being shot even speaking to Caroline. So what could he do? Already the walls of this little cabin were beginning to close in.

After a moment, Rees picked up the bucket. But he didn't have any of his tools or leather straps with which to repair it, and he put it aside again. He went outside to the back and sat on the top step. From here, all he could see was the orchard, rows and rows of apple trees. Behind them was the sky, the clouds boiling up over the red of sunrise, so it looked as though the sky was on fire. He thought it might rain today. He hoped so; the fields needed it.

Realizing his thoughts were drifting, Rees pulled them back to the problem at hand. Oh, how he missed his loom! Weaving always made it easier for him to think.

As Rees considered all those who might be involved, he found it painful to realize how many people disliked him enough to want to do him harm. Why, his own sister was probably involved. Rees didn't want to believe she hated him that much but he knew that she could be so utterly consumed with anger that she just reacted, damn the consequences. Yet *she* could not have shot Ward, that much was certain. The climb up Bald Knob would be impossible for a woman in skirts and she was inexperienced with guns. Would Sam take this kind of direction from his wife? And, if the command did not slip out of his disordered brain, would he actually shoot another man without hesitation or remorse? Rees nodded. The old Sam certainly would have and he had the experience with a rifle to accomplish it. Would Farley? Rees slowly shook his head. He was less convinced of Farley's ability than of Sam's.

Rees turned his attention to the second murder. Caroline would have needed help, but if she'd had it? Well then, that could explain the manner of Mac's death. Rees pinched the bridge of his nose and tried to will away the burning in his eyes. What had Caroline done? But Elijah had claimed he'd driven Sam home. Sworn, in fact, that he'd seen Sam go through the farm gate. So, unless he was lying, Sam could not be guilty. Rees shook his head and scattered his thoughts. While the boy might have wanted to murder his father—the relationships between fathers and sons could be difficult—the possibility that Elijah murdered two other men was too much for Rees to swallow.

He considered the location of Sam's farm. There was no direct road from it to the mill; the only path was down to West Road and then north onto Mill Street. Duck Swamp occupied the land between, so-called because it flooded in the spring and hosted flocks of migrating fowl. Now, in the summer, the soil was damp but the vast pond had shrunk to scattered puddles. Maybe Sam could have crossed it on foot. Since he had been at the mill earlier, he would have known that the miller would be working late. But while Rees could visualize Sam tramping through the mud to reach the mill, imagining his dainty sister crossing the swamp was difficult. And there would have been no alternative to walking, not with the buggy, the horses, and the mules all sold.

Rees jumped to his feet and paced around the dusty yard. If Caroline was the architect of the plan, Rees would have to believe his sister capable of laying out a complicated plot, with Ward's death only the first scene. Could she have done it? Unconsciously he shook his head. He didn't think so. As children, when they sneaked into Winthrop's orchards in the late fall to steal the last of the apples, Caroline would stockpile an enormous hoard to use against her brother and then wait for him to approach. Rees's strategy was different. He would fill his pockets and then slip up behind her. The apple would hit with a satisfying smack and she would start to cry. Usually one of his parents would stop the game then, exclaiming over the round bruise forming on Caroline's arm and scolding their son. Rees did not think Caro had changed so much. But Sam, Sam had had that malevolent cunning. Maybe Rees had been right all along and Sam was merely pretending to be injured.

But that would mean Caroline had shot and killed her husband and partner, knowing her brother would be accused.

Shaking his head, Rees sat back down again upon the dusty step. All he had was supposition and guesswork. Concentrate on what was real, he told himself. That was the only way he would discover the truth.

So, the deaths of Zadoc Ward, Thomas McIntyre, and Sam Prentiss—no doubt at all they were murders. The accusations against Lydia, while untrue, had certainly occurred. Someone had burned her beehives and destroyed Rees's loom, both events arguing for someone familiar with Rees's farm.

Rees jumped to his feet. He couldn't stay here, trapped at this shack. Right now he wished he had left this mystery alone, given the farm to David, and moved on with Lydia, abandoning Dugard forever. But he was truly in the center of the whirlwind now.

He began walking south, toward the wall that separated the

Winthrop farm from Rees's own. He had to risk visiting David to borrow paper and pencil. Rees hoped to sketch out a timeline and write down everything that had happened. Maybe then, after he saw the events of the last few weeks laid out on paper, he could order his thoughts and determine the killer. Or killers.

Chapter Thirty-two

Rees began walking through the orchard. Mr. Winthrop would be horrified by the lack of care for his trees, evident in the weeds trailing up the trunks and the damage left by deer. But Rees thought the apple harvest would be a good one this year; the branches were heavy with reddening globes. The orchard could be brought back, with time and attention.

From this elevation, Rees's farmhouse was clearly visible through the thicket of trees and underbrush. He saw a familiar buggy tied up in front and was almost certain that it and the two brown cobs pulling it belonged to the Bristols. Farley had lost no time in revealing David's secret to Abigail's parents. Rees was so curious about what was being said that he almost walked down despite the risk. But this was David's problem to resolve. Besides, Rees couldn't know how the Bristols felt about him. Mary Martha had assured him that they did not believe in the charge of witchcraft leveled at Lydia. Was that true? Rees couldn't know. But there was also the accusation of murder laid against Rees himself. Until he could prove his innocence, he must keep away from everyone.

He knew David would be trying to be a good host; Rees could smell burning wood and he saw the faint thread of smoke floating out of the chimney and sifting through the air in a gossamer thread. David had lit a small fire and was probably offering tea or coffee. Rees could not imagine what else David would have to offer, without Lydia to bake for him.

Suddenly, something Farley had said popped into Rees's mind. He stared transfixed at the faint smoky trail, barely noticeable against the blue sky. All the facts suddenly lined up in his mind. Everything made sense. He no longer needed paper, he knew exactly what had happened and could not deny it. "Oh no," Rees said, the agony of betrayal sweeping over him. "Oh Lord, no." He had to talk to Caroline, in the presence of witnesses so she could not repudiate the truth.

Moving with sudden purpose, Rees walked back to the place where Sam's body had been discovered. By the time he reached the edge of the forest he regretted his impulsive decision. The cuts and scrapes on his feet were beginning to sting. But he plowed on, determined to finally reach the end of what had been a very emotionally charged investigation.

The grass and vegetation had started growing up, hiding the broken stems and the dark stain left by Sam's blood. Now this hollow seemed almost identical to the meadow around it. In another week no one would ever know anything had happened here.

Rees walked in a circle around the area. It had been carefully chosen—the final piece in a plan to destroy him. Struggling to understand the depth of anger and hatred behind the scheme, Rees reconstructed the steps of the plan. It had all been so easy.

Shaking his head with reluctant belief, he began limping back to Winthrop's shack. Rees stuck to the shelter of the brush at forest's edge. Farley's arrival the previous night had scared him. Although he doubted the new constable and his deputies had returned, it was possible. And Rees was too close to the resolution to take any risks. But when he inspected the shack from the screen of trees, the cabin looked exactly the same. By now his feet were throbbing. He should have taken the old mare. The long walk had rubbed open some of the scabs on his feet. Groaning, he crossed the dilapidated porch to his temporary refuge. Everything was just as he'd left it. He drank down the cold coffee with the last of the milk and ate the remainder of the cheese. He tried not to think of Caroline.

As dusk set in, a lantern came bobbing up through the trees. Rees withdrew to the far side of the cabin, watching from around the corner, but as he suspected, the light belonged to David. Rees moved out in front and waited, slapping at the mosquitoes swarming around him.

David carried another basket, a smaller one this time, and he walked as though he was very tired. He nodded at his father but didn't speak as he stepped over the rotting porch and went into the cabin.

The lantern made a homey golden glow upon the table. "I brought some candles for you," David said, gesturing to the basket. Rees moved the napkin and peered inside. Most of them were stubs, leftovers of Lydia's fine beeswax tapers. He missed her suddenly with a physical pain. What was she doing now? How was she feeling? Had the baby come? It would be early but that happened sometimes. His eyes began to burn and he hastily thrust away his emotional thoughts.

He knew he would blame Caroline all his days for putting Lydia in danger and forcing him to send her away. David sat in the chair, which creaked at the sudden weight, and put his head in his hands. "The Bristols came to see me," he said.

"I know. I saw the buggy." Rees paused, and sat down across the table. He looked into the basket. Fresh bread, white bread too, not the injun loaf Lydia usually made. A quarter of a chicken pie and another quarter of cherry. Rees looked up at David in astonishment. "Where did you get this food?"

"I went into town this morning, right after I finished milking. When I finished with Mr. Potter, I stopped at the Contented Rooster. Mrs. Anderson asked after you. She, at least, believes you're innocent," David said.

"You didn't tell her where I'm staying?" Rees sounded panicky. He didn't want to put Susannah into danger.

"No." David shook his head. "She didn't ask. But she gave me the food and said if I saw you I was to wish you well."

Rees thought now that he'd underestimated her; she would not have turned her back on him as George Potter had.

"I signed those papers," David said. He took off his hat and laid it on the table. As Rees tore off a hunk of bread and stuffed it into his mouth, the boy continued. "Mr. Potter told me the farm officially belongs to me. And a good thing, I daresay. Mr. and Mrs. Bristol were angry." His tone of voice told Rees that David was minimizing their reaction.

"Was Abby there?"

"Yes. She too insisted that nothing had happened." David stumbled over his words. Rees couldn't see his son's face clearly in the gathering gloom but guessed David was blushing. "But they didn't believe her either. I told them I owned the farm and that I could and would marry her. I showed them a copy of the paper Mr. Potter gave me. The only concession I managed to wring from them was the date of the wedding. They wanted us to marry right away, by September at the latest. I asked them to wait until early November. All the harvest will be in by then. And I hope this difficulty of yours will be over."

"Did they agree?" Rees's voice sounded rusty. His son would be only sixteen in November, young to wed. And Abigail was barely fourteen, a mere child in Rees's eyes.

"Finally. They were reluctant. They believe by then Abby will show . . ."

Rees nodded, too embarrassed to speak. "So we, Abby and I, will be married at their farm by a Quaker minister. We don't know what time as yet. There are always chores to be done and the wedding must be fit in around them." The excitement in his voice flattened out. For a moment both men were silent. Rees felt events were moving much too quickly. Finally David spoke again. "Anyway," he continued, "I thought Abby could move into the cottage with me. It is big enough for two. And you have all the children, and Lydia will have had her baby by then."

And what happens when you and Abby begin having babies, Rees wondered. *Where will Lydia and I live then?* But instead of asking that question, he tried to force some excitement into his voice. "I'll be a grandfather someday." He shivered involuntarily.

David looked at his father and said in a much quieter voice, "I know this isn't what you wanted."

Rees managed to smile although his lips felt stiff and unnatural on his face. "I knew this day would come. Everything is changing." He couldn't help thinking that he and Lydia might not even live in Dugard much longer—he did not think he would ever be able to forget what had happened here or forgive those who had been involved. "Does Charlie know? About you and Abby I mean."

David nodded. "He heard it in town. People are talking." He stopped. Rees didn't know what to say. "He teased me about it," David added in a flat voice. Rees understood that Charlie had not been kind. "I'm supposed to help him tomorrow, but I really don't want to. He treats me like a joke."

"Could you tell him that you suspect me of staying here at night? That I usually arrive just before dusk."

"I can't do that," David said in horror. "He'll tell Aunt Caroline. You know he will. She'll probably come over."

"I know," Rees said. "I'm counting on that, in fact."

"She might try to shoot you again," David said. "And she'll probably alert Constable Farley."

Rees hadn't thought of that. Caroline might also inform Piggy Hanson; in fact, Rees would be surprised if she didn't. He rubbed his forefinger down his nose, thinking. "Well, that may not be a bad thing. More witnesses." He forced a grin. "But I suspect she will not. Especially not if she's planning to shoot me."

"I won't do it," David said. "I won't. Not if it means you're likely to be shot and killed."

"It's the only way to clear not only my name but Lydia's," Rees said, leaning forward and clasping his son's hand. "Please."

"No." David wrenched free of his father's grasp. "I want to know you're still alive, even if you're on the run."

Rees was silent a moment. David's fear was justified. And Rees didn't really want to die. "Very well. Take my rifle and hide in the underbrush; I'll show you where. Anyone lifts a gun to me, shoot him. Can you do that?"

David hesitated. Rees had not realized how late it had grown. The sun was almost below the horizon and shadows wreathed the inside of the cabin in darkness. David's face was now just a white blur. Very white, and Rees knew his son was scared.

"I can do it," David said at last, his voice shaking.

"Good. Let's go outside and I'll show you where to hide."

Chapter Thirty-three

The next morning Rees left at daybreak for his sister's farm. He needed to see Caroline at the Winthrop shack this evening and was determined to ensure she arrived. It was early enough that few would be on the roads and he thought he would escape notice. He'd spent an anxious night reviewing his plans and trying to decide how much to leave to chance. Very little—Rees was not the kind of man who assumed everything would proceed as planned. Although Farley and Magistrate Hanson might still believe Lydia was a witch and Rees was guilty of three murders, he wanted to make sure he told his sister that he knew the truth. He might have to run for his life afterward, but in the end, it was all about the truth.

Rees again elected to slip up to his sister's farm from the back. When he could see the back of the barn he tied the mare to a branch and continued on alone. Pausing in the thick undergrowth, he examined the yard before him. A few chickens scratched in the dust but he saw no other movement.

After several seconds of study, Rees crept through the brush until he was as near the house as he could be. Charlie had done his best with the fields. There were two of corn and at least one of winter rye. Someone, probably Charlie, had made some effort with the kitchen garden as well. It looked as though he'd replanted the squash and put in second plantings of cabbage and beets.

Rees made his way into the cornfield and around to the back of the house, where he knelt among the stalks and waited. Finally, Phoebe came down the back steps with an egg basket over her arm. *Collecting eggs from* my *chickens,* Rees thought sourly. Although he saw no one else, he scuttled forward at a crouch. Phoebe went first into the chicken house. When she returned outside, she began searching the yard, looking under a wagon as well as in the wagon bed, and moving closer and closer to Rees with each pass.

"Phoebe," he hissed, when she came within earshot. She jumped, stifling a little scream. Rees rose so she could see his face and then crouched down once again.

"What in heaven's name are you doing here, Will?" she whispered, crossing to stand by the wall of green. "If Caro sees you she might shoot at you again."

"This is important," Rees replied. "Can you get Caroline to the Winthrop cottage tonight? About six?"

"Winthrop?" She looked at him, her brows drawn together in puzzlement.

"Yes. You remember, he owned the farm next to us. Had the big orchard."

"Oh yes. I thought he'd died."

"He did. He's been dead a few years at least. But that's not important. Tell Caro I sleep there. Tell her anything you want, but get her there. This is really important, Phoebe."

"Why? Why is it so important?"

"Do you think I'm guilty of murder?" Rees asked. His sister

did not respond. "If you had to say which of us, either me or Caro, was a murderer, which would you pick?"

He watched guilt sweep across her face. "Caro," she whispered.

"I want Caroline to hear me tell her the truth. Then I'll leave Dugard, probably forever."

Phoebe shifted the egg basket from one arm to another. "If you're going to risk your life, why don't you just walk inside and tell her what you want her to know?"

"Because I want it on my terms. And somewhere I can control the meeting. I'd like to increase my chances of living beyond today, if at all possible," Rees said. "Please, Feeb."

She sighed. "All my life I've been put between the two of you. All my life. And I'm tired of it." Rees couldn't think of anything to say so he said nothing. "All right, Will. I'll have her there at about six." Sudden tears filled her eyes and she wiped them away with the back of her hand. "You better not be accusing Caro of the murders. And I don't want to see either of you end up dead. I'd never forgive you, Will."

"Don't forget. And don't change your mind," Rees said sternly. He backed away, still at a crouch, and moved farther into the shelter of the corn. As he retreated he heard Caroline's voice.

"Who were you talking to, Phoebe?"

"No one."

"I thought I heard a man."

"No." Her voice took on a snap. "Let me finish collecting these eggs or you and the girls won't have any breakfast."

By four-thirty Rees was in position. He knew he was too early, that no one would arrive before chores were done, while it was still daylight. But he didn't want to be caught unawares either. He burrowed farther back inside the screen of shrubs and bracken and a long stick jabbed him. He carefully pushed it aside and nestled his back against the tree trunk. His butt rested upon a variety of stones, but most were flattish and some were even softened by a mixture of dirt and vegetation.

He thought he was too nervous to relax, but he settled in so completely that he fell into a doze, awakening only at the sound of someone moving furtively through the overgrown clearing. Rees came to alertness, jerking into position so abruptly he knocked into a branch. To Rees's ears, it sounded as loud as a gunshot. The whisper of movement halted and Rees tensed. He couldn't see his visitor, who was out of sight behind the shack. After a moment the discreet passage resumed. Rees might not have noticed it if he had not been listening for it.

The back step creaked. Rees hoped the scene he'd set so artfully was appreciated. The coffeepot, left in the middle of the table, with a cup and wooden plate in front of it as though he might return at any minute.

Rees's heart began to pound. He saw movement through the glass window at the front but the form was not identifiable. The murderer would walk out of the cabin any second. Any second. He held his breath. But no one appeared. What had happened? Rees was so impatient he almost jumped to his feet and ran to the cabin. He took a few steps forward, his feet crackling over the dried leaves.

Charlie stepped out onto the front porch.

Although Rees had expected it, he involuntarily closed his eyes in a spasm of regret. He'd realized that the boy had as much reason to hate him as Caroline and Sam. And Charlie, with his unlimited access to his uncle's farm and none of the disadvantages of either parent, could have most easily accomplished all three murders. Rees had kept hoping he was wrong. Now he couldn't deny it anymore. Charlie was here, and he held his father's pistol casually in his hand. Rees had planned for the pistol. All pistols contained only one shot, and he would dive for the ground as soon as Charlie cocked the gun. Rees prayed he was fast enough.

Rees hoped David was in position. The boy must be reeling with shock. Rees had known the possibility and he was still incredulous.

He went to his knees and slowly backed deeper into the woods. Through the screen of leaves and branches Rees saw Charlie disappear into the shack. Rees did not stand up until he was well hidden inside the shelter of the trees.

He began moving forward, running from trunk to trunk. Every now and then he would stop and peer cautiously around the trees as though he did not know Charlie was inside. Rees paused on the very edge of the clearing and waited. He realized he had not thought this step through sufficiently. What if Charlie did not act until his uncle stepped out of the trees? Yet if Rees did not exit the forest, wouldn't Charlie suspect this was a trap? Caught by indecision, Rees hesitated.

Charlie stepped out onto the cabin porch. "Come out, Uncle Will," he said, his right hand held behind his back. "It's only me."

Heart pounding, Rees looked around the tree trunk. "What are you doing here?" He tried to speak in an innocent and unsuspecting voice, but to his own ears he sounded false. "How did you know I was staying in the cabin? Did David tell you?"

"Yes. I thought I would come and see if you needed anything." Charlie sounded completely natural, and if Rees had not already seen the pistol he would have trusted his nephew without hesitation. Trembling, he stepped away from the tree.

"I asked David to tell no one," he lied.

"David and I tell each other everything," Charlie said. "Why don't we go inside?"

Rees pretended to consider it. He took one step forward. As he suspected and hoped, Charlie couldn't wait. The pistol came out of hiding, the metal barrel gleaming in the long brassy rays of the western sun. "Charlie," he gasped.

"You were cleverer than I thought you would be," Charlie said.

Rees heard a quickly muffled scream and wondered if Phoebe had managed to bring Caroline here as promised.

"Before you shoot me," Rees said, "tell me why. You owe me that much."

"How can you even ask?" Charlie shouted.

"Was it for the farm?"

"Your farm? No. That's what my mother wants. I don't care about this farm. It belongs to David and I have my own farm."

"Then why? Was this for your father? I don't understand."

"You are so stupid," Charlie said.

"Did you kill Zadoc Ward and Thomas McIntyre? And Sam, your own father?" Rees's voice broke. "Why kill them if it's me you wanted?"

Charlie laughed, a hoarse, ragged sound that shivered down Rees's spine. "You really don't understand? My father always said you were a fool."

"So, explain it to me." Rees had tried to ensure Caroline's presence, but he no longer cared about that. He wanted to understand Charlie. "Did you kill Zadoc Ward?" Then, as he looked at the boy standing twenty feet from him and smiling, Rees's thoughts leaped to understanding. "No. You didn't. You aren't a sharp-shooter. Your father killed Ward."

Charlie nodded. "This was all my father's plan. He got tired of Ward's bullying and arranged to meet him on Little Knob. Told him some story. Ward never suspected a thing."

The ice in Rees's stomach spread out to fill his body with cold. He could understand murder committed in the heat of anger—understand although not condone. But this cold-blooded taking of another's life—that Rees could not comprehend. "So you helped him murder Tom McIntyre?"

"No. Mr. McIntyre was already dead when I arrived." The pistol in Charlie's hands began shaking. "Mr. McIntyre was good to us but my father thought his death would inflame public opinion against you and your wife. And it did." Rees, his gaze fixed on the trembling weapon, made as if to approach, but Charlie brought the gun up.

"Stop. I will shoot you."

Rees froze but continued talking in a soft voice. "When Elijah McIntyre let Sam off at your farm, he walked back to the mill by way of Duck Swamp?"

Charlie nodded. "I followed as soon as I finished my chores. By the time I arrived Mr. McIntyre was lying on the floor." His voice began to tremble and he stopped.

"You helped your father tie the miller to the post?"

Charlie nodded. "And I spread around Miss Lydia's candles . . ." His words trailed off. Rees stared into the ashen face, the horror of that experience visible in the pinching around the boy's eyes. "It was terrible. But my father said . . ."

"It was necessary." Rees supplied the rest of the sentence. Charlie nodded.

"Then you shot your father?"

Tears fell from Charlie's eyes. He wiped his sleeve across his face. "I had to. We knew you suspected him. Anyway, what kind of life would he have? You saw him. The only thing he had left was his hatred of you."

"You planned this elaborate charade to set me up for murder and my wife for witchcraft," Rees said. He was struggling to keep his tone calm.

"My father thought of it in the beginning. He had his lucid moments, although they were becoming fewer and fewer. But I helped, and I picked up where he left off." Was that pride Rees heard in the boy's voice?

"I daresay you were the one who set fire to my wife's beehives and opened the door to the dairy? Did you break my loom?" Rees could not prevent his anger from leaking into his questions.

Charlie nodded. "That part was fun. All of you running around scared."

Rees recalled his wife's grief at the destruction of the hives and felt like leaping across the yard and punching the boy. He controlled himself with an effort.

"My father wanted to destroy you. And I wanted to help; you stole my father from me. My mother gave me the idea for accusing Miss Lydia of witchcraft. A lot of people were willing to believe it because of that strange faith she belonged to. And your arrogance and the number of people who already dislike you made it easy to persuade them you were guilty of murder."

"You almost succeeded," Rees said. His voice was thin with

hurt. He could not understand this betrayal. He had tried to help Caroline and her children. Tried to be a good brother and a good man. What had he done that was so terrible his sister and her family hated him?

"I did succeed," Charlie said, raising the pistol and sighting along the barrel. "I'll tell that idiot Farley I found you and shot you. The magistrate is offering a reward. Did you know that? So, not only will I finish my father's work, but I will earn the reward at the same time."

Rees tensed, preparing to throw himself down to the ground. If Rees timed his dive correctly, Charlie would miss. He heard the sharp click as the pistol was cocked.

"Charlie. Don't." Caroline hurled herself through the shrubbery, wrenching her arm free of Phoebe's grasp. "Please."

Charlie jerked. "What are you doing here?" he cried.

At the same moment a rifle shot cracked, Charlie spun around and dropped to the ground with blood pouring from his shoulder. David stood up, his face so contorted with sobbing he was almost unrecognizable.

Caroline shrieked and ran for her son. She flung herself to the ground beside him. "Oh, Charlie."

Rees turned to David and held out an arm. He didn't think he could run, not even for David. Rees's legs were trembling so, he wasn't sure they would hold him up. David staggered to his father's side and clung to him.

Then Farley said from behind Rees, "I'll have to take the boy in."

"What are you doing here?" Rees asked, turning to look at the constable and the two men behind him. Rees couldn't muster the energy to be shocked.

"I heard a rumor." Farley glanced at Rees and then quickly away. "You know how it is in Dugard. All you have to do to hear everything is lean into the wind."

"My sister told you, didn't she?" Rees said. He looked over at Caroline, kneeling beside Charlie. Although the boy's face was white with pain, he was awake. Caroline turned a look of hatred upon Rees.

"This is your fault," she said.

"I wouldn't have believed this if I didn't see it with my own eyes," Farley said. "He'll hang, I don't doubt." Farley regarded Rees for several seconds. "And you, you're so sharp you're gonna cut yourself one day. I just hope I'm there to see it."

"Magistrate Hanson won't be pleased," said one of Farley's companions. Rees recognized the voice from their visit to Winthrop's shack.

"Ahh, he won't care," Farley replied. "He's gettin' ready to go on circuit anyway."

"You'll release Caldwell now, I hope," Rees said.

"You know this doesn't prove nothin' about your wife," Farley said, leaning forward so Rees could smell the constable's fetid breath. "She's still a witch in my book."

He turned and made his way through the tall grass, "You'll live," he said, looking down at Charlie. "The doctor will patch you up. Come on." He helped the boy rise, pulling him none too gently to his feet. Charlie groaned.

"I told him almost everything," David said, his voice muffled by the arm he swiped across his face. "He was as close as a brother."

Rees turned and tugged his son to his chest. "You should know he loves you. That's partly how I guessed he was involved. Neither Sam nor Caro would have spared you, but Charlie did. Nothing happened, no petty destruction, no thefts, nothing, when you were alone at the farm. He couldn't bear to harm you."

"So how did you know?"

"You told Charlie I'd gone off with Caldwell, didn't you?" Rees asked gently. David's face crumpled as though he would begin crying once again.

"I didn't even suspect . . ."

"I wondered how Farley and his men were always just one step behind. Of course Charlie was telling them. He didn't know I was here, in the cabin, but he told them he saw smoke from the chimney. Only someone on my farm could see that, so it had to be either you or Charlie. That's when I understood everything."

Rees looked across the field at his sisters. Caroline was sobbing wildly, her face in her hands. The malice had been hers but she was innocent of everything else. And she'd lost both her husband and son to her angry resentment. It was a heavy price.

Rees's feet turned toward her of their own accord. She would always be his baby sister. He walked across the field and stretched out his arms to hold her. To comfort her. But she flinched away and with one last furious glare at her brother, she ran after Farley and her son. Rees hoped one day she would forgive him.

Epilogue

I wish you would come with me," Rees said, looking up at his son standing on the porch above him. "You'll be safe at Zion." Two days had passed since Charlie had admitted his part in the murders. Although Rees had wanted to leave immediately for the Shaker community—and his wife and other children—Farley and Piggy Hanson had insisted on keeping Rees in Dugard and asking questions. He suspected the two men did not want to believe in either his or Lydia's innocence, despite Charlie's confession. At least the two days had enabled Rees to clean up and pack some food before setting off.

"I don't want to leave the farm," David said, his gaze going to the barn across the drive and the fields behind it. "I'll be fine. Some of Mother's kin have offered to help me." They had said the same things to each other several times these past few days. But they hadn't spoken about Charlie.

"But Farley . . ." Rees stopped. What if Farley went after David?

"He's not interested in me," David said.

Rees sighed. "I hope not. I'll return in a week or two," he said. David turned his gaze to his father.

"Checking up on me?" he asked with a faint smile. Rees was

heartened to see this first sign of David's recovery from Charlie's betrayal.

"Yes," Rees said, with an answering grin. "I'd stay, but . . ."

"Of course," David said quickly. "Lydia may have had the baby." Rees nodded.

"You belong here," Rees said. Although he'd been born in Dugard and lived here most of his life, he would never be as much a part of the community as David was already.

"Say hello to Squeaker for me," David said. "Tell him I miss him. And don't forget my wedding."

"We will all be here," Rees promised. "You'll talk to Simon yourself." He stared at his son. There was so much Rees wanted to say, but he didn't know how to begin. "I know I was not here as often as I should have been," he said. "I regret that. I will for the rest of my life. But you have become a man any father would be proud of."

David put his hands in his pockets and took them out again. "You better let me know whether I have a brother or sister," he said. Then he came running down the porch steps and into Rees's embrace.

"I understand better now," David said, his voice muffled against Rees's shoulder. "About why you left." David was almost as tall as his father, a man grown. "You'll always have a home here." Rees hugged David to him. He had never thought he would see this day; David was not only his son but also his friend.

"I'll return," Rees said. Although he doubted he would ever live in Dugard again, his bond with David would always draw him back for visits. "I may not have been a good father," he said, his voice trembling as he fought to control his emotions, "but I love you." David squeezed his father hard and then stepped back.

"You'd better get going," he said, wiping his eyes with the backs of his hands. "You've got a long trip as it is."

Rees nodded and inhaled a deep, shaky breath. Now that he knew he would meet Lydia and his children in just a few days, the desire to see them had become too urgent to ignore. "I'll see you soon," he promised as he climbed into his wagon. With one last look at David, Rees drove down the drive. His heart was already lifting at the thought of seeing Lydia and his other children again. Had Lydia had the baby yet? He hoped not. He wanted to be there.

Author's Note

The belief in witches and witchcraft has a long history. The motivations behind accusations are many, from true belief, to hatred of women, to a desire for gain. Witchcraft, which is probably (and I think most likely) the remnants of ancient religions that worship the feminine, earthly, and masculine aspects of God, was considered anti-Christian heresy. In 1200 Pope Gregory IX authorized the killing of witches. In 1498 Pope Innocent VIII issued a declaration confirming the existence of witches and inquisition increased. Full-fledged killing of witches truly began in the 1500s and 1600s. Thousands, mainly women, were burned at the stake.

Salem is the name associated with witch hunts in the colonies. As most people know, the outbreak began in 1692 and by its end nineteen people—mainly women—as well as two dogs had been hanged, and one eighty-year-old man pressed to death with stones. (Witches were hanged, not burned, in the New World.) One hundred and fifty more were accused. Although reparations to the families were paid out beginning in the early 1700s, the bitterness broke up the community. PTSD was not a term coined at that time but I suspect the survivors lived it. The legacy of those times affected everyone. Families of those accused moved to a new village they called Salem Neck. Many of those involved changed their names. Nathaniel Hawthorne, for example, a descendant of one of the hanging judges, added the *w* to his name to distance himself from the witch trials.

Although the end of the outbreak in Salem seemed like the end of the hysteria, belief in witchcraft continued. As described in this book, Ann Lee, the spiritual heart of the Shakers, was herself accused of "blasphemy," but that accusation took place in New York State one hundred years later, and she was released.

Accusations of witchcraft continued into the 1800s. In West Nyack, New York State, herbalist Jane (Naut) Kannif, a widow of a Scottish physician, was accused of practicing witchcraft. At a gristmill, Naut was weighed against a large brass-bound Dutch Bible on the large flour balance. Jane outweighed the Bible, was judged innocent, and set free.

But accusations of witchcraft and the murders of the women so suspected continue worldwide.

About the Author

ELEANOR KUHNS won the 2011 Minotaur Books/Mystery Writers of America First Crime Novel Competition. She lives in New York, received her master's in library science from Columbia University, and is currently the assistant director at the Goshen Public Library in Orange County, New York.

6-16